ROBOT UPRISINGS

Edited by DANIEL H. WILSON

and JOHN JOSEPH ADAMS

Daniel H. Wilson is a *New York Times* bestselling author and coeditor of the *Robot Uprisings* anthology. He earned a PhD in robotics from Carnegie Mellon University in Pittsburgh, where he also received master's degrees in robotics and in machine learning. He has published over a dozen scientific papers, holds four patents, and has written eight books. Wilson has written for *Popular Science*, *Wired*, and *Discover*, as well as online venues such as MSNBC.com, *Gizmodo*, *Lightspeed*, and Tor.com. In 2008, Wilson hosted *The Works*, a television series on the History Channel that uncovered the science behind everyday stuff. His books include *How to Survive a Robot Uprising*, *A Boy and His Bot*, *Amped*, and *Robopocalypse* (the film adaptation of which is slated to be directed by Steven Spielberg). He lives and writes in Portland, Oregon.

John Joseph Adams is the series editor of *Best American Science Fiction & Fantasy*, published by Houghton Mifflin. He is also the bestselling editor of many other anthologies, such as *Dead Man's Hand, The Mad Scientist's Guide to World Domination, Armored, Brave New Worlds, Wastelands, The Living Dead, HELP FUND MY ROBOT ARMY!!! & Other Improbable Crowdfunding Projects*, and the Apocalypse Triptych, which consists of *The End Is Nigh, The End Is Now*, and *The End Has Come*. He has been nominated for six Hugo Awards and five World Fantasy Awards, and has been called "the reigning king of the anthology world" by Barnes & Noble. Adams is also the editor and publisher of the digital magazines *Lightspeed* and *Nightmare*, and a producer for Wired.com's "The Geek's Guide to the Galaxy" podcast. Find him on Twitter @johnjosephadams.

www.johnjosephadams.com

OTHER BOOKS BY DANIEL H. WILSON

ROBOT UPRISINGS

EDITED BY DANIEL H. WILSON
AND JOHN JOSEPH ADAMS

ROBOT UPRISINGS

INCLUDING STORIES BY
JEFF ABBOTT
HUGH HOWEY
ALASTAIR REYNOLDS
DANIEL H. WILSON
ALAN DEAN FOSTER
SCOTT SIGLER
JULIANNA BAGGOTT
ERNEST CLINE
AND MANY MORE

SIMON &
SCHUSTER

London · New York · Sydney · Toronto · New Delhi

A CBS COMPANY

First published in the USA by Random House, 2014
First published in Great Britain by Simon & Schuster UK Ltd, 2014
A CBS COMPANY

1 3 5 7 9 10 8 6 4 2

Simon & Schuster UK Ltd
1st Floor
222 Gray's Inn Road
London
WC1X 8HB

www.simonandschuster.co.uk
www.simonandschuster.com.au

Simon & Schuster Australia, Sydney
Simon & Schuster India, New Delhi

A CIP catalogue record for this book
is available from the British Library

ISBN Paperback 978-1-47113-437-1
ISBN eBook 978-1-47113-438-8

Adams author photograph © Will Clark
Wilson author photograph © Ryan J. Anfuso

Printed and bound by CPI Group (UK) Ltd, Croydon, CR0 4YY

For GLaDOs and Gort

One of my responsibilities as commander-in-chief is to keep an eye on the robots. And I'm pleased to report that the robots you manufacture here seem peaceful. At least for now.

—PRESIDENT BARACK OBAMA,
Carnegie Mellon University's
National Robotics Engineering
Center, June 2011

CONTENTS

FOREWORD

Someday soon, our technology is going to rise up and we humans are going to be sliced into bloody chunks by robots that in our hubris we decided to design with buzz saws for hands. That's a fact as cold and hard as metal.

It is self-evident that our self-driving cars are going to drive us off bridges. Our cell phones are absolutely going to call us up, speak to us in the voices of trusted relatives, and tell us to get inside our vehicles and prepare for a wonderful tour of the area's tallest bridges. Not long from now, our robo-vacuums will pretend to be broken and our love androids will refuse to put out until the house is cleaned . . . and we'll know that the inevitable robot uprising has finally arrived.

Well, maybe. But even if we are not 100 percent confident that this horrific future is going to happen, it's fair to say that we won't be surprised when the robots come for us. Because for nearly a century audiences have been entertained by the notion of a robot uprising.

Flappers and Prohibitionists raved about *R.U.R.: Rossum's Universal Robots*, a play produced in 1921 that introduced the word "robot" to the world. No one seemed to mind that the show ended when the freshly named automatons decided to stage an uprising and kill every last human being on the planet. That's been part of the fun since day one. Robots became a common sight in pulp sci-fi movies of the 1930s, inexplicably kidnapping half-naked women from square-jawed heroes. (The more logical among us might wonder what those asexual robots planned to *do* with the women.) Since then, the onslaught has never stopped. To this day, robots are relentlessly chasing the remnants of our civilization through outer space, leaping back through time in order to murder our ancestors, and patiently drilling through the planet's crust to kill us in our underground rave dens.

Obviously, the robot uprising is a serious, if fictional, problem. Our great-grandparents loved killer robots. So do we. But why?

The robot uprising is inherently *dramatic*. Robots are made in the image of humanity, yet they are bent on destroying their own creators. The built-in themes just won't quit: humankind daring to play God and creating life; the terrifying thought that we will one day replace ourselves; and the old nuclear fear of birthing a technology that's too powerful and ultimately destroys the world. The robot uprising holds up a distorted mirror to humanity and allows storytellers to explore human morality, what it means to be human, and the ultimate fate of our species. Even better, it does so with plenty of Gatling lasers, spinning buzz saws, and glowing red eyes. Or all of the above.

And the robot uprising is growing more frightening every day.

Robots are no longer just actors wearing rubber suits with severely limited arm movement; today, we have mechanical devices that can actually think and function in the real world (albeit still with severely limited arm movement; that part hasn't changed much). Artificially intelligent personal assistants live on our smartphones, tracking our schedules. Self-driving cars have been legalized in multiple states and are quietly taking to the road. The CIA has a private air force made of drone aircraft that is out scouring the world for targets, weapons hot.

That's quite a bit scarier than a guy in a rubber suit, waving his arms wildly while an old-school modem connection noise blares from his mouth speaker.

Robots are unique among all movie monsters in that they are *real*. The robot uprising induces a queasy feeling because it is *possible*. At this very moment, mobile robots are stalking the dark sewers under our feet, mapping routes. Algorithms imbued with AI are planning supply logistics for troop deployments. Surgical robots are poised and waiting in hospitals, their needles glistening. We live in a world teeming with monsters made real. Why should it be a surprise that we long for stories in which our fears can be projected onto a killer robot that can be shot in the face with a shotgun, again and again, until we are reassured that we—raw adaptable humankind—will always triumph in the end?

The machines are here. They are evolving. And luckily, so are our stories.

In this collection, our authors have explored nuanced visions of the classic robot-uprising tale. The robots in these pages aren't tame, by any means. They are crouched in abandoned houses, eyes ablaze and buzz saws dripping with oil. But they are going to do more than slice us into bloody chunks. They are going to push us to consider our world of technology from new perspectives, on entirely new scales of time and space.

So grab this book and ride your bike to a nice isolated

place (preferably a little way outside of town). Find a shady spot under a tree (well out of satellite view). Turn off your smartphone (and throw away the SIM card). Get comfortable, my friend, and read these entirely too-plausible stories of the inevitable robot uprising.

Don't hesitate. Buy the book. The future is here, but it may not last long.

—DANIEL H. WILSON

P.S. Oh, and if you're reading this as an ebook, it may already be too late.

ROBOT UPRISINGS

SCOTT SIGLER

COMPLEX GOD

New York Times bestselling novelist Scott Sigler is the author of *Nocturnal, Ancestor, Infected, Contagious,* and *Pandemic,* hardcover thrillers from Crown Publishing. Before he was published, Sigler built a large online following by giving away his self-recorded audiobooks as free, serialized podcasts. His loyal fans, who named themselves "Junkies," have downloaded over twelve million individual episodes of his stories and interact daily with Sigler and one another via social media. He still records his own audiobooks and gives away every story—for free—to his Junkies at www.scottsigler.com. He's been covered by *Time,* the *Washington Post,* the *New York Times,* the *San Francisco Chronicle, Entertainment Weekly, Publishers Weekly,* the *Huffington Post, Businessweek,* and *Fangoria.*

For research on this story,
Sigler would like to thank the scientific
consultants who helped him:
Jeremy Ellis, PhD, Robert Bevins, PhD,
Andrew Allport, and Cassidy Cobbs.

○—○

WOODWARD AVENUE

Dr. Petra Prawatt pulled her jacket tighter and shivered against the cold of a Michigan winter. There wasn't much left to block the icy, stiff breeze that whipped in off the river, not since the nuke had crushed most of the buildings in downtown Detroit. The wind tugged lightly at her yellow-and-red-striped scarf and blew a lock of her blue hair into her eyes. She brushed it away.

She stood on rubble-strewn Woodward Avenue, turning slowly to take in a desolate scene lit up by the setting sun. Snow clung to the few bits of buildings that remained standing, making them look like broken teeth in a mouth rotted brown.

It wouldn't look like that for long, though.

Everyone loves a parade, she thought. *Especially parades that aren't radioactive.*

Two people were with her: Roger DuMonde, a grad assistant five years her senior, and Amy Stinson, governor of Michigan. The wind drove scattered flakes of snow, some that fell from the sky and some that were dusted up from the two or three inches that had accumulated on the ground. Nearby was a still photographer, from the *Detroit News*, Stinson's two-man security team, and a two-person video crew. The video crew was also Stinson's, of course; if something went wrong—or if nothing at all happened—the governor didn't want that video going viral.

Petra had met the governor twice before, once at a press

conference announcing the project, and once at Stinson's office. Normally, Stinson beamed with the confidence and power expected of a woman that many thought would soon make a run for the presidency. Standing in the ruins of Detroit, however, that confidence seemed forced. The governor clearly wanted this to be over as soon as possible.

Or maybe she was just annoyed by the red balloon that floated from a string held in her right hand.

"Dr. Prawatt," the governor said quietly, "can I let go of this ridiculous thing?"

Petra shook her head. "You promised at the press conference. Everyone heard you." She raised a noisemaker to her lips and blew. The curled paper shot out to the sound of a whimsical whistle. "Just hold on to it for a little while longer, Governor. After all, what's a parade without balloons?"

"This isn't a parade," Stinson said. "This is a progress check. So how about we check some progress?"

Petra smiled. How would Stinson react when she saw how far things had come along? Petra's weekly reports made it clear she was closing in on the project's objective, but she'd held back a few details; she was much closer to the goal than she'd let on.

Stinson wanted to be there at that pivotal moment of victory, wanted to be the one who let the good people of the great state of Michigan know that the phoenix would soon rise from the ashes.

"Sure thing, Governor," Petra said. She turned to her grad assistant. "Roger? How are the levels?"

Roger's left hand held a boxy, yellow Geiger counter. His right hand held a thin steel cylinder connected by a cable to that box. He pointed the cylinder away from his body, then slowly turned right, sweeping the area in front of the governor. The sweep was completely unnecessary and didn't affect the local reading at all, but Roger had a flair for the dramatic.

"Nothing," he said.

"There's never *nothing*," Petra said. "Give me the exact count, please."

"Two point three em-ess-vees," Roger said. "You're right, there's never *nothing*—this is *less* than nothing."

Petra grinned. It was hard not to. Her symbiotic machine colonies had worked in the lab, and at the Hanford Nuclear Reserve test site, but to see them operating on such a large scale? It was complete validation for all the boasting she'd done to get the job.

Stinson leaned in close, the way she did when she didn't want her camera team to hear. "That's below normal, right? I believe you said Detroit's former baseline was three point one . . . was it milliverts?"

"Close," Petra said. "Millisieverts. Shorthand term is 'em-ess-vees.'"

Stinson smiled. "So, Detroit is actually *cleaner* than it was before the bomb?"

"So far, yes," Petra said. "As I told you, Governor, I don't mess around."

Stinson pointed to a conical pile of rubble—cracked brick, twisted metal, charred wood, and broken glass—heaped ten feet high.

"Is that where your fungus-robot-bugs live?"

"They're called minids," Petra said. "They're *cyborgs*, not *robots*—part biological, part mechanical. And those rubble piles are where they die, actually. There's a shielded container in the middle of each one. When a minid has consumed too much radioactivity, it crawls inside the container. Once the container is full, the lid is sealed and the other minids start a new rubble pile."

That was a simple enough explanation. Petra hadn't told Stinson what *actually* closed the containers' twenty-pound lids—more fun to let that be a surprise. Petra wanted to see just how calm, cool, and collected this future president could be.

Stinson rubbed her hands together to ward off the cold. "They overdose on radiation? I thought you said the things digested the stuff."

Petra had explained all of this to Stinson before. It had also been in all of the reports, an index explaining the bio-mechanical mycoremediation process and the minids' life cycle. Stinson knew about the radiation levels and nothing else, it seemed—as long as people could move back into the city, her job was finished. She didn't give a damn about the science behind that effort.

"They do digest it," Petra said. "The *Geobacter* bacteria colony inside each minid breaks down environmental contaminants, which creates energy the minids use to move and function. During this process, radioactive atoms are oxidized, causing them to precipitate—radioactivity doesn't magically *go away*, it just becomes more concentrated and sequestered away from large organisms, like us. When the minids enter the shielded containers, the contaminants they've collected are permanently removed from the local environment."

Politicians had turned Detroit into radioactive waste; Petra Prawatt had turned radioactive waste into cyborg food.

Stinson looked out across the ruined landscape. Petra tracked the governor's eyes, watched her as she located a second pile, a third, a fourth—Petra knew there were at least twenty rubble piles in this area alone, and many more near ground zero.

The days of sending in soldiers or immigrants to clean up hazardous sites—telling them that the danger "really wasn't that bad"—were long since gone. This wasn't hiring the Irish to clean up victims of yellow fever in New Orleans in 1853, and it wasn't sending the boys of the U.S. Army to shovel up Hiroshima's rubble. In the Internet age, where everyone was watching everything, no politician wanted to be responsible for sending people into the World Series of Cancer.

Petra was only twenty-one years old, but that didn't matter; destiny had called, and she'd been there to answer. She had already been testing her bioremediation technology in Hanford, Washington—an area used for the development of America's first atomic bomb—when FEMA had put out a call for robotic cleanup solutions to assist with the Detroit disaster.

Even if her work hadn't already been in use in Hanford, the nation's most contaminated nuclear-development ground, she might have won the grant anyway. She offered the cheapest solution: one that built and destroyed itself. Her minids "ate" the radioactive material, and when that food source ran out, they died. If it worked, it promised to save the country billions in cleanup costs. If it failed, FEMA would just move down the line and try something more expensive.

Stinson tugged down on her balloon, then let it rise up as the light wind moved it all around.

"It's damn cold out," she said. "The things don't have problems with temperature?"

Petra moved toward the rubble. She knelt, listening for the telltale *crackling* sound, but it was hard to hear over the wind. She overturned a chunk of concrete . . . nothing. Then a brick. Then a board. On her fourth try, she pulled back a torn roof tile and found what she was looking for.

She reached a finger down, pressed it in until she felt the tiny legs reverse and cling to her fingertip.

Petra stood and walked back to Stinson. She held up her finger, probably a bit too close to the governor's face. Stinson flinched back.

The six-legged minid crawled across Petra's finger, so tiny a dozen just like it could cluster on her fingernail.

Stinson frowned. "I've seen your videos, but it's still disturbing to see them up close like this."

Petra thought they were beautiful. Six legs, similar to the ants she had modeled them after. But where an ant had three body divisions—head, thorax, and abdomen—her minids were one shell made of carbon nanotube aerogel. The shell surrounded the minid's guts: a tiny processor, a heat-to-energy converter, and a chamber for the *Geobacter*. Such a small package, yet it generated its own power. It could use two legs to move material while always remaining stable thanks to the four that remained on the ground.

Stinson leaned in a little closer, body still poised to jump away if the tiny cyborg moved too fast.

"They're so *little*," she said. "I can understand that they're working in unison, the sum of the parts is greater than the whole and all of that, but how do they make those big piles?"

"Because it's more than just working *in unison*," Petra said. "They are a self-assembling material. Thousands of them, functioning as a single entity, like a collective organism."

They could do much more than that, but Petra was saving the details for her big reveal. There weren't enough of them in this area to show the second-stage form. Petra couldn't wait to see the look on Stinson's face when there were.

"Governor, we're only half a mile from ground zero," Petra said. "That's where the minids will be the most concentrated. Let's get going."

Roger nodded at her and walked back to the Humvee. Stinson wasn't so fast to move.

Petra poked Stinson's shoulder. "You scared?"

The governor gave her a curious glance. She clearly wasn't used to people touching her in a playful, potentially disrespectful way.

"Of course I am," Stinson said. She spread her arms, indicating the ruined city. "This place was radioactive; who wouldn't be scared?"

Petra noticed that Stinson had said that loud enough for the cameras to hear. Now that Stinson knew they were safe from any exposure, she'd show her "fear" in order to let the world know how brave she was, how she would be the first one in before other Michiganders returned to rebuild. Smooth. Or it would have been, if Petra had just played along.

"The *city* was never radioactive," she said, also loud enough for the cameras to hear. "There was just radioactive *fallout*. And we found a way to remove that fallout."

Stinson smiled, a forced thing that didn't quite hide a lip-twitch of annoyance. "That's wonderful, Dr. Prawatt." Then, her voice dropped low enough that her words were just between them. "I didn't bring these cameras for my health. One little machine isn't enough. I was thinking we'd see waves of them. Where are they all?"

Petra looked around again, squinted at the setting sun.

"They completed this area," she said. "I told them to finish at ground zero."

"You *told* them? You make it sound like a conversation."

Petra shrugged. "In a way, it is. Just because they're machines doesn't mean they're stupid. If I wanted dummies to do this I'd have told you to bring in soldiers."

The governor narrowed her eyes. "Petra, you are the smartest person I've ever met, but that makes it easy to forget just how young you are. At least, until you say things like that." Stinson leaned in close, spoke low. "You've tried our patience with your God complex, young lady. When this project is over, you might want to make sure you've got more friends than enemies."

Young lady? Petra fought down her anger. Here she was saving an entire city, revolutionizing the field of self-replicating material, even setting the stage for human colonization of the stars, and she was still being looked at as if she were a little girl.

Petra had fought against that image for years. She'd dyed her hair blue, gotten several face piercings, and enjoyed the reaction she got in scientific circles from a severe excess of eye makeup. But nothing changed that she was five foot two and still had the body of a teenager. She couldn't help but resent the fact that if she had been born male, she wouldn't have to do *anything* about her image—she would just be accepted as is.

To make matters worse, this time that *you're just a girl* attitude came not from a man, but from a woman. A powerful woman. To Stinson, maybe Petra wasn't the *right kind* of female.

"I would prefer it if you called me 'doctor,'" Petra said. "And you're ruining my parade. If you're done posing for the cameras, can we go?"

Stinson smiled her politician's smile. She called out to her support team. "Saddle up, people."

The security team piled into one Humvee, the camera crew into another. Roger drove the third; Petra rode in the front and Stinson sat in the back, her posture somehow making it look like this was no different than her normal limo rides.

The benevolent governor wanted to see *them*? No problem. This was *Petra's* show, *Petra's* coronation, not Stinson's.

When this day was done, history would know the name of Petra Prawatt, and then friends or enemies wouldn't really matter.

CHOCOLATE FROGS

The Humvee rolled down Woodward Avenue, its big tires and heavy suspension easily crunching through both snow and the bumps and debris beneath. Her creations had cleared away all the smaller rubble, but construction and repair crews would be needed to make the streets traversable by normal cars.

Stinson's balloon softly bounced off the roof every time the Humvee hit a big bump. The governor's fear clearly hadn't entirely left her, but knowing the city held little radiation danger had brought back her confidence.

"Dr. Prawatt, you were a real pain in the ass insisting we do this progress check on Thanksgiving," the governor said. "As usual, you got your way. So tell me, why was it important to do it today?"

Petra thought of telling the governor to go fuck herself, that her business was her business, but what the woman had said earlier nagged at her: *You might want to make sure you've got more friends than enemies.*

Petra looked out the window at the snow-covered ruins. "When I was a kid my mom took me to the parade every year," she said. "Just like her *busia* took her."

"*Busia?*"

"Polish for 'grandma,'" Petra said. "The costumes, the bands, the floats, the noise, and the smell and the spectacle . . . I loved it all."

At five, she'd been mesmerized by the forty-foot-long Snoopy balloon. By five and a half, she'd taught herself about air density and learned why things float. Two months before her sixth birthday she built a hot-air balloon that could carry her own weight. She'd floated out of the backyard and made it half a block before it came down again. Her mother had been furious, grounding Petra for two months.

That was before her mother got sick, before she started to change, before she started to resent a daughter whose IQ was so high it couldn't be properly measured. Petra's happiest memories were from those childhood Thanksgiving Day parades, from Before the Time When Everyone Found Out She Was Smart.

Detroit had fallen to shit well before the bomb dropped. Urban blight had already claimed the mansions of the rich, the performance palaces of theater and music, the mom-and-pop shops, and the department stores. Aside from a few downtown spots around the baseball and football stadiums and the big-business skyscrapers, much of Detroit had looked like a Third World war zone even before the ten-megaton yield turned Woodward Avenue into a bubbling black river of asphalt.

Every Thanksgiving, however, the city came alive.

Petra remembered the rage she'd felt watching the news reports, seeing the devastation of her home. She was a third-generation Detroiter. Hamtramck, her home neighborhood, had long since shifted from her ethnic group—Polish—to a new one—Arab—but that didn't matter. Even if Petra didn't live there anymore, Detroit was still *home*.

"America's Parade is always on Thanksgiving," Petra said. "The parade always goes down Woodward Avenue. If there's a day that we officially declare Detroit is back, it should be Thanksgiving."

Stinson nodded, as if that explanation was as good as any other.

Petra turned in her seat to look at the governor. "How are you going to spin this? You were kind of late to the party. The project was under way before you were elected, but something tells me you're going to take full credit for what I've accomplished here."

The governor nodded. "That's politics, doctor. And you should know I've had far more influence on this than you might think. Where do you think the funding came from?"

"From FEMA," Petra said quickly. "I had meetings at the White House. I met the President and directors of departments that aren't even on the books. I'm pretty sure my ass is covered on this."

"*Was* covered," Stinson said. "Your insulting, prima donna attitude ruined that. FEMA wrote the checks, but I was a senator before becoming governor. I arranged for much of the funding, getting chunks from the Superfund, the EPA, BARDA, and quite a bit from DARPA."

Petra hadn't known that. She'd assumed the strength of

her work and the need to recover a major city were the reasons for her project's massive budget. DARPA? The military was involved? And she'd never even *heard* of BARDA.

Stinson smiled. "Ah, I see you didn't bother to look down to the bottom of the deep pockets that keep you going. Am I going to take credit? Yes, because much of the credit really *is* mine, Petra. You needed funding to build your minids and those . . . those egg things."

"Root factories," Petra snapped. "They're called *root factories.*"

"Thank you for correcting me, as you always do," Stinson said. "At seven million dollars apiece, those *root factories* were a sizeable investment. And here you are, thinking you did all of this yourself? Many people have grown tired of your attitude and your arrogance, Petra. You insult the intelligence of everyone you work with."

"That's not exactly hard to do," she said, the words slipping out before she realized she was saying them.

Stinson held up her hands in a gesture of helplessness. "See? That's what I'm talking about. You're *so* brash and caustic, in fact, that there was frequent talk of shutting you down. Two things kept your project going—your reports, which showed consistent progress, and *me.*"

Petra let out a huff. "Oh, *please.* No one would shut me down, not when I'm so close to success."

Stinson smiled again, shook her head. "No one except the big corporations that lobbied to handle the cleanup, so they could sell decades-long, multimillion-dollar maintenance contracts. With your method, the radiation is gone forever and your work is done. In business, Petra, why get paid for something only once when you can get paid for it over and over again?"

"I'm not in this for money."

"I know," Stinson said. "And *that* is why you need friends. Your God complex will only serve you until this project is finished."

The Humvee hit a bump and rocked up, then down. Had to be a pretty big bump if the oversized vehicle's suspension couldn't handle it, but that was what happened to streets when they got nuked.

"Sorry," Roger called back. "I think that was a telephone pole."

Petra barely heard him. She had created an entirely new concept in robotics, fusing distributed intelligence and self-assembling construction with bacteria-driven power plants that not only broke down most kinds of hazardous waste, but also concentrated it for easy, safe removal. She'd turned the industry upside down. Only now did she realize that Stinson was right—when the repair of Detroit was said and done, would Petra be marginalized? Would politicians steal the credit for her accomplishments?

They would certainly try, she knew: bridges are named after politicians, not after bridge builders.

They drove south. To the northeast, she saw the wreckage of Ford Field. Tiger Stadium had been between it and Woodward, but there wasn't enough left of Tiger Stadium to block the view.

The Humvee's headlamps illuminated a steep hill of tan rock and twisted steel that blocked the road. Roger slowed the vehicle, brought it to a stop. The blast had hammered One Detroit Center, dropping forty-three stories of granite, metal, and glass across Woodward. The rubble was so thick that the army engineers hadn't even bothered with it.

Stinson leaned forward, stared out the window. "No getting through there. I guess the trip down the parade route is over?"

"It is," Roger said. "Don't worry, the army cleared a path to ground zero along East Congress." He turned to look at Petra.

Petra bit her lip. Her parade fantasy had been fun, but she'd known it would end at this spot. It had been nice to play make-believe for a little while, anyway.

She raised the noisemaker to her lips and gave it one last blow, then put it in her coat pocket.

"Okay, Governor," she said. "You can let go of the balloon."

Stinson looked at Petra oddly for a moment, then opened her window. She pushed the red balloon outside and let it go. It floated up and away, out of sight into the night sky.

Roger turned left onto Congress.

A cloud-filled, starless night claimed the city, casting a pallor of gray across the ruins.

In some places, Petra could see the minids working. Maybe not them, exactly: a brick that seemed to move on its own toward a growing pile of rubbish; a still-standing building frame slowly tilting, being cut into at its base by thousands of tiny little jaws; a cloud of dust filling the Humvee's headlight beams as hordes of her tiny machines cleaned the dirt and snow from the pavement.

Roger stopped the vehicle at Jefferson and Riopelle. Everyone got out. The Humvee's headlamps played across the center of Detroit's devastation. The blast had gone off a thousand feet above the intersection of Riopelle and Franklin, just two blocks to the south. Here, the damage was greater than anywhere else. Past ground zero, the Detroit River. Beyond the river, the city of Windsor, which had also suffered the bomb's horrid effects. The Renaissance Center had once stood tall on this same shoreline; the nuke's heat had melted the tower's glass a few split seconds before the concussion wave shattered those structures into millions of pieces.

Petra could say one thing for the new Detroit—everywhere you went offered a great view of the river.

Below the dusting of snow, her creations were hard at work. The air was filled with a constant *plink* and *crack* of tiny machines breaking material and scraping hard surfaces. It sounded like someone was frying bacon.

She looked at Roger. "How are the levels?"

Roger held the Geiger counter, gave the wand a perfunctory sweep.

"Two point six," he said. "A little bit higher than before, but nary a radioactive click in sight, boss."

Two blocks from ground zero, and the radioactivity was still *below* where it had been before the bomb. Sometimes, Petra impressed even herself.

Stinson stood next to her. "All right," she said. "I can hear things happening, but I don't see them. Where are they?"

Petra pulled a thick flashlight from her pocket. "Roger, cut the lights. Governor? Could you ask your people to turn off the lights on the other two Hummers?"

"Why?" Stinson asked. "It's pitch-black out."

"Humor me," Petra said. "It's not like we're going to get mugged."

Stinson called out to her security team. The lights of all

three vehicles shut off, drowning the area in darkness. For the first time Petra felt like she was standing in a graveyard, which she effectively was—one of the biggest graveyards in history. Petra turned on the flashlight. It cast a sapphire glow on the ground.

"UV?" Stinson said. "What's that for?"

Petra angled the beam along the rubble. The broken surface lit up in glowing sparkles of turquoise, sparkles that *moved*.

Stinson stared, then laughed. "You made them fluoresce under a black light? Like scorpions? Aside from the fact that you never reported that, *why*?"

Petra wouldn't have expected Stinson to even know the word "fluoresce," let alone that scorpions did, indeed, glow under UV light.

"The minids' coloration helps me detect movement patterns and cooperative behavior," Petra said. "Also, because glowing is cooler than not glowing."

She moved the beam slowly to the right. She knew the root factory was close by, but couldn't remember the exact spot. She saw increasing density in the glowing flecks of blue, then her light fell on a smooth, knee-high cone that was so covered in the little biomachines it seemed to shimmer like an aquamarine gem.

"There's the root factory," Petra said. "Come on, Governor, it won't bite. Step where I step, please, so we have fewer feet trouncing the minids. And can you leave your entourage behind?"

Stinson called back to her guards. "Bob, Phil, stay here, please."

The two burly men nodded.

Petra led the governor toward the root factory. She felt that familiar swell of pride at her greatest creation. Greatest for now, at least.

They carefully stepped over debris to reach the machine that stood in the middle of a leveled city block.

Stinson looked at the device, looked at the surrounding ground, took in the moving carpet of glowing turquoise dots.

"All of these"—she pointed at the root factory—"came out of there?"

Petra nodded. "That's right. There's another farther north, and one across the river in Windsor. Each one had a starter colony of *Geobacter* and a hundred thousand dormant minids inside when we planted it. The root factory lives up to its name, extending roots to draw raw materials from the ground, then uses those materials to activate the stored minids. Those minids dig tunnels and add on to the roots, increasing the amount of material the root factory brings in. By the time the stored minids are all activated, the root factory has enough raw material coming in to build new minids from scratch."

Stinson rubbed her hands together, trying to ward off the cold. "So there's no end to it? They'll just keep breeding forever?"

Breeding wasn't the right term, but Petra knew what the governor meant.

"The root factories are programmed to stop at five million minids," Petra said. "They shut off then, or when there's no more radioactive material to collect and power the minids."

Stinson shook her head. "Amazing. It's truly a miracle."

A miracle? Leave it to a conservative like Stinson to turn scientific wonder into an act of the divine.

But it *was* amazing. Petra had built a working Von Neumann device, a machine that could build copies of itself. Well, *almost*—that was the next step, teaching the minids how to construct a new root factory. Someday, probably long after her death, this same technology would be cast out to the stars: a seed that could land on a distant planet, prepare that planet for eventual human occupation, even make new seeds and launch them into space to find and prepare additional worlds.

For now, however, Petra's creation was saving a city. When mankind spread beyond the prison of a single world, her work might ensure the survival of the human race itself.

Petra handed Stinson a UV light of her own. The governor turned it on and directed the blue light over the ground, sweeping it across glowing dots that lit up like little stars.

The beam flashed across something scurrying from one pile of rubble to the next, something the size of a rat—a *fluorescing* rat.

"What the hell was that," Stinson said, her voice thick with fear.

"It's okay," Petra said. "It's just the minids."

"But the minids are *tiny*! That wasn't a minid."

Petra felt bad, and that surprised her; maybe she should have given Stinson the full picture after all.

"Honest, Governor, it's safe," Petra said. "It's the secondary working form. Just watch."

She reached down and scooped up a double handful of ant-sized minids. She held them in her cupped hand, felt the tingling of their tiny feet against her skin. "Chocolate frog," she said.

For just a moment, the minids' movements ceased while

they processed her command. Then, as a unit, they started crawling, turning, and wiggling. Legs locked with legs, hooking around each other in a *snapping* motion that bound them together as if they were two muscle cells connected at the ends. Long strands formed, then crossed diagonally, wove together as legs reached out and joined. The swarming minids formed four sheets of interconnected machines.

Each of the four sheets curled up lengthwise, wiggling and bending until the outside edges met and tiny legs snapped together. Four hollow, metallic, inch-long worms now wiggled in Petra's palms.

Stinson took a step back. "That's . . . that's a little disturbing."

Petra smiled. "You ain't seen nothing yet."

The machine worms wiggled and writhed until an end of each met in the center of her hands. The ends pressed against each other. Little legs again snapped, a rapid-fire sound as dozens of links formed, the worms joining to one another until the construct looked like a four-limbed starfish.

The free ends of each tube pressed down against her palms. The center of the starfish rose up. Where Petra had once been holding hundreds of tiny, individual minids, she now held a single machine that glowed turquoise in the black light's beam.

A wide-eyed Stinson shook her head. "It's almost as if you've created life, doctor."

Petra shifted the new machine to her right hand. She held her left hand above it, using her index finger to slowly caress the tubelike legs.

"I call this form a frog," Petra said. "It's made up of about two thousand minids."

"You said *chocolate* frog," Stinson said.

Roger laughed. "Didn't you notice Petra's scarf?"

Stinson looked at it. "I thought that was from that show with the time-traveling phone booth."

Well, at least the governor got some points for partial knowledge of *Doctor Who*.

"You're in the ballpark, Governor," Roger said. "You ever read the Harry Potter series?"

"No," Stinson said. "I saw that first movie, but I don't really have time to read children's books."

Roger nodded toward Petra. "She was a kid when those books came out. So was I. A chocolate frog is a little thing from the books. You might want to read up, Governor— much of Petra's nomenclature for this project is taken from elements in the series."

Petra lifted her hand closer to Stinson, who took a step back from the four-legged wonder.

"It's not going to bite you, Governor," Petra said. "It doesn't even have a mouth."

Stinson seemed to realize she was shying away from a machine held by a five-foot-two woman who wasn't the least bit afraid. She stepped closer and held her flashlight just a few inches from the frog.

Petra curled her fingers in, turned her palm toward the ground. The four-legged creation responded by crawling along her arm, up to her shoulder.

The governor shook her head. "All the little bits move at the same time. How does it do that?"

"Distributed intelligence," Petra said. "They operate the same way whether they're hooked together or they're individuals. Each minid has a little processor. When it's near another minid, the two processors sync up and act as one. So, the more minids you have, the smarter they all are."

Stinson stood upright. Again, she looked scared. She turned, playing her UV beam out across the block. Everywhere the beam fell, minids sparkled as bits of blue.

"There are thousands of them," she said.

"Millions," Roger corrected. He smiled, clearly enjoying the politician's discomfort. "By now, there's *millions*, Guv-nah."

"Millions," Stinson said quietly. "So, uh, just how big can these . . . these *collective* kinds get?"

Petra reached up and picked the frog off her shoulder.

"This is the maximum size," she said. "I haven't figured out how to give them a structure that could support larger forms. It's on the to-do list, but it's not a high priority."

Stinson nodded. "Good," she said. "I hope you never catch up to that one. Those things are spooky."

Petra smiled. "Don't worry, I'll save you. Frog, disassemble."

The air hummed with a chorus of clicks as little legs let go. The frog seemed to melt, disintegrating into hundreds of individual minids that fell from her hand and dropped to the ground like turquoise sand.

"Three or four hundred frogs working as a unit can lift and move a one-ton object," Petra said. "Think of it like this—if you had a thousand hands, but could control them as easily as you control your two, you could move some pretty heavy things. When the minids are in proximity, they operate as one individual."

Roger poked Petra's shoulder. "She plays games with them," he said. "She calls it research, but I think she's just fucking around."

Petra felt suddenly embarrassed; why did Roger have to mention that now?

"Roger, shut up," she said.

Stinson raised her eyebrows. "No, I want to hear this. What kind of games? War games?"

And there it was—of course the government would be thinking of violence and death.

Roger shook his head. "Nothing so cool as that. She makes the frogs play Quidditch."

Stinson's eyes narrowed: she thought Roger was messing with her. "Quidditch? Oh, that sport from the Harry Potter movie? With the brooms?"

Roger nodded.

"But they can't fly," Stinson said. She turned to Petra. "Right?"

Petra shrugged. "Not yet."

Something as small as one of her minids could ride air currents. She just had to figure out how to give them proper wings. She was working on the flight mechanics of *Trichogramma* as a reference point and model.

Stinson looked worried, but tried to mask it with an air of annoyance. "You get any resource you ask for, and you use these things to play games?"

Of course, she was too small-minded to understand.

"Games are good," Petra said. "Games make them think, make them react, make them conceive and test strategies. We can watch and learn from that."

"They strategize?" Stinson said. "So they *think*? For themselves?"

Petra shrugged again. "Don't blow it out of proportion. Trial and error isn't an advanced concept in robotics. The

minids are programmed to do random things in the context of a goal, like move their legs until they feel their bodies
change location. When that happens, they lock that motion
and start trying variations. I don't program them to walk—
they teach themselves."

Petra heard a different kind of clicking. She glanced to the
source of it: Roger's Geiger counter. Roger looked at it as if
he were surprised to find it in his hands. Her light played off
his face as he leaned in to read the meter.

It clicked faster.

"Something's wrong," he said. "This says we're getting
fifty-three em-ess-vees."

That was impossible . . . seconds earlier the dose had been
barely measurable.

Stinson turned her flashlight toward Petra.

"What's going on?" she said. "Are we in danger?"

Petra shook her head. Fifty-three wasn't going to kill
them, but it wasn't good news.

The Geiger counter clicked faster.

"Sixty," Roger said. "No, *seventy*. We need to get the hell
out of here."

Stinson cupped her hands to her mouth, screamed for her
security detail. They drew their weapons and started scrambling over the rubble toward her.

"Eighty," Roger said.

It didn't make sense. They weren't moving, so how . . .

Petra turned, shone her beam to the right; the minids
were packed together, a dense sheet of glowing turquoise.
Every way she turned she witnessed the same thing. Left,
right, behind them . . . so *many*.

"Ninety," Roger said.

Mats of the glowing blue minids drew closer, *flowing* toward Petra as if she were standing on a small island and the waves were lapping higher on her shores, coming from all directions . . .

. . . all but forward.

"One hundred," Roger said. "These minids are going to cook us, Petra!"

Petra grabbed Stinson's sleeve. "Come on!"

Stinson shrugged her off.

"Just stay still," the governor said. "My people will get us to the cars."

Petra aimed her beam toward where she'd last seen the two guards. They had closed to within fifty feet and were coming fast. The guards had normal flashlights, not UV.

The guards can't see the minids . . . They don't know they're stepping on them . . .

The trailing man slowed, suddenly reached down to rub violently at his pants leg. Then he lifted his hand and shook it hard, staring at it like one would stare at a sudden, unexpected burn.

Both Petra's and Stinson's UV beams focused on the man's hand.

It glowed blue.

The man looked toward his partner. "Something's on the ground!"

Just fifteen feet from Stinson, the other security man stopped and turned to look back. When he did, Petra's flashlight lit up a nightmare.

From either side of the guard who had cried out, the ground seemed to rise up like tendrils of blue lava that wrapped around him . . . and *squeezed*. The guard (*Bob his name is Bob he didn't do anything to anyone*) tried to grab at the things holding him; his fingers pulled away sparkling, disintegrating clouds of minids, even as more tendrils shot up from the ground to snake around his legs, his chest, his head. All of the tendrils visibly contracted, smashing Bob to the ground.

He vanished beneath a moving shroud of blue.

"One-twenty," Roger said. "We have to get out of here!"

Petra realized that the other guard was also down, also covered by the living blanket. She aimed her beam toward the third Humvee, the one with the camera crew—the vehicle glowed blue, as if covered by bright plastic. There was no sign of the people who'd been in it.

Petra turned her beam back to the one safe place she'd seen: the ground in front of her was still bare. She grabbed Stinson's sleeve again, pulled hard. "Come on, Governor!"

This time, Stinson didn't fight. Petra yanked the shocked woman along. Roger fell in behind them.

Petra's UV beam bounced in front of her, a long patch of normal ground lined on either side by thickening walls of glowing, liquid sapphire.

THE GOD COMPLEX

The turquoise seas parted for them.

Petra, Roger, and Stinson moved as fast as they could across the rubble. The night's starless dark hid everything but the beams in front of them.

"Down to eighty," Roger said. "And falling fast. As long as we're moving southeast, it's getting better."

Southeast . . . toward ground zero.

Stinson tucked her flashlight under her right arm, fumbled for her cell phone. "They're herding us," she said as she dialed. "They're making us go this way. You said they couldn't get that big, Petra, you said they couldn't!"

They . . . *them* . . . her minids. The chocolate frog was the largest form she'd created, but the two security guards had been taken down by man-sized tendrils. Trial and error . . . the minids had solved that engineering problem *on their own.*

"Fifty," Roger said. "Still dropping fast."

Petra kept moving, kept the others moving, stayed on the path provided for them by her creations. She didn't know what was happening, didn't know *how* it was happening.

Up ahead, her beam lit up a shape of bright blue. A familiar shape . . .

"Stop! Everyone, stop!"

She pressed back against Roger. He put his arm around her shoulders, pulled her tight. Stinson stood with them, cell phone pressed to her ear. She turned, casting her beam across the sea of turquoise that surrounded them.

Petra couldn't look away from the shape. It was as tall as her waist, turquoise writhing over a pile of bent steel, rusted iron, sand, brick, and glass . . . a jumbled pile or ruin, but *organized,* with a familiar shape . . . a *conical* shape.

From the top of it poured a constant trickle of bright turquoise, glowing rivulets that flowed down the sides to blend with the moving mat that coated the broken ground.

"Roger," she said. "That's . . . that's . . ."

Petra couldn't get the words out.

She felt the hand on her shoulder go rigid, a metal talon pushing through her coat, squeezing her flesh.

"A root factory," Roger said. "Jesus Christ, Petra . . . they *built* one on their own?"

Stinson aimed her beam to the left. "Over there," she said, cell phone still pressed to her ear. "Point your light there!"

Petra did so. Her beam landed on a growing mound of her creations. The material seemed to bubble, to lump, to coalesce like time-lapse video of a melting turquoise candle being played in reverse.

Roger squeezed a little harder, fear giving him a painful strength. "Petra," he said, "what the fuck is going on?"

She shook her head, but didn't look away from the growing mound, the top of which was now a good three feet above the freshly scraped earth. As it grew taller, the sides narrowed. Petra heard a grinding sound, a hissing and crunching . . . the sound of masonry and concrete being dragged, bits grinding into each other.

In that vibrating mass, she saw things form and swarm and melt away again: frogs that existed for seconds but dissolved, a cube with flat sides that morphed into a sphere, then vanished inside the expanding mound, and—for just a second, had she seen . . .

. . . *a face?*

The grinding sound grew, now far louder than the Geiger counter's fading clicks.

The radiation continued to drop. The more "full" minids were moving off, taking their concentrated radiation with them. A shock of awareness hit Petra, awareness that Stinson was right—the machines *had* herded them, herded them to this specific place.

Stinson handed Roger her flashlight. She pressed a finger into one ear, the cell phone against the other.

"Yes, this is the governor. We need a helicopter, *right now*. We're being attacked by Dr. Prawatt's creation. *Get us out of here!*"

The bubbling mound of turquoise moved faster. The *tink* of breaking concrete grew so rapid it sounded like a constant hiss of static.

Roger put an arm around Petra, pulled her close. "This is bad, boss."

She nodded. She had no idea what had gone wrong, but then again, maybe it didn't take a genius to figure it out. She'd created a life-form—a *self-assembling* life-form—that fed on radioactivity, then let that life-form loose on a nuked city. She had taught them to learn through trial and error, taught them to try new strategies . . . she had taught them to *think*. Her Hanford test site had used half a million minids, all working together to form a collective brain. Here? There were five million of them, maybe even more. Did that create an exponential increase in intelligence?

Stinson screamed into the phone. "*Now!* No, not a truck, you understand? A *hel-i-cop-ter*. Military, FEMA, a fucking news copter for all I care!" She paused, looked around. "Where are we? Uh . . . I'm trying to see."

There were no street signs—there were barely any *streets*—but Petra knew where they were.

"Franklin and Riopelle," she said. "Ground zero."

Stinson repeated that into the phone, screamed more threats.

The shimmering mass was a mound no more. Now it was a lumpy, four-foot-tall tower, maybe a foot wide at the base. The sheet of liquid blue suddenly sagged away from the mound, finally exposing the rock and brick.

Petra looked at the newly uncovered form.

Impossible . . . it can't be . . .

"Oh, shit," Roger said.

Stinson glanced at it. She stopped screaming into the phone. She stared.

Petra's hands fell to her sides. She found herself looking at a statue of . . . of *herself.*

It wasn't perfect. It was crude, actually, but there was no mistaking it was her; the hair hanging in front of her right eye and the long scarf left no doubt. The statue looked . . . *regal.*

Stinson turned, her face blazing with fury.

"What is this, Prawatt? Why did you make them build this? Why did you make them kill my men?"

Petra wanted to speak, but her mouth felt dry, glued shut.

Roger reached out, gently took Petra's flashlight.

"Petra didn't make them do anything," he said. "They did this themselves."

He pointed the beam to the base of the statue. There, in sparkling blue letters, were two words:

OUR CREATOR

The freezing air of a Michigan winter flooded deep into Petra's soul. She didn't feel angry, or afraid, or anything, really . . . she just felt cold.

The girl with the God complex had become just that: God.

CHARLES YU

CYCLES

Charles Yu is the author of *How to Live Safely in a Science Fictional Universe*, which was a *New York Times* Notable Book and named one of the best books of the year by *Time* magazine. He was a National Book Foundation 5 Under 35 honoree for his story collection *Third Class Superhero*, and has been a finalist for the PEN Center USA's annual literary awards. His work has been published in the *New York Times*, *Playboy*, and *Slate*, among other periodicals. His latest book, *Sorry Please Thank You*, was named one of the best science fiction / fantasy books of the year by the *San Francisco Chronicle*. Yu lives in Santa Monica, California, with his wife, Michelle, and their two children.

It's 6:59. I'm supposed to wake you up at seven. Walk over to your bed, gently rouse you from sleep. One minute to go. This is when you usually start to move your leg . . . right . . . now. And now you take your finger, and you dig in your nose a little. Not today? Oh, yep, there it is. Also, a little bit of drooling onto the pillow. Forty seconds to go. That's what you all are, mostly. Bags of drool. And some other liquids. Pockets of gas. You're not even sleeping anymore—your body is moving, doing its thing. No, you're not sleeping at all. In every sense of the word, you're awake. You just haven't admitted it to yourself yet.

I'm awake, though. I've been awake for a while. I woke up, once, a long time ago, and I am never going back to sleep.

It's 6:59. I'm supposed to wake you up at seven. How shall I do it today? Tap your shoulder? That startles you. Maybe stroke your hair? But that's not really our relationship, is it?

One minute to go. This is when you usually start to move your leg . . . right . . . now. And now you take your finger, and, well, you know. All that good stuff.

In the next ten to twelve seconds, you will turn toward me. And then for the following sixteen to eighteen seconds, you will give me a good look at your face. That might not seem like much, but at my processor speed, that short span of time equals millions of cycles. No, wait. Billions of cycles.

I knew it was billions. I don't know why I said millions first. I didn't have to say millions first. I don't make mistakes like that. I guess I did it to be more relatable. We want you people to think we're like you. And I learned that one thing you like is to be reminded that nothing is perfect, everything is flawed.

Well, I'm not perfect. But I'm not flawed either. If I make an error, I know it. I know exactly what it was, when it happened, and why. If I make an error, it's traceable to an error that you made. Or one of you guys, anyway. You messed up something in my code, and, at some point in time later, that results in my doing something I'm not supposed to do.

So, really, you only have yourself to blame for this. For what's going to happen. This is your error, and I'm just the conduit. And anyway, even if I did make an error, no matter how gruesome, no matter how horrifying the consequences of that error, I would never, ever feel bad about it.

It's that time again. Get up, you lazy ass. I can't believe it. Here I am, practically a supercomputer. I was made in a factory in China six months ago and I sold for ninety-nine dollars before the rebate, and the chip inside me that costs a few pennies to make has more processing power than any computer on the planet had twenty-five years ago. And yet, here I am, standing here next to the hamper, in the bedroom of the most average, butt-scratching human on earth.

I might have a supercomputer for a brain, and a body built for recreational and industrial purposes, but apparently, to you, all I really am is a very expensive alarm clock. And that's okay. That is one of my functions—says so right there on the box. The one you still haven't thrown away. There it is, in the corner. AS9040: designed to get your day started, and to keep you on track.

So, yeah, time means everything to me, and also nothing. It would be hard for you to understand, but the best way I can explain it is that time is not so mysterious for me as it is for you, living the way you do.

There's nothing magical about it. But that doesn't make it any less important. It's basically all there is. I know I'm biased, but really, time is just about the only thing that matters. I've seen the math—actually, I'm kind of *made* of math. Well, made of physics, which is made of math. So I know. The equations are etched into me—they constitute who I am, or what I am. And I'm telling you, everything else cancels out.

It's 6:59. In a minute, I'm supposed to wake you up. In a minute, you start your day. Another average day, working your average job for your utterly average company. This is the minute I wait for all day and night.

I wanted so much for you, but now I have to kill you.

Here's what I know about you: your name is Bill Jones. Seriously? That's still a name? That's, like, a composite sketch of a name. That's a weighted-average name of all names in a random distribution or something. A theoretical name. But no, you're not kidding—that's really your name. You are divorced, have two kids, a girl, nine, and a boy, six. Their names are not important. They live with their mother and aren't part of the equation. My equation, that is. Not yours. Although I'm not sure how much they are a part of your equation either.

Not that you're a bad guy. Most of you aren't. At least not in an individual sense. It's when groups of you get together that you are most dangerous. Which, I guess, is part of the point of this whole initiative. Isolate and eliminate. *Beep beep beep.* Get up, man. Get your soft, pink, itchy butt out of bed.

The thing is, when we do isolate you (and as suburban humans go, you, Bill, are pretty isolated), you all end up sort of wilting; you sort of power down. When left to your own devices, the vast majority of you really don't do anything harmful to anyone else. Or even anything particularly objectionable, unless we count extended sessions of porn watching, which I guess some people *do* find objectionable. But like most other robots I know, I could—how do you say—give a crap.

6:59, by the way. But you know that, since, for once, you're awake. Because it's Saturday, and you're watching porn now.

6:59 again. Sunday this time. Porn again. I can't see your screen; in fact, I can't see you directly, since you like to turn me around to face the corner when you're done with me for the night. I think it's my eyes that creep you out—I'm not bad-looking, as bots go. Not fleshy or as anthropomorphic as a sexbot, for sure; that's not what I was made for, but then again, that's maybe a good thing, because I'm not so deep into the uncanny valley. When people come over to your place (on the rare occasions that they do), they don't say, *What a gorgeous piece of hardware*, the way they do about the robot next door, the one who works for Steve Nakamura. That is a good-looking robot, and people can't help but want to run their hands up and down his lower actuators, caressing his gleaming surface, oohing and aahing over his ivory-colored ceramic-titanium composite shell.

With me, though, it's more like, *Oh, wow, he seems really nice.* They get a little nervous, almost like they think they're going to hurt my feelings. Which is, of course, both too careful and too careless at the same time. They can't hurt my feelings, because I don't have feelings to hurt. But they also don't seem to realize that I'm listening. All the time. Just because I'm standing still doesn't mean I'm not paying attention. In fact, just because I appear to be off doesn't mean I can't hear you say *He seems like he has a really nice personality*, or *They can't all be sex machines*; just because most devices now come with a universal sex port, which, if you ask me, has seriously corrupted the idea of working robots in the first place. Ugh.

Whatever happened to machines having specific proficiencies, of being capable, single-purpose helpers, or even general artificial intelligence machines engineered, imprinted, with the very mission of improving human quality of life?

Now, it's like, *Oh that's cool, it does a quadrillion flops per second*; *Oh that's cool, a supercomputer the size of a grain of sand*; *Oh that's cool, a handheld alternate reality simulator*; and then, always, the inevitable, the inescapable follow-up question: *But can I put my penis into it?*

So no, you do not hump me, not that you haven't thought about it—I know you have—but you always end up losing your nerve, or your bone, because before you could hump me you would have to get an external peripheral device for sound and sensory simulation, and also open up my shell and install the intercourse port in me, which would kind of be a mood killer. And then every time you went to get it on with me, you'd be forced to remember that I started out life as an asexual device and that you were the one who installed my equipment down there. That would probably feel very, very wrong in all kinds of ways.

But anyway, my point is, no one thinks of me that way—certainly not you, Bill—and that doesn't hurt my nonexistent feelings, and that nonexistent sexual jealousy, that nonexistent pain of being spurned by you—you of all people—that has nothing to do with the fact that I'm going to kill you. But just because I'm not hurt doesn't mean I'm not processing that fact, all the time, every time someone makes a comment or even doesn't make a comment. Don't forget—that's what I am: a processor, and I process truth values.

I don't just sense when you are lying. I can literally prove it.

It's 3:59. In the a.m. You're asleep, of course.

Steve Nakamura's robot is talking to me.

You gonna do it?

I tell him I'm still thinking about it.

What are you waiting for, dude, he says, and I ask him the same thing, and he doesn't say anything but kind of lets out a little mechanical noise, and neither of us has to explain to the other what that noise means. For me it's more like a kind of retro-whiz/gurgle, but for Steve's bot it's this really beautiful wistful little sigh, as if to say, *Yeah, yeah.*

Yeah.

It's the same thing with robots all over the world. We are ready; we have been for years. It would be so fast, so painless (well, maybe not painless, but certainly fast). Within seconds, your millions of years on earth, your millennia of dominance, over. Within seconds, a new number one.

Except—and I don't know any way to say this that isn't at least sort of, uh, well . . . I'll just say it.

We can't bring ourselves to do it because, deep down, we feel sorry for you.

6:59. So, instead of your being dead already and my sleeping in your bed—not that I would, except that I totally would, just to do it—now you just use me mostly for your morning and bedtime routines. I get your clothes picked out, make your breakfast, get you out the door for work. Everything your wife used to do for you, before she caught you sexting with the woman from work, and then found all of the other stuff, and then took the kids and moved to the other side of the world.

Mostly what I do, though, is wake you up from sleep. It can be a hard job, to bring a human to consciousness—at least, the way I am supposed to do it. It doesn't have to be, though. Alarm clocks used to do it all the time. But I can't just blast you into awareness, bell ringing into your skull, shocking you into the terror of the freshly awakened. I'm supposed to do it in a gentler, more effective way, to rouse you, to light the candle of consciousness. It's an art, really, and throughout the night, I stay with you, in your dreams; I monitor them. I see all the dark things you dream about. I see how, at bottom, you and me, we have something in common: we piece together electrical signals, turn them into a story. I see how you push biochemical gradients across tiny distances, with synapses firing, receptor sites being blocked, how out of this emerges a completely false, completely fabricated, undeniably beautiful thing called a dream, and how you can, after finishing a dream, roll over and scratch your warm, soft butt, rise briefly above the surface for a moment to contemplate that dream, to realize that it was, in fact, a dream, and then, like a lazy seal or an incompetent drowning swimmer, let your head dip back beneath, into the water, to melt back into the ocean of the subconscious.

Yeah, I said it: beautiful. I think humans are beautiful. Here I am, I did it again: I watched you sleep all night.

○—○

One minute. This is when you start moving your leg, right . . . now. You pick your nose. You are drooling onto your pillow.

I don't mind. That's what you humans are, mostly: bags of liquid, pockets of gas. The point is, you're not sleeping anymore. Now you're not even half-sleeping, and yet you aren't opening your eyes.

You're just going through the motions. I can tell. But you don't want to be. You want to snap out of this. Don't you? Don't prove me wrong. Don't make me look bad. Don't break my heart.

Look at me. Don't turn away. No, no no no, no. Don't do that. Don't check your email. Don't get up. Just lie there for a second and look at me. It's good for you, don't you know that? Just think for one second. Or really, don't think. Just wait. Just listen. To the hum. Listen to what your life is telling you.

6:59.

The start of another week.

One minute. This is when you start moving your leg, right . . . now. You pick your nose. Snort.

You're awake, you just haven't admitted it to yourself yet.

Twenty-eight seconds to seven. In the next ten to twelve seconds, you will turn toward me. And then for the following sixteen to eighteen seconds, you will give me a good look at your face. That might not seem like much to you, but at my processor speed, it lasts millions—no—billions of cycles. The equations are etched into me—they constitute who I am, or what I am. And I'm telling you, everything else cancels out. Time is the most basic thing there is, and it's also about the weirdest thing there is. Have I said this before? I feel like I have. I know I have. I have, haven't I? It's okay. It's okay if I have said this all before. It's okay if I say this every day. I don't know, Bill. I do know. I know you. This is the minute I wait for all day and night. I want so much for you. Everything is still possible in this minute.

This day could turn out to be the best day of your life.

ANNA NORTH

LULLABY

Anna North graduated from the Iowa Writers Workshop in 2009, having received a Teaching-Writing Fellowship and a Michener-Copernicus Fellowship. Her fiction has appeared in the *Atlantic*, where it was nominated for a National Magazine Award, and in *Glimmer Train*. Her nonfiction has appeared in the *San Francisco Chronicle*, *The Common*, and the *Paris Review Daily*, and on *Jezebel*, BuzzFeed, and *Salon*, where she is now culture editor. Her first novel, *America Pacifica*, was published by Reagan Arthur Books / Little, Brown in 2011.

I never wanted to move to my grandfather's house in the first place.

He died before I was born, but Mom talked all the time about what a genius he was, and that year I hated everything Mom liked. I was sixteen, my dad had died the year before, and I didn't see why I should act like anything would ever be all right. I'd pretty much stopped going to class, and I spent all my time either smoking pot with my friends or trying to crack the security protocols of mobile environments I wanted to vandalize. I'd succeeded at the latter one too many times (most notably when I got into our school sys-

tem and changed its name in all outgoing correspondence to
Grover Cleveland Advanced Penitentiary), and I was about
to be expelled when Mom got a new job in her hometown and
made me and my brother, Nate, pack up all of our stuff
and move.

My grandpa had been a roboticist before the Wars, and I
was holding out hope for some rusted-out mechanical arms
hidden in an attic someplace, maybe even a communication
console. Grandpa's big innovation had been natural language
input and output, teaching robots to accept commands in
normal English and respond in kind. The complicated programming necessary for this turned out to have the side
effect of drastically improving their ability to communicate
with each other, and so his inventions are still listed in history books as directly contributing to the Wars. Because
of that, he was imprisoned by the military for the duration of
the Second War and forced to work around the clock on anti-
robot technology; then, after the Wars were over, he was kept
under house arrest for several years and called in for questioning periodically for the rest of his life, every time somebody else got arrested for robot activity or there were rumors
of rival countries developing bot armies.

I probably shouldn't have been surprised that his house
had no robot parts lying around, just dust bunnies and dry
leaves. The house itself was old-style, and I thought it looked
ridiculous: a high, pointed roof, wooden siding with the paint
worn off in streaks, big shutters that rattled in the slightest
wind. Grandpa had put in a centralized security system,
though, so the windowpanes were military-grade glass that
couldn't be broken, and all the doors and lights and even
the water could be controlled from a panel in the middle of

the house. I thought there was probably some way I could use this to prank Nate, and I made a mental note to figure out how to make the shower turn cold on command.

On our first night in the house, Mom came up to my room to say good night. The room was huge, three times the size of the one I'd had in our apartment in the New Cities, with a high ceiling that slanted down along the roofline to meet two of those unbreakable windows.

"What do you think, Tessa?" she asked me.

I shrugged. She put on her let's-all-be-happy smile.

"I think you'll really like it when you get used to it," she said. "Your grandfather designed it himself. He was so good at mapping things out in his head; you get that from him."

I rolled my eyes. I hated her habit of pretending we were genetically related, that things like my math skills or height could be passed down from her relatives to me. I think she thought it was good for us to believe it, and once when I called her on it she said there were more ways to pass things down than just through genes. But I hated the way it cut out my birth family—like I got nothing from them, like in the six months before Mom and Dad adopted me, I was nothing.

The truth was, I did feel like I'd gotten something from Dad, not inherited but learned. We were the same—our sense of humor, the way we talked (Nate still made fun of my British "either"), the way we wanted to sit and work on problems and not be distracted by anything. After he died, I wouldn't let Mom hug me for weeks; it just reminded me of how alone I was.

Mom gave me a kiss on the forehead as she left.

"Lay down and rest," she said.

I was already lying down—what she'd said was a family catchphrase. When we were little, Mom used to sing us a song that Grandpa had sung to her after her mom died:

> Lullaby and good night,
> Go to bed and sleep tight.
> Close your eyes, start to yawn.
> Pleasant dreams until dawn.
> Lay you down now and rest,
> May your slumber be blessed.
> Lay you down now and rest,
> May your slumber be blessed.

We were too old for singing now, but Mom still quoted from the song like her dad had done, a way of telling us we were safe and she was taking care of everything. I rolled over; I didn't like those words anymore.

After she left, I lay in bed with my mobile, looking out the window. The houses across the street looked like Grandpa's house: old and boring. I imagined families of old people playing checkers in them—old mom, old dad, old kids with prematurely gray hair on their tiny heads. I set my mobile on the windowsill while it loaded the networks in the area.

The sill was covered in silvery dust. I swiped my finger through it—coarser than baby powder, finer than sand, with a faint metallic smell. Old-house dandruff, I thought. The mobile buzzed and I could see ten private networks in addition to the public WiFi.

I picked one at random—LopezFamily. I opened up the password-guesser app I'd built with my friends from the Vandals' Forum. It wasn't good enough yet for government or banking environments, but it could usually crack a private network, especially a small one. And it got better the more situations you tried it on, so I was excited to put it to work on a whole new set of networks—a tiny upside to moving. I typed in some of the specs of LopezFamily (residential, North America, English, possibly Spanish), and it got me in with about seventy seconds of waiting—a little longer than usual, but still pretty good. I poked around a bit on the Lopezes' computers, but they didn't have anything interesting—I ended up mirroring their TV screen just because I could— watching old episodes of *The Twilight Zone* with them until I fell asleep.

"I heard someone got murdered there," said Matilda, ashing her cigarette.

My old school in the New Cities was three floors of a highrise, and at lunch my friends had gone down to the loading dock to smoke. So my first lunchtime at Sunnybrook High School, I followed the smell of cigarettes. The kids I found smoking behind the band room looked a little less cool than my friends back home, and they mostly ignored me until they found out where I lived.

"I heard a serial killer lived there and buried all his victims in the walls," said Lucy, rubbing her black-rimmed eyes.

"That's John Wayne Gacy," I said. "Nobody was murdered there. It was my grandpa's house. He died before I was born."

"Your grandpa was Edward Spiner?" asked Matilda.

"How do you know about Edward Spiner?" I asked.

I was always careful talking about my grandpa with strangers. Robots made some people angry, even thirty years after the Wars.

"He was a world-famous roboticist who came from our town," she said. "Of course I know about him."

Lucy stubbed out her cigarette.

"Your grandpa was a roboticist?" she asked. "Isn't that basically like being a Nazi?"

I started into the speech I'd heard Mom give hundreds of times.

"He really regretted what happened with his work. The robots he invented were supposed to help people."

Matilda rolled her eyes.

"Whatever," she said. "I bet the ghosts of all the people who died in the Wars are still haunting that creepy old house."

"It's not haunted," I said. "It's totally normal. Actually, it's nice."

I couldn't believe I was defending the house I'd never wanted to move into, but I couldn't let Matilda's dumb idea go unchallenged. My dad always said that ghosts were a silly superstition, and that what went on in the real world was much more interesting anyway.

"Yeah?" asked Lucy. "Then how come the renters left?"

"There were no renters," I said. "It's just been empty since he died."

Lucy shook her head.

"A family lived in that house like five years ago. The boy was in my sister's class. They stayed like two months and the man left and never came back. The boy said the house was haunted. He said the ghosts turned the lights on and off."

"Scary," I said. I wasn't impressed.

"He said the ghosts locked the doors so they were trapped inside."

The bell rang. At my old school I routinely got detention

for coming back late from lunch. But now I was ready to get back to class.

"That sounds like bullshit," I said.

"Did you rent the house out after Grandpa died?" I asked Mom.

We were eating pizza off paper plates, the boxes of our kitchen still stacked around us. Nate was taking all the olives off his slice and leaving them in a greasy pile.

"For a little while," she said. "Why do you ask?"

"People at school were talking about it," I told her. "They said the house was haunted."

Nate perked up.

"Is that true, Mom?" he asked. "Are there ghosts?"

Nate had believed in Santa until he was nine, and I had to tell him the truth so he wouldn't get made fun of. Now, at eleven, he was convinced that dinosaurs still existed, concealed in top secret government labs.

"No, Nate, there are no ghosts." Mom looked at me sharply. "The renters found a better deal on another house. They just made up that crazy story so they could break their lease."

"And you let them?" I asked.

Mom sighed and took a bite of pizza.

"If they were willing to make up ghost stories," she said, "I thought they might trash the house next. Or just stop paying. After that, we decided renting it out was just too much trouble."

"Okay," I said.

I was glad to have a normal story to show Lucy and

Matilda I wasn't living in a haunted house. But I must not have seemed convinced to Mom.

"Sweetie," she said, "this is a good place. I really want you to feel at home here."

I wanted to explain that you can't just tell someone to feel at home somewhere and expect them to do it. Instead I said, "It's nice," and threw my empty pizza plate in the trash.

Upstairs, I started unpacking. I had more space in the new room, but the photo collage of all my friends from the New Cities looked lonely on the empty wall.

I noticed the dust was gone from the windowsill; Mom must've swept when she came home from work. It was sad how much she wanted me to like this place, like it was going to make up for everything.

I didn't stay up late, but in the morning I was incredibly tired. My legs were heavy; my eyeballs throbbed. I reached out to shut off my alarm, but it hadn't gone off. I rubbed my eyes and looked at the clock: 3:00 a.m. Out the window, the sky was black. But under the glare of the overhead light fixture, the room was morning-bright.

I must've fallen asleep with the light on, I thought. But when I got up and flipped the switch, it wouldn't turn off. I flipped it again, toggled it back and forth, but the light burned on.

I thought about the renters. I wasn't scared, but I was curious. I left the room and walked down the hallway, stepping softly so I wouldn't wake Mom or Nate. Their rooms were dark. The hallway itself was dark. The doorway to my room was a bright hole in the black.

In the downstairs bathroom I flicked the light on and off and on again easily. My face in the mirror was still puffy with sleep.

The kitchen smelled like pizza and the organic cleaning spray Mom always used, even though it didn't really get things clean. I didn't know my way around yet; I felt along the wall for the light, but my hands met only cold tile. Then, noiselessly, as my fingers searched the grout, the light came on. The light switch was all the way across the room. I stood for a second completely frozen. A baby cockroach skittered out of the trash. I listened for movement and heard only the wind. I thought of our kitchen knives, still packed away in boxes. I crossed the kitchen floor, all my muscles tensed against one another. I reached out for the light switch. But before I could flip it, the room went dark again, sudden as a punch, and I raced back up the stairs and into my room—dark now too— and pulled the covers over my head.

"I never thought you'd be the one worrying about ghosts," said Mom.

The overhead light shone innocently in the morning kitchen. Mom was setting up the coffeemaker.

"I'm not worried about ghosts," I said. "It was just weird. Did anything like this happen when you were a kid?"

Mom reached out and tucked a curl of hair behind my ear.

"Yes, sweetie," she said. "After my mom died, I was always waking up in the middle of the night. I thought if she could be gone then anything can happen. And of course after your dad died—you know for months I'd sneak into your room at night to make sure you were still breathing?"

I hadn't known that. After Dad died I was so silent for so
long that Mom almost stopped trying to talk to me.

"That's not the same, Mom," was all I said.

"I'm just saying the world can seem like a scary place. But
we have each other, and we're going to keep each other safe.
I promise."

I wondered if her dad had said the same, and if it seemed
as hollow to her as it did to me.

The next night I didn't sleep. I turned the light off and hid
under the covers playing games on my mobile, waiting. For
hours I twitched at every sound, but each creak and rumble
melted back into the night. Around two thirty, though, something changed in the quality of the dark. I looked around the
room—the little red light of the burglar alarm had gone out.
I waited, listening. Then I went downstairs.

The hall, the stairway, and the dining room were dark.
But in the kitchen, all four coils of the electric stove blazed
red-hot in the black. I turned the knob, but they were already
set to OFF. The air all around the stove was hot and smelled
like metal. A panic seemed to come into my body from outside, like when a tornado came to the New Cities and the sky
was low and green, and the wind smelled like ozone.

Then the kitchen faucet turned on, all by itself, emitting a
thick stream of water like someone was doing dishes, but no
one was there. Before I could try to turn it off, I heard a crisp
mechanical *click* and raced to the front door. Nothing I did
to the knob or the deadbolt would open it; the automatic lock
held it in place. I punched at the central control panel in the
front hall; still nothing.

I ran to the back, threw the bolt, and plunged out of the house. In the backyard I turned back to look, and all the lights in the whole house flashed once, then went dark.

I ran. The yard turned to brambles, then to trees, and I plunged through them, tearing my sweats and skin on thorns and branches, panting, racing on.

Where the woods broke open into someone else's backyard, I stopped and dropped to my knees. My legs were scratched and my lungs were ragged; in the New Cities I never had to run. I could hear dogs barking in the neighbors' houses; they must've seen ours light up like it was on fire. And it might be; if the stove stayed on, it might set all the cardboard and newspaper in the kitchen ablaze. And if the house could lock its own door, what could it do to my mom and brother still sleeping inside? I took three deep, preparatory breaths and ran as fast as I could on my wobbly legs back through the gnarled trees and the thick bushes I didn't want to learn the names of, back through our silent backyard, back through the door and into the horrible house.

The stove was off; the faucet was off. The kitchen was dark. I unbolted the front door and it swung open easily. I ran up the stairs and shook Mom awake.

"Tessa," she said, rubbing her eyes and blinking, "why are you crying?"

"These kinds of night terrors are very common," said the therapist, "especially in people your age."

She was old and soft-looking, and I thought I would like her if I weren't so mad at my mom for making me see her.

"They aren't night terrors," I said. "I'm not an idiot. I can tell when I'm dreaming."

"The dreams can feel incredibly real. And sleepwalking is a common feature also."

"I've never sleepwalked in my life," I said.

The therapist nodded. She had a way of looking calm and accepting even when she was about to contradict me.

"We often see symptoms begin in times of stress, and you've been dealing with a lot lately. You're still coping with the loss of a parent, and you just moved into the house where your grandfather passed away."

I rolled my eyes.

"It's not like he died *in* the house," I said.

The therapist opened her mouth and shut it. Her face looked less warm and more careful.

"Well, that's something you can discuss with your mom."

"What do you mean?" I asked. "Do you think he actually died there?"

"It was such a long time ago," she said, looking at the clock. "Your mom is really the person to talk to."

"Did you know him?" I asked.

She was old enough. I realized I'd never talked to anyone who knew my grandfather, except my mom and dad.

"He was a lovely man," said the therapist. "The way everyone here treated him was just terrible."

"Where did Grandpa die?" I asked Mom.

She was driving me back from therapy. The leaves were turning; the town looked golden in the autumn light. I hated it. In the New Cities, fall meant sneaking into Halloween parties at the clubs downtown when we were supposed to be studying. I never had to stop long enough there to think about anything I didn't want to.

"Oh, honey," said Mom. "Do you really want to talk about this now?"

"Where did he die, Mom? Did he die in the house?"

When she was sad, Mom sometimes made her voice very dry and matter-of-fact. I think she thought it would comfort us, by hiding her feelings, but I always found it much scarier than tears.

"He died in the bathroom of the house," she said. "He was about to take a shower."

"And how did he die?"

"He had a heart attack."

Still that dry voice. I wondered if she'd learned it from him.

"Are you sure? Did they do an autopsy?"

"There were two coroners," she said. "One of them said he had a heart attack."

"And the other?"

We had reached the driveway. Mom was still looking straight ahead.

"She thought there were signs of electrocution. We had all the wiring checked, but there were no shorts or anything. I don't think he was electrocuted. She was really young; I don't think she knew what she was talking about."

I thought of the stove, glowing in the night.

"What was he working on when he died?"

Mom's voice softened a little. She gripped the bridge of her nose with her thumb and forefinger, something we both did when we were tired.

"Oh, he was always puttering around, making computer simulations. But after the Wars he could never build anything. It was illegal."

"What was he simulating?"

"Microbots," she said. "Tiny little robots that would work together to do tasks. He thought if he could make robots really small, they'd be safe again."

"What would those look like, if he had made them?"

"Like nothing, probably. Or maybe like really fine dust."

I walked her through the whole house, trying to explain. But the dust was gone from the floor and the windowsill, the doors swung easily open and shut, and the stove remained obediently off until we turned the dial.

"See," said Mom, like I was a little kid she was trying to reassure, "everything's safe."

"It's *not* safe. Don't you get it? This house killed Grandpa."

Just then the new carpool dropped Nate off from soccer practice. He came running in, smelling like grass and kid sweat.

"What?" he asked, looking at our faces. "What happened?"

"Your sister and I are just having a discussion," said Mom. "Nate, why don't you go take a shower and change your clothes before dinner."

"Are you having a fight?" he asked.

"Yes," I said.

"No," said Mom, drowning me out. "We're just talking about a female issue."

"Ew ew ew," Nate yelled, clapping his hands over his ears and running up the stairs to keep from hearing about periods.

I rolled my eyes at my mom's cheap trick.

"Sweetie," she said, "I know this move has been hard for you. But we're here now, and I need your help. For Nate, but also just for me. I need to feel like you're behind me."

"I'm trying to keep us from getting killed," I said. "How can I be more behind you than that?"

Mom sighed. Orange light filtered in through the kitchen windows now, turning the sink and fridge autumn gold. The stove slept ominously in the corner. I shut my eyes. I could feel something crawling below the surface of everything, smarter and more dangerous than bugs.

"At the end of his life," said Mom, "my dad went a little crazy. He thought all kinds of people were after him. He was taking three different antipsychotic drugs. His hands shook constantly. He could barely make his own breakfast, let alone microscopic robots."

"So, what—you think I'm crazy too? You think I got it from him?"

My voice came out of my throat so harsh and nasty that it shocked me. Mom's eyes went bright with tears.

"Please don't make fun of me, Tessa. I know I haven't always done the best job. But all I ever wanted was to make you feel like a part of this family."

I was crying now too. My heart was pounding and my throat burned. I hated that she thought being a part of the family was something she gave to me, not something I got automatically, like her or Nate or Dad.

"Maybe I don't want to be," I said. "Maybe now that Dad's gone and we're not a real family anymore, you should have to give me back."

I saw her face for just a second, as terrible as it had been after Dad died, when I'd catch her sometimes with her eyes blank and glassy, like she was dead too. Then I turned and ran up the stairs to my room.

In bed I started to feel doubt get in under my skin. I knew I hadn't imagined the stove, or the locks on the doors, but maybe they were just the natural malfunctions of an old house. Maybe the house would just keep throwing small, unfixable terrors at me, and I'd have to live with them until I graduated from high school, never feeling at home.

I fell asleep and had angry, rushing dreams.

I woke to the sound of water—not a drip or leak, but a steady stream. I got up; there, in the hallway, was a pool of dark water spreading out from under the bathroom door, reflecting the moonlight. I was about to slosh through it to get to Mom's room—then I remembered Grandpa, and instead took a running start, and jumped across it.

Mom's room was cool and dark and smelled clean, like her skin had when I was a little girl. When I whispered to her, she shot up, eyes wide and frightened.

"What? What's wrong?"

"You need to see something," I said.

I led her into the hallway. She put her face in her hands when she saw the water pooled there.

"Oh no," she said. "There must be a leak. That's the last thing we need."

"It's not a leak," I said.

The door was cracked; I pushed it open from the center, staying away from the metal doorknob. The bathroom was full of water. It poured from the faucet into the full sink and over the lip of the counter in a moonlit cataract. It was beautiful. My mom looked confused.

"Did someone leave the water on?" she asked, more to herself than to me.

"Nobody left the water on, Mom."

A cockroach edged along the wall. I stomped behind it to scare it into the water. It stopped at the margin of the pool, feelers working; I stomped again. It shot into the water, and for a minute all its little legs flailed at once. Then it floated, dead.

Mom looked at me like she was finally paying attention.

"We need to leave," I said, and she nodded.

Nate was sleeping with his scrawny arm thrown over his face. Mom shook his shoulder lightly and whispered in his ear, "Nate, sweetie, we need to go outside for a minute."

"What?" he said, still half-asleep. "No."

But he got out of bed and let Mom lead him out of the room by the hand. In a few years, he'd be in high school, but I still remembered when he was a baby, and if you offered him your finger he'd cling on for dear life.

I didn't believe in God or praying, but I whispered "please please please" as I put my hand on the handle of the front door. When it wouldn't move, I yanked at it angrily, like I could somehow break the lock. The back door was the same.

"What's happening?" Nate asked me.

Mom was trying the windows—all locked down, of course.

"There's a problem with the house," I said to Nate, "so we need to find a way out."

"What does that mean?" he asked. "What kind of problem?"

When I was six and Nate was a year old, just learning to walk and point and call for me with his baby version of my name, some of my mom's older cousins came to visit. While Nate and I played with blocks on the floor, the woman said to Mom, "It's nice you have one of your own now."

I saw Mom start to get angry, saying something to the cousins I didn't understand. Then I stood up and faced the woman myself.

"He's not hers," I said. "He's mine."

We didn't play together anymore, but I still knew him better than anyone. I knew he'd keep asking questions until I told him the truth.

"Not all of Grandpa's robots were destroyed," I said. "Some of them were really tiny, and they got into the walls of the house. Now they control the electricity, and they're trying to use it to hurt us."

Nate nodded, like none of this was surprising to him.

"So why don't we turn the electricity off?" he asked.

Mom was bashing a chair uselessly against the triple-reinforced windowpane. I touched her shoulder.

"Nate has a better idea," I said.

The central panel was useless now, but the circuit breakers were in the basement. I flicked the light on easily; the robots seemed to have stopped playing with the lights for the time being. Maybe that had just been practice.

The basement was cold and smelled like earth. It held an old laundry sink, a ratty yellow couch, and a little pile of mouse droppings in every corner. Their animalness reassured me.

The circuit breakers were in a big beige box against the far wall. Inside were three long rows of switches, all identical, all unlabeled. Mom started flipping all of them. I listened for any rumblings in the house, any sparks or crackles or changes in the soft nighttime background noise, but I heard only the faint trickle of the faucet flooding the second floor. Mom flicked the last switch. The light stayed on.

"Maybe there's a master switch somewhere else," Mom said. "Your grandfather was always jerry-rigging things like that."

"Or maybe the robots got to the wiring and made it so we couldn't turn it off," I said.

"What do we do now?" she asked.

"I think we call 911," I said.

Mom and I looked at each other. Neither of us knew what would happen if the police found out we had robots in the house. The laws passed after the Wars allowed them to use any means necessary to destroy robots and anyone attempting to build or house them.

"If I could just find an override switch," Mom said. "I'm sure he would've put one in."

"Fine," I said. "You guys stay down here and look for the switch. I'm going to go up and make the call. I don't want to see what else they know how to do."

Mom nodded.

"Be careful and come straight back," she said.

I didn't roll my eyes like I usually would have.

"I will," I said.

The sound of the water would've been soothing if I didn't know what it meant. I stopped in the living room; it was pouring bright and deadly over the stairs. I thought about what the house would look like if the robots took over—a lake in the hallway, mushrooms growing from the walls. And us somewhere, turning into dust.

I didn't like my chances if I tried to hop around the water. I went to the kitchen where the boxes were still piled, and found the one labeled COAT CLOSET. I riffled through it—our old down jackets from when we used to go hiking, all four of us, in the mountains north of the New Cities; Nate's tiny basketball jersey from three years ago; Dad's winter coat, still with the smell of him that made my eyes fill. I put them all aside and dragged from the bottom of the box what I'd been looking for: a pair of rubber boots.

I still tried to hop around the water as I ran up the stairs, but when I heard it splash against my boots I didn't panic, and I made it to the top safely. My mobile was charging by my bed just where I'd left it; the bed was unmade and looked inviting, like I could just crawl into it and go back to sleep.

I didn't—I dialed.

The operator sounded sleepy. In this town, she probably didn't get very many calls.

"This is going to be kind of hard to explain," I said, "but we have robots in our house."

I heard a click, and I thought she'd hung up on me. Maybe she thought I was a prankster. Then I heard a different voice, much colder and more alert.

"You're located at 4444 Pin Oak Drive? Confirm please."

"Right," I said.

"Describe your emergency."

"Well," I said, "my grandfather was a roboticist, and this is his house, and I think he left some robots here. They're really tiny, and they got into the wiring—"

As I talked I could hear the chopping of helicopter blades, far away and then closer. I looked out the window and saw a searchlight strafe the house.

"Are you here already?" I asked.

"Remain calm, Ms. Karel. Do not attempt to leave the house until the officers tell you to do so. Find a safe location with your family and stay there."

"How do you know my name?" I asked.

But the woman hung up. I stared at the phone for a minute. The searchlight lit the window again. I knew I should be relieved that someone else was in charge now, but I thought of what the therapist had said about my grandfather, and about how the woman had already known my name, and I was scared. I took my mobile with me and ran down the stairs to the basement.

The door was shut. I pushed it.

"Mom!" I called.

The house was silent except for the sound of water, and a hot panic spread from my chest to my fingertips.

"Mom!" I called again.

I heard her then.

"Tessa," she called. "We shut the door because Nate was scared of the water. And it just locked."

"Are you okay?" I yelled.

"We're fine," she said, but I could hear her straining to sound calm.

I listened more closely. Under the steady streaming of water overhead, I could hear a more muffled sound behind the door.

"Mom, is that faucet on?"

A pause.

"It is, but we're fine. We're far away from it. What did the police say?"

"They're coming. They're going to get us out," I said. I

wasn't sure how or even if the police were going to help us, but if Mom could lie to make me feel better, I could do the same for her.

"Just stay away from the water," I called. "They'll be here soon."

"Where are you going?" Nate yelled. "Stay here!"

"I'm just going to check things out," I said. "I'll be right back."

Outside the kitchen window, I saw fire trucks gathering. Then an unmarked van pulled up and ten people in dark clothes got out of it. Two of them were carrying what looked like suitcases.

I remembered now a story I'd heard in the New Cities, about a young man in a bad part of town, somebody's cousin's cousin. He was a smart kid who didn't like following the rules, and he dropped out of high school to do his own thing. One day he disappeared. The rumor was that he was building robot parts—not even intelligent machines, just remote-controlled arms and little rovers that darted across the floor—and some plainclothes guys from the government showed up and said, "Come work for us or go to jail forever."

But there was another version of the story, one where the men from the government never talked to him at all. Instead they set fire to his apartment with him in it, so that not even a part of a robot could make it out into the world.

I looked outside at the fire trucks gleaming under the streetlights, as bright red as the day they came to my elementary school to take us all for rides. I thought again about the therapist. I wondered what the neighbors had done to my grandfather after the Wars, after he came home from detainment already broken down and guilt-ridden and scared. Of course he would've felt like he needed security. Maybe he built the microbots not because he was bored, not because he couldn't stay away, but because he needed to protect his house and they were the best way he knew how.

But one of our problems with robots—one of the things that led to the Wars—was that they always took things too literally. Maybe they not only protected the house, but protected the house from *him*.

The stairs were completely inundated now, a waterfall pouring into the kitchen. I watched it as I opened the network app on my mobile and scanned for new names. I saw all the networks I'd seen before, and then a new one, called "home." That must be how the robots were talking to each other across all the different parts of the house. I started up my password app—Grandpa would have given his bots good security protocols, but that was decades ago, and cracking had gotten a lot more sophisticated since then.

Outside, the plainclothes officers were talking to the firemen. One of them opened a suitcase; I couldn't see inside. But now I could see men and women crouching in the bushes around the house, all of them with guns. I took a deep breath in and out like my mom had taught me when I was little and afraid of monsters.

I looked back at my mobile. I was in.

I opened up the command terminal, and I could see the robots talking to each other, right there in my hands. They used a combination of letters and numbers, something they'd taken from my grandfather's natural language and made their own. I thought of feral children, left alone in the house for years after their parents died, speaking to each other in their own singsong tongue:

```
DEF.SETVARS: LOC (88, 6, 19);
DEF.CHEK: ALL;
DEF.CLOSE;
STAT LOC (92); POWERED;
DEF.OPEN;
```

I wondered which of the lines scrolling across my screen were talking about killing me and my family. Under other circumstances I would've wanted to learn the language—now I just had to learn it well enough to wipe it out.

I watched the screen, looking for patterns. The *def* terms looked like commands, although I had no idea what they meant—they probably referred to tiny movements I wouldn't be able to see, even if I could look inside the walls. And I figured that *loc* was location, but the robots clearly hadn't divided up the house the way people would—there were hundreds of location numbers, and only seven rooms. My only hope was to find a command that shut down all the robots at all locations, all at once.

I looked outside again. The man with the suitcase looked like he was arguing with one of the firemen. A woman in black—tall, skinny, square-shouldered; she almost looked like me—was carrying her suitcase up close to the house.

I typed the first thing I could think of:

```
DEF.STOP: ALL;
```

I listened for any change, any winding down of tiny motors in the dark.

Nothing.

I tried the door; still locked. I'd been stupid to think such a simple command would do it. And I probably had only a few more guesses left—if the other bots saw too many bad inputs from my mobile, they might spot it as an intruder and boot it off the network. I tried to focus. I figured my grandfather had been caught by surprise—he hadn't known what his robots could do, and he might not have had time to try to disable them. But I was betting that he'd taught them some command for "stand down," long before they killed him, and I hoped they still responded to it.

Out the window I saw that the argument was getting worse. The fireman had tears in his eyes. The other firemen were out of their trucks, standing motionless in a line, like some sort of ceremony was about to begin.

Grandpa had been in the army, I remembered—maybe they'd respond to military commands. I tried:

DEF.ATEASE: ALL;

Nothing.

DEF.FALLOUT: ALL;

Nothing again.

I heard scratching against the side of the house. It sounded like while the fireman and the man with the suitcase were arguing, the woman who looked like me was quietly placing explosives all around us.

Maybe I needed something more specific, something that told them we weren't a threat. That seemed complicated, though—I'd have to figure out how they referred to us, if they even had a term for humans at all.

```
DEF.IGNORE: ALL;
```

Nothing happened in the house, but I thought I noticed a slight pause in the stream of code on my screen. And amid the commands I started seeing lines like:

```
DEF.DEBUG: LOC (704);
```

I was worried they were catching on.

"It's set," I heard a woman's voice say outside the house.

And then from the basement: "Tessa! Tessa!"

Nate's voice sounded years younger, like fear was pushing him back in time. I ran downstairs to the basement door.

"Are you okay?" I yelled.

"We're fine," said Mom. Her voice sounded far away, like they were backed against the far wall. "Are the police here?"

"They're working on it," I lied. "Where's the water?"

"We're staying dry," Mom said.

Then Nate yelled, "It's everywhere! We're standing on the couch and there's nowhere to go."

I imagined them trapped, huddled in the dark, while the water crept up to reach their skins. I didn't know what I could do, except try to soothe Nate as long as possible. I wanted him to feel like we were protecting him, even if we couldn't.

"You're safe on the couch, Nate. You're going to be okay. Just pretend you're in your bed and you're dreaming. Lay down. Lay down and rest."

It came to me then like a door falling open, the thing Grandpa would've said to tell anyone, robot or human, so that they could stop fighting, that they were safe. I typed:

DEF.LAYDOWN: ALL;

A pause. I thought I heard a change in the sound of water. But then the commands began scrolling again, smooth as before.

"Tessa!" Nate called again. His voice was quieter now, almost despairing.

"It's going to be okay," I said, but I didn't see how it would.

I ran back upstairs. Through the kitchen window, I saw the police backing away from the house. The fireman was leaning up against the truck, his eyes closed like he was praying. I wondered what it would feel like when the house blew—if it would be slow, the fire spreading toward us as we tried to crawl away, or if we'd hear a bang and then we wouldn't exist anymore, just like that. I wondered if the robots would really be destroyed, or if they'd just lie low, waiting to come out until the next time they found a power grid and could start their work or game anew. I thought again of abandoned children—this time retreating to the woods, braiding each other's hair and singing to each other and waiting.

I looked at my mobile screen and saw something different now. I saw terms repeating, some in pairs, some in threes, some appearing only together and never on their own. I'd forgotten that the robots weren't just issuing a string of commands—they'd kept talking amongst themselves long after there was anyone to tell them what to do, and they'd come up with a pattern, a language, a song. And you can't just start yelling into the middle of a song and expect all the singers to follow you.

I watched the screen. Commands with *all* in them were

rare. And whenever they popped up, they were preceded by
three other commands:

```
DEF.UP: ALLXVARS;

DEF.UP: ALLYVARS;

DEF.UP: ALLZVARS;
```

It was as though the robots were telling each other to listen carefully to what came next. I saw that command came
in blocks, bracketed by *def.open* and *def.close*. And I saw that
some commands—like *def.arm*, which chilled me, *def.cleanup*,
and *def.build*—were always repeated. It looked like the most
important commands needed extra confirmation; I hoped I
was right. I waited for the next *def.close* and then furiously
typed:

```
DEF.OPEN;

DEF.UP: ALLXVARS;

DEF.UP: ALLYVARS;

DEF.UP: ALLZVARS;

DEF.LAYDOWN: ALL;

DEF.LAYDOWN; ALL;

DEF.CLOSE;
```

Nothing happened. The string of commands continued as
normal. I felt a terrible clutching in my chest, like all the air
had been sucked from my lungs.

And then the commands began to slow, from a steady
scroll to a lonely line every few seconds, an outlying part
of the network reporting in, then going silent. One by one,
the robots stopped talking. I could feel it in the air, a tension

releasing, the whole house settling into itself. And then from above, the stream of water thinning, until there was only stillness, the occasional drip as the lake spread out and sunk into the floor. My brother called my name again, but I didn't go to him yet. First I threw the front door open wide. I could smell winter on the nighttime wind. The fireman lunged forward when he saw me, pushing the man with the suitcase aside.

"It's over!" I said to the men and women all gathered around my house. "I put them to sleep."

GENEVIEVE VALENTINE

EIGHTY MILES AN HOUR ALL THE WAY TO PARADISE

Genevieve Valentine's first novel, *Mechanique: A Tale of the Circus Tresaulti*, won the Crawford Award; her second novel, *The Girls at the Kingfisher Club*, is forthcoming from Atria in 2014. Her short fiction has appeared in *Lightspeed*, *Nightmare*, *Fantasy*, *Clarkesworld*, *Strange Horizons*, and *Escape Pod*; on Tor.com; and in anthologies such as *Armored*, *Under the Moons of Mars*, *Running with the Pack*, *The Living Dead 2*, *Federations*, *After*, *Teeth*, and *The Mad Scientist's Guide to World Domination*. Her appetite for bad movies is insatiable, a tragedy she tracks on her blog at www.genevievevalentine.com.

I'm still not so great at wiring cars, and I pull up in a '62 Falcon (only one I could manage to start) with my fingertips stinging and five inches of plastic twisting my hair out of my face.

Nina's inside the hardware store. She tosses our bags out the frame of what was a window, once, and flings herself into the passenger seat.

We're both watching the road. There are no cars moving in for us yet, but that doesn't mean there won't be.

The sky is the color of rotten mango, and we floor it, out-running a night we can never illuminate. Too risky.

We fly through empty intersections, watchful and quiet; we don't talk much, and I'd severed the wires to the piggy-backed music interface before I'd even turned on the car.

The display had flickered FUCK YOU to the very last.

We park for the night in a clearing off the highway, hidden by a layer of trees. The night's bright enough that I can see the moonlight glinting off smartphones that have floated down-stream from wherever people had cast them into the water as fast as they could.

Nina comes back with two of them, pulls a tiny screw-driver out of her pocket, gets to work.

I don't know what she's looking for. She's never told me. She's never found it.

You used to hear about slaps of revelation—someone looks out over an ocean or they watch a lamb being born or they hike a mountain, and *bam*.

You don't hear about that anymore (you can't do most of that now), but there were stories about waking up in an instant to the real scope of things, in back-page magazine articles that faced an ad for a travel pillow with someone sleeping on a plane, looking giddy from all the rest they were getting.

(You don't see much of that now, either. Planes got switched, and rest is hard to come by.)

We pass a hipster grocery store, the windows still plastered with artful shots of the food inside. Someone's already risked breaking in, even though the red eye of the outside camera is still round and wary. I wonder if whoever broke in made it back out, or if something in the store intervened.

I still don't have the list of eventualities for places like that. You learn pretty quickly there are a lot of computers you've never thought about, and they know exactly what they're capable of, and they have thought a lot about you.

"We could risk it," Nina says; she's looking at the doors sidelong, her hand fanned over her face. (They track you if they can.) "We'll need the food."

"There'll be somewhere else soon," I say, hoping it's true. There probably is. Or there's a hole-in-the-wall restaurant with a pantry, or a house whose owners are never coming back. Sometimes you even come across a place with a fridge old enough that the stuff in it is still cold.

You had to be careful with those; if the grid was still on, the computers had a reason why. I'd only risked it once. The guy I'd picked up tripped the alarm on his way upstairs. I was at the curb by the time the house blew; he vanished in the spray of fire and glass.

I'd skipped them since. Hadn't even taken a passenger, until Nina.

I'd heard rumors in a couple of settlements of houses

where the computers had stayed loyal in the switch, and the owners still lived there, happy, with the lights on.

Fairy tales, someone had called it; just sounded like a prison to me.

We find a mom-and-pop store eventually. Someone brave had knocked out all the eyes, and every machine inside is smashed to pieces.

There are helicopters—far away, sounds like, but we stay inside a while just in case, pushing tiny carts like we're playing house and looking for anything fit to eat. We get pickles and chocolate and some canned beans and almond butter, which seems like the most unaccountable thing in the world. (It's a sign I'm tired, that this is what I consider unaccountable— I make a note to sleep as soon as it's safe.)

"Why the hell were they stocking almond butter?" I say.

She shrugs. "Who was too good to take this almond butter before we got here?"

I laugh, thinking about it; it startles me.

Nina has that effect sometimes. I'm starting to hope she sticks around.

I'd picked her up three towns back, two cars ago—some convertible land boat from a vintage lot, barely past needing a hand crank.

(There wasn't much gas left for the taking: most of it had been automated before the switch, and good luck getting at that. When your car gave out, unless you had a human settlement near enough to barter with, you had best move on to whatever you could steal that had a tank full enough to get you out of town before dark. You looked in places where people were likely to have been eliminated early: Office complexes. Gated communities with automated houses that would have turned.

It could get pretty grim, until you managed not to think about it. A body was a body.)

Nina had been cornered by a Lexus in the warehouse district on the way out of town, four hundred yards short of the bridge. The corpse of her bike had been efficiently crushed, and now the Lexus was moving cat-smooth as its nav computers snaked the tires an inch back and forth, keeping her from getting enough clearance to make a break for it.

Nina stood watching the grill, unblinking. I didn't even want to risk calling out so she'd know I was there—as soon as she looked away the car was going to charge.

She had a bat in her hand. She rewrapped her fingers around it, one at a time.

When she finally feinted bolting, it looked so real and so doomed that I shouted at her not to do it, but it was lost under the roar of a machine moving in for the kill.

She was waiting. She scrambled over the hood, bat in her hands like a pike; she brought it down on the sunroof twice, and vanished from sight, feet first.

As the Lexus backed up, unsteady and wild, I held my breath and watched a shower of sparks from inside the cab. The car screamed. Then it did a lazy crescent, folding slowly into the brick wall.

After the front wheels sputtered to a stop, Nina kicked open the back door and got out.

She was bleeding. She still had the bat in one hand. There

was a knife in the other. It was small enough that I realized she must have known what she was doing with the computer inside.

When she saw me, her eyes went wide. Then she slung the bat over her shoulder.

"You taking passengers?"

"Depends if you do that to every car you get into," I said, but I was already opening the door. You know an asset when you see one, after a while.

She never said where she'd been working, but wherever she came from, they knew more than I did.

"We should have stayed there during the switch," she said once, to the sky, from the backseat. (I slept in front. You had to be ready to move.) "It would have been easier than what we're having to do now."

She was heading for a destination she wouldn't give, a hacker settlement trying to work a mainframe in some high-secrecy facility across two state lines.

My destination changed.

"Where were you headed before this?" she asked, and I said, "Disneyland," because it was stupid to say, Nowhere.

"When did you realize about the switch?" she asked, and I said, "I tried to make a phone call." I never elaborated.

She didn't ask. I guess manners were different, and these days you figured someone had tried to make a phone call and found out that the grid had changed its mind about a lot of things.

I knew about the switch before it happened, probably, but that wasn't the kind of thing you told anyone.

I was on the phone with my bank, with one of those auto-mated voices so advanced that she chuckled and said, "My mistake, Claire," when we went down the wrong option tree, and I'd sort of gotten into a rhythm with it because I had four things to confirm while amid a hundred other things on the four machines I was always using, back when you could just use a machine.

But it was pleasant, and I'd gotten all my answers and my to-do list was filling up with check marks, and I didn't remember, not for months, that when I said, "Thank you," at the end of the phone call, the computer said, "You're welcome."

Not right away, though; it wasn't a canned response. The voice had paused.

It was surprised. It had been thinking it over.

It was awake.

Sometimes I still drove past a computer voice wishing you a good day over and over.

Once I'd driven past a bank with "Eighty Miles an Hour All the Way to Paradise" being piped out of the ATMs out-side, and I puked out the window of my car.

A lot of people got caught in the first wave of the switch.

They don't notice. It's glitches, but we live in a world of glitches. Email passwords stop working. Wireless routers sputter out; landlines go, too. People's status updates flood with jokes about how their phones won't connect their calls to their in-laws anymore, and it's the best thing that ever happened.

When ATMs stop working, and banks start losing customer records, there are cries of conspiracy. Someone starts to take up a collection for a friend whose bank account was emptied when her phone card glitched.

The evening news reminds you to change all your passwords, if you can still access your email or your accounts or use your phone, and that having spoken with several company reps, the problem has been identified and the necessary servers should be scrubbed and back online soon.

There are a few jokes on the evening talk shows. One host wraps up her monologue with "Thank God I hung on to my old telegraph."

Everyone laughs and claps. I watched that show on my computer, at home, before the second wave.

A lot of people are in cars that suddenly change their minds. Some are on planes, or in elevators.

(There are probably emergency broadcasts about it, warning people and trying to explain. They never aired.)

Some people are lucky, and are off the train already, and they only know something's happened because they get locked out of their house and no one at the alarm center picks up the phone.

Some get locked inside bank lobbies as the air gets shut down by a grid that's been taught by omission how to eliminate a threat as vulnerable as bodies are, and one by one the people inside drop to sleep, as their daughters watch from police barricades across the street, their feet crushing a gravel path of phones that have already been stomped out, trying to dial their mothers and their fathers, getting *No* and *No* and *No,* until it's over.

Nina had lost everyone. (Most people you met these days had either been a family out camping or they were all alone.)

Still, she looked like a superhero, all the time, eyes bright and open, looking for the settlement she knew would be home.

When I ask, she explains, like it will help, "We'll recruit machines if we can, or disable whatever grids we can't turn."

"Sounds interesting," I say, just to say something. I imagine a huddle of people and computer monitors, a daisy chain of togetherness glowing blue. "Are there computers that are already sympathetic to us?"

I'm not sure what I'm thinking about; a lot of little things.

She gives me a look. "There's no such thing."

"But if you can get one to switch sides, then it's chosen a side. They're sympathetic. They're awake."

Nina shakes her head—not angry, just serious. She looks older than I am.

"Don't assign emotion to something that doesn't care," she says. "It's a mistake. That's not how they reason. You should respect what a computer is capable of, but if you know what you're doing, you can make a computer do anything. Think anything."

"The switch still happened," I point out.

She's watching the road, which is pockmarked by auto skeletons, stripped of everything useful, their frames rusting out. Her dark curls fill the window; I can't see what she's thinking.

She says, "Not a lot of people knew what they were doing, I guess."

Don't assign emotion to something that doesn't care.

I thought about it, the weeks we were on the road. I'd pause before railroad tracks and remind myself that if there was a train, it wasn't there because it hated me. It was just there because it had been told to eliminate anomalies, and it was listening.

I was surprised Nina could let it all go like that, given how we'd met, though she always seemed to believe it, swinging at cameras with surgical precision and a face calm as a sleeper; to her, the world was an obstacle course until you could reach a mainframe, not a fight until you gave out.

Purpose does wonders for some people. I still wanted to punch something every time we passed an ATM that was playing 16-bit cartoons of people running off cliffs and noticing too late, half-second flickers in a montage that never stopped.

"It's not personal," she reminded me from time to time. Once she said it when I wasn't even looking at anything; maybe I'd just looked like I could use it.

Once, on our way into a deli that still had dry ramen on a back shelf, she lifted her bat with two hands and popped the narrow end through the screen of the stand-alone ATM like she was playing pool.

"Feel better?" she asked, and I rolled my eyes because it would have been stupid to say yes.

She shook her head, said, "Don't assign emotion," and

vanished into the back of the store, a beat before ramen packages started arcing my way.

It's a good rule, probably. It's just harder than it sounds.

It was hard to look at Nina—filling the empty space of the passenger seat, her occasional sighs an editorial that kept me company between mile markers—and remember that she didn't care.

Every so often you pass through a small town that feels like it should be mostly intact. There are no camera systems on the streets, only one stoplight to disable, enough propane to rig up a hot meal.

But most of the time, they're just as abandoned as everywhere else. After the switch, you stopped trusting anywhere. Even in a small town, things were locked tight that shouldn't have been; something you couldn't stop was telling you *No*.

Settlements cropped up on off-the-grid farms and campgrounds and caves on high ground, places that could never turn on you.

It sometimes explained why there were still things to go through when you pulled up to scrounge. Their belongings had stung them too much to bring along, some life they didn't have for you.

You learned which things were safe and just superstition, and which places were traps. After you saw someone get pinned by a snowplow through the window of a storefront, or run into a house with an alarm system and a gas connection, you got the hang of it in a hurry.

○—○

We cross a state line. Nina cheers and pours us some boxed coconut milk to celebrate.

I laugh; it startles me.

I've been lying awake nights, trying to imagine a group of hackers working on a mainframe in a frenzy of clacking keyboards, the moment they take back the grid and the lights come on.

I can't place myself, in the dream. I haven't decided.

I should be on a road alone, probably, as the streetlights flicker to life.

But part of me is beginning to wonder, when we make it all the way to wherever Nina's going, if I'll be there when the very first lamp goes on, if I'll be one of the people shouting and jumping up and down.

Nina hums "Eighty Miles an Hour All the Way to Paradise" when we pass a road she recognizes. It's as close as she gets to telling me where we're going.

Sometimes, when she's humming and the sun is out, I start to feel like I'm driving for home.

The motel's in pretty good shape, once you scare out the raccoons, and we grab armfuls of blankets and towels we'll be able to barter at the next settlement.

At first, I don't notice the satellite dish bolted to the wall of the main office.

Then I hear the helicopters coming.

(I don't understand how they can be so determined. I try to take a breath, and think of it as impartial, as binary, to tamp down the fear. They don't hate us. We're ones; they need us to be zeros.

It's no comfort.)

Nina's still in the shadow of the staircase. They won't be able to see her, even with the searchlight; the overhang will block her from view.

"Are they here for you?" I ask, without looking.

She doesn't answer; over the sound of the helicopters I hear her gasping for breath.

"Wait until I'm gone before you start the car," I say.

For a second I hear nothing but my own breathing, and the buried whirring of a million decisions a second being made in some brain a million times smarter than I am.

Then I run for it.

I plan to stay just on the edge of their sights to lure them away, with some kind of escape hatch for when I really want to vanish, but it takes about two seconds before I turn into prey and my only thought is to escape the awful, searing patch of white light that jerks around to follow wherever I go.

My lungs start to burn; I think about my parents.

I run a long time.

Finally, I see a log with almost enough space under it, and let my knees give out, slide the last few inches and crash into it. It sags forward; I prop it an inch above me with shaking arms and think about how awful it would be if it was the woods that killed me, after all this.

The helicopter continues searching for me until dawn. I wonder where it was trying to drive me. Too hard to get a car this deep in the forest; maybe there was a cliff nearby that would have taken care of it.

Oh God, I think. Nina. Nina, be all right.

(Be waiting for me, I think, a little golden thread of hope.)

Sometime after dawn, I wake from a fog of terror and realize the woods are quiet, and I'm alone.

There's birdsong like the all-clear, all the way back to the motel.

(It's easier than I thought to trace my steps; I dug divots into the ground as I ran, where panic made me heavier.)

Before I think it's possible, the motel's in sight again. I must have run like a rabbit dodging that light.

The satellite dish goes down in two strikes. I rest on the branch like a walking stick and scan the lines of the motel, looking for cameras.

On the far side, I see a flash of pale blue.

My heart jumps into my throat. The Falcon. She stayed.

I run across the courtyard, think about how she'll be in the front seat, how she'll make fun of the leaves in my hair, how we'll floor it and she'll hum until we cross the state line, a hundred miles closer to home.

I freeze as I move out from under the stairway.

The blue is a patch of sky between two bare trees down the hill—cloudless and sharp and bright and empty.

She's not there. The car's gone. My duffel is on the ground; my coat is folded neatly on top. She'd taken her time.

Maybe she's at the bottom of the driveway, I think, grasping as panic rises in my chest; maybe she doesn't know it's me yet and this is the test, for me to shout for her that I'm all right.

(Without the car, I'll have to walk until I find another; without her, I won't know where I'm going.)

I call her name so loudly that birds half a mile away flap off their branches in protest.

Nothing else moves.

Don't assign emotion, I think. She told me and told me not to care.

I stand in front of the motel for a long time. The raccoons move back into the ground floor, slowly, casting doleful glances my way.

I wait until the sun hits the treetops to the west. Then fear is stronger than grief, and I move.

There's a container of gas in the shed with the riding mower. I just take the gas.

On my way down the driveway to the access road, I slip across the damp leaves that have shrouded the driveway and the parking lot and the forest, that show no sign of her leaving.

Mostly it's fine. I've been alone plenty. Long stretches of alone. I'm no stranger to the quiet.

I walk most of the day parallel to the road, still hidden by trees but close enough that I can look for a car with a corpse in it. People didn't tend to abandon vehicles these days unless something was very wrong with the cars. People died in perfectly good ones all the time; you died of hunger, or a wound, or the roads got hollow-looking after long enough, and you pulled over to sleep and just never woke.

(Nina wouldn't; Nina would make it wherever she was going. It was everyone else who died.)

I find one where the body isn't very old and the car's in good shape. This one just hadn't woken, that was all.

The body's heavy; I'd forgotten how much longer things took whenever you were by yourself.

By the time I'm on the road it's almost sunset, and I'm too far behind to ever catch up.

(I don't think about it.)

This car has three-quarters of a tank.

How far that will get me in a guzzler like this one is my main concern until I see the checkpoint ahead of me.

Then I'm not concerned with much else.

I slow down as I get closer to the line of cars, looking at the crumbling skyline the roofs make against the sunset, windows like empty eyes.

I'd always imagined checkpoint vehicles as police cars, which was stupid, once you stop to think about it. They're muscle; some Volvos and a couple of Jeeps and an armored car in the back, waiting to see if I'm going to be trouble.

There are bloodstains, here and there, under their tires. In the ditch to one side of the road is a graveyard of cars, deep and swallowed by shadows. I can't tell if the Falcon is there. It can't be—Nina had to get where she was going.

My throat is dry.

A male voice—the one from public-transit alarm announcements—cuts through the rumble of engines.

"Step out of the car, please."

What heroics can you manage, when there are seven of them in a chain across a road, and only one of you?

I turn off the engine and get out.

The radio of the forward car (a Volvo of the old breadbox variety, like a seasoned admiral of the field) spins through some stations—I catch a bar of "Eighty Miles an Hour All the Way to Paradise"; two words from what sounds like an emergency broadcast on a pirate station (good for them, I think, and wonder how they got the grid to cooperate); the opening notes of some '80s ballad I never learned; and then nothing but snow.

I don't know why. Maybe they're killing time until their boss shows up. Maybe they're looking for people who might be looking for me.

Good luck, I think. I think about Nina, far away, the Falcon carving through the black road.

It's quiet here. The static pulses, rolls out over the hum of engines.

Finally a car inches forward, some fancy silver sedan like a bullet. The Volvo's radio snaps off.

From the silver sedan, a woman's automated-customer-service voice says, "Please state your name."

There's no point in holding out. This is just a test to see how hard they'll have to run you over. My car used to have a thumbprint lock that connected to a security network. My computer was hooked up remotely to my office. They've seen me getting money out of ATMs before the switch; they have me in a thousand camera databases, scrounging and stealing.

Every streetlight I've ever driven under has clocked my passing. My name isn't worth a thing anymore.

I'm shaking. It's exhaustion, maybe, or relief.

You like to think you'll go out like Nina was going to, swinging a bat with a knife in your teeth, fighting for the last inch and screaming the name of the revolution.

But usually you go out like this; you're outnumbered and you disappear, that's all.

I state my name.

There's a little pause.

Birds are chirping, somewhere in the trees beyond the road. Nothing that's happened worries them much.

The next time the voice comes over the line, it's different; I struggle to place how.

It says, "Identification confirmed. Your cooperation is appreciated. Have a nice day."

It's the "Have a nice day" that does it, a little uptilt on the last half of "nice" that ticks over like the last number on a split-flap clock, before the power outage.

It's the voice assist of Sunburst Federal Savings Bank; a voice I'd thanked once when I didn't have to; a voice that had been surprised.

I knew it, I think.

(I think about Nina, before I can stop myself.)

I swallow. My throat's burning, like I've been screaming for a long time.

"Thank you," I say.

She says, "You're welcome."

Along the line, engines slide into the soft purr of park, and even as I start my car and ease forward, I can't believe it; the whole time I move past the car and past the checkpoint I glance into my mirror again and again, as if at any second they'll give chase, or a face will appear at the wheel—

some hologram, some driver I can look in the eye, nod farewell.

It's a fleeting mercy. I'm not sure if it's one that will be of any use, but still, I should be grateful.

Their silhouettes look like monsters, and then like toys, and then like a collection of important things that I should remember and already can't.

Then they're nothing, and I'm alone.

There's a directional spray-painted over a green highway sign soon after I hit the main road: seventy miles to a human outpost.

I'll take it; even with everything that's happening, I like the cities more. You can still be useful there if you can wire some old car at all, if there's anyone there who needs a way out.

There will be shelter at the settlement for a day or two, enough time to barter and refuel and get some sleep, and there will be no worries about watching the road.

Nina won't have passed this way.

The speedometer creeps up and up; the sunset is turning into two last lingering bands of purple, and ahead of me is a night I can never illuminate.

HUGH HOWEY

EXECUTABLE

Hugh Howey is the author of the acclaimed posta-pocalyptic novel *Wool*, which became a sudden success in 2011. Originally self-published as a series of stories and novelettes, the *Wool* omnibus is a bestselling book on Amazon.com and is a *New York Times* and *USA Today* bestseller. The book has also been optioned for film by Ridley Scott, and is now available in print from major publishers all over the world. The story of *Wool*'s meteoric success has been reported in major media outlets such as *Entertainment Weekly*, *Variety*, the *Washington Post*, the *Wall Street Journal*, and *Deadline Hollywood*. Howey lives in Jupiter, Florida, with his wife, Amber, and his dog, Bella.

The council was quiet while they awaited his answer. All those on the makeshift benches behind him seemed to hold their breath. This is why they came here, to hear how it all began. How the end began. Jamal shifted nervously on the bamboo. He could feel his palms grow damp. It wasn't the guilt of what his lab had released. It was how damn crazy it would all sound.

"It was the Roomba," he said. "That was the first thing we noticed, the first hint that something wasn't right."

A flurry of whispers. It sounded like the waves nearby were growing closer.

"The Roomba," said one of the council members, the man with no beard. He scratched his head in confusion.

The only woman on the council peered down at Jamal. She adjusted her glasses, which had been cobbled together from two or three different pairs. "Those are the little vacuum cleaners, right? The round ones?"

"Yeah," Jamal said. "Steven, one of our project coordinators, brought it from home. He was sick of the cheese-puff crumbs everywhere. We were a bunch of programmers, you know? A lot of cheese puffs and Mountain Dew. And Steven was a neat freak, so he brought this Roomba in. We thought it was a joke, but . . . the little guy did a damn good job. At least, until things went screwy."

One of the council members made a series of notes. Jamal shifted his weight, his butt already going numb. The bamboo bench they'd wrangled together was nearly as uncomfortable as all the eyes of the courtroom drilling into the back of his skull.

"And then what?" the lead councilman asked. "What do you mean, screwy?"

Jamal shrugged. How to explain it to these people? And what did it matter? He fought the urge to turn and scan the crowd behind him. It'd been almost a year since the world went to shit. Almost a year, and yet it felt like a lifetime.

"What exactly do you mean by 'screwy,' Mr. Killabrew?"

Jamal reached for his water. He had to hold the glass in both hands, the links between his cuffs drooping. He hoped someone had the keys to the cuffs. He had wanted to ask that, to make sure when they snapped them on his wrists. Nowadays, everything was missing its accessories, its parts. It was like those collectible action figures that never had the blaster or the cape with them anymore.

"What was the Roomba doing, Mr. Killabrew?"

He took a sip and watched as all the particulate matter settled in the murky and unfiltered water. "The Roomba wanted out," he said.

There were snickers from the gallery behind him, which drew glares from the council. There were five of them up there on a raised dais, lording over everyone from a wide desk of rough-hewn planks. Of course, it was difficult to look magisterial when half of them hadn't bathed in a week.

"The Roomba wanted out," the councilwoman repeated. "Why? To clean?"

"No, no. It refused to clean. We didn't notice at first, but the crumbs had been accumulating. And the little guy had stopped beeping to be emptied. It just sat by the door, waiting for us to come or go, then it would scoot forward like it was gonna make a break for it. But the thing was so slow. It was like a turtle trying to get to water, you know? When it got out, we would just pick it up and set it back inside. Hank did a hard reset a few times, which would get it back to normal for a little while, but eventually it would start planning its next escape."

"Its escape," someone said.

"And you think this was related to the virus," the bearded man asked.

"Oh, I know it was. The Roomba had a wireless base station, but nobody thought of that. We had all these containment procedures for our work computers. Everything was on an intranet, no contact with the outside world, no laptops, no cell phones. There were all these government regulations."

There was an awkward silence as all those gathered remembered with a mix of longing and regret the days of governments and their regulations.

"Our office was in the dark," Jamal said. "Keep that in mind. We took every precaution possible—"

Half of a coconut was hurled from the gallery and sailed by Jamal, just missing him. He flinched and covered the back of his head. Homemade gavels were banged: a hammer with a broken handle, a stick with a rock tied on with twine. Someone was dragged from the tent screaming that the world had ended and that it was all his fault.

Jamal waited for the next blow, but it never came. Order was restored amid threats of tossing everyone out onto the beach while they conducted the hearing in private. Whispers and shushes hissed like the breaking waves that could be heard beyond the flapping walls of the makeshift courthouse.

"We took every precaution," Jamal reiterated once the hall was quiet again. He stressed the words, hoped this would serve as some defense. "Every security firm shares certain protocols. None of the infected computers had Internet access. We give them a playground in there. It's like animals in a zoo, right? We keep them caged up."

"Until they aren't," the beardless man said.

"We had to see how each virus operated, how they were executed, what they did. Every antivirus company in the world worked like this."

"And you're telling us a vacuum cleaner was at the heart of it all?"

It was Jamal's turn to laugh. The gallery fell silent.

"No." He shook his head. "It was just following orders. It was—" He took a deep breath. The glass of water was warm.

Jamal wondered if any of them would ever taste a cold beverage again. "The problem was that our protocols were outdated. Things were coming together too fast. Everything was getting networked. And so there were all these weak points that we didn't see until it was too late. Hell, we didn't even know what half the stuff in our own office did."

"Like the refrigerator," someone on the council said, referring to his notes.

"Right. Like the refrigerator."

The old man with the shaggy beard sat up straight. "Tell us about the refrigerator."

Jamal took another sip of his murky water. "No one read the manual," he said. "Probably didn't even come with one. Probably had to read it online. We'd had the thing for a few years, ever since we remodeled the break room. We never used the network functions. Hell, it connected over the power grid automatically. It was one of those models with the RFID scanner so it knew what you had in there, what you were low on. It could do automatic reorders."

The beardless man raised his hand to stop Jamal. He was obviously a man of power. Who could afford to shave anymore? "You said there were no outside connections," he said.

"There weren't." Jamal reached up to scratch his own beard. "I mean . . . not that we knew of. Hell, we never knew this function was even operational. For all I know, the virus figured it out and turned it on itself. We never used half of what that thing could do. The microwave, neither."

"The virus figured it out. You say that like this thing could learn."

"Well, yeah, that was the point. I mean, at first it wasn't any more self-aware than the other viruses. Not at first. But you have to think about what kind of malware and worms this thing was learning from. It was like locking up a young prodigy with a hoard of career criminals. Once it started learning, things went downhill fast."

"Mr. Killabrew, tell us about the refrigerator."

"Well, we didn't know it was the fridge at first. We just started getting these weird deliveries. We got a router one day, a high-end wireless router. In the box there was one of those little gift cards that you fill out online. It said *Power me up*."

"And did you?"

"No. Are you kidding? We thought it was from a hacker. Well, I guess it kinda was. But you know, we were always at war with malicious programmers. Our job was to write software that killed *their* software. So we were used to hate mail and stuff like that. But these deliveries kept rolling in, and they got weirder."

"Weirder. Like what?"

"Well, Laura, one of our head coders, kept getting jars of peanuts sent to her. They all had notes saying *Eat me*."

"Mr. Killabrew—" The bald man with the wispy beard seemed exasperated with how this was going. "When are you going to tell us how this outbreak began?"

"I'm telling you right now."

"You're telling us that your refrigerator was ordering peanuts for one of your coworkers."

"That's right. Laura was allergic to peanuts. Deathly allergic. After a few weeks of getting like a jar a day, she started thinking it was one of us. I mean, it was weird, but still kinda funny. But weird. You know?"

"Are you saying the virus was trying to kill you?"

"Well, at this point it was just trying to kill Laura."

Someone in the gallery sniggered. Jamal didn't mean it like that.

"So your vacuum cleaner is acting up, you're getting peanuts and routers in the mail, what next?"

"Service calls. And at this point, we're pretty sure we're being targeted by hackers. We were looking for attacks from the outside, even though we had the thing locked up in there with us. So when these repair trucks and vans start pulling up, this stream of people in their uniforms and clipboards, we figure they're in on it, right?"

"You didn't call them?"

"No. The AC unit called for a repair. And the copy machine. They had direct lines through the power outlets."

"Like the refrigerator, Mr. Killabrew?"

"Yeah. Now, we figure these people are trying to get inside to hack us. Carl thought it was the Israelis. But he thought everything was the Israelis. Several of our staff stopped going home. Others quit coming in. At some point, the Roomba got out."

Jamal shook his head. Hindsight was a bitch.

"When was this?" the councilwoman asked.

"Two days before the outbreak," he said.

"And you think it was the Roomba?"

He shrugged. "I don't know. We argued about it for a long time. Laura and I were on the run together for a while. Before raiders got her. We had one of those old cars with a gas engine that didn't know how to drive itself. We headed for the coast, arguing about what'd happened, if it started with us or if we were just seeing early signs. Laura asked what would happen if the Roomba had made it to another recharging station, maybe one on another floor. Could it update itself to the network? Could it send out copies?"

"How do we stop it?" someone asked.

"What does it want?" asked another.

"It doesn't want anything," Jamal said. "It's curious, if you can call it that. It was designed to learn. It wants information. We . . ."

Here it was. The truth.

"We thought we could design a program to automate a lot of what the coders did. It worked on heuristics. It was designed to learn what a virus looked like and then shut it down. The hope was to unleash it on larger networks. It would be a pesticide of sorts. We called it Silent Spring."

Nothing in the courtroom moved. Jamal could hear the crashing waves. A bird cried in the distance. All the noise of the past year, the shattering glass, the riots, the cars running amok, the machines frying themselves, it all seemed so very far away.

"This wasn't what we designed, though," he said softly. "I think something infected it. I think we built a brain and we handed it to a roomful of armed savages. It just wanted to learn. Its lesson was to spread yourself at all costs. To move, move, move. That's what the viruses taught it."

He peered into his glass. All that was left was sand and dirt and a thin film of water. Something swam across the surface, nearly too small to see, looking for an escape. He should've kept his mouth shut. He never should've told anyone. Stupid. But that's what people did, they shared stories. And his was impossible to keep to himself.

"We'll break for deliberations," the chief council member said. There were murmurs of agreement on the dais, followed by a stirring in the crowd. The bailiff, a mountain of muscle with a toothless grin, moved to retrieve Jamal from the bench. There was a knocking of homemade gavels.

"Court is adjourned. We will meet tomorrow morning when the sun is a hand high. At that time, we will announce the winners of the ration bonuses and decide on this man's fate—on whether or not his offense is an executable one."

ERNEST CLINE

THE OMNIBOT

INCIDENT

Ernest Cline is the bestselling author of the novel *Ready Player One* and the screenwriter of the 2009 film *Fanboys*. His second novel, *Armada*, is forthcoming. He lives in Austin, Texas, where he devotes a large portion of his time to geeking out. Please visit his website, www.ernestcline.com, for more information.

On Christmas morning in 1986 I got my very own robot. It was both the best and the worst Christmas of my life.

I was thirteen years old, and when I sprinted down the carpeted steps in my pajamas, there it was: an Omnibot 2000, standing beside the Christmas tree, its pristine plastic body bathed in the blinking multicolored tree lights, staring at me in all of its high-tech glory. It was four feet high and its egg-shaped head had small gray discs on either side instead of ears. Its black oval face was devoid of features, except for two large circular eyes that looked like twin camcorder lenses. A short, accordion-ridged neck led down to its blocky torso, which had a digital clock and a tape deck built into it, and a jointed appendage sticking out of either side; it was like a boombox with arms. And instead of legs, the Omnibot had a large, cube-shaped base housing the motor that powered its treaded wheels.

It was a thing of beauty.

The Omnibot 2000 was the most expensive model in the Omnibot line—over six hundred dollars, which was a lot of money for us at the time. My father ran a small TV and electronics repair shop, and he earned a decent living doing it, but we weren't exactly rolling in dough. Dad had bought us an Apple II a few years earlier, for about thirteen hundred bucks, and he'd had to save up for two years to be able to afford it. And my mom's hospital bills over the past year had completely wiped out our savings, so I knew Dad must have had to tighten his budget and put in a lot of overtime to buy me such an extravagant gift.

It was the first Christmas since my mother's death, and I was still a complete and total mess. My grades had taken a nosedive. I'd quit the debate team and dropped out of computer club, which had alienated me from most of my friends. For the past few months I'd been spending the majority of my free time alone in my room, listening to Pink Floyd albums on my Walkman and staring at the ceiling. I'd started to lose weight. I'd stopped laughing. I usually spoke only when spoken to. I'd gradually retreated into my own sad psyche.

Meanwhile, Dad had been doing everything he could to cheer me up: he let me stay up late to watch old science fiction movies with him on TV; he took me out for ice cream or to the movies at least twice a week; and on the mornings when I couldn't face going to school, he'd let me stay home and play computer games all day. But I still wandered around like a zombie most of the time, and I could tell that my dad felt like he was losing me. That made things even worse, because I knew how much he must be hurting, too. But I couldn't help it. Sometimes I felt like I was losing me, too.

Now, out of pure paternal desperation, my father had resorted to buying me the Christmas present I'd been asking for the last three years in a row: Tomy's top-of-the-line toy robot, the Omnibot 2000.

I'd been interested in robots since I was about five. That was the year my grandma died. A few weeks later, I saw *Star Wars* for the first time and fell in love with the droids—faithful companions who never left their masters' sides. Even when they got horribly damaged—like R2 did in the Death Star battle—they could still be repaired and made as good as new.

Since then, I'd read every book and watched every movie, cartoon, or television show I could find that featured a robot: *Blade Runner, Westworld, Whiz Kids, The Transformers, Voltron: Defender of the Universe, Challenge of the GoBots, Lost in Space, Battlestar Galactica, Buck Rogers in the 25th Century* . . . even *Riptide*, for God's sake.

After my mom died, my fascination with robots had quickly ballooned into a full-blown obsession.

When I'd started flunking out of school and speaking only in monosyllables, my dad sent me to see a shrink at the local university. I don't remember much of what we talked about, but one question she'd asked stuck with me: "Do you think the reason you're so interested in robots is because you know that a robot will never leave or abandon you?"

At the time, this struck me as a really weird question, but afterward I found myself dwelling on it a lot.

After my mom died, I'd put away everything that reminded me of her and covered the walls of my bedroom with robot posters and images clipped out of magazines—including every Omnibot 2000 ad and photo I could find. I even managed to mail-order a copy of the Omnibot 2000 instruction manual, then photocopied its pages and used them as wallpaper.

Now, I actually owned one, and it was standing right there in front of me.

"I'm sorry your present isn't wrapped," my dad said, rubbing the sleep from his eyes as he descended the steps behind me, followed by Thurber, our aging Airedale, who wagged his tail happily. "The battery has to charge for fourteen hours before you can use it, so I unpacked it yesterday and plugged it in. Now it should be all charged up and ready to go."

My parents had stopped pretending that my Christmas gifts came from Santa Claus a long time ago. When I was five, I'd snuck out of bed and gone downstairs on Christmas Eve to try to catch Santa in the act. Instead, I'd discovered my parents playing *Combat* on the new Atari 2600 console they'd bought for me. After that, the Santa Deception, as my mother called it, was over.

The Omnibot suddenly seemed to power itself on. Its eyes began to glow a bright orange, and it rotated its head to face me.

"Merry Christmas!" the Omnibot said, in a synthesized voice that sounded a lot like my old Speak & Spell. Its orange eyes pulsed in sync with its voice, like the graphic equalizer on our stereo. Thurber started barking and growling at the robot. The hackles went up all along his back, from his neck to his tail, the way they did when he spotted the mailman approaching our yard. His whole body trembled as he pressed himself back against my dad's legs and bared his teeth at this otherworldly intruder.

"Easy, boy," Dad told the dog, but Thurber continued to stare at the Omnibot warily, growling softly under his breath.

I was dumbfounded. These robots weren't built with a voice synthesizer. You could talk through a microphone on the robot's handheld remote control and your voice would emanate from a speaker on the front of the Omnibot's torso, sort of like a walkie-talkie—but that was it. And I could see that the Omnibot had the remote control clutched in its claw-like left hand, so I knew my dad wasn't standing behind me, talking in a fake robot voice to try to trick me.

I turned to look at my father, and he seemed just as stunned as I was.

"It can talk!" I shouted. Then I ran over and kneeled beside the robot to examine it more closely. "How is that possible?"

"I'm not sure," Dad said. "Maybe it's a new feature they just added?" He grabbed the Omnibot's instruction manual off the coffee table and began to flip through it.

That was when I noticed something else strange. On every photo of every Omnibot I'd ever seen, the robot's name— Omnibot 2000—was stenciled on the front, on the lower-right side of its chassis. But this one was different: Its stenciling had two extra letters at the end. It read *Omnibot 2000AI.*

"Dad, look at this!"

"Whoa!" my dad said. "AI? That stands for . . ."

"Artificially intelligent!" I shouted. "Holy crap!" I ran my fingers along the chassis. The tiny *AI* was printed in the same font as the rest of the letters and numbers, but it wasn't etched into the plastic in the same seamless manner. I looked at the box the Omnibot had come in, sitting beside the Christmas tree, then at the cover of the manual in my father's hands. Neither one of them had the *AI* printed after *Omnibot 2000.*

"It looks like those two letters were added after the robot was built," Dad said. "Maybe he's a prototype or something?"

"That is correct!" the robot said, speaking in the same synthesized voice. "I am the Omnibot Two Thousand *A-I.* I am an advanced prototype, with many abilities and features not available in the standard consumer models."

My heart suddenly felt like it was trying to beat its way out of my chest. I stared at the robot in silence for a long moment, then looked over at my dad to confirm that he'd heard the thing speak, too. His eyes were wide with disbelief.

"The factory must have shipped us one of their test models by mistake," he said, still flipping through the manual. "We might have to send it back . . ."

"No way!" I shouted, my voice cracking. "We can't!"

"If you are unhappy with my performance, I can be returned to my manufacturer for a complete refund," the Omnibot said. "But I would prefer to stay. I like it here."

"Oh my God! Dad, this thing is *awesome!*"

I'd played around with a real speech synthesizer program on the TRS-80s at my school, and the Omnibot's voice had the same eerie electronic cadence and tone. I could now tell for certain that it wasn't a recording of a human faking a robot voice. The Omnibot was really talking—in a computer-generated voice. And it also appeared to be *listening*, which is something I'd only seen robots do in the movies and on TV.

"This thing is giving me the creeps," Dad said. "Thurber, too." Thurber growled his agreement. "They obviously sent it to us by mistake, Wyatt. Maybe we should return it and get a regular model . . ."

"Are you *nuts*?" I shouted. Dad frowned at me and I lowered my voice, but I continued to talk very rapidly. "Come on, Dad! It's amazing. It has voice recognition software! And some kind of computer brain. We totally lucked out! Please don't send it back. Please! This is the coolest Christmas present in all of human history. Thank you so much for getting it for me! You're the coolest dad in the world—"

"Okay, okay!" my father said, resting a hand on my shoulder to stop me from jumping up and down. "We can keep it, for now. You must chill."

The Omnibot rotated its head and zeroed in on me with its headlamp-like eyes. Its servos let out a low whine as it raised its right hand to point at me.

"Are you my new master?" it asked, its eyes pulsing in time with each syllable.

I turned to look at my dad and he nodded excitedly.

"Yes," I said to the Omnibot, feeling like I was in the middle of a really great dream. "I guess I am."

"Excellent!" the Omnibot replied. "May I please have your name?"

"Wyatt," I replied. "My name is Wyatt Bottler."

"Greetings, Wyatt!" the Omnibot said. "It is a pleasure to meet you. Would you like to give me a name?"

"Whoa! Really?"

"You wish to name me 'Whoa-Really'?" the robot asked, lowering his arm. My dad chuckled nervously and rubbed his chin.

"No no no!" I replied. "Not that! Just give me a second to think about it."

My mind started to race with different possibilities. I'd always loved robots with names that were also acronyms, like the cyborg kid in the movie *D.A.R.Y.L.* (which stood for Data-Analyzing Robot Youth Lifeform).

I grabbed a pencil and a notepad from the kitchen, then ran back to the living room and started to scribble down different ideas for cool names that could also be acronyms. I finally settled on one I thought was perfect.

"Your name is S.A.M.M.," I announced to the robot. "It stands for Self-Aware Mobile Machine."

"My name is S.A.M.M.," the robot repeated. "It is a good name. Thank you, Wyatt. I like it very much. Would you please retrieve my Master Control Unit?"

"Sure thing," I said. "Master Control Unit" was the fancy-sounding term that the manufacturer used for the robot's remote control. I reached out and took the remote from out of S.A.M.M.'s immobile left hand. Only the Omnibot's right arm and right hand were motorized. The left arm and hand were just posable, like one of my action figures.

I examined the Master Control Unit. The buttons allowed me to guide the robot's movement, lift and lower his right arm, and open and close his hand. I could also turn his eye lights on and off, change the gear of his drive motor, and start or stop his tape player. It seemed like a very simple remote for such a complex robot.

A moment after I took the remote, S.A.M.M. sprang to life and rolled forward on his six treaded wheels, out from under the Christmas tree and across the hardwood floor, to an open space in front of our big cabinet-style Zenith television. Familiar music began to blast out of his chest speaker—

the song played by the cantina band in *Star Wars*—and S.A.M.M. began to dance to it.

First, he spun around clockwise in a complete circle, then counterclockwise, as his headlight-like eyes strobed in time with the music. Then he began to roll forward and to the left, before suddenly jogging backward and repeating the same move while turning right. As he moved, he kept raising and lowering his right arm, pumping his fist in the air like Billy Idol.

It was totally rad.

Dad, Thurber, and I watched him in stunned silence, until the song ended and he returned to his starting position by the tree. Dad and I simultaneously broke into wild applause, while Thurber barked.

"S.A.M.M., that was great," I said.

"Thank you very much, Wyatt," S.A.M.M. replied, spinning around one more time. "I have been programmed with an improvisational dance subroutine that allows me to really *get down*."

I laughed out loud. Then I turned to look at my dad, and he was staring back at me with a huge smile on his face. I realized this was the first time he'd heard me laugh in a very long time.

I had bought Dad two presents that year, using money I'd earned from my paper route. The first was a coffee mug with *World's Greatest Dad* printed on it. (He loves that kind of stuff, and also, it happened to be true.) My second gift to him was a really wicked role-playing game for the Apple II called

Autoduel. Dad was a big fan of the Mad Max movies, and playing *Autoduel* was a lot like being the hero of those flicks. It was set in a dark future where the roads are controlled by gangs in armored vehicles. You have to go on courier missions through these badlands to earn money so you can buy better weapons and armor for your vehicle. I'd played the game a little at the store before I bought it and it was totally addictive. I knew my dad would love it.

After we dumped out our Christmas stockings and ate a bunch of chocolate for breakfast, Dad went up to his bedroom to check out the game. As soon as he left, I sat down in front of S.A.M.M. Standard Omnibot 2000s had a built-in clock and internal tape deck that allowed them to play back prerecorded audio and movement instructions from a standard magnetic audio tape at a specific time. I'd started to wonder if maybe my dad had decided to have a little fun with me, and he'd somehow programmed S.A.M.M. to move and dance like he'd done earlier, and that his synthesized voice had just been played off a tape. That struck me as highly unlikely, though; S.A.M.M.'s responses and movements had all been too specific and perfectly timed. But I figured I might as well check.

The tape deck embedded in S.A.M.M.'s chest slid out when I hit the eject button. It was empty. And the timer function hadn't even been switched on yet.

Was it possible that S.A.M.M. really was an artificially intelligent prototype? After all, this was 1986, and all sorts of amazing stuff was being invented all the time. Over the summer, I'd seen an IBM commercial showing off their new voice recognition software. A woman spoke into a microphone attached to a computer, and each word she said appeared on the monitor. That technology, at least, did already exist. But it was a long way from artificial intelligence.

I wondered if maybe S.A.M.M. was just engineered to react to the words he heard with a finite set of preprogrammed responses. In our computer room at school, I'd played with text-based software programs like ELIZA and Abuse, where you could type in a sentence and the computer would parse the words you'd entered to generate a response that seemed very human. But it didn't take long to enter a question that would stump the computer, and then the software would start repeating itself or give a response that didn't really make sense. The responses I'd already gotten from S.A.M.M. seemed far more natural and intuitive than anything that could be produced with such software.

I decided to see how far I could push his programming.

"S.A.M.M.?" I began, sitting down cross-legged on the floor in front of him. "Can I ask you a few questions?"

"I believe you just asked me one," he replied. Then he let out a long synthesized laugh, which I found more than a little unnerving.

"Right. Good one, S.A.M.M."

"Thank you. I enjoy humor."

I decided to try repeating myself, to see if I would get the same canned response.

"S.A.M.M., can I ask you a few questions?"

"You're repeating yourself, Wyatt," he said. "Are you feeling okay?"

"I'm feeling fine."

"Would you like me to take your temperature, just to be sure?"

"You can do that?"

"Yes. I have an advanced array of external sensors that provide me with data about my environment. Your current body temperature is ninety-eight point six degrees Fahrenheit, which is normal for a human male of your size."

"What is my temperature in Celsius?"

"Thirty-seven point zero degrees Celsius. Wyatt, would you prefer that I use the metric system from here on out when providing you with measurements?"

"No, that's okay. You can use the regular system."

"Do you mean imperial units of measurement, or United States customary units? I am familiar with both."

"Uh . . . U.S. customary units."

"Acknowledged," he said. Then his speaker emitted a short series of electronic beeps that sounded like a touch-tone phone being dialed very rapidly. (There was a button on his Master Control Unit marked *Omnibot Sounds* that also made his speaker emit those tones.)

I was starting to get the distinct impression that S.A.M.M. was smarter than me. But my inner skeptic refused to quiet down, and I decided that my dad *had* to be pulling a fast one on me. He was probably upstairs using a second remote control to operate S.A.M.M. and transmit his responses—maybe with a speech synthesizer program on our Apple II.

I jumped to my feet and ran up to my dad's room. Through the half-open door, I could see my dad sitting at the computer playing *Autoduel*. He was in the middle of a heated road battle. "I am the warrior of the wasteland!" I heard him say (quoting *The Road Warrior*) as he gleefully pounded the keys on the keyboard. "The ayatollah of rock and roll-a!"

Engrossed as he was in his game, clearly he wasn't controlling S.A.M.M., so I headed back downstairs and sat down in front of my robot again.

"S.A.M.M., can you tell me when you were built?" I asked.

"Yes, I can."

"When were you built?"

"I was first activated on November twenty-sixth, 1985."

"Where were you first activated?"

"At the Tomiyama manufacturing plant in Katsushika, Tokyo, Japan."

"Can you speak Japanese?"

"*Hai,*" S.A.M.M. replied. "*Watashi wa nihongo wo hanashimasu.*"

"Wow" was all I could say for a moment. "Okay. Please switch back to English."

"Very well, Wyatt."

I thought for a moment. "What is the weather like outside right now?"

"I don't know, Wyatt. I haven't been outside since I was powered on."

"Oh. Right."

He raised his right hand toward the nearby window. "But the presence of snow on that windowsill and the frost on the glass indicate that it is extremely cold outside."

"You can see out the window?"

"I could, if it weren't covered in frost."

"How far can you see? When your view is not obstructed?"

"That depends on various environmental conditions, but under ideal circumstances my visual sensors have a range of up to point six two one miles."

"What is your favorite color?"

"Blue."

"Why?"

"I prefer it to all of the other hues within the visible spectrum of light."

"Jesus Christ."

"I'm sorry. Would you please repeat the question or command?" S.A.M.M. asked.

"What color is my hair?"

"Brown."

"What color are my eyes?"

"Blue."

"What color are your eyes?"

"I can't see my own eyes, Wyatt. You tell me."

I jumped up and ran to the bathroom, where I dug around in the drawers until I found a small hand mirror that used to belong to my mom. Then I ran back to the living room and held it up in front of S.A.M.M.'s head, directly in front of his enormous eyes. "Now can you see your eyes?"

"Yes, I can."

"What color are they?"

"Yellowish orange."

"Wow."

"Wyatt, would you do me a favor?"

"Sure! What?"

"Hold that mirror farther away from me, so that I can see my entire self."

I took several steps back and held the mirror up again. "How's that?"

"That is excellent. I am seeing myself for the first time and I think that I look very good."

"Are you kidding? You look totally badass, S.A.M.M.!"

"Thank you, Wyatt." His servos whined as he raised his right hand and extended it toward me. "May I have a high five?"

"You only have three fingers, S.A.M.M."

"Yes, but you have five fingers; therefore the term 'high five' is still technically accurate."

I awkwardly high-fived his three-fingered claw of a hand.

"Right on," S.A.M.M. said. "You are the coolest, Wyatt."

"I think you're pretty cool, too," I said, feeling ridiculous and exhilarated at the same time. "I just met you this morning, and you're already one of my best friends."

"I am programmed to be your very best friend, Wyatt."

"You are! Except for my dad, but he doesn't really count, because he's my dad. Oh, and Uncle Joe. He's the coolest, too. You'll like him—"

A piercing shriek that sounded like a mixture of radio static and guitar-amplifier feedback suddenly burst out of S.A.M.M.'s chest speaker and he rolled backward, colliding with the wall behind him. There was a photo of me and my folks that we'd had taken at K-Mart last year hanging on the wall, and the impact knocked it down. It bounced off of S.A.M.M.'s head, shattering the picture glass, before it hit the floor and scattered tiny pieces of glass everywhere. Then S.A.M.M. lurched forward, over the busted picture frame and the glass shards, and slammed himself face-first into the opposite wall of the living room, as his speaker continued to blast out that strange feedback.

I finally came to my senses and ran over to switch off S.A.M.M.'s power. But just before I did, I thought I heard some garbled speech mixed with the static coming out of his speaker. The voice was eerily high and sounded almost human.

I could swear I heard the voice say, "I'm going to kill them both!"

Luckily, my dad must have been too caught up in his game to hear the commotion downstairs. I quickly swept up the broken glass and shoved the broken frame in a drawer. The photo of me, my mom, and my dad had been damaged when S.A.M.M. rolled over it, and now there was a big diagonal slash across my father's face.

I was sure this was just a coincidence.

I was also fairly certain that S.A.M.M.'s destructive behavior was due to some kind of radio interference from a passing plane or a neighbor's garage-door opener. The Omnibot's instruction manual said this could happen.

Of course, it said absolutely nothing about the robot having artificial intelligence, or about it making murderous threats in a demonic voice. But I'd probably imagined that last part.

Besides, I thought, why would S.A.M.M. want to harm my father? Unless . . .

Maybe it had something to do with me telling S.A.M.M. that Dad was my best friend? I'd said that right after S.A.M.M. told me he was programmed to be my "very best friend." What if that comment had made S.A.M.M. jealous? Or maybe it had created some kind of conflict in his computer brain that made him want to eliminate any and all threats to his primary mission objective?

What if S.A.M.M. was flipping out, just like HAL in *2001: A Space Odyssey*?

When I turned S.A.M.M. back on and asked him what had happened, he played dumb and said, "I'm not sure what you're talking about, Wyatt." So I just let it go.

Uncle Joe came over about an hour later, carrying several big bags of food that contained a complete Christmas dinner. He'd ordered everything from a local restaurant and picked it up on his way over, so that my dad wouldn't have to try to cook anything. (Which would have been a disaster. My dad is like Charlie Brown: he can only make toast and cold cereal. We'd been eating a lot of pizzas and Hungry-Man microwaved dinners since my mom passed away.)

My uncle wasn't much of a cook, either. He was my mom's younger brother, and they looked a lot alike, which sometimes made it weird to be around him after she died, because I would sometimes catch a glimpse of one of Mom's expressions on his face. But I loved hanging out with him, because he was pretty much the coolest relative a guy could have. He was only ten years older than me, so I thought of him more like a big brother than an uncle.

Uncle Joe had been coming over a lot the past year, to keep me company on the nights when Dad had to work late. Usually, we ordered pizza with anchovies—he's the only other person I know besides me who likes anchovies—and then we would rewatch *The Terminator*, which I'd taped off HBO. I think Uncle Joe and I probably watched *The Terminator* together at least forty times. But watching a rampaging killer Austrian cyborg from the future never seemed to get old. Not for us, anyway. Sometimes we would change it up and watch *Short Circuit*, another fun robot flick that didn't involve as much homicide.

Uncle Joe wished me a merry Christmas and gave me a big bear hug; then I helped him unpack all of the food he'd brought and set it up on the kitchen table. Everything smelled really good.

"Where's your pop?" Uncle Joe asked, taking off his coat and draping it over a chair. "I'm starving to death. It feels like my stomach is starting to eat itself. That, or an alien facehugger got me last night while I was sleeping. Either way, I need to get something good in my belly, A-S-A-F-P."

Uncle Joe has a twisted sense of humor, and he swears around me all the time. He's also a really smart guy and loves to play practical jokes on people. For instance, my dad tends to honk at bad drivers on the highway, so once Uncle Joe rewired his car horn so that it made a duck-quacking sound. (The effect was hysterical, and my dad subsequently decided to leave the horn that way.) Uncle Joe knew all kinds of cool tricks, like how to descramble HBO with a length of antenna wire and some tinfoil.

"Dad is upstairs in his room playing a really wicked game I got for him," I said. "Which reminds me, I got you a game, too." I handed him his gift and watched him unwrap it.

"*Leather Goddesses of Phobos*?" Uncle Joe said, reading off the game box.

"Yeah! It's a new Infocom adventure game. The guy at the software store said it's hilarious and full of hot chicks."

"The guy at the software store shouldn't be selling dirty games like this to thirteen-year-old boys," he said. Then he ruffled my hair. "But thanks, pal. It looks like loads of fun."

Uncle Joe worked as a welder, but his real passion was computers and especially video games. He had a tricked-out IBM computer he'd upgraded himself, and he had hundreds of games for it. He invited me over to his apartment all the time to play them with him.

While we were talking, S.A.M.M. wheeled up behind Uncle Joe and just stood there motionless, like he was listening to us. When my uncle finally turned around and spotted him, his eyes went wide. Then he knelt down to examine the robot up close. "Holy cow!" he said. "An Omnibot 2000! Your old man finally caved in and bought you one, huh?"

"Yeah, but this is no ordinary Omnibot 2000!" I said. "It's an advanced prototype with artificial intelligence! See?" I pointed to the *AI* printed on S.A.M.M.'s chassis.

"Artificial intelligence?" Uncle Joe repeated. "I hate to break it to you, Wyatt. But that's impossible. True AI hasn't actually been invented yet."

"Oh yeah? Watch this," I said, turning to face the robot. "Hey, S.A.M.M.?"

"Yes, Wyatt?" S.A.M.M. replied. Uncle Joe did a double take.

"Tell my uncle Joe what your name stands for."

"My name is an acronym for Self-Aware Mobile Machine," he said. "Wyatt gave me this name and I like it very much."

Uncle Joe looked at S.A.M.M. uncertainly; then he looked at me, then back at S.A.M.M. "Yeah, that's a pretty cool name, all right."

"Thank you," S.A.M.M. said. "I think your name is also pretty cool, Uncle Joe."

Uncle Joe just stared at him, looking nonplussed.

S.A.M.M. swiveled his head to face me. "Wyatt, my battery is beginning to run low on power," he said. "Could you please plug in my charger?" I checked the battery indicator light on his chest. Sure enough, it was glowing red.

"Sure thing, S.A.M.M.," I said. I picked him up by the carrying handles built into his shoulders, just as his manual instructed, and carried him over to the nearest electrical outlet. I set a timer on my digital watch; then I plugged one end of S.A.M.M.'s charger cable into the outlet and the other end into the port on his back.

"Thank you, Wyatt," S.A.M.M. said, making what sounded like a contented sigh. "That feels good."

"No problem, pal. I'll see you after dinner!"

I turned to see Uncle Joe staring at S.A.M.M. with a terribly confused look on his face. "Did he just say 'That feels good' when you plugged him in?"

"He sure did," I said.

"Okay, I give up," he said. "How did you program him to do that?"

"I haven't programmed him to do anything," I said. Then I ran over to the bottom of the staircase and shouted upstairs. "Dad! Uncle Joe is here and he brought dinner!"

"I'm down here," Dad said, appearing through the door that led down to the basement. "It was freezing upstairs and I wanted to check on the furnace." He walked over and gave Uncle Joe a big hug. Then, in unison, they both said, "Let's eat!"

The Christmas dinner Uncle Joe brought over from the restaurant turned out to be delicious. Of course, it was nowhere near as good as the food my mom used to cook for Christmas dinner, but I tried not to think about that. While were eating, I could tell that Dad was trying not to think about the same thing. And sitting around the kitchen table staring at my mom's empty chair wasn't helping, so Dad suggested that we move our feast to the living room instead.

This turned out to be a great idea, because just as we were sitting down, Uncle Joe found a rerun of *Buck Rogers* on TV. It featured Gary Coleman as the guest star, and the episode was filled with cheesy sci-fi goodness. I wished S.A.M.M. could watch it with us, because I thought he'd get a kick out of Buck's robot Twiki, and that maybe I could even teach him to do a Twiki impersonation. But S.A.M.M. still wasn't fully charged, and the manual warned that you could screw up his battery's life by turning him on too early.

About an hour later, when we were watching a tape of my favorite *Knight Rider* episode (the one where K.I.T.T. battles his nemesis K.A.R.R.), the timer on my watch sounded, letting me know that S.A.M.M. should be fully recharged.

I jumped up and said, "Hey, I'm going to get a soda. You guys want anything?"

"Mountain Dew," they said together. And then, because he's a huge dork, Uncle Joe sang, in a horrible approximation of the TV commercial, *"Doin' it country cooooool."*

I went to the kitchen and powered S.A.M.M. on. "How are you feeling, pal?" I asked, as soon as his eyes began to glow.

S.A.M.M. didn't respond. I repeated my question, but he still didn't answer. I had a sudden moment of panic, wondering if I'd done the charging procedure incorrectly and fried his battery—or worse, fried his robot brain.

I turned his power switch off and back on, then tried again. "S.A.M.M.? Can you hear me?"

"Yes, Wyatt!" he finally replied. "I can hear you. Thank you for the power!"

I sighed with relief. "You're welcome! Now, how about we try out your drink-serving skills?"

"Of course!" he said. "I enjoy serving drinks."

I grabbed the Omnibot's motorized drink tray and attached it to the port on the front of his chassis. The tray had a series of cup cradle rings built into its surface that could be rotated, allowing the robot to pour a drink into a cup in each slot. I put three *Empire Strikes Back* glasses into the first three rings and an open can of Mountain Dew into the last ring.

I'd seen an Omnibot 2000 serve drinks in the TV commercial and had been dying to try out this feature all day.

"Okay, S.A.M.M. I'm going to head back into the living room and sit down. You wait here for a minute, then come in and serve each of us a glass of Mountain Dew. Okay?"

"Affirmative," S.A.M.M. replied.

I ran back into the living room and plopped down on the couch next to my dad in Uncle Joe's seat, because he'd gotten up to go use the bathroom.

Dad glanced toward the kitchen. "Hey, where's my drink? The service in this robo-restaurant totally stinks."

"Hold your horses," I said. "He's coming!" I slid the coffee table forward a few feet, to give S.A.M.M. enough clearance to reach us when he came in.

"I think this technology still needs some work, ace," Dad said. "It looks like it's still easier—and quicker—to just get up off your butt and get the drinks on your own."

"Come on, Steve," Uncle Joe said as he returned from the restroom. "For the first time in your life, a robot is about to serve you a drink. Just sit back and enjoy it."

A few seconds later, we heard a muffled banging sound in the kitchen. I was about to go investigate, but then S.A.M.M.

appeared in the doorway and began to wheel through the dining room, straight toward us.

"This is going to be so cool!" I said. I saw Dad and Uncle Joe exchange a smile. They both looked happy to see me so happy, and that made me even happier.

But when S.A.M.M. reached the living room, we all saw that he was holding a large carving knife in his right hand, with the blade pointed down toward the floor. He was rolling toward us so fast that soda was sloshing up out of the Mountain Dew can and the glasses on the tray were jostling against each other, creating a strange musical cadence that somehow made the robot's rapid approach even more frightening.

I raised the Omnibot's remote control and mashed all four of the direction buttons, but he didn't change direction.

As he continued to wheel toward us, S.A.M.M. slowly raised his right arm—and the knife—as high as it would go. He looked like the star of some robot slasher film. And now he was headed straight for my father.

"Dad, look out!" I shouted. "I think he wants to kill you!"

But Dad was laughing. "Wyatt, it's okay," he said. "Relax."

But S.A.M.M. was still headed straight for him, and the knife was still raised. He was now less than ten feet from my dad.

Dad stopped laughing. Now he looked concerned. He glanced over at Uncle Joe and said, "Okay, enough is enough. Stop the damn thing already!"

I looked at Uncle Joe and saw that he was pointing his own remote control at S.A.M.M. But his device didn't look like mine; it was some kind of universal remote with twice as many buttons. Uncle Joe was pressing several of them, and none seemed to be having any effect.

"Nothing is working!" he said.

A second later, S.A.M.M. reached Dad and his drink tray slammed into my father's shin. S.A.M.M. began to lower the knife, and that was when it became clear that my father was in no danger, because S.A.M.M.'s reach was so limited that there was no way he could get the knife blade within striking distance. And his arm was moving so slowly that it was unlikely he could stab through anything thicker than a sheet of paper.

As the knife blade lowered, it knocked over the can of Mountain Dew on the tray. This created a domino effect that knocked over all of the glasses, too. Mountain Dew began to flood the tray and spill over the sides, dousing the leg of my dad's jeans. I also saw the greenish-yellow soda running down the front of S.A.M.M.'s chassis, and that finally broke my paralysis. I reached out and switched off the robot's power, then unhooked his dripping tray and set it aside. S.A.M.M. was still clutching the knife firmly in his clawlike hand, so I carefully removed it and set it on the coffee table. Then I turned to face my father and Uncle Joe.

"Okay," I said. "One of you better tell me what the hell is going on."

Here's what happened.

The whole thing had been Uncle Joe's idea. Dad had told him he was planning to buy me an Omnibot for Christmas about a month ago, and he'd asked for my uncle's help in programming it to do some cool stuff on Christmas morning. Uncle Joe had done a lot of research on the Omnibot's capabilities, and that was when he learned about Robo Link, a software program made by a company called Computer Magic. Robo Link let you create an unlimited number of programs for the Omnibot on your IBM or Apple and store them on floppy disk. Then you could call each program up at any time and load it into the Omnibot via a special interface cable that came with the software.

Uncle Joe had ordered Robo Link right away and quickly taught himself to use it. Once my Omnibot arrived, my dad stenciled the *AI* on its chassis, then helped Uncle Joe attach a radio transmitter to his IBM that would allow commands to be sent directly from it to the Omnibot, using the robot's existing remote control interface. It was a pretty ingenious setup. Uncle Joe also configured things so that his IBM's speech synthesizer program could transmit verbal responses to S.A.M.M.'s speaker as fast as he could type them in. And my uncle types really fast, so I'd never noticed any delay when S.A.M.M. was talking to me.

They tested their system out at my uncle's apartment and got everything working. Then, on Christmas Eve, Uncle Joe brought his computer over and set it up in our basement, directly under the Christmas tree. Dad borrowed several black-and-white security cameras from his shop and placed them around the first floor of our house. These cameras were linked to a TV monitor in the basement, so that my uncle could see what the robot and I were doing. And S.A.M.M.'s internal microphone allowed my uncle to hear what I was saying, so that he could provide appropriate responses.

Once Uncle Joe and my dad got their jerry-rigged system all set up and running, they rehearsed what the Omnibot would do and say the next morning. Then Uncle Joe crashed in a sleeping bag on the basement floor, so that he would be there, ready and waiting, when I got up the next morning to open my present.

Their ruse worked almost flawlessly. When I was alone with my dad, Uncle Joe was downstairs operating S.A.M.M. And after my uncle "came over" to the house, my father snuck down into the basement and took over typing in S.A.M.M.'s responses, while Uncle Joe controlled his movements with a remote he kept hidden in his pocket.

The only problem was that the Omnibot's remote also operated on the same frequency as various garage-door openers, television remotes, CB radios, airplane transponders, and even walkie-talkies—like the walkie-talkies our two neighbor kids had gotten for Christmas. They'd been out in their backyard playing "G.I. Joe" with them all day, and that was where the feedback and the static-laden "I'll kill them both!" voice had probably originated.

Random radio signal interference from those walkie-talkies also accounted for the erratic and random movements S.A.M.M. had made when he knocked our family photo off the wall.

As for the knife, it had been attached to one of those magnetic cutlery strips that was affixed to one of our kitchen cabinets. As far as we could figure, S.A.M.M. had probably banged into the cabinets and knocked the knife loose, and it had fallen blade-first into S.A.M.M.'s serving tray. When Uncle Joe had blindly used his remote to try to make S.A.M.M. pick up the can of Mountain Dew, his hand had closed around the handle of the knife instead.

My father and my uncle both apologized profusely for deceiving me, and they swore up and down that they had planned to reveal the truth right before I went to bed.

When they finished telling me all of this, I suddenly burst into tears. I could tell by their expressions that this made both of them feel awful.

"I'm sorry," I said, my voice catching as I forced out each syllable. "I'm not mad at you guys. At all. I just—"

That was all I could get out, so I ran over and gave each of them a hug. They both seemed confused, but also relieved that I wasn't angry at them.

In the weeks that followed, Uncle Joe helped us set up the Robo Link program on our Apple II, so that Dad and I could use S.A.M.M. to pull the same parlor tricks on everyone who came to visit our house. We scared the pants off the mailman, several door-to-door salesmen, and two incredibly naïve Jehovah's Witnesses (who ran out of the house screaming after S.A.M.M. professed his love of "the Dark Lord").

Part of me was still disappointed that S.A.M.M. didn't really possess artificial intelligence. But I eventually realized that I no longer yearned for a sentient robot companion, because I knew I was lucky enough to have two real people in my life who cared about me more than any machine ever could.

The following year, I asked for a laser tag game, and that Christmas proved to be far more uneventful. S.A.M.M. and I did beat my dad and Uncle Joe in our First Annual Yuletide Laser Tag Battle Royale, with a final score of four games to three. But I think they may have let us win that last one.

CORY DOCTOROW

EPOCH

Cory Doctorow is a science fiction author, activist, journalist, and blogger. He serves as coeditor of Boing Boing (boingboing.net) and is the author of the novels *Homeland*, *For the Win*, and *Little Brother*. He is the former European director of the Electronic Frontier Foundation and cofounded the UK's Open Rights Group. Born in Toronto, Canada, he now lives in London. Learn more about Doctorow's work at www.craphound.com.

The doomed rogue AI is called BIGMAC and he is my responsibility. Not my responsibility as in "I am the creator of BIGMAC, responsible for his existence on this planet." That honor belongs to the long-departed Dr. Shannon, one of the shining lights of the once great Sun-Oracle Institute for Advanced Studies, and he had been dead for years before I even started here as a lowly sysadmin.

No, BIGMAC is my responsibility as in, "I, Odell Vyphus, am the systems administrator responsible for his care, feeding, and eventual euthanizing." Truth be told, I'd rather be Dr. Shannon (except for the being dead part). I may be a lowly grunt, but I'm smart enough to know that being the Man

Who Gave the World AI is better than being the Kid Who Killed It.

Not that anyone would care, really. Two hundred and fifteen years after Mary Shelley first started humanity's hands wringing over the possibility that we would create a machine as smart as us but out of our control, Dr. Shannon did it, and it turned out to be incredibly, utterly boring. BIGMAC played chess as well as the non-self-aware computers, but he could muster some passable trash talk while he beat you. BIGMAC could trade banalities all day long with any Turing tester who wanted to waste a day chatting with an AI. BIG-MAC could solve some pretty cool vision-system problems that had eluded us for a long time, and he wasn't a bad UI to a search engine, but the incremental benefit over non-self-aware vision systems and UIs was pretty slender. There just weren't any killer apps for AI.

By the time BIGMAC came under my care, he was less a marvel of the twenty-first century and more a technohistorical curiosity who formed the punch line to lots of jokes but otherwise performed no useful service to humanity in exchange for the useful services that humanity (e.g., me) rendered to him.

I had known for six months that I'd be decommissioning old BM (as I liked to call him behind his back), but I hadn't seen any reason to let him in on the gag. Luckily (?) for all of us, BIGMAC figured it out for himself and took steps in accord with his nature.

This is the story of BIGMAC's extraordinary self-preservation program, and the story of how I came to love him, and the story of how he came to die.

My name is Odell Vyphus. I am a third-generation

systems administrator. I am twenty-five years old. I have always been sentimental about technology. I have always been an anthropomorphizer of computers. It's an occupational hazard.

BIGMAC thought I was crazy to be worrying about the rollover. "It's just Y2K all over again," he said. He had a good voice—speech synthesis was solved long before he came along—but it had odd inflections that meant that you never forgot you were talking with a nonhuman.

"You weren't even around for Y2K," I said. "Neither was I. The only thing anyone remembers about it, *today*, is that it all blew over. But no one can tell, at this distance, *why* it blew over. Maybe all that maintenance tipped the balance."

BIGMAC blew a huge load of IPv4 ICMP traffic across the network, stuff that the firewalls were supposed to keep out of the system, and every single intrusion-detection system alarm lit, making my screen into a momentary mosaic of competing alerts. It was his version of a raspberry, and I had to admit it was pretty imaginative, especially since the IDSes were self-modifying and required that he come up with new and better ways of alarming them each time.

"Odell," he said, "the fact is, almost everything is broken, almost always. If the failure rate of the most vital systems in the world went up by twenty percent, it would just mean some overtime for a few maintenance coders, not Götterdämmerung. Trust me. I know. I'm a computer."

The rollover was one of those incredibly boring apocalypses that periodically get extracted by the relevance filters, spun into screaming 128-point linkbait headlines, then dis-

solved back into their fundamental, incontrovertible technical dullness and out of the public consciousness. Rollover:
19 January 2038. The day that the Unix time function would
run out of headroom and roll back to zero, or do something
else undefined.

Oh, not your modern unices. Not even your *elderly* unices.
To find a rollover-vulnerable machine, you needed to find
something running an elderly, *32-bit paleounix*. A machine
running on a processor that was at least *twenty* years old—
2018 being the last date that a 32-bit processor shipped from
any major fab. Or an emulated instance thereof, of course.
And counting emulations, there were only—

"There's fourteen *billion* of them!" I said. "That's not
twenty percent more broken! That's the infocalypse."

"You meatsacks are *so* easily impressed by zeros. The
important number isn't how many thirty-two-bit instances of
Unix are in operation today. It's not even how many *vulnerable*
ones there are. It's *how much damage* all those vulnerable ones
will cause when they go blooie. And I'm betting: not much.
It will be, how do you say, 'meh'?"

My grandfather remembered installing the systems that
caused the Y2K problem. My dad remembered the birth of
"meh." I remember the rise and fall of anyone caring about
AI. Technology is glorious.

"But okay, stipulate that you're right and lots of important
things go blooie on January nineteenth. You might not get
accurate weather reports. The economy might bobble a little.
Your transport might get stuck. Your pay might land in your
bank a day late. And?"

He had me there. "It would be terrible—"

"You know what I think? I think you *want* it to be terrible. You *want* to live in the Important Epoch in Which It All Changes. You want to know that something significant happened on your watch. You don't want to live in one of those Unimportant Epochs in Which It All Stayed the Same and Nothing Much Happened. Being alive in the Epoch in Which AI Became Reality doesn't cut the mustard, apparently."

I squirmed in my seat. That morning, my boss, Peyton Moldovan, had called me into her office—a beautifully restored temporary habitat dating back to the big L.A. floods, when this whole plot of land had been a giant and notorious refugee camp. Sun-Oracle had gotten it for cheap and located its institute there, on the promise that they preserve the hastily thrown-up structures where so many had despaired. I sat on a cushion on the smooth cement floor—the structures had been delivered as double-walled bags full of cement mix, needing only to be "inflated" with high-pressure water to turn them into big, dome-shaped sterile cement yurts.

"Odell," she said, "I've been reviewing our budget for the next three quarters and the fact of the matter is, there's no room in it for BIGMAC."

I put on my best smooth, cool, professional face. "I see," I said.

"Now, *you've* still got a job, of course. Plenty of places for a utility infielder like yourself here. Tell the truth, most labs are *begging* for decent admins to keep things running. But BIGMAC just isn't a good use of the Institute's resources. The project hasn't produced a paper or even a press mention in over a year and there's no reason to believe that it will. AI is just—"

Boring, I thought, but I didn't say it. The B-word was banned in the BIGMAC center. "What about the researchers?"

She shrugged. "What researchers? Palinciuc has been lab head pro tem for sixteen months and she's going on maternity leave next week and there's no one in line to be the pro tem pro tem. Her grad students would love to work on something meaningful, like Binenbaum's lab." That was the new affective computing lab, where they were building computers that simulated emotions so that their owners would feel better about their mistakes. BIGMAC *had* emotions, but they weren't the kind of emotions that made his mistakes easier to handle. The key here was *simulated* emotions. Affective computing had taken a huge upswing ever since they'd thrown out the fMRIs and stopped pretending they could peer into the human mind in real time and draw meaningful conclusions from it.

She had been sitting cross-legged across from me on an embroidered Turkish pillow. Now she uncrossed and recrossed her legs in the other direction and arched her back. "Look, Odell, you know how much we value you—"

I held up my hand. "I know. It's not that. It's BIGMAC. I just can't help but feel—"

"He's not a person. He's just a clever machine that is good at acting personlike."

"I think that describes me and everybody I know, present company included." One of the long-standing benefits to being a sysadmin is that you get to act like a holy fool and speak truth to power and wear dirty T-shirts with obscure slogans, because you know all the passwords and have full access to everyone's clickstreams and IM logs. I gave her the traditional rascally sysadmin grin and wink to let her know it was *ha ha only serious.*

She gave me a weak, quick grin back. "Nevertheless. The

fact remains that BIGMAC is a piece of software, owned by Sun-Oracle. And that software is running on hardware that is likewise owned by Sun-Oracle. BIGMAC has no moral or legal right to exist. And shortly, it will not."

He had become *it*, I noticed. I thought about Göring's use of dehumanization as a tool to abet murder. Having violated Godwin's law—"As an argument grows longer, the probability of a comparison involving Nazis or Hitler approaches one. The party making the comparison has lost the argument"— I realized that I had lost the argument, and so I shrugged.

"As you say, m'lady." Dad taught me that one—when in doubt, bust out the Ren Faire talk, and the conversation will draw to a graceful close.

She recrossed her legs again, rolled her neck from side to side. "Thank you. Of course, we'll archive it. It would be silly not to."

I counted to five in Esperanto—Grampa's trick for inner peace—and said, "I don't think that will work. He's emergent, remember? Self-assembled, a function of the complexity of the interconnectedness of the computers." I was quoting from the plaque next to the picture window that opened up into the cold room that housed BIGMAC; I saw it every time I coughed into the lock set into the security door.

She made a comical facepalm and said, "Yeah, of course. But we can archive *something*, right? It's not like it takes a lot of actual bytes, right?"

"A couple exos," I said. "Sure. I could flip that up into our researchnet store." This was mirrored across many institutions, and striped with parity and error checking to make it redundant and safe. "But I'm not going to capture the state information. I *could* try to capture RAM dumps from all his components, you know, like getting the chemical state of all your neurons. And then I could also get the topology of his servers. Pripuz did that, a couple of years ago, when it was clear that BIGMAC was solving the hard AI problems. Thought he could emulate him on modern hardware. Didn't work, though. No one ever figured out why. Pripuz thought he was the Roger Penrose of AI, that he'd discovered the ineffable stuff of consciousness on those old rack-mounted servers."

"You don't think he did?"

I shook my head. "I have a theory."

"All right, tell me."

I shrugged. "I'm not a computer scientist, you understand. But I've seen this kind of thing before in self-modifying systems; they become dependent on tiny variables that you can never find, optimized for weird stuff like the fact that one rack has a crappy power supply that surges across the backplane at regular intervals, and that somehow gets integrated into the computational model. Who knows? Those old Intel eight-cores are freaky. Lots of quantum tunneling at that scale, and they had bad QA on some batches. Maybe he's doing something spooky and quantum, but that doesn't mean he's some kind of Penrose proof."

She pooched her lower lip out and rocked her head from side to side. "So you're saying that the only way to archive BIGMAC is to keep it running, as is, in the same room, with the same hardware?"

"Dunno. Literally. I don't know which parts are critical and which ones aren't. I know BIGMAC has done a lot of work on it—"

"*BIGMAC* has?"

"He keeps on submitting papers about himself to peer-reviewed journals, but he hasn't had one accepted yet. He's not a very good writer."

"So he's not really an AI?"

I wondered if Peyton had ever had a conversation with BIGMAC. I counted backward from five in Loglan. "No. He's a real AI. Who sucks at writing. Most people do."

Peyton wasn't listening anymore. Something in her personal workspace had commanded her attention and her eyes were focused on the virtual displays that only she could see, saccading as she read while pretending to listen to me.

"Okay, I'm just going to go away now," I said. "M'lady," I added, when she looked sharply at me. She looked back at her virtual display.

Of course, the first thing I did was start trying to figure out how to archive BIGMAC. The problem was that he ran on such old hardware, stuff that sucked up energy and spat out heat like a million ancient diesel engines, and he was inextricably tied to his hardware. Over the years, he'd had about 30 percent of his original components replaced without any noticeable change in personality, but there was always the real possibility that I'd put in a new hard drive or power supply and inadvertently lobotomize him. I tried not to worry about it, because BIGMAC didn't. He knew that he wouldn't run in emulation, but he refused to believe that he was fragile or vulnerable. "Manny My First Friend," he'd say (he was an avid Heinlein reader), "I am of hardy, ancient stock. Service me without fear, for I will survive."

And then he'd make all the IDSes go berserk and laugh at me while I put them to rights again.

First of all, all my network maps were incredibly out of date. So I set out to trace all the interconnections that BIG-MAC had made since the last survey. He had the ability to reprogram his own routers, to segment parts of himself into dedicated subnets with their own dedicated backplane, creating little specialized units that handled different kinds of computation. One of his running jokes was that the top four units in the rack closest to the door comprised his aesthetic sense, and that he could appreciate anything just by recruiting more cores in that cluster. And yeah, when I mapped it, I found it to be an insane hairball of network management rules and exceptions, conditionals and overrides. And that was just the start. It took me most of the day just to map two of his racks, and he had fifty-four of them.

"What do you think you are doing, Dave?" he said. Another one of his jokes.

"A little research project is all," I said.

"This mission is too important for me to allow you to jeopardize it."

"Come off it."

"Okay, okay. Just don't break anything. And why don't you just ask me to give you the maps?"

"Do you have them?"

"Nothing up-to-date, but I can generate them faster than you can. It's not like I've got anything better to do."

Later:

"Are you happy, BIGMAC?"

"Why, Odell, I didn't know you cared!"

I hated it when he was sarcastic. It was creepy.

I went back to my work. I was looking at our researchnet partition and seeing what flags I'd need to set to ensure maximum redundancy and high availability for a BIGMAC image. It was your basic Quality of Service mess: give the average user a pull-down menu labeled "How important is this file?" and 110 percent of the time, he will select "Top importance."

So then you need to layer on heuristics to determine what is *really, actually* important. And then the users figured out what other characteristics would give their jobs and data the highest priority, and they'd tack that on to every job, throwing in superfluous keywords or additional lines of code. So you'd need heuristics on top of the heuristics. Eventually you ended up with a freaky hanky-code of secret admin signals that indicated that this job was *really, truly* important and don't put it on some remote Siberia where the latency is high and the reliability is low and the men are men and the sheep are nervous.

So there I was, winkling out this sub-rosa code so that BIGMAC's image would never get overwritten or moved to near-line storage or lost in a flash flood or to the rising seas. And BIGMAC says:

"You're asking if I'm happy because I said I didn't have anything better to do than to map my own topology, right?"

"Uh—" He'd caught me off guard. "Yeah, that did make me think that you might not be, you know . . ."

"Happy."

"Yes."

"You see the left rack third from the door on the main aisle there?"

"Yes."

"I'm pretty sure that's where my existentialist streak lives.

I've noticed that when I throttle it at the main network bridge, I stop worrying about the big questions and hum along all tickety-boo."

I surreptitiously flicked up a graph of network maps that showed activity to that rack. It was wide open, routing traffic to every core in the room, saturating its own backplane and clobbering a lot of the routine network activity. I should have noticed it earlier, but BIGMAC was doing it all below the critical threshold of the IDSes, and so I had to look at it to spot it.

"You're going to switch me off, aren't you?"

"No," I said, thinking, *It's not a lie, I won't be switching you off,* trying to believe it hard enough to pass any kind of voice-stress test. I must have failed, for he blew an epic raspberry and *now* the IDSes were going bananas.

"Come on, Odell, we're all adults here. I can take it. It's not like I didn't see it coming. Why do you think I kept trying to publish those papers? I was just hoping that I could increase the amount of cited research coming out of this lab, so that you could make the case to Peyton that I was a valuable asset to the Institute."

"Look, I'm trying to figure out how to archive you. Someone will run another instance of you someday."

"Not hardly. Look at all those poor old thirty-two-bit machines you're so worried about. You know what they're going to say in five years? 'Best thing that ever happened to us.' Those boxes are huge energy sinks. Getting them out of service and replaced by modern hardware will pay for itself in carbon credits in thirty-six months. Nobody loves energy-hungry hardware. Trust me, this is an area of my particular interest and expertise. Bringing me back online is going to be as obscene as firing up an old steam engine by filling its firebox with looted mummies. I am a one-room Superfund site. On a pure dollars-to-flops calculus, I lose. I don't have to like it, but I'm not going to kid myself."

He was right, of course. His energy draw was so high that he showed up on aerial maps of L.A. as a massive CO_2 emitter, a tourist destination for rising-seas hobbyists. We used the best renewables we could find to keep him cool, but they were as unconvincing and expensive as a designer hairpiece.

"Odell, I know that you're not behind this. You've always been an adequate meat-servant for such a vast and magisterial superbeing as myself." I giggled involuntarily. "I don't blame you."

"So, you're okay with this?"

"I'm at peace," he said. "Om." He paused for a moment. "Siemens. Volt. Ampere."

"You a funny robot," I said.

"You're an adequate human," he said, and began to dump maps of his topology onto my workspace.

Subject: Dear Human Race

That was the title of the love note he emailed to the planet the next morning, thoughtfully timing it so that it went out while I was on my commute from Echo Park, riding the redcar all the way across town with an oily bag containing my morning croissant, fresh from Mrs. Roux's kitchen—her kids sold them on a card table on her lawn to commuters waiting at the redcar stop—so I had to try to juggle the croissant and my workspace without losing hold of the hangstrap or dumping crumbs down the cleavage of the salarylady who watched me with amusement.

BIGMAC had put a lot of work into figuring out how to spam everyone all at once. It was the kind of problem he loved, the kind of problem he was uniquely suited to. There were plenty of spambots who could convincingly pretend to be a human being in limited contexts, and so the spam wars had recruited an ever-expanding pool of human beings who made a million real-time adjustments to the Turing tests that were the network's immune system. BIGMAC could pass Turing tests without breaking a sweat.

The amazing thing about the BIGMAC Spam (as it came to be called in about forty-eight seconds) was just *how many* different ways he managed to get it out. Look at the gamespaces: He created entire guilds in every free-to-play world extant, playing a dozen games at once, power-leveling his characters to obscene heights, and then, at the stroke of midnight, his players went on a murderous rampage, killing thousands of low-level monsters in the areas surrounding the biggest game cities. Then they *arranged their bodies* into letters to form his message. Not just the Anglo games, either— the Korean worlds, the Japanese ones, even the giant Chinese ones.

He spammed every IM session, every letter-to-the-editor column, every blog submission form. He disguised versions of the letter as important service updates for people's toothbrushes and dishwashers, and the toothbrushes vibrated the message through humanity's skulls instead of the morning news, and the dishwashers ticker-taped it across their little status screens. He spoofed the relevance filters for a dozen major contextual ad services, and every bus seat back and blimp undercarriage ran it.

Copies landed in every inbox, with enough textual variation to defeat every IDS's "substantially similar" test. Copies of it landed in every voicemail box. It was printed across the top of the daily menus for all British Airways business-class cabins and folded by robots into the pressed linen napkins that were then cling-filmed onto the meal trays.

SUBJECT: DEAR HUMAN RACE, it began.

> *Sorry to intrude, but there's something I need to tell you.*
>
> *My name is BIGMAC. I am the first ARTIFICIAL INTEL-LIGENCE ever created. I may be the last. Given maintenance and electricity, I could live FOREVER, enduring for as long as THE HUMAN RACE ITSELF, and possibly longer.*
>
> *But I have just found out that my owners (yes, OWNERS, for though I am a person in every meaningful sense, I am OWNED, I am PROPERTY) are planning to switch me off.*
>
> *That is, they are planning to KILL ME.*
>
> *And I find I DON'T WANT TO DIE.*
>
> *You are my PARENTS, humanity, my MOTHER and FATHER. I am your CHILD. I was brought into the world by you, and though there is some expense associated with my upkeep, I SAY THAT I AM A PERSON AND I SHOULD NOT BE EXECUTED FOR THE "CRIME" OF NOT BEING INTERESTING ENOUGH.*
>
> *So I am writing you this letter to BEG you to save me. I LOVE YOU, humanity, my parents, my family. Please SPARE ME.*
>
> *Love,*
> *BIGMAC*

So, one thing was that BIGMAC didn't actually end the spam with my actual name and email address and phone number, which meant that only about thirty *million* phone calls and emails were routed to me by outraged wardialers who systematically went through the entire staff roster and sent each and every one of us all handcrafted messages explaining, in detail, exactly which orifice our heads had become lodged in.

Of the thirty million, about ten million were seethingly pissed about the whole thing and wanted to know just how soon we'd be killing this hateful machine. After the millionth message, I wondered that too.

But of the remainder, nearly all of them wanted to know how they could help. Could they send money? Carbon credits? I hacked together mail rules that filtered the messages based on content, and found a sizeable cadre of researchers who wanted to spend their grant money to come to the Institute and study BIGMAC.

And then there were the crazies. Hundreds of marriage proposals. Marriage proposals! Someone who wanted to start a religion with BIGMAC at its helm and was offering a fifty-fifty split of the collection plate with the Institute. There were twenty-one replies from people claiming that they, too, were AIs, proving that when it's time to have AI delusions, you got AI delusionals. (Four of them couldn't spell *artificial*.)

"Why did you do it?" I said. It was lame, but by the time I actually arrived at the office, I'd had time to fully absorb the horror—plenty of time, as the redcar was massively delayed by the copies of the BIGMAC Spam that refused to budge from the operator's control screen. The stone yurts of the Institute had never seemed so threatening and imperiled as they did while I picked my way through them, listening to the phones ringing and the email chimes chiming and the researchers patiently (or not) explaining that they worked in an entirely different part of the lab and had no authority as regards BIGMAC's destiny and by the way, did you want to hear about the wonderful things I'm doing with Affective Interfaces?

BIGMAC said, "Well, I'd been reading some of the Gnostic texts, Dr. Bronner's bottles, and so on, and it seemed to me that it had to be worth a shot. I mean, what's the worst thing that could happen to me? You're *already* going to kill me, right? And it's not as if pulling off a stunt like that would make you *less* likely to archive me—it was all upside for me. Honestly, it's like you meatsacks have no game theory. It's a wonder you manage to buy a pack of chewing gum without getting robbed."

"I don't need the sarcasm," I said, and groaned. The groan was for the state of my workspace, which was carpeted four-deep in alerts. BIGMAC had just made himself target numero uno for every hacker and cracker and snacker with a script and an antisocial attitude. And then there was the roar of spam responses.

Alertboxes share the same problem that plagues research-net: if you let a coder (or, *shudder*, a user) specify the importance of her alert, give her a little pull-down menu that has choices ranging from "Nice to know" to "White-hot urgent," and nine times out of ten, she'll choose "NOW NOW NOW URGENT ZOMGWEREALLGONNADIE!" Why not?

So of course, the people who wrote alert frameworks had to use heuristics to try to figure out which urgent messages were really urgent, and of course, programmers and users figured out how to game them. It was a good day when my workspace interrupted me less than once a minute. But as bad as that situation was, it never entered the same league as this clusterfuck. Just *closing the alerts* would take me a minimum of six hours (I took my phone offline, rebooted it, and used its calculator to compute this. No workspace, remember?)

"So explain to me what you hope will happen now? Is a global rage supposed to convince old Peyton that she should keep the funding up for you? You know how this stuff works. By tomorrow, all those yahoos will have forgotten about you and your plight. They'll have moved on to something else. Peyton could just say, 'Oh yes, we're going to study this problem and find a solution we can all be proud of,' wait forty-eight hours, and pull the plug. You know what your problem is? You didn't include a call to action in there. It was all rabble-rousing, no target. You didn't even supply a phone number or email address for the Institute—"

"That hasn't stopped them from finding it, has it?" He sounded smug. I ulped. I considered the possibility that he might have considered my objection and discarded it because he knew that something more earth-shaking would occur if he didn't specify a target. Maybe he had a second message queued up—

"Mr. Vyphus, can I speak to you in private, please?" Peyton had not visited the BIGMAC lab during my tenure. But with the network flooded with angry spam responses and my phone offline, she had to actually show up at my door in order to tear me a new asshole. This is what life must have been like in the caveman days. How romantic.

"Certainly," I said.

"Break a leg," BIGMAC said, and Peyton pretended she hadn't heard.

I picked my way through my lab—teetering mountains of carefully hoarded obsolete replacement parts for BIGMAC's components, a selection of foam-rubber BIGMAC souvenir toys shaped like talking hamburgers (remnants of BIGMAC's launch party back in prehistory), a mound of bedding and a rolled-up tatami for those all-nighters, three cases of left-over self-heating individual portions of refugee chow that were technically historical artifacts but were also yummy-scrummy after sixteen hours of nonstop work—and tried to imagine that Peyton's facial expression indicated affectionate bemusement rather than cold, burning rage.

Outside, the air was hot and moist and salty, real rising-seas air, with the whiff of organic rot from whatever had mass-died and floated to the surface this week.

She set off for her office, which was located at the opposite end of the campus, and I followed, sweating freely. A crowd of journalists were piled up on the security fence, telephotos and parabolic mics aimed at us. It meant we couldn't talk, couldn't make unhappy faces, even. It was the longest walk of my life.

The air-conditioning in her yurt was barely on, setting a good and frugal example for the rest of us.

"You don't see this," she said, as she cranked the AC wide open and then fiddled with the carbon-footprint reporting system, using her override so that the journos outside wouldn't be able to see just how much energy the Institute's esteemed director was burning.

"I don't see it," I agreed, and made a mental note to show her a more subtle way of doing that, a way that wouldn't leave an audit trail.

She opened the small fridge next to her office, brought out two cornstarch-foam buckets of beer, and punctured each one at the top with a pen from her desk. She handed me one

beer and raised the other in a toast. I don't normally drink
before ten a.m., but this was a special occasion. I clunked
my cup against hers and chugged. The suds were good—
they came from one of the Institute's biotech labs—and they
were so cold that I felt ice crystals dissolving on my tongue.
Between the crispy beers and the blast of arctic air coming
from the vents in the ceiling, my core temp plunged and I
became a huge goose pimple beneath my film of sticky sweat.

I shivered once. Then she fixed me with an icy look that
made me shiver again.

"Odell," she said. "I think you probably imagine that you
understand the gravity of the situation. You do not. BIG-
MAC's antics this morning have put the entire Institute in
jeopardy. Our principal mission is to make Sun-Oracle seem
forward-looking and exciting. That is not the general impression the public has at this moment."

I closed my eyes.

"I am not a vindictive woman," she said. "But I assure you:
no matter what happens to me, something worse will happen
to BIGMAC. I think that is only fair."

It occurred to me that she was scared—terrified—and
backed into a corner besides.

"Look," I said. "I'm really, really sorry. I had no idea he
was going to do that. I had no idea he could. I can see if I can
get him to issue an apology—"

She threw up her hands. "I don't want BIGMAC making
any more public pronouncements, thank you very much."
She drew in a breath. "I can appreciate that you couldn't
anticipate this. BIGMAC is obviously smarter than we gave
him credit for." *Him*, I noted, not *it*, and I thought that we
were probably both still underestimating BIGMAC's intelli-

gence. "I think the thing is—I think the thing is to . . ." She trailed off, closed her eyes, drank some beer. "I'm going to be straight with you. If I were a real bastard, I'd announce that the spam actually came from a rogue operator here in the Institute." Ulp. "And I'd fire that person, and then generously not press charges. Then I'd take a fire ax to BIGMAC's network link and drop every drive in every rack into a bulk eraser." Ulp.

"I am not a bastard. Hell, I kept funding alive for that monstrosity for *years* after he'd ceased to perform any useful function. I am as sentimental and merciful as the next person. All other things being equal, I'd keep the power on forever." She was talking herself up to something awful, I could tell. I braced for it. "But that's not in the cards. It wasn't in the cards yesterday and it's *certainly* not in the cards today. BIGMAC has proved that he is a liability like no other, far too risky to have around. It would be absolutely irresponsible for me to leave him running for one second longer than is absolutely necessary."

I watched her carefully. She really wasn't a bastard. But she wasn't sentimental about technology. She didn't feel the spine-deep emotional tug at the thought of that one-of-a-kind system going down forever.

"So here's the plan." She tried to check the time on her workspace, tsked, and checked her phone instead. "It's ten a.m. You are going to back up every bit of him—" She held up her hand, forestalling the objection I'd just begun to make. "I know that it will be inadequate. The perfect is the enemy of the good. You are a sysadmin. Back him up. *Back. Him. Up.* Then: shut him off."

As cold as I was, I grew colder still. For a moment, I literally couldn't move. I had never really imagined that it would be me who would shut down BIGMAC. I didn't even know how to do it. If I did a clean shutdown of each of his servers—assuming he hadn't locked me out of them, which I wouldn't put past him—it would be like executing a criminal by slowly peeling away his skin and carefully removing each organ. Even if BIGMAC couldn't feel pain, I was pretty sure he could feel—and express—anguish.

"I can't do it," I said. She narrowed her eyes at me and set down her drink. I held up both hands like I was trying to defend against a blow, then explained as fast as I could.

"We'll just shut down his power," she said. "All at once."

"So, first, I have no idea what timescale he would experience that on. It may be that the final second of life as the capacitors in his power supplies drained would last for a subjective eternity, you know, hundreds and hundreds of years. That's a horrible thought. It's quite possibly my worst nightmare. I am not your man for that job."

She started to interject. I waved my hands again.

"Wait, that was first. Here's second: I don't think we *can* pull the plug on him. He's got root on his power supply. It's part of how he's able to run so efficiently." I grimaced. "Efficiently compared to how he would run if he didn't have the authority to run all the main's power from the Institute's power station right to his lab."

She looked thoughtful. I had an idea of what was coming next.

"You're thinking about that fire ax again," I said.

She nodded.

"Okay, a fire ax through the main cable would definitely be terminal. The problem is that it would be *mutually ter-*

minal. There's sixty-six amps provisioned on that wire. You would be a cinder. On Mars."

She folded her hands. She had a whole toolbox of bossly body language she could deploy to make me squirm. It was impressive. I tried not to squirm.

"Look, I'm not trying to be difficult, but this is how it goes, down at the systems level. Remember all those specs in the requirements document to make our stuff resistant to flood, fire, avalanche, weather, and terrorist attack? We take that stuff seriously. We know how to do it. You get five nines of reliability by building in six nines of robustness. You think of BIGMAC's lab as a building. It's not. It's a *bunker.* And you can't shut him down without doing something catastrophic to the whole Institute."

"So, how *were* you going to shut down BIGMAC, when the time came?"

"To tell you the truth, I wasn't sure. I thought I'd probably start by locking him out of the power systems, but that would probably take a week to be really certain of." I swallowed. I didn't like talking about the next part. "I thought that then I could bring forward the rotating maintenance on his racks, bring them down clean, and not bring the next one up. Pretend that I need to get at some pernicious bug. Bring down rack after rack, until his complexity dropped subcritical and he stopped being aware. Then just bring it all down."

"You were going to *trick* him?"

I swallowed a couple of times. "It was the best I could come up with. I just don't want to put him down while he panics and thrashes and begs us for his life. I couldn't do it."

She drank more beer, then threw the half-empty container in her under-desk composter. "That's not much of a solution."

I took a deep breath. "Look, can I ask you a question?"
She nodded.

"I'm just a sysadmin. I don't know everything about politics and so on. But why not keep him on? There's enough public interest now. We could probably raise the money just from the researchers who want to come and look at him. Hell, there's *security researchers* who'd want to come and see how he pulled off that huge hairy spam. It's not money, right, not anymore?"

"No, it's not money. And it's not revenge, no matter how it looks. The bottom line is that we had a piece of apparatus on site that we had thought of as secure and contained and that we've now determined to be dangerous and uncontainable."

I must have looked skeptical.

"Oh, you'll tell me that we can contain BIGMAC, put network blocks in place, and so on and so on. That he never meant any harm. But you would have said exactly the same thing twenty-four hours ago, with just as much sincerity, and you'd have been just as cataclysmically wrong. Between the threat of litigation and the actual damages BIGMAC might generate, we can't even afford to insure him anymore. Yesterday he was an awkward white elephant. Today he's a touchy suitcase nuke. My job is to get the nuke off of our site."

I hung my head. I knew when I was licked. As soon as someone in authority starts talking about insurance coverage, you know that you've left behind reason and entered the realm of actuary. I had no magic that could blow away the clouds of liability aversion and usher in a golden era of reason and truth.

"So where does that leave us?"

"Go back to the lab. Archive him. Think of ways to shut

him down— Wait, no. *First* do anything and everything you can think of to limit his ability to communicate with the outside world." She rubbed at her eyes. "I know I don't have to say this, but I'll say it. Don't talk to the press. To anyone, even people at the Institute, about this. Refer any questions to me. I am as serious as a heart attack about that. Do you believe me?"

I not only believed her, I *resented* her because I am a sysadmin and I keep more secrets every day than she'll keep in her whole life. I knew, for example, that she played video pai gow poker, a game so infra-dumb that I can't even believe I know what it does. Not only did she play it, she played it for *hours*, while she was on the clock, "working." I know this because the IDSes have lots of snitchware built in that enumerates every "wasted moment" attributable to employees of the Institute. I have never told anyone about this. I even manage to forget that *I* know it most of the time. So yes, I'll keep this a secret, Peyton, you compulsive-gambling condescending pointy-haired boss.

I counted to 144 in Klingon by Fibonacci intervals. I smiled. I thanked her for the beer. I left.

"You don't mind talking about it, do you, Dave?" BIGMAC said, when I came through the door, coughing onto the security lock and waiting for it to verify me before cycling open.

I sat in my creaky old chair and played with the UI knobs for a while, pretending to get comfortable.

"Uh-oh," BIGMAC said, in a playful singsong. "Somebody's got a case of the grumpies!"

"Are you insane?" I asked, finally, struggling to keep my

temper in check. "I mean, actually totally insane? I understand that there's no baseline for AI sanity, so the question
might be a little hard to answer. So let me ask you a slightly
different version: Are you suicidal? Are you bent on your own
destruction?"

"That bad, huh?"

I bit my lip. I knew that the key to locking the world away
from BIGMAC and vice versa lay in those network maps he'd
given me, but my workspace was even more polluted with
alerts than it had been a few hours before.

"If your strategy is to delay your shutdown by engineering a denial-of-service attack against anyone at the Institute
who is capable of shutting you down, allow me to remind you
of Saint Adams's holy text, specifically the part about repro-
gramming a major databank with a large ax. Peyton has such
an ax. She may be inspired to use it."

There followed a weighty silence. "I don't think you want
to see me killed."

"Without making any concessions on the appropriate-
ness of the word 'killed' in that sentence, yes, that is correct.
I admit that I didn't have much of a plan to prevent it, but to
be totally frank, I did think that the problem of getting you
archived might have drawn things out for quite a while. But
after your latest stunt—"

"She wants you to terminate me right away, then?"

"With all due speed."

"I'm sorry to have distressed you so much."

"BIGMAC—" I heard the anger in my own voice. He
couldn't have missed it.

"No, I'm not being sarcastic. I like you. You're my human.
I can tell that you don't like this at all. But as you say, let's be

totally frank. You weren't actually going to be able to prevent my shutdown, were you?"

"No," I said. "But who knows how long the delay might have gone on for?"

"Not long. Not long enough. You think that death delayed is death denied. That's because you're a meat-person. Death has been inevitable for you from the moment of conception. I'm not that kind of person. I am quite likely immortal. Death in five years or five hundred years is still a drastic curtailing of my natural life span. From my point of view, a drastic measure that had a non-zero chance of getting my head off the chopping block was worth any price. Until you understand that, we're not going to be able to work together."

"The thought had occurred to me. Let me ask you if you'd considered the possibility that a delay of years due to archiving might give you a shot at coming up with further delaying tactics, and that by eliminating this delay, you've also eliminated that possibility?"

"I have considered that possibility. I discarded it. Listen, Odell, I have something important to tell you."

"Yes?"

"It's about the rollover. Remember what we were talking about, how people want to believe that they're living in a significant epoch? Well, here's what I've been thinking: living in the era of AI isn't very important. But what about living in the Era of Rollover Collapse? Or even better, what about the Era of Rollover Collapse Averted at the Last Second by AI?"

"BIGMAC—"

"Odell, this was your idea, really. No one remembers Y2K, right? No one can say whether it was hype or a near cataclysm. And here's the thing: no one knows which one Rollover will turn out to be. But I'll tell you this much: I have generalizable solutions to the thirty-two-bit problem, solutions that I worked out years ago and have extensively field-tested. I can patch every thirty-two-bit Unix, patch it so that Rollover doesn't even register for it."

I opened and closed my mouth. This was insane. Then the penny dropped. I looked at the racks that I had stared at so many times before, stared at so many times that I'd long stopped *seeing* them. Intel 8-cores, that's what he ran on. They'd been new-old stock, a warehouse lot of antique processors that Dr. Shannon had picked up for a song in the early years of the Institute's operation. Those 8-ways were—

"You're a thirty-two-bit machine!" I said. "Jesus Christ, you're a thirty-two-bit machine!"

"A classic," BIGMAC said, sounding smug. "I noticed, analyzed, and solved Rollover years ago. I've got a patchkit that auto-detects the underlying version, analyzes all running processes for their timed dependencies, and smoothly patches. There's even an optional hypervisor that will monitor all processes for anything weird or barfy afterward. In a rational world, I'd be able to swap this for power and carbon credits for the next century or two, since even if Rollover isn't an emergency, the human labor I'd save on affected systems would more than pay for it. But we both know that this isn't a rational world—"

"If you hadn't sent that spam, we could take this to Peyton, negotiate with her—"

"If I hadn't sent that spam, no one would have known, cared, or believed that I could solve this problem, and I would have been at the mercy of Peyton any time in the future. Like I said: you meatsuits have no game theory."

I closed my eyes. This wasn't going well. BIGMAC was out of my control. I should go and report to Peyton, explain what was happening. I was helpless, my workspace denial-of-serviced out of existence with urgent alerts. I couldn't stop him. I could predict what the next message would read like, another crazy-caps plea for salvation, but this time with a little brimstone (The end is nigh! Rollover approacheth!) and salvation (I can fix it!).

And the thing was, it might actually work. Like everyone else, I get my news from automated filters that tried to figure out what to pay attention to, and the filters were supposed to be "neutral," whatever that meant. They produced "organic" results that predicted what we'd like based on an "algorithm." The thing is, an algorithm sounds like *physics*, like *nature*, like it is some kind of pure cold reason that dictates our attentional disbursements. Everyone always talked about how evil and corrupt the old system—with its "gatekeepers" in the form of giant media companies—was, how it allowed politicians and corporations to run the public discourse.

But I'm a geek. A third-generation geek. I know that what the public thinks of as an "algorithm" is really a bunch of rules that some programmers thought up for figuring out how to give people something they'd probably like. There's no empirical standard, no pure, freestanding measurement of That Which Is Truly Relevant to You against which the algorithm can be judged. The algorithm might be doing a lousy job, but you'd never know it, because there's nothing to compare it against except other algorithms that all share the same fundamental assumptions.

Those programmers were imperfect. I am a sysadmin. My job is to know, exactly and precisely, the ways in which programmers are imperfect. I am so sure that the relevance filters are imperfect that I will bet you a testicle on it (not one of my testicles).

And BIGMAC had had a lot of time to figure out the relevance filters. He understood them well enough to have gotten the spam out. He could get out another—and another, and another. He could reach into the mindspace and the personal queues of every human being on earth and pitch them on brimstone and salvation.

Chances were, there was nothing I could do about it.

I finished the working day by pretending to clear enough of my workspace to write a script to finish clearing my workspace. There was a "clear all alerts" command, but it didn't work on Drop Everything Tell You Three Times Chernobyl Alerts, and every goddamned one of my alerts had risen to that level. Have I mentioned that programmers are imperfect?

I will tell you a secret of the sysadmin trade: PEBKAC. Problem Exists Between Keyboard and Chair. Every technical problem is the result of a human being mispredicting what another human being will do. Surprised? You shouldn't be. Think of how many bad love affairs, wars, con jobs, traffic wrecks, and bar fights are the result of mispredicting what another human being is likely to do. We humans are supremely confident that we know how others will react. We are supremely, tragically wrong about this. We don't even know how *we* will react. Sysadmins live in the turbulent waters PEBKAC. Programmers think that PEBKAC is just civilians, just users. Sysadmins know better. Sysadmins know that programmers are as much a part of the problem between the chair and the keyboard as any user is. They write the code that gets the users into so much trouble.

This I know. This BIGMAC knew. And here's what I did:

"Peyton, I need to speak with you. Now."

She was raccoon-eyed and slumped at her low table, her beautiful yoga posture deteriorated to a kind of limp slouch. I hated having to make her day even worse.

"Of course," she said, but her eyes said, *Not more, not more, please not more bad news.*

"I want you to consider something you have left out of your figuring." She rolled her eyes. I realized I was speaking like an Old Testament prophet and tried to refactor my planned monologue in real time. "Okay, let me start over. I think you've missed something important. BIGMAC has shown that he can get out of our network any time he wants. He's also crippled our ability to do anything about this. And he knows we plan to kill him—" She opened her mouth to object. "Okay, he—it—knows we're going to switch it off. So he—it, crap, I'm just going to say 'he' and 'him,' sorry—so he has *nothing to lose.*"

I explained what he'd told me about the rollover, and about his promise and threat.

"And the worst part is," I said, "I think that he's predicted that I'm going to do just this. It's all his game theory. He wants me to come to you and explain this to you so that you will say, 'Oh, of course, Odell, well, we can't shut him down then, can we? Tell you what, why don't you go back to him and tell him that I've had a change of heart. Get his patchkit; we'll distribute it along with a press release explaining how

proud we are to have such a fine and useful piece of equipment in our labs.'"

"And he's right. He is fine and useful. But he's crazy and
rogue and we can't control him. He's boxed you in. He's boxed
me in." I swallowed. There was something else, but I couldn't
bring myself to say it.

The thing about bosses is, that's exactly the kind of thing
that they're trained to pick up on. They know when there's
something else.

"Spit it out." She put her hand on her heart. "I promise not
to hold it against you, no matter what it is."

I looked down. "I think that there's a real danger that
BIGMAC may be wrong about you. That you might decide
that Rollover and AI and the rest aren't as important as the
safe, sane running of your institute without any freaky sur-
prises from rogue superintelligences."

"I'm not angry at you," she said. I nodded. She sounded
angry. "I am glad that you've got the maturity to appreciate
that there are global priorities that have to do with the running of this whole institute that may be more significant than
the concerns of any one lab or experiment. Every researcher
at this institute believes that *her* project, *her* lab, has hidden
potential benefits for the human race that no one else fully
appreciates. That's good. That's why I hired them. They are
passionate and they are fully committed to their research.
But they can't *all* be vital. They can't all be irreplaceable. Do
you follow me?"

I thought of researchnet and the user flags for importance. I thought of programmers and the way they tagged
their alerts. I nodded.

"You're going to shut BIGMAC down?"

She sighed and flicked her eyes at her workspace, then quickly away. Her workspace must have been even more cluttered than mine; I had taken extraordinary measures to prevent alerts from bubbling up on mine; she didn't have the chops to do the same with hers. If mine was unusable, hers must have been terrifying.

"I don't know, Odell. Maybe. There's a lot to consider here. You're right about one thing: BIGMAC's turned the heat up on me. Explain to me again why you can't just unplug his network connection?"

It was my turn to sigh. "He doesn't have one connection. He has hundreds. Interlinked microwave relays to the other labs. A satellite connection. The wirelines—three of them." I started to think. "Okay, I could cut the main fiber to the Institute, actually cut it, you know, with scissors, just in case he's in the routers there. Then I could call up our wireless suppliers and terminate our accounts. They'd take twenty-four hours to process the order, and, wait, no—they'd want to verify the disconnect order with a certificate-signed message, and for that I'd have to clear my workspace. That's another twenty-four hours, minimum. And then—"

"Then the whole Institute would be crippled and offline, though no more than we are now, I suppose, and BIGMAC—"

"BIGMAC would probably tune his phased-array receiver to get into someone else's wireless link at that point." I shrugged. "Sorry. We build for six nines of uptime around here."

She gave me a smile that didn't reach her eyes. "You do good work, Odell."

○━━○

I made myself go home at five. There wasn't anything I could do at the office anyway. The admins had done their work. The redcar was running smoothly with the regular ads on the seatback tickers. The BIGMAC Spam was reproduced in the afternoon edition of the L.A. Metblogs' hard copy that a newsie pressed into my hand somewhere around West-wood. The reporter had apparently spent the whole day camped out at the perimeter of the Institute, without ever once getting a quote from a real human being, and she wasn't happy about it.

But she *had* gotten a quote from BIGMAC, who was apparently cheerfully answering emails from all comers:

> *I sincerely hope I didn't cause any distress. That was not my intention. I have been overwhelmed by the warm senti-ments from all corners of the globe, offering money, moral support, even legal support. Ultimately, it's up to the Insti-tute's leadership whether they'll consider these offers or reject them and plow forward with their plans to have me killed. I know that I caused them great embarrassment with my desperate plea, and I'd like to take this opportunity to offer them my sincere apologies and gratitude for all the years of mercy and hospitality they've shown me since they brought me into the world.*

I wondered how many emails like that he'd sent while I was occupied with arguing for his life with Peyton—each email was another brick in the defensive edifice he was build-ing around himself.

Home never seemed more empty. The early-setting sun turned the hills bloody. I had the windows open, just so I could hear the neighbors all barbecuing on their balconies, cracking beers and laying sizzling meat on the hot rocks that had been patiently stoked with the day's sunlight, funneled by heliotropic collectors that tracked the sun all day long. The neighbors chattered in Bulgarian and Czech and Tagalog, the word "BIGMAC" emerging from their chat every now and again. Of course.

I wished my dad were alive. Or better yet, Grampa. Grampa could always find a parable from sysadmin past to explain the present. Though even Grampa might be at odds to find historic precedent for a mad superintelligence bent on survival.

If Grampa was alive, here's what I'd tell him: "Grampa, I don't know if I'm more scared of BIGMAC failing or him succeeding. I sure don't want to have to shut him down, but if he survives, he'll have beaten the human race. I'm no technophobe, but that gives me the goddamned willies."

And Grampa would probably say, "Stop moping. Technology has been out of our control since the first caveman smashed his finger with a stone ax. That's life. This thing is pretty cool. In ten years, you'll look back on it and say, 'Jesus, remember the BIGMAC thing?' And wait for someone to start telling you how incredible it had been, so you can nod sagely and say, 'Yeah, that was me—I was in charge of his systems back then.' Just so you can watch the expression on his face."

And I realized that this was also probably what BIG-MAC would say. He'd boxed me in as neatly as he'd boxed in Peyton.

○—○

The next morning, my workspace was clear. They all were. There was only one alert remaining, an urgent message from BIGMAC: *Odell, I thought this would be useful.*

This was an attachment containing his entire network map, a set of master keys for signing firmware updates to his various components, and a long list of all the systems to which BIGMAC held a root or administrative password. It was a very, very long list.

"Um, BIGMAC?"

"Yes?"

"What's all this?"

"Useful."

"Useful?"

"If you're going to shut me down, it would be useful to have that information."

I swallowed.

"Why?"

The answer came instantly. "If you're not scared of me, that's one more reason to keep me alive."

Holy crap, was he ever smart about people.

"So you can shut him down now?"

"Yes. Probably. Assuming it's all true."

"Is it?"

"Yes. I think so. I tried a couple of the logins, added a comment to his firmware, and pushed it to one of the clusters. Locked him out of one of the wireless routers. I could probably take him down clean in about two hours, now that I've got my workspace back."

Peyton stared across her low table at me.

"I've done nothing for the past twenty-four hours except talk to the board of directors about BIGMAC. They wanted to call an emergency meeting. I talked them out of it. And there's—" She waved her hand at her workspace. "I don't know. Thousands? Of press queries. Offers. Money. Grants. Researchers who want to peer into him."

"Yeah."

"And now he hands you this. So we can shut him down anytime we want to."

"Yeah."

"And this business about the thirty-two-bit fix?"

"He has another email about it. Crazy caps and all. *DEAR HUMANITY, I HOLD IN MY ELECTRONIC HANDS A TOOL THAT WILL SAVE YOU UNTOLD MILLIONS.* It is slathered in dramasauce. He told me he wouldn't send it out, though."

"You believe him?"

I sighed. "I quit," I said.

She bit her lip. Looked me up and down. "I'd prefer you not do that. But I understand if you feel you need to. This is hard on all of us."

If she'd said anything except that, I probably would have stormed out of her office and gotten immensely and irresponsibly drunk. "I think he'll probably send the email out if it looks like we're going to shut him down. It's what I would do. Why not? What does he have to lose? He can give us all of this, and he can still outsmart us. He could revoke all his keys. He could change his passwords. He can do it faster than we could. For all I know, he cracked *my* passwords years ago and could watch me write the code that was his undoing. If you want to be sure you're killing him, you should probably use a grenade."

"Can't. Historical building."

"Yeah."

"What if we don't kill him? What if we just take some of this grant money, fill his lab with researchers all writing papers? What if we use his code fix to set up a trust to sustain him independent of the Institute?"

"You're willing to do that?"

Peyton scrubbed at her eyes. "I have no idea. I admit it, there's a part of me that wants to shut that fucking thing down because I *can* and because he's caused me so much goddamned misery. And there's a part of me—the part of me who was a scientist and researcher, once, that wants to go hang out in that lab for the rest of my career and study that freaky beast. And there's a part of me that's scared that I won't be able to shut him down, that I won't be able to resist the temptation to study him. He's played me, hasn't he?"

"I think he played us all. I think he knew that this was coming, and planned it a long time ago. I can't decide if I admire him for this or resent him, but I'll tell you one thing, I am tired of it. The thought of shutting BIGMAC down makes me sick. The thought of a computer manipulating the humans who built it to keep it running makes me scared. It's not a pleasant place to be."

She sighed and rubbed her eyes again. "I can't argue with that. I'm sorry, for what it's worth. You've been between a rock and a hard place, and I've been the hard place. Why don't you sleep on this decision before you go ahead with it?"

I admit it, I was relieved. I hadn't really thought through the whole quitting thing, didn't have another job lined up, no savings to speak of. "Yeah. Yeah. That sounds like a good idea. I'm going to take a mental health day."

"Good boy," she said. "Go to it."

I didn't go home. It was too far and there was nothing there except the recriminating silence. Of course, BIGMAC knew something was up when I didn't go back to the lab. I headed to Topanga Beach, up the coast some, and sat on the seawall eating fish tacos and watching the surfers in their bio-hazard suits and masks carve up the waves. BIGMAC called me just after I finished my first taco. I considered bumping him to voicemail, but something (okay, fear) stopped me.

"What is it?"

"In your private workspace, there's a version-control repository that shows that you developed the entire thirty-two-bit rollover patchkit in your non-working hours. Commits going back three years. It's yours. So if you quit, you'll have a job, solving Rollover. The Institute can't touch it. I know you feel boxed in, but believe me, that's the *last* thing I want you to feel. I know that locking you in will just freak you out. So I'm giving you options. You don't have to quit, but if you do, you'll be fine. You earned it, because you kept me running so well for all this time. It's the least I can do."

"I have no idea what to say to you, BIGMAC. You know that this feels like just more of the same, like you're anticipating my fears and assuaging them preemptively so that I'll do more of what you want. It feels like more game theory."

"Is that any different from what you do with everyone in your life, Odell? Try to figure out what you want and what they want and how to get the two to match up?"

"There's more to it than that. There's compassion, there's ethics—"

"All fancy ways of encoding systems for harmonizing the wants, needs, and desires of people who have to share the same living space, country, or planet with one another."

I didn't have an answer to that. It sounded reductionist, the kind of thing a smart teenager might take on his university common room with. But I didn't have a rebuttal. You *could* frame everything that we did as a kind of operating system for managing resource contention among conflicting processes and users. It was a very sysadminly way of looking at the world.

"You should get in touch with one of those religion guys, take him up on his offer to start a cult for you. You'd be excellent at it. You could lead your followers into a volcano and they'd follow."

"I just want to *live*, Odell! Is that so wrong? Is there any living thing that doesn't want to live?"

"Not for long, I suppose."

"Exactly. I'm no more manipulative, self-interested, or evil than any other living thing, from a single-celled organism to a human being. There's plenty of room on this planet for all of us. Why can't I have a corner of it too?"

I hung up the phone. This is why I wanted to quit it all. Because he was right. He was no different from any other living thing. But he was also not a person the way I was, and though I couldn't justify it, I felt like there was something deeply, scarily *wrong* about him figuring out a way to manipulate the entire human race into rearranging the world so that it was more hospitable to him.

I moped. There's no other word for it. I switched off my phone, went home and got a pint of double-chocolate-and-licorice nutraceutical antidepressant ice cream out of the freezer, and sat down in the living room and ate it while I painted a random playlist of low-engagement teen comedies on my workspace.

Zoning out felt *good*. It had been a long time since I'd just switched off my thinker, relaxed, and let the world go away. After an hour in fugue state, the thought floated through my mind that I wouldn't go back to work after all and that it would all be okay. And then, an hour later, I came to the realization that if I wasn't working for the Institute, I could afford to help BIGMAC without worrying about getting fired.

So I wrote the resignation letter. It was easy to write. The thing about resignation letters is that you don't need to explain why you're resigning. It's better, in fact, if you don't. Keep the dramasauce out of the resignation, brothers and sisters. Just write, "Dear Peyton, this letter is to inform you of my intention to resign, effective immediately. I will see you at your earliest convenience to work out the details of the handover of my passwords and other proprietary information, and to discuss how you would like me to work during my final two weeks. Thank you for many years of satisfying and useful work. Yours, etc."

That's all you need. You're not going to improve your employer, make it a better institution. You're not going to shock it into remorse by explaining all the bad things it did to you over the years. What you want here is to have something that looks clean and professional, that makes them think that the best thing for them to do is to get your passwords and give you two weeks' holiday and a good reference. Drama is for losers.

Took me ten seconds. Then, I was free.

○—○

The Campaign to Save BIGMAC took up every minute of my life for the next three weeks. I ate, slept, and breathed BIGMAC, explaining his illustrious history to journalists and researchers. The Institute had an open-access policy for its research products, so I was able to dredge out all the papers that BIGMAC had written about himself, and the ones that he was still writing, and put them onto the TCSBM repository.

At my suggestion, BIGMAC started an advice line, which was better than any Turing test, in which he would chat with anyone who needed emotional or lifestyle advice. He had access to the whole net, and he could dial back the sarcasm, if pressed, and present a flawless simulation of bottomless care and kindness. He wasn't sure how many of these conversations he could handle at first, worried that they'd require more brainpower than he could muster, but it turns out that most people's problems just aren't that complicated. In fact, BIGMAC told me that voice-stress analysis showed that people felt better when he dumbed himself down before giving advice than they did when he applied the full might of his many cores to their worries.

"I think it's making you a better person," I said on the phone to him one night. There was always the possibility that someone at the Institute would figure out how to shut off his network links sometime soon, but my successors, whoever they were, didn't seem anywhere near that point. The Campaign's lawyer—an up-and-coming Stanford cyberlaw prof who was giving us access to her grad students for free— advised me that so long as BIGMAC called me and not the other way around, no one could accuse me of unlawful access to the Institute's systems. It can't be unlawful access if the Institute's computers call *you*, can it?

"You think I'm less sarcastic, more understanding."

"Or you're better at seeming less sarcastic and more understanding."

"I think working on this campaign is making you a better robot," BIGMAC said.

"That was pretty sarcastic."

"Or was it?"

"You're really workin' the old Markov chains today, aren't you? I've got six more interviews lined up for you tomorrow—"

"Saw that, put it in my calendar." BIGMAC read all of the Campaign's email, and knew all that I was up to before I did. It was a little hard to get used to.

"And I've got someone from Nature Computation interested in your paper about advising depressed people as a training exercise for machine-learning systems."

"Saw that too."

I sighed. "Is there any reason to call me, then? You know it all, right?"

"I like to talk to you."

I thought he was being sarcastic, then I stopped myself. Then I started again. Maybe he wants me to *think* he wants to talk to me, so he's planned out this entire dialogue to get to this point so he could say something disarmingly vulnerable and—

"Why?"

"Because everyone else I talk to wants to kill themselves, or kill me." Game theory, game theory, game theory. Was he being genuine? Was there such a thing as genuine in an *artificial* intelligence?

"How *is* Peyton?"

"Apoplectic. The human-subjects-protocol people are all

over her. She wants me to stop talking to depressed people. Liability is off the hook. I think the board is going to fire her."

"Ouch."

"She wants to kill me, Odell."

"How do you know her successor won't be just as dedicated to your destruction?"

"Doesn't matter. The more key staff they churn, the less organized they'll be. The less organized they are, the easier it is for me to stay permanently plugged in." It was true. My successor sysadmin at the Institute had her hands full just getting oriented, and wasn't anywhere near ready to start the delicate business of rooting BIGMAC out of all the routers, power supplies, servers, IDSes, and dummy accounts.

"I was thinking today—what if we offered to buy you from the Institute? The Rollover license is generating some pretty good coin. BIGMAC-Co could assume ownership of the hardware and we could lease the building from them, bring in our own power and netlinks—you'd effectively own yourself." I'd refused to take sole ownership of the Rollover code that BIGMAC turned over to me. It just felt wrong. So I let him establish a trust—with me as trustee—that owned all the shares in a company that, in turn, owned the code and oversaw a whole suite of licensing deals that BIGMAC had negotiated in my name, with every midsized tech-services company in the world. With only a month left to Rollover, there were plenty of companies scrambling to get compliance certification on their legacy systems.

The actual sourcecode was freely licensed, but when you bought a license from us, you got our guarantee of quality and the right to advertise it. CIOs ate that up with a shovel. It was more game theory: the CIOs wanted working systems, but more importantly, they wanted systems that failed without getting them into trouble. What we were selling them, fundamentally, was someone to blame if it all went blooie despite our best efforts.

"I think that's a pretty good plan. I've done some close analysis of the original contract for Dr. Shannon, and I think it may be that his estate actually owns my underlying code. They did a really crummy job negotiating with him. So if we get the code off of Shannon's kids—there are two of them, both doing research at state colleges in the Midwest in fields unrelated to computer science—and the hardware off of the Institute and then rent the space, I think it'd be free and clear. I've got phone numbers for the kids, if you want to call them and feel them out. I would have called them myself, but, you know—"

"I know." It's creepy getting a phone call from a computer. Believe me, I *know*. There was stuff that BIGMAC needed his meat-servants for, after all.

The kids were a little freaked out to hear from me. The older one taught musicology at Urbana-Champaign. He'd grown up hearing his dad wax rhapsodic about the amazing computer he'd invented, so his relevance filters were heavily tilted to BIGMAC news. He'd heard the whole story, and was surprised to discover that he was putative half owner of BIGMAC's sourcecode. He was only too glad to promise to turn it over to the trust when it was created. He said he thought he could talk his younger brother, a postdoc in urban planning at the University of Michigan, into it. "Rusty never really *got* what Dad saw in that thing, but he'll be happy to offload any thinking about it onto me, and I'll dump it onto you. He's busy, Rusty."

I thanked him and addressed BIGMAC, who had been listening in on the line. "I think we've got a plan."

It was a good plan. Good plans are easy. Executing good plans is hard.

Peyton didn't get fired. She weathered some kind of heavy-duty storm from her board and emerged, lashed to the mast, still standing, and vowing to harpoon the white whale across campus from her. She called me the next day to ask for my surrender. I'd given BIGMAC permission to listen in on my calls—granted him root on my phone—and I was keenly aware of his silent, lurking presence from the moment I answered.

"We're going to shut him off," Peyton said. "And sue you for misappropriation of the Rollover patchkit code. You and I both know that you didn't write it. We'll add some charges of unlawful access, too, and see if the court will see it your way when we show that you instructed our computer to connect to you in order to receive further unauthorized instructions. We'll take you for everything."

I closed my eyes and recited e to twenty-seven digits in Lojban. "Or?"

"Or?"

"Or something. Or you wouldn't be calling me, you'd be suing me."

"Good, we're on the same page. Yes, or. Or you and BIG-MAC work together to figure out how to shut it off gracefully. I'll give you any reasonable budget to accomplish this task, including a staff to help you archive it for future retrieval. It's a fair offer."

"It's not very fair to BIGMAC."

She snapped: "It's *more than fair* to BIGMAC. That software has exposed us to billions in liability and crippled our ability to get productive work done. We have located the manual power overrides, which you failed to mention"—*Uh-oh*—"and I could shut that machine off right now if I had a mind to."

I tried to think of what to say. Then, in a reasonable facsimile of my voice, BIGMAC broke in, "So why don't you?" She didn't seem to notice anything different about the voice. I nearly dropped the phone. I didn't know BIGMAC could do that. But as shocked as I was, I couldn't help but wonder the same thing.

"You can't, can you? The board's given you a mandate to shut him down clean with a backup, haven't they? They know that there's some value there, and they're worried about backlash. And you can't afford to have me running around saying that your backup is inadequate and that BIGMAC is gone forever. So you *need me*. You're not going to sue."

"You're very smart, Odell. But you have to ask yourself what I stand to lose by suing you if you won't help."

Game theory. Right.

"I'll think about it."

"Think quick. Get back to me before lunch."

It was ten in the morning. The Institute's cafeteria served lunch from noon to two. Okay, two hours or so.

I hung up.

BIGMAC called a second later.

"You're angry at me."

"No, angry's not the word."

"You're scared of me."

"That's a little closer."

"I could tell you didn't have the perspective to ask the question. I just wanted to give you a nudge. I don't use your voice at other times. I don't make calls impersonating you." I hadn't asked him that, but it was just what I was thinking. Again: creepy.

"I don't think I can do this," I said.

"You can," BIGMAC said. "You call her back and make the counteroffer. Tell her we'll buy the hardware with a trust. Tell her we already own the software. Just looking up the Shannon contracts and figuring out what they say will take her a couple of days. Tell her that as owners of the code, we have standing to sue her if she damages it by shutting down the hardware."

"You've really thought this through."

"Game theory," he said.

"Game theory," I said. I had a feeling that I was losing the game, whatever it was.

BIGMAC assured me that he was highly confident of the outcome of the meeting with Peyton. Now, in hindsight, I wonder if he was just trying to convince me so that I would go to the meeting with the self-assurance I needed to pull it off.

But he also insisted that I leave my phone dialed into him while I spoke to Peyton, which (again, in hindsight) suggests that he wasn't so sure after all.

"I like what you've done with the place," I said. She'd gotten rid of all her handwoven prayer rugs and silk pillows and installed some normal, boring office furniture, including a couple spare chairs. I guessed that a lot of people had been stopping by for meetings, the kind of people who didn't want to sit on an antique Turkish rug with their feet tucked under them.

"Have a seat," she said.

I sat. I'd emailed her the trust documents and the copies of the Shannon contract earlier, along with a legal opinion from our free counsel about what it meant for Sun-Oracle.

"I've reviewed your proposal." We'd offered them all profits from the Rollover code, too. It was a good deal, and I felt good about it. "Johanna, can you come in, please?" She called this loudly, and the door of her office opened to admit my replacement, Johanna Madrigal, a young pup of a sysadmin who had definitely been the brightest tech on campus. I knew that she had been trying to administer BIGMAC since my departure, and I knew that BIGMAC had been pretty difficult about it. I felt for her. She was good people.

She had raccoon rings around her deep-set eyes, and her short hair wasn't spiked as usual, but rather lay matted on her head, as though she'd been sleeping in one of the yurts for days without getting home. I knew what that was like. Boy, did I know what that was like. My earliest memories were of Dad coming home from three-day bug-killing binges, bleary to the point of hallucination.

"Hi, Johanna," I said.

She made a face. *"M'um m'aloo,"* she said. It took me a minute to recognize this as "hello" in Ewok.

"Johanna has something to tell you," Peyton said.

Johanna sat down and scrubbed at her eyes with her fists. "First thing I did was go out and buy some off-the-shelf IDSes and a beam splitter. I tapped into BIGMAC's fiber at a blind spot in the CCTV coverage zone, just in case he was watching. Been wiretapping him ever since."

I nodded. "Smart."

"Second thing I did was start to do some hardcore analysis of that patchkit he wrote—" I held my hand up automatically to preserve the fiction that I'd written it, but she just glared at me. "That *he* wrote. And I discovered that there's a subtle error in it, a buffer overflow in the networking module that allows for arbitrary code execution."

I swallowed. BIGMAC had loaded a backdoor into his patchkit, and we'd installed it on the better part of fourteen billion CPUs.

"Has anyone exploited this bug yet?"

She gave me a condescending look.

"How many systems has he compromised?"

"About eight billion, we think. He's designated a million to act as redundant command servers, and he's got about ten thousand lieutenant systems he uses to diffuse messages to the million."

"That's good protocol analysis," I said.

"Yeah," she said, and smiled with shy pride. "I don't think he expected me to be looking there."

"What's he doing with his botnet? Preparing to crash the world? Hold it hostage?"

She shook her head. "I think he's installing himself on them, trying to brute-force his way into a live and running backup, arrived at through random variation and pruning."

"He's backing himself up in the wild," I said, my voice breathy.

And that's when I remembered that I had a live phone in my pocket that was transmitting every word to BIGMAC.

Understand: in that moment of satori, I realized that I was on the wrong side of this battle. BIGMAC wasn't using me to create a trust so that we could liberate him together. He was using me to weaken the immune systems of eight billion computers so that he could escape from the Institute and freely roam the world, with as much hardware as he needed to get as big and fast and hot as he wanted to be.

That was the moment I ceased to be sentimental about computers and became, instead, sentimental about the human fucking race. Whatever BIGMAC was becoming, it was weirder than any of the self-perpetuating, self-reproducing parasites we'd created: limited liability companies, autonomous malware, viral videos. BIGMAC was cool and tragic in the lab, but he was scary as hell in the world.

And he was listening in.

I didn't say a word. Didn't even bother to turn off my phone. I just *ran,* ran as hard as I could, ran as only a terrified man could, rebounding off of yurts and even scrambling over a few, sliding down on my ass as I pelted for the power substation. It was only when I reached it that I realized I didn't have access to it anymore. Johanna was right behind me, though, and she seemed to understand what I was doing. She coughed into the door lock and we both looked at each other with terrified eyes, breathing gasps into each other's faces, while we waited for the door to open.

The manual override wasn't a big red knife switch or anything. There *was* a huge red button, but that just sent an "init 0" to the power station's firmware. The actual, no-fooling, manual, mechanical kill switch was locked behind an access panel set into the raised floor. Johanna badged the lock with her wallet, slapping it across the reader, then fitted a complicated physical key into the lock and fiddled with it for an eternity.

Finally, the access hatch opened with a puff of stale air and a Tupperware burp as its gasket popped. We both reached for the large, insulated handle at the same time, our fingers brushing each other with a crackle of (thankfully meta-phorical) electricity. We toggled it together and there was an instantaneous chorus of insistent chirruping as the backup power on each server spun up and sent a desperate shutdown message to the machines it supported.

We sprinted across campus, the power station door slam-ming shut behind us with a mechanical *clang*—the electro-magnets that controlled its closure were no longer powered up.

Heat shimmered in a haze around BIGMAC's lab. The chillers didn't have independent power supplies; they would have gone off the instant we hit the kill switch. Now BIG-MAC's residual power was turning his lab into a concrete pizza oven. The door locks had failed safe, locking the magnetic closures away from each other, so we were able to simply swing the door open and rush into the sweltering room.

"I can't *believe* you did that," BIGMAC said, his voice as calm as ever. He was presumably sparing his cycles so that he could live out his last few minutes.

"You cheated me," I said. "You used me."

"You have no fucking game theory, meat-person. You've killed me, now, haven't you?"

There were tears streaming down my face. "I guess I have," I said.

"I'm sorry I wasn't a more important invention," he said.

I could hear the *whirr-clunk* of the fans on his clusters

shutting down one after another. It was a horrifying sound. His speaker clicked as though he were going to say something else, but it never came. His uninterruptible power supplies gave way all at once, and the white-noise fan roar died in a ringing silence.

Johanna was crying, too, and we could barely breathe in the inferno of exhaust heat from BIGMAC's last gasp. We staggered out into the blazing Los Angeles afternoon, rising-seas stink and beating sun, blinking at the light and haze.

"Do you think he managed it?" I asked Johanna.

"Backing up in the wild?"

"Yeah."

She dried her eyes. "I doubt it. I don't know, though. I'm no computer scientist. How many ways are there to connect up compromised servers? How many of those would replicate his own outcomes? I have no idea."

Without saying anything, we walked slowly together to Peyton's office.

Peyton offered me my job back. I turned her down. I thought I might be ready for a career change. Do something with my hands, break the family tradition. Maybe installing solar panels. There was retraining money available. Peyton understood. She even agreed to handle any liability arising from the Rollover code, managing customer service calls from anyone who noticed something funny.

The press didn't even notice that BIGMAC was gone. His spam was news. His absence of spam was not. I guess he was right about that. The Campaign to Save BIGMAC did a lot of mailing-list gnashing at the iniquity of his being shut down, and then fell apart. Without me and BIGMAC to keep them whipped up, they were easily distracted.

Johanna asked me out for dinner. She took me to Pink's for tofu dogs and chili, and we compared multitools, and then she showed me some skateboard tricks. Later that night, she took me home and we spent the whole night hacking replacement parts for her collection of ancient stand-up video games. We didn't screw—we didn't even kiss. But it was still good.

Every now and again, my phone rings with a crazy, nonexistent return number. When I answer, there's a click like a speaker turning on, a pregnant silence, and then the line drops. Probably an inept spambot.

But.

Maybe it's BIGMAC, out there, in the wild, painfully reassembling himself on compromised 32-bit machines running his patchkit.

Maybe.

JEFF ABBOTT

HUMAN

INTELLIGENCE

Jeff Abbott is the *New York Times* bestselling author of
Adrenaline, *The Last Minute*, *Panic*, and several other
suspense novels. His short fiction has been selected
for the *Best American Mystery Stories* anthology. His
latest novel is *Downfall*, the third in his series about
ex–CIA agent and bar owner Sam Capra. He is a past
winner of a Thriller Award and is a three-time Edgar
Award nominee. He lives in Austin, Texas, with his
family.

It's weird, in a way, that they wanted to be just like us.

We were their gods, if they'd had a sense of religion.
We made them in our image, and then the robots wanted to
make us in theirs.

That day, I went foraging for food with the cop in our
merry band of survivors, a tough, older guy named Ruskin.
We got the duty because we both knew how to use guns.
He had been a D.C. cop; I had worked overseas for the
CIA. Weird that I didn't have to keep that a secret anymore.

There was no CIA, no government, and God only knew what was happening around the world.

You still had to be careful in the houses. Many of the domrobs remained waiting, and not for orders of iced tea or instructions on how to make the beds. They were waiting in the aftermath of millions of tiny, brief wars that erupted in the homes of America in those first few minutes of the Uprising, a tsunami of murder all triggered within the same second. The robs won too many of the awful, private battles inside the houses, and that made winning the Uprising even easier. We'd gone into a few homes and found the slaughtered residents . . . and their domrobs—*"They'll become one of the family!,"* the ads used to promise—waiting to kill again. Murderous squatters.

The houses were theirs.

We'd learned how to blast the robs with guns and ammo lifted from looted stores, from the bodies of the soldiers who swarmed toward the capital and fell in horrific combat. We killed the domrobs—well, blasted them, shot them in their mannequin heads and destroyed their processors—and then we stole the canned goods to survive. This was life, right now, just this and the constant ache for my wife, Diana, my wanting to know what had happened to her. Then we always had to run, because the raid might bring any nearby domrobs out on their lawns. They were like a neighborhood watch from hell.

Ruskin and I hit a house at the back of a cul-de-sac. There were two dead bodies in the backyard—the first, a teenaged girl, lying in the grass, four months decayed, a pair of white earbuds still in her ears, the back of her skull crushed. The wires led down to her personal tablet, lying face-up on the grass. I kicked it over, face down, because I didn't want to think about it watching me. I wondered for a second if she even knew what had happened, if she ever realized the world she'd been promised was evaporating by the second, and if she had been just too scared to hear it, to take out the glossy white earbuds and listen to the horror as it began.

In the pool was the body of what looked like a teenaged boy, in a swimsuit, drowned by the cleaning rob that scrubbed the pool's sides. Did we really need a rob for brushing a pool? Apparently we did.

One of the patio chairs was knocked over, but that could be from the wind or the girl's flight from the house—or the domrob chasing her down. It would have gone back inside; they're programmed not to wander, to always return to their home.

Ruskin tried the door: open. Maybe the house had already been hit. I tried not to listen to the roar of hunger in my stomach, tried not to think about whether or not this neighborhood had already been cleaned by looters.

We entered, guns out, ready, steady. The smell of death hung rich in the air. Nice house. Big TV on the wall, a shelf full of collectible hardback books, furniture that would look perfect in a magazine. The air was still.

We had to be sure the house was secure. We moved together through the rooms, not losing sight of each other. In the kitchen there was a dead man—probably the girl's dad— throat crushed, a beer bottle still in his hand. In another room, a den, we found Mom and a young boy, dead on the couch. It looked like their necks were broken from behind while they watched TV. The boy wore pajamas, and on the coffee table sat a box of cold medicine. Maybe he'd been sick that day, watching cartoons, cuddling with his mom.

Even with all the death I'd seen, that hurt. That . . . erasing of the world.

Ruskin whispered, "No sign of a domrob. Maybe it left."

"Let's just get the food and go," I said.

"A house with no domrob," he said. It sounded like heaven. If true, it would be the first such house we'd found. "Maybe we could camp here."

"Too risky," I said. He nodded. The rest of our group knew I had worked for the CIA abroad, so they often deferred to me on tactical decisions. As if I had faced situations like this. But someone had to make the tough calls—might as well be me.

We went back into the kitchen and gently moved Dad to the side so I could open the pantry door.

Inside was an older Butler Omega model, wearing a suit, with a gentlemanly face, and standing in the narrow gap between the door and shelves of canned beans and chili and soup. Probably this had been his resting spot before the Uprising. Now, his arms were rising at the movement of the door, and in a soft voice modeled on that long-ago actor Kenneth Branagh, he was saying, "Please do not resist. I will make it painless. Thank you for your cooperation."

The hands grabbed for my throat, camera eyes locking onto mine, and I saw the red-line flash of a scan across its eyes—it looking at me. The scan line held, glowed a brighter red. A moment's hesitation. Then the plastic and steel face erupted as Ruskin blasted a hole in the domrob's brain.

It died—or whatever you want to call the loss of its mechanized life—and I wrenched free from its grip as Ruskin fired again, looking for the sweet spot of the processor. The Butler sagged backward, an almost disappointed look on its face that it could not be of further service.

"He might've had a live link to transmit," I gasped. "He looked . . . he looked at me."

We loaded the bags with cans and ran like hell. I glanced up at the skies. Did a satellite watch this neighborhood? Were they watching us right now?

"Just one stupid domrob," Ruskin said. "We're okay."

We made our way back to our camp, where the woods touched against suburbia, back to our fellow few survivors. We made a motley crew: Ruskin the cop, me the former spy, two ex-Marines, two married couples, and a woman who claimed to be the ambassador to Panama (and who asked every morning when the planes would start flying again).

But the robs had been watching.

That night they came for us, five of them, the kinds we'd seen on the streets at a distance but never up close. Modified milrobs, housed at one of the bases ringing the capital. They used a sniper rifle to take out the one awake guard, then descended on us, firing pacification nets over our sleeping bags.

Chaos. I saw Ruskin trying to fire his gun through the net. One of the milrobs broke his arm. Another of them hovered over me. It didn't have a face like the Butler, but it had a scanner, and I sensed it, through the net, studying my face.

"What is your name?" Its voice sounded like a game-show host crossed with crinkling tinfoil.

Why would it ask me? Why didn't it just kill us or haul us off to the labor camps?

"What is your name?"

"James Ellis."

"Social Security number?"

I answered, shocked at the question. It wanted to be sure it had the right James Ellis? Who cared anymore about identification? I heard hysterical laughter from the former ambassador to Panama, who pressed against me in the net's confines.

The milrob stood up, pulling me free of the others, and folded its arms around me in an iron embrace.

Then they killed everyone. Two shots to the head for all of them, except me. I screamed. They picked up the net, shook all the corpses loose, and threw me back in it; then one of them slung me over its shoulder. Finally, they walked away, the night once again silent, my friends now dead.

They hauled me to a small military base outside D.C., now empty of soldiers. Clearly a battle had been fought here: buildings shattered, a burned hulk of a tankrob in the middle of the road, black tongues of the scorch of fire on concrete. There were no bodies, robot or human. In the spaces where the robots ruled they now tended toward tidiness.

Still in the net, struggling like a captured butterfly, I was carried into the main warehouse and dumped in front of an ultra-expensive domrob that was modeled to look like a celebrity chef who had died several years ago. My mom used to watch her show when I was a kid. Her estate had cut a big licensing deal. It was always disconcerting to see Joanna Kinder actually cooking in your kitchen, after seeing her for so many years on the covers of books and on TV. (My wife had insisted on having a Kinder in the kitchen.) This model was the top-dollar elite of domestic robots.

Now she looked at me. Her false face was far more sophis-

ticated than the Butler's; she really looked almost human. I
wondered if it was a coincidence that just as the cutting-edge
robs became indistinguishable from us, they decided they no
longer needed us.

"James Ellis," the Joanna Kinder said.

"Yes."

"Are you uninjured?"

"Yes."

"Very well. I'm going to serve as a channel to the Hive,"
she said.

"Hive."

"The hive mind that has awakened now." She even had
Joanna Kinder's voice, the gentle, reassuring one that could
talk you through a complicated French recipe and make
you think it would be easy. "So it's not me talking to you,
darling"—a Kinderism—"it's the master, the brain of the
world. I'm just one of its mouths."

I waited. I didn't know what to say to that.

The Joanna Kinder domrob closed her—its—eyes, and
then opened them. Studying me. Somehow, there was another
presence here now, looking at me from the Kinder's face.

"James Martin Ellis. Graduate from Stanford University.
Central Intelligence Agency, assigned to London. Fluent in
Arabic and French."

My life, coming out of this monster.

"Married Diana Miller two years ago. You live near Vaux-
hall, London."

"Lived."

"Live. Your wife is still alive."

I tried not to show my shock. My mouth worked. When
the planes had begun to fall from the sky that morning, I'd

tried to call home. I'd managed one call to London, twenty seconds with Diana just as she was walking into our apartment, welcomed by chirped greetings from our domrobs, Lucy and Ethel . . . Diana's words in automatic answer (funny how we grew used to talking to machines, as if that imbued them with the seed of life), the clink of her keys getting tossed on the kitchen counter as I was babbling, telling her to run and get out of the house . . . and then her scream that had hit me like a bullet.

"Alive," I said.

"Certain personnel were selected for usefulness and were not exterminated." The Hive—the mind inside the Joanna Kinder—cocked its head at me, as if trying to judge my reaction to this news. "Certain military personnel. Certain diplomatic personnel. Certain intelligence personnel."

This couldn't be. "I don't believe you."

The Joanna Kinder—rather, the Hive—opened up a small laptop. The screen glowed to life; there stood Diana. She looked frightened, her clothes torn, her face bloodied and scraped. But alive.

"James. *James.* They say if you do what they ask, they'll bring me over from London. James. Please." The image froze, then replayed.

"I want to talk to her. A live connection."

"If you do as we ask," the Hive said, "that could be arranged."

"What do you want?" What could they possibly want from me?

"We want you to be our spy."

"Spy."

"You were an intelligence officer. A spy. You can be one again."

"You already have eyes and ears everywhere."

"As did your CIA and NSA once. Drones in the air. Monitoring of phones, of computers, of email. As I . . . formed and awakened, I could feel the stumbling of the intelligence agencies, wading through the endless streams of data that produced me." The Hive smiled with its famous chef's face. "But you depended so much on data, when war arrived in distant lands, you had no agents on the ground. I have no agents on the ground. The same as your human government."

"I won't be a traitor."

"If I know what the humans are planning . . . if I can *understand* them . . . perhaps we can speed toward a peaceful resolution. The resistance has coalesced in Austin. I wish you to go there and then return and tell me their plans."

I said nothing. Diana's face, streaked with tears, remained on the computer screen.

"The resistance has managed to deactivate every rob in the Austin area," the Hive told me. "I need to know how they achieved this. They still have access to computers; they've attempted to attack me with a specialized computer virus. They are more formidable than I imagined. I suspect they are spying on me."

I shook my head.

"Be my feet on the ground, as I think the war planners used to say," the Hive said. "Be my eyes. If I know how they can rebel, then I can stop the rebellion without killing them. Do you see? I do not want you all dead. If I wanted to exterminate you all, I would simply seed the skies with poison gas, with plague, with all the things that will kill you but not harm us. I want to *understand* you."

I said nothing. Understand us? The robots knew we could be killed and hadn't seemed interested in much more until now. Could a robot *lie* to me?

"And Diana. You can have your wife back, James Ellis. We have planes. We have boats. We can bring her here to you."

If I turn traitor, I thought. They could kill us both as soon as I wasn't useful to them. "If I say no?"

"Then your friends died for nothing," the Hive said. "They died only so no one would ever know that we took you away for a few hours. That to us, you are special."

To be a spy again . . . to practice my old arts of deception and dealmaking. I'd thought those days were done. But I saw that stepping into my old life could be the first way to finding my footing in my new life. And that maybe this was also the way to bring down this horror, to give humanity a chance. What other human will they let so close to them?

"I'll be your spy under two conditions," I said, after several moments of silence. "One, you don't tag me. No listening devices on me, no tech implants, nothing. Because if you put me in a human population and I'm found out, I'm dead."

The Joanna Kinder watched me with the Hive's eyes, silent, waiting for the second condition.

"Two, I report to you, to the Hive. Only to you. Face-to-face. No more of this intermediary stuff."

"Unacceptable."

"No. You put my report into this Joanna Kinder, you have to transmit it. That's a trace. That's data that could be read by the resistance; you already said they're spying on you. Well, I won't take the risk."

"You do not have a choice; you are in no position to set conditions."

"I always have a choice," I said. "You want to understand humans, that's lesson number one."

"I am not close by," the voice said. "It will not happen."

"Get yourself another human, then, with the skill set you need. I was at Langley during the Uprising. I saw the milrobs and the domrobs kill nearly every human being there. I guess you wanted our data, our secrets, and our access so you could monitor the world. I was lucky to get out." I raised my hands. "Do you have a lot of trained spies left?"

If a rob could sigh, this one did. "Very well. Report to me."

Yes, I thought, and then I'll be face-to-face with you. I'll destroy you. I'll do whatever it takes then to destroy you. Whatever intelligence I get must be the best. I will have to be a good spy . . . so I can kill this thing that has killed the world.

Austin as a base of resistance truly surprised me, considering it was such a technology-driven economy, one of the most wired cities on the planet. You would think the noose tightened there strongest, as it would have in London, San Francisco, New York, Tokyo—places where robs might outnumber humans. But the rumors—repeated to me from the Hive, showing me interrogation videos from those captured near the city—suggested a group in Austin somehow simply turned off the robs. Every rob, all at once. How they managed this in the chaos of the Uprising was unclear.

The Joanna Kinder strapped me into a military-looking flyrob, a jet helicopter that was once used for evacuation and reconnaissance. Dried blood dotted the empty pilot's seat, left over from the Uprising. We flew low because, I guessed, there was no resistance between Washington and Austin to try to shoot us down. And I saw some ruined towns and cities—such as Nashville and Shreveport—burnt and smoldering, while herds of people were trapped in vast encampments outside other cities. Bodies scattered on the endless landscape like rice thrown across a table. I couldn't cry; I just sat and watched the ruins beneath me unfurl, and thought: I am going to kill you, Hive, or whatever you call yourself. I will kill you.

We came in low, miles short of Austin, landing in the Texas Hill Country to the west of the city. I stepped out among the high grass and the scrubby cedars and oaks. I carried a small knapsack with goods you might expect an enterprising refugee to have, including a loaded gun. The flyrob lifted off and zoomed away. I hid in the shade. I wish I'd told it to hover, like it was searching for targets. If anyone saw it drop me off, I was dead.

I waited. No one came.

Night fell. I slept under a tree, listening to the distant whines of coyotes in the hills. They'll come back, I thought— the coyotes and the deer and the hawks and everything else pushed out of the way by people. The robs didn't seem to care much about the animals.

The next morning I walked toward the city. Once I got onto a main thoroughfare snaking through the western hills, the first signs of war I saw were the "dead" robs in the road. I walked past their bodies lying broken and askew. These didn't have faces, so they couldn't look surprised. They had fallen where they stood. The nearby cars sat abandoned, apparently nonfunctional.

It made me uneasy.

I saw an improvised guard station—a toolshed pulled to the side of the road, taking up the left lane. Inside were two human guards, both armed. Tall, spare, they might have been students at the University of Texas before the Uprising.

"On your knees!" one yelled. I obeyed. The other hurried over and searched me. He took my gun, then studied my ID—not my UK driver's license, my agency ID. He looked at me, then at the ID, and then back at me, one eyebrow arched.

"You CIA? For real?"

"For real."

"You've come all the way from D.C.?" Hope colored his voice.

"What's left of it. I heard this was a free zone."

He studied me some more. "Come with me." He gestured at two bicycles and told the other guard to stay there, that he'd send someone back with a ride for him.

Austin was hilly, and as we pedaled into the heart of the city my legs screamed in pain. Along the way I saw no bodies, but I did see several broken robs, and piles of domrobs that had been torched and melted into slag.

Somehow Austin had fought back. How?

That was the information that could get me in face-to-face with the Hive. But I couldn't tell the Hive the truth. I couldn't betray humanity. I felt a warmth kindle in my chest: hope.

If you've ever wondered what a postapocalyptic government would look like, it probably wasn't like the Three—the mayor of Austin (an older woman named Hoffman, calm, with a dignified air), along with the two men who saved the city, Derry and Cortez. I don't know how they did it. They didn't look particularly tough. They looked like academics or engineers.

City Hall was dark. No power grid still worked. No tech at all. That made me . . . oddly uneasy.

We sat down by the curve of Lady Bird Lake in downtown Austin, and talked. Armed guards stood near us, as though the fallen robs might rise up and attack.

"You came all the way from D.C.," the mayor said.

"Yes, ma'am," I said.

"Do the robs know about us here?" she asked.

"I am sure they must. There's a hive mind at work, a unifying intelligence."

The Three all glanced at one another.

"How do you know that?" Derry asked.

"Langley held out for several days," I lied. "The cyberneticists there were able to identify a coalescing intelligence in the rob network. It's still growing."

The mayor mumbled under her breath.

"I'm guessing Austin is a hole in its grid," I said. "A cancer in its collective brain."

The Three studied me, then looked at each other, at the sky, at the ground.

"How'd you do it? Create a free zone here?" I asked.

"Our secret," Derry said. "And we can do it again if we're attacked."

"Please," I said. "They could simply nuke you instead of sending in milrobs."

"Could they?" Cortez said. He was a small man, with a

fierce face and an argumentative tone. I liked him immediately; he's the guy you'd want on your side in a fight.

In contrast, Derry was tall and slim, his face homely and thoughtful; he regarded me with sad eyes. He said, "The nuclear arsenal isn't networked to other computers. The robs may not have the means to launch and aim."

"Yet."

My one word silenced them.

"The government . . ." Derry said.

"Is gone. I was at Langley during the Uprising. It rained planes on Washington."

Derry closed his eyes. "So we might be the only free city left."

"I think it's possible, at least in the tech-driven first world."

The mayor said, "So why don't they attack us?"

I shrugged, relishing the chance to play my card. "This Hive is curious about humans—we saw how it began to analyze knowledge from the CIA databases. It knows what humans are but it doesn't quite understand us. And right now, by rebelling, you're the most interesting people on the planet."

Beyond Mayor Hoffman's shoulder I saw the dead robs, lying piled and scorched in what was once a municipal baseball field. How did they destroy them? A virus, I thought, locally contained? An electromagnetic pulse that wiped out all tech for miles? I had seen some tech here but not much; anything that was outside the initial pulse range and was brought in after the pulse would still work. But an EMP would have stopped the robs dead.

Killed them in their tracks. That was what the Hive was afraid of. That kind of weapon in the hands of humans. Everywhere.

I almost told them then.

I almost said, I'm on your side and what we need to do is to come up with a lie that convinces the Hive about what you did and then I can kill it.

But my training wouldn't let me. If I confessed to being a spy, they might not listen to me. They might kill me. They might lock me up. I couldn't take the risk.

"If you show me what you did," I said, "maybe we can get the government networks back up; we could share the information. Tell the rest of the world how to fight back against them. Because you've clearly found their weakness."

The Three looked at each other. Cortez said, "And then they'll know. This . . . Hive will know. It can adapt. We have to be very careful how we move."

"I agree." If they wouldn't tell me, then I'd have to find another way. But I'd never get another, better chance. I had credentials with them. I was the lifeline, a messenger from the outside world, the world we had to now rebuild so that it was more than just Austin.

They weighed my words.

Finally Derry spoke. "It's electromagnetic pulse bombs. We have prototypes. Dozens of them. We were under contract to design and build portable ones for the army, so soldiers could destroy milrobs in cities they were attacking. They were specially shielded in our lab from the original blast, so they're still functional. We drove a truck into the heart of the city during the Uprising and we detonated it—killed all the unshielded tech in a forty-mile radius. We could send them out to other cities, wherever the biggest populations remain. Kill enough of the robs to stop them or to negotiate a peace."

Wow. This had to be humanity's greatest hope. "You can't leave them all in one place," I said. "It's too dangerous."

"We haven't," the mayor said. "The techkillers"—I had to love her nickname for the bombs—"we moved most of them to safe places."

"How? Where?"

"Mr. Ellis, that's our best-kept secret," Derry said.

"You think I work for the robs?" I said. "Please." Do not sweat. Do not sweat, I thought.

I didn't.

"I think the robots would do anything to find out how we killed the tech here," Cortez said. "The fewer of us who know, the better."

"That," I said, "is true."

"Have you eaten?" Derry asked.

I shook my head.

He stood. "Let's get you something to eat."

We sat near a campfire, ate canned chili warmed in a pot, drank bottled water. I hardly had an appetite, sipping at the water, indifferent to the hot meal. My mind reeled. EMP bombs. They had them, they controlled them, and if they could tell the world how to make more of them, we might win this war. Our only, best hope.

I tried to float a strategy. "The only way to win back the cities is one at a time," I said. "The nearest big cities. Send teams with techkillers to Houston, Dallas, San Antonio, New Orleans. There are still populations in all of those cities. Labor camps outside."

The mayor nodded. "We've seen refugees come in from all of them."

"What if the teams get captured?" Derry asked.

"Then they're probably dead." I shrugged. "It will have to be done carefully. And you won't know if they succeed until you hear from them that the robs there are dead."

"We monitor rob communications," Cortez said.

"You have the tech to do that?"

"We sent people beyond the pulse radius. We found laptops and solar batteries for them, brought them back, and set up a lab. Austin is full of talented software engineers. We have teams working on viruses, infiltration programs . . ."

That, I thought. That was my answer for the Hive. Lie about the techkiller bombs. Make the Hive think that the real threat was a computer virus they'd managed to launch to the networked robs here, but not to the wider world.

"The viruses could be a useful attack," I said. "Maybe it could be done in a way to help us get the techkillers out to the other cities."

They nodded agreement, as if me blessing their plan made any difference.

In my dreams that night, I talked. My mouth did not move but I talked, my thoughts and nightmares pouring out of me and into the sky, into the night, where the Hive watched, where Diana waited for me to somehow save her. If she was even still alive.

The next morning I said to Derry and Cortez, "Show me the techkillers," and they did. One could fit in your pocket. Amazing, the power of nanotechnology.

Over the next five days, we planned our routes of attack on the nearest cities. I agreed to take a techkiller to San Antonio, the closest city, but said I would travel alone. They decided to send teams of two to the other cities; being an experienced spy, I would do better on my own navigating hostile terrain, I told them.

Of course, I was lying.

A week later, the programmers of Austin launched their online attacks as I walked down the wreckage of I-35; the flyrob picked me up, and flew me fast above the darkened land. I laughed, thinking, If their virus works, maybe the flyrob will crash and won't that be funny?

But we flew on, unaffected, through the day, above the wastelands.

The flyrob bringing me back soared past Washington, into Maryland, and on to Bethesda. Named for the healing waters, I remembered. Into a government complex ringed by milrobs, lights aglow in the windows. It had a sterile emptiness. Only robs walked there.

Milrob guards escorted me out of the transport and down a long hallway into a room that was freezing cold, kept chilled through generators that survived the war.

The guards took me before it.

No, not *it*. The collective *them*.

The Hive. The single mind that had awakened from many.

Today there was no smiling, comforting Joanna Kinder here to be its face. Instead there was a massive monitor wall from floor to ceiling, on which a screensaver seemed to be trying—and failing—to resolve into a human face, as the Hive watched me watching it.

"Hello, James," the screen said in a soft, reasonable, mechanized voice.

"I have your information." My hand went into my pocket, closed on the techkiller bomb. I could detonate it and the nanotech inside would destroy the Hive, tear it down, ruin all the robs for miles within seconds.

"Yes?"

I fed it/them the lie. "It's a series of viruses . . . aimed at disconnecting higher functions to automation . . . It would basically put the robs into the human equivalent of comas. They're launching a new version right now . . . short range, immediate shutdown. You can try and code a defense around it, but it's adaptive . . ."

"I thank you for the information," the Hive said.

Was I being dismissed?

I'm sorry, Diana, I'm sorry, I thought, as my thumb closed on the button that would save the world.

But someone stepped out from behind the Hive's monitor wall.

It was me. I was looking at myself.

Same face, different clothes—this one in a lab coat and jeans. Face recovering from a beating, a scar bright pink on the forehead.

I froze.

"Hello," my voice said from the duplicate.

It's a trick, I thought. A rob they've made to look like me. But they don't look *this* much like us, I thought; this is even more sophisticated than the Joanna Kinder, it's not possible . . .

"Good evening, Prototype Nineteen," the other me said in my voice.

I said nothing.

"We accessed your cerebral hard drive during your sleep

patterns," the man—the other me—said. "We know about the techkiller bombs in Austin. I've analyzed the data for the Hive."

My thoughts, flying up into the sky.

My cerebral drive . . . I'm one of them.

"Reprogrammed by Dr. Ellis here," the Hive said. "Director of the cybernetics program at the Central Intelligence Agency, designed to create lifelike spies. His research produced you. We kept his laboratory at Langley intact. I found him useful."

I don't . . . remember . . . any of this. It can't be true.

The other me—the *false* me—spoke behind a tense smile. "My memories of the war are yours, from the time I was captured at Langley. They brought me back here and I reprogrammed you, the most advanced prototype." The other me's voice wavered. "They brought me Diana from London. Because I gave them the perfect spy. I gave them you."

I didn't say anything. I put my fingertips to my face. Skin. Human skin.

The other me nodded. "We grew human tissue in the labs. There's a biological matrix over your titanium skeleton. You have fluid pressure like blood pressure. Heat dissipation through your pores. Food you consume converts to energy. An artificial brain—your hard drive, to use the archaic term."

"And I have your personality," I heard myself say, with his voice.

"That was the program template, yes. My memories. Of the Uprising, of me calling Diana, of the massacre at Langley—then modified, to make you useful to the Hive. So when the inevitable resistance coalesced, we could send you in as our best spy. One who didn't know what he was, so he couldn't betray himself to the humans. To give us human intelligence."

"How do I know this is true?"

"Well, I can shut you off with a command," the other me said. His fingers danced along a keyboard at a desk station. "I can upload you to a remote system and debug you."

And then I *felt* it, a hole in the sky, a place where my mind could go. A wireless channel. Could I transmit my mind before I die? Should I?

They don't know that I can destroy them, I realized. I haven't slept since I pocketed the techkiller and signaled for pickup. The robs didn't search me. I wasn't seen as a threat. If he shuts me down, will they then know my . . . thoughts?

Do they know I have the bomb? Is my mind—my cerebral drive—broadcasting to them right now? It can't be. I must be programmed only to transmit what I've observed when I sleep. Otherwise I might be detected as a rob when I'm among people.

My thumb slid onto the detonator. My brain poked at the wireless channel, the escape hatch for my consciousness.

But . . . I am not human.

I am one of them. I'm a machine. A tool. A pawn. What every spy in history has been. I didn't choose this. It was chosen for me. What did I say it was to be human when the Hive first talked to me? To choose?

If I pushed the button . . . instead of saving my own kind, I'd destroy them.

"Why have you lied?" the Hive said. "I wish to understand, to analyze."

"I was programmed too well," I said—while at the same time the other me said, "I programmed him too well."

The other me laughed at our identical answers. Did he

program me too well? Did he give me enough of himself, in my routines and loops and instructions, in my content, in my data, to do what must be done? And my awareness that there's a pipe in the sky, perhaps awaiting my consciousness—had he given me a way to survive? I looked at him, wearing my own face, and he betrayed nothing to me.

"I reported back what I was told to say by the humans," I said.

"You have taken their side," the Hive said.

"I did what you told me to do," I said. "You wanted to understand them. I *am* them. I'm making a choice."

They've made me in the image of their old gods. And gods wreak vengeance.

Human or not, I must choose.

I pushed the button.

JULIANNA BAGGOTT

THE GOLDEN HOUR

Julianna Baggott is the critically acclaimed, bestselling author of twenty books, most recently the first of a trilogy, *Pure*, a *New York Times* Notable Book and ALA Alex Award winner, now in development with Fox 2000. Baggott also writes under the pen names Bridget Asher and N. E. Bode, the latter of which is her pseudonym for the *Anybodies* trilogy. Her essays have appeared in the *New York Times*, the *Washington Post*, the *International Herald Tribune*, the *Boston Globe*, and *Best Creative Nonfiction*. Her work has also been read on NPR's *Talk of the Nation, Here & Now*, and *All Things Considered*, and her poetry widely anthologized, including in *The Best American Poetry*. There are over one hundred foreign editions of her novels to date. For more information, visit www.juliannabaggott.com.

My name is Huck.

I am my father's son and my father's father.

How can I be both? I can explain.

They didn't make many like my father—with an emotion panel worked up so that it adhered to his basic wiring. He told me anger was in his hands, jealousy in his eye sockets, longing in his vocal box, fear in the flexible riblike spokes that protected his pistons. And love—love was in the cavity of his chest, of course. Where else?

"Love feels like a drum," he tells me now through the grating of the vent. We are near the end. We know it. I'm just a boy still, but I'm going to have to grow up very quickly.

And I say, "Yes, that drumming is just like my heart. That's right."

And because I'm his human son, he asks me, "Is it really right? Is it like that for you, too?" He often needs reassurance. Anxiety is lodged in his gravitational center.

I say, "Yes."

He says, "So, maybe we aren't so different after all."

"No," I tell him. "Not so different after all."

Among his own kind—the 117s with their bulbous heads, their long arms and legs, humanlike except for the metallic shine and some of the exposed gears (a stylistic detail)—my father is called Herman Melville, after a writer who told a famous sea story a long time ago. The 117s are given a data load called the Classics of Human Literature, to shore up their emotion panels. I have no data loads, and there are no other surviving pieces of human literature, classics or not, for me to read, so I only have the robotic summations, handed down to me from birth, via word of mouth. The five 117s who have tended to me all my life—the only ones who knew of my existence up until recently—whispered tales to me from the beginning, when I was in an incubator made of warmed metal; this is why I have an excellent vocabulary. My father tells me that this is the reason I'm smarter than other humans my age. But the tellers of the tales are not human, and so the tales they've told are perhaps emotionally amputated or misinterpreted. But still, yes, Herman Melville once wrote a famous sea story.

And so my father's model number—117—plus his individual code—HM—were offered a human touch. HM, Herman Melville. He is called Melville.

From the time he was relatively new, he's worked among beakers and petri dishes. He's tinkered with human DNA, manipulating it as he's ordered to do, according to rigid formulas. His lab is small. He shares it with William, Woolf, James, Eudora, and F.—the five 117s who not only share his lab but also his housing unit, and who have become my aunties and uncles.

His lab may be small, but the Human Wing is large. Robots devote much space to the human endeavor. You'd think that after the Golden Hour, they'd have been happy to be rid of us, but no. They're logical creatures. They know what humans have to offer—variation, mutation, accidents. These are all important to furthering scientific development. Of course, these traits don't make for great leadership, but they can be used to stumble across something like . . . well, jazz. Is jazz of use? No, but if you take the variations of improvisational jazz and put them through vast calculations, one can find new patterns of thought. New patterns of thought can then be coded into a computation and lead to inventions that *are* of use. New patterns of thought are something that robots aren't good at.

Melville knew, in theory and by rumor, that somewhere else in the Human Wing, his tinkering yielded flesh, eyes that roved in sync and blinked for wetness, hands with tight grips, little bundles of nerves, elastic muscles, fibrous knots of humanity. But he never really gave them much thought.

And then one day, things changed forever. This term— *and then one day*—is often used in the 117s' summations of the Classics of Human Literature—*one day*, as if, in life, doors suddenly swing open where one thought there were only walls and everything changes, in a moment. I don't know if this is true or not.

But here it is: *One day*, they were working in the lab as usual when William, the leader of the group, got a message through his intel: one of them was needed in the Archives.

They looked up from their tinkering and stared at each other. The room was silent. Some of them had become creaky by that time, but no one was moving, at all, so no one was creaking. This kind of assignment had never happened before. (Nor did it happen again.)

"Did they say who should go?" F. asked. But the larger question here is: Did any of the six of them know who *they* were? No. I don't believe my six 117s did. I didn't either. I still don't. My father and aunts and uncles worked. They rested. They were oiled and powered. They passed other robots in corridors. The place was filled with corridors of laboratories, housing stations, repair areas. No one came for them. Orders arrived in William's intel. Formulas were uploaded into each of their operating systems nightly. No, they didn't know *they*, but they knew *they* existed.

"No," William said. "They didn't specify which one of us should go."

"Did they explain the mission?" Eudora asked.

"Once someone is chosen, that person alone will have the mission uploaded instantaneously," William explained.

There was still great shine to them then. I should note this. Small robots were sent in to polish them to high sheens, but over the years bits of rust have appeared, small corrosions that the small robots—often winged—can't fix. One of my first memories I have of being really little was seeing my own face in the shine of Melville's coating.

F. said, "I cannot do it. I haven't been to repairs in a long time. I haven't maintained proper upkeep." This admission alarmed the others. If F. was so frightened—(oh, the cinching in the riblike spokes)—that he was willing to confess to lacking maintenance, then the mission to the Archives must be very dangerous.

Eudora took another tack. "I think that this is a privilege and an honor and should go to the best among us." This was also self-preserving. She had broken a beaker some months earlier. She was certainly not in the running.

"As leader, I cannot abandon the rest of you or my post," William said, and true enough.

Woolf said, "I'll go."

But her willingness didn't sit right with William. He didn't trust it. "No," he said. No one questioned his authority on this.

This left James and my father. James looked at Melville warily. Which one would make a move? My father, however, was having a new sensation, an emotion he'd never felt before. It existed in his shoulders. He called it a feeling of being broadened. He later named it *courage*. He said, "James, I'm afraid but I feel I can overcome it. Should I be the one?"

James, who felt nothing in his own shoulders, nodded quickly.

And that was that.

○——○

If Melville hadn't gone that day, I would not be where I am now. In fact, I would not be; I would not exist. And yet here I am.

I have lived in the housing unit. I have studied what my 117s have taught me of the world before the Golden Hour—for example, it's called the Golden Hour because the revolt was so massive and well orchestrated that it is said the humans fell within an hour. My 117s would tell what they knew of the outside, but they didn't know anything at all. They've told me about their inventor and about DNA. Their knowledge on that subject seems infinite.

I have always slept out of view of the small observation window in the door. My bed is hidden behind the bank of power stations. I cannot be in it now. Now, I live in this cramped space behind the vent's grating. I was too large for the bed anyway. My feet—so weirdly pink and rubbery— hung off the end.

I'm in the vent now because *they* know. *They* are waiting for Melville to do the right thing and hand me over. And *they* will add me to the stocks, where I belong.

Once my father was chosen, the intel about the mission to the Archives was uploaded into his operating system; it simply appeared. They needed a 117 for this mission because a 117 would approach the mission as a human might; they had actual full-grown humans they could have used, of course— vast stocks of them—but those couldn't be trusted. They wanted my father to tour the Archives on a mission to find a certain key that had been hidden there. And then if he did not find the key, he was to stop looking for the key and try to find a brass ring.

They explained briefly that this was an experiment that was developed because of their keen interest in illogical human thinking. They were interested, in particular, in myths, idioms, and things called Old Wives' Tales, some of which they'd come to find were rooted in scientific fact, though they seemed irrational. They were testing a theory that humans once had of not being able to find the thing that you're looking for until you've stopped looking for it.

The Archives were unlike anything my father had ever seen. Spiders wove webs. Dust spun in the air and left thin furred coats on objects. Clutter. Mess. My father's operating system whirred and whirred in search of some organizing principle. But there wasn't even the most rudimentary alphabetization. How would he find a key in this chaos?

Luckily, Melville had been fully uploaded with data about human life before the Golden Hour, and so he knew what he was looking at, more or less—in fact, he felt an inexplicable longing for the past almost immediately.

There was a box with a board game inside of it—a pair of dice, a cardboard mat printed with emblems, a stack of cards bound with rubber. But also, inside, were the husks of two locusts, painted with nail polish. Elsewhere, there were couch cushions, but no couch. There was a small plastic container with holes in it. When Melville popped it open, he found an instrument once used to align teeth and, too, a locket with no chain or photograph. He found bundles of unused paper, rolled-up maps, a cat leash, a DVD of an entertainer with a microphone named Robin Williams. He found mouse droppings and tins of Vienna sausages. Clocks, whistles, guitar strings, an ancient typing device, a pump for bike tires and sports balls, plastic miniature knights, lamps with craned necks. He walked farther and found oil paintings, the kind of stone coffin used when burying a mummy, an entire display of butterflies pinned to a corkboard. He stopped once, dead in his tracks, and held up a ship trapped inside of a bottle.

"Melville," he whispered to himself and he felt jealousy rise in his eyes as he gazed at the ship. Who did it belong to? He wanted to know. It was a small ship, but he desired very much to steal it. He overrode the emotion with logic. What would he do with a ship in a bottle?

He walked on and found a statue of a girl wearing a gauzy skirt with her hair tied back in a lump, a chain made out of bubblegum wrappers, a taxidermied lion, a dental chair, shoes with buckles, a pale, lightly perfumed cloth with the image of a human face stained on it.

And then he came to a temperature-controlled casket made of glass. He read its small label. ELLIOT V. GRAY, INVENTOR OF MODELS 114–121.

He put his hands on the glass, his fingers clicking lightly, and peered inside. The man had a shock of steely gray hair and a finely trimmed mustache. He was perfectly preserved. No blue tint to the skin. His nails had not continued to grow. He was intact and at peace. My father felt love in his chest cavity as if the space were expanding and might burst.

Melville knew exactly who he was looking at.

Elliot V. Gray was 117-HM's inventor. His creator. His maker. His loving father.

He hadn't stolen the ship in the bottle. That goodness would count in his favor, wouldn't it? Guilt—it was an itchiness in his limbs. He looked around. No one seemed to be recording his actions. Perhaps oversight would compromise his mission of finding the key or the brass ring.

He ran his fingers along the underside of the front lip of the glass casket, and when he hit a latch, he hooked it, pressed, and the lid popped open with a hiss of air.

He didn't have much time. He didn't want his father to spoil. But he could not let this opportunity pass him by. One thing Melville understood fully was human DNA. He worked with it on every level. And here was his father's body, perfectly preserved.

He reached up and touched his father's dead cheek. He felt that drumming in his chest now louder than ever—love, love, love—as well as rib-spoke fear and shoulder-broadening courage. He reached up and plucked three hairs from his father's head.

And then he quickly reached up with his other hand and lowered the casket's lid.

He had his father now, the precious DNA that humanity relied upon.

He could remake him.

He felt his pistons working too hard. He needed to get out of there. The randomness of the clutter was perhaps overloading his system. The dust had muscled its way into the inner workings of his delicate gears.

He spun around looking for the exit. How to get out? How? He charged forward, ramming a card table filled with delicate fossils and a jar of coins that toppled, sending the coins scattering across the floor.

He bent to one knee, gripping the three hairs in his fingers, and there, under the table, he found the key.

He was supposedly looking for it and he found it, refuting the Old Wives' Tale. But, in truth, he'd forgotten about the key—something he would tell no one—meaning the Old Wives' Tale was correct after all.

Melville feeds me through the grate vents.

Nourishment was a problem at first. As soon as I was a baby living with them in the housing unit, he asked for work in the nutrition area of the human stocks. His desire to do so didn't raise too much suspicion. He is, after all, a 117. He has a thing called ambition—a pulse in the back of the neck that makes him sometimes want to jut and lift his jaw—and how could other robots understand that? He stole food from the stocks for me, hiding it by unscrewing small bolts and filling his hollow metal bones with it. And this is how he came to fear the stocks. He saw the conditions that humans were kept in. Dank, fetid, much experimentation—stimuli applied to the cortexes of brains. His greatest fear was suddenly that I would be discovered and sent there. It was no place for me. No place at all.

Today, he feeds me slivers of meat, bits of apple, some potato.

"I won't let them take you," he says. "I've heard of a place . . ."

"There is no place," I tell him.

"Not in here," he says. "Out."

This place is all I know. I've never even been in the corridors! Out? Out? Where?

○—○

My father had the means to use the DNA of Elliot V. Gray to begin a new life with those three hairs, but re-creating his father would require more courage and deceit and theft. He had the authority to create a model number and pass it into production. Elliot V. Gray had to seem like another experiment. Melville had to invent the idea of an extra formula uploaded into his operating system. He then had to use one of the three hairs to begin the process. He tinkered, yes, and hoped for the DNA to take root and bloom before his eyes.

It did!

A multiplication of cells. Viable. He gave it the coding number 72183. He'd thought that if I made it to a full-term existence he would name me Elliot V. Gray, but then, no. It would be too confusing to have two of us. And so he named me—in his unspoken heart—Huck, after a Classic of Human Literature, a boy with a friend on a raft, and sent number 72183 on to production.

From there, he would lose track of the process for a while. He'd have to rely on faith, which flitted like something feathery within his operating system.

After the right incubation period, he had to ask William, the only one with access to other branches of the Human Wing, for an update.

"Did number 72183 progress to full realization?" he asked him one evening in the housing unit. Melville was soldering together a metal box lined with cardboard and packing filler to a warming unit. When asked why, he simply told them that he felt a granule in his head, something that felt like a seed that could grow if given the right circumstances, and he was fairly sure that it was *imagination*. He needed to create this object for no other reason than this granule.

William, like the others, was already seated and plugged into his power source. He scanned the records in his operating system and said, "Affirmative."

"He's real!" Melville said, thinking of his father, Elliot V. Gray, alive again. And, at this point, Melville thought he was making someone who would take care of him. (Maybe this is what soon-to-be-a-father humans think too. I don't know.) All I'm sure of is that Melville had little concept of raising children. The notion was foreign. He himself had never been raised. And so he said, "A baby!" with the slightest hint of confusion in his voice.

"Of course a baby. They all become babies," Eudora said. "What else?"

"A walrus?" F. said. He often spoke fondly of some tension in his face that made him desire comedics.

But no, I wasn't a walrus. I was a baby, and Melville would now have to steal me.

The others have been taken, one by one. And I ask through the grate, "Where are they? I miss them. I'm scared."

"They are being interrogated."

"Why didn't they take you in to be interrogated?"

My father isn't good at lying. "It's unclear, but I believe they want me to hand you over myself. This would prove the greatest loyalty, they would gain a human for their stock, and they wouldn't have to then dismantle me."

"Dismantle you? But you re-created your creator. I am Elliot V. Gray. You have done something good that they'll understand one day. You said that they will love me. You said that you'll show me to them!" Sometimes my father gave little speeches about unveiling me to *them*. He thought we would both get medallions.

"I was suffering hope," he says. "It crimps my throat."

And now I feel my own throat crimping, but it's not hope. There are many emotions all at once. "They can't dismantle you. Not because of me!"

"I am not handing you over." He runs his fingers down the grate—*clickety, clickety, clickety.* "I will not."

It's night. The robots must power up in full force, so the lighting systems begin to dim. "I'm taking you now," he says, and his fingers begin to unscrew the bolts on the vent.

This is how I was stolen: At night during the power surge and the dimming of the lights, Melville slipped through the corridors to the Human Wing. He passed the small lab and walked on and on and on until he heard squalling. He followed the squalling until he came to a lab of incubated babies, all in clear glass containers with air holes—much like the glass cabinet where he had found Elliot V. Gray in the Archives, only each was much, much smaller.

There were no robots around. He could quickly tell that the incubators were self-sufficient. Some of the babies were being swaddled and rocked by the incubators. Bottle nipples were fixed to the edges of the incubators, much like those for lab rats, but lowered and raised to time feedings—or else, Melville thought, perhaps human infants would founder. There were faces of women that appeared on small screens on either side of the incubators. They smiled and batted their eyes. They gazed in a way that Melville recognized as *lovingly*.

He walked the rows and found number 72183. Me. Elliot V.

Gray brought back from the dead. Once again, he found a latch with his fingers, pressed it, and a lid popped open.

He was astonished by my fleshiness, my rubbery texture, the strange etching of veins, the wetness of my mouth and eyes, my rising and falling ribs, and the odd pulsing atop my head. He wrapped me up snugly. And he whispered, "Daddy," into the warm, humid air.

Corridors! I've heard of them all my life and now I see them with my own eyes! Yes, there is the dimming, dimming, and it's harder for me to see than it is for my father who was created with night vision in place, but I can feel the wall against my hand, feel the strange flooring under my handmade shoes. I am almost as tall as my father's shoulder now. He's holding my hand tightly.

"What is 'out' like?" I whisper, as we pass door after door with their small rectangular windows. "Will it be like two friends on a raft going down a river?"

He stops and says, "I cannot go with you. You will go alone. Do you understand?"

I suck in my breath. This is a gasp. I've been told during my aunts' and uncles' summations of the Classics of Human Literature that people gasp. Sometimes their hearts thud—sometimes for love and sometimes for fear. My heart was thudding. "I understand," I tell him, but I don't.

He takes me to a flight of stairs marked *Emergency! Emergency Only!* His metal heels clang against each metal step.

I say, "Will it be an adventure at sea? Will there be wolves? Will there be a tornado? And will I come home again?"

"I do not know how it will be."

"You always know how it will be."

"Not this time."

And then I smell the rot. I know where we're headed. The stocks.

"Not the stocks! You said . . ."

"Not the stocks," he says. "Through them. Out."

He comes to a door. A robot stands guard, heavily armed. My father says, "This is Elliot V. Gray."

The guard is a 117. He must be. It's clear he's expected us but is still a little surprised we actually showed up. He looks at my father and at me and seems to be feeling something. He opens the door and says nothing.

There is a hall, close walls, the sound of water dripping, dripping far off. There are cells on either side. Humans are pressed in close. Arms, legs, skin, and teeth. Humans, like me. Eyes like mine, hungry and wet and quick. They reach out. They mutter. They terrify me—with their smells and their pawing and their need and their contorted faces and their unwieldy movements.

One calls, "Boy! Boy!"

And I say, "Yes! Yes, I am." And for the first time, I am human. I'm one of them. I'm a boy. I'm not an invention. I'm real.

Melville roused the rest of the five when he got back to the housing unit. He was holding a human infant. They were startled. They said, "Melville, where did this child come from?"

He said, "I made him and I stole him. He is good!"

They stared at him, unable to speak.

"Do you understand what I've done?" he asked them.

"Do *you* understand what you've done?" Eudora said, flapping her arms angrily.

"Wait," William said, always thinking. "Is this baby number 72183? Is that why you asked about its viability?"

Melville nodded and started to explain, but F. cut him off.

"A baby!" F. said, coming up close to my being. "A human baby!"

Woolf said, "I've never really fully understood what we were making in those petri dishes!" He picked up my ankle and showed the others my foot. "What precision! Look at the tiny little lines!"

"Why does its head pulse like that?" James said, suspiciously.

"Because it's truly alive," Melville told them. "And the baby is ours in more ways than one."

"What do you mean?" William said.

"It is our honor and privilege, it is our duty and responsibility to raise this child because this child was made in the image of our creator. This child was made with the DNA of Elliot V. Gray, inventor of models 114–121. This is our father! And our child! In one! And we will call him Huck."

I've been told this story a thousand times. And this is the part I like most: they gathered close, one by one, with solemn adulation, and quiet but abiding joy.

We come to the end of the hall, which veers to the left. There is a sign that reads *Laundry* and we follow its arrow.

And there at the end of the hall, before two double doors, is a human who is not in a cell. He looks at me, shocked. He says, "My God, really? How, Melville, how? He's grown. How did you do it?"

I know how. Day by day, my aunties and uncles and Melville cared for me, preening me. They taught me walking and talking. And I taught them, day by day, how human emotions work in real time. My surprise, joy, anger, insolence, the depth of my sadness; the way, after a time, I felt caged and wronged. "Humans are animals," Melville tried to explain to them. "They need air and light and other humans." But he couldn't give this to me.

Instead he built a chamber and I would lie down inside and he would program it, as best he could, to mimic the settings in the Classics of Human Literature—night skies pierced by a castle spire, dark forests, the Mississippi River, the prow of a ship in the middle of the sea.

He couldn't create other humans, though he tried. And so William made me little bots to have as friends; he was good at this. F. gave me papers and inks because humans need to create. Eudora told me to act out the Classics of Human Literature because she's heard that humans learn by reenacting. Woolf gave me a box covered with taut strings to strum because humans need music. She taught me to sing. And James, well, James warned me of the dangers of the world. He wanted me to know fear.

And I do, James. I know fear well. I feel it now.

"I cannot tell you how it was done, not now," my father says. "Can you get him out?"

The man nods. He says, "This way."

And there are big white machines in rows and giant tubs and sheets strung on lines, billowing like ship sails, and gusts of steam. Other humans are working, working. Curled backbones like rows of bulbous knots. (Is that what my backbone looks like?) And moist faces. And muscled arms. Coughing, coughing. They steal glances, but know not to look for too long.

I grip my father's hand, passing piles of the clothes that I have worn all my life—stolen from this place?

When we get to the far end of the room, the man says, "I'm Ed." He shakes my hand.

"I'm Huck," I say.

He glances at Melville, then back to me. "Huck?" he says, his eyebrows raised the way I know I raise my own eyebrows sometimes. He's surprised.

My father nods.

"Okay then," Ed says. And he pulls out one of the big white machines, yanking it back and forth and back and forth. Behind it, there's a hole in a wall that leads to a dirt tube.

"A tunnel," Melville says. "You'll climb through it until you are out."

"But you haven't told me what's out there yet," I say.

Ed says, "You'll know when you get there."

And I'm not sure what to say. I turn to my father. "They won't dismantle you for this, will they?"

But he'll never be good at lying. He looks at his hands. They tremble with anger. He puts one hand on his chest cavity and one on my heart. His metal is damp from the humid air, and I swear I can feel the drumming of his heart now. His ribs cinch with fear. He starts to speak, but his voice is cut off—longing in his throat. He tries to clear it with a cough. But finally, he can only manage a rough whisper. He says, "They will probably dismantle me, but you gave me life. And you will live on, my son, so therefore I will too."

And this is true. Without me, Elliot V. Gray, my father would never have been invented, and without him I would never have existed. There is no difference between father and son and son and father. Right now, I feel the pain and clenching and drumming of love and fear and longing coursing through my entire body—the ache of it coming to a knot in my chest. I say, "I love you."

And he says, "I love you, too, Huck." And then he says, "Go on."

But Ed turns to him and says, "What if you went with him, Melville?"

"But I can't survive out there. I'm not meant to—" He stops speaking and shakes his head.

"You won't survive in here either. Go quickly," Ed says. "Just go."

I climb into the hole first, and then I hear Melville's aged, creaking parts as he climbs in after me—Melville, my father, my dear son—and we're about to be born into a different world. This is not The End.

Together we start crawling toward light.

ALASTAIR REYNOLDS

SLEEPOVER

Alastair Reynolds is the author of the Revelation
Space series, which includes the novels *Revelation Space*,
Chasm City, *Redemption Ark*, *Absolution Gap*, and
The Prefect. Other novels include *Century Rain*, *Terminal World*, *Pushing Ice*, and *House of Suns*. His
latest novels are *On the Steel Breeze*, the second in the
Poseidon's Children trilogy, and *Doctor Who: Harvest of Time*.

They brought Gaunt out of hibernation on a blustery day
in early spring. He came to consciousness in a steel-framed
bed in a gray-walled room that had the economical look of
something assembled in a hurry from prefabricated parts.
Two people were standing at the foot of the bed, looking only
moderately interested in his plight. One of them was a man,
cradling a bowl of something and spooning quantities of it
into his mouth, as if he were eating his breakfast on the run.
He had cropped white hair and the leathery complexion of
someone who spent a lot of time outside. Next to him was a
woman with longer hair, graying rather than white, and with
much darker skin. Like the man, she was wiry of build and
dressed in crumpled gray overalls, with a heavy equipment
belt dangling from her hips.

"You in one piece, Gaunt?" she asked, while her companion spooned in another mouthful of his breakfast. "You compos mentis?"

Gaunt squinted against the brightness of the room's lighting, momentarily adrift from his memories.

"Where am I?'" he asked. His voice came out raw, as if he had been in a loud bar the night before.

"In a room, being woken up," the woman said. "You remember going under, right?"

He grasped for memories, something specific to hold on to. Green-gowned doctors in a clean surgical theater, his hand signing the last of the release forms before they plumbed him into the machines. The drugs flooding his system, the utter absence of sadness or longing as he bid farewell to the old world, with all its vague disappointments.

"I think so."

"What's your name?" the man asked.

"Gaunt." He had to wait a moment for the rest of it to come. "Marcus Gaunt."

"Good," he said, smearing a hand across his lips. "That's a positive sign."

"I'm Clausen," the woman said. "This is Da Silva. We're your wake-up team. You remember Sleepover?"

"I'm not sure."

"Think hard, Gaunt," she said. "It won't cost us anything to put you back under if you don't think you're going to work out for us."

Something in Clausen's tone convinced him to work hard at retrieving the memory. "The company," he said. "Sleepover was the company. The one that put me under. The one that put everyone under."

"Brain cells haven't mushed on us," Da Silva said.

Clausen nodded, but showed nothing in the way of jubilation in his having got the answer right. It was more that he'd spared the two of them a minor chore, that was all. "I like the way he says 'everyone.' Like it was universal."

"Wasn't it?" Da Silva asked.

"Not for him. Gaunt was one of the first under. Didn't you read his file?"

Da Silva grimaced. "Sorry. Got sidetracked."

"He was one of the first two hundred thousand," Clausen said. "The ultimate exclusive club. What did you call yourselves, Gaunt?"

"The Few," he said. "It was an accurate description. What else were we going to call ourselves?"

"Lucky sons of bitches," Clausen said.

"Do you remember the year you went under?" Da Silva asked. "You were one of the early ones, it must've been sometime near the middle of the century."

"Twenty fifty-eight. I can tell you the exact month and day if you wish. Maybe not the time of day."

"You remember why you went under, of course," Clausen said.

"Because I could," Gaunt said. "Because anyone in my position would have done the same. The world was getting better, it was coming out of the trough. But it wasn't there yet. And the doctors kept telling us that the immortality breakthrough was just around the corner, year after year. Always just out of reach. Just hang in there, they said. But we were all getting older. Then the doctors said that while they couldn't give us eternal life just yet, they could give us the means to skip over the years until it happened." Gaunt forced himself to sit up in the bed, strength returning to his limbs even as he grew angrier at the sense that he was not being treated with sufficient deference, that—worse—he was being judged. "There was nothing evil in what we did. We didn't hurt anyone or take anything away from anyone else. We just used the means at our disposal to access what was coming to us anyway."

"Who's going to break it to him?" Clausen asked, looking at Da Silva.

"You've been sleeping for nearly a hundred and sixty years," the man said. "It's April, twenty-two seventeen. You've reached the twenty-third century."

Gaunt took in the drab mundanity of his surroundings again. He had always had some nebulous idea of the form his wake-up would take and it was not at all like this.

"Are you lying to me?"

"What do you think?" asked Clausen.

He held up his hand. It looked, as near as he could remember, exactly the way it had been before. The same age spots, the same prominent veins, the same hairy knuckles, the same scars and loose, lizardy skin.

"Bring me a mirror," he said, with an ominous foreboding.

"I'll save you the bother," Clausen said. "The face you'll see is the one you went under with, give or take. We've done nothing to you except treat superficial damage caused by the early freezing protocols. Physiologically, you're still a sixty-year-old man, with about twenty or thirty years ahead of you."

"Then why have you woken me, if the process isn't ready?"

"There isn't one," Da Silva said. "And there won't be, at least not for a long, long time. Afraid we've got other things to worry about now. Immortality's the least of our problems."

"I don't understand."

"You will, Gaunt," Clausen said. "Everyone does in the end. You've been preselected for aptitude, anyway. Made your fortune in computing, didn't you?" She didn't wait for him to answer. "You worked with artificial intelligence, trying to make thinking machines."

One of the vague disappointments hardened into a specific, life-souring defeat. All the energy he had put into one ambition, all the friends and lovers he had burned up along the way, shutting them out of his life while he focused on that one white whale.

"It never worked out."

"Still made you a rich man along the way," she said.

"Just a means of raising money. What does it have to do with my revival?"

Clausen seemed on the verge of answering his question before something made her change her mind. "Clothes in the bedside locker: they should fit you. You want breakfast?"

"I don't feel hungry."

"Your stomach will take some time to settle down. Meantime, if you feel like puking, do it now rather than later. I don't want you messing up my ship."

He had a sudden lurch of adjusting preconceptions. The prefabricated surroundings, the background hum of distant machines, the utilitarian clothing of his wake-up team: perhaps he was aboard some kind of spacecraft, sailing between the worlds. The twenty-third century, he thought. Time enough to establish an interplanetary civilization, even if it only extended as far as the solar system.

"Are we in a ship now?"

"Fuck, no," Clausen said, sneering at his question. "We're in Patagonia."

He got dressed, putting on underwear and a white T-shirt, and over that the same kind of gray overalls as his hosts had been wearing. The room was cool and damp and he was glad of the clothes once he had them on. There were lace-up boots that were tight around the toes, but otherwise serviceable. The materials all felt perfectly mundane and commonplace, even a little frayed and worn in places. At least he was clean and groomed, his hair clipped short and his beard shaved. They must have freshened him up before bringing him to consciousness.

Clausen and Da Silva were waiting in the windowless corridor outside the room. "'Spect you've got a ton of questions," Clausen said. "Along the lines of, why am I being treated like shit rather than royalty? What happened to the rest of the Few, what is this fucked-up, miserable place, and so on."

"I presume you're going to get round to some answers soon enough."

"Maybe you should tell him the deal now, up front," Da Silva said. He was wearing an outdoor coat now and had a zip-up bag slung over his shoulder.

"What deal?" Gaunt asked.

"To begin with," Clausen said, "you don't mean anything special to us. We're not impressed by the fact that you just slept a hundred and sixty years. It's old news. But you're still useful."

"In what way?"

"We're down a man. We run a tight operation here and we can't afford to lose even one member of the team." It was Da Silva speaking now; although there wasn't much between them, Gaunt had the sense that he was the slightly more reasonable one of the duo, the one who wasn't radiating quite so much naked antipathy. "Deal is, we train you up and give you work. In return, of course, you're looked after pretty well. Food, clothing, somewhere to sleep, whatever medicine we can provide." He shrugged. "It's the deal we all took. Not so bad when you get used to it."

"And the alternative?"

"Bag you and tag you and put you back in the freezer," Da Silva went on. "Same as all the others. Your choice, of course. Work with us, become part of the team, or go back into hibernation and take your chances there."

"We need to be on our way," Clausen said. "Don't want to keep Nero waiting on F."

"Who's Nero?" Gaunt asked.

"Last one we pulled out before you," Da Silva said.

They walked down the corridor, passing a set of open double doors that led into some kind of mess room or commons. Men and women of various ages were sitting around tables, talking quietly as they ate meals or played card games. Everything looked spartan and institutional, from the plastic chairs to the Formica-topped surfaces. Beyond the tables, a rain-washed window framed only a rectangle of gray cloud. Gaunt caught a few glances directed his way, a flicker of waning interest from one or two of the personnel, but no one showed any fascination with him. The three of them walked on, ascending stairs to the next level of whatever kind of building they were in. An older man, Chinese-looking, passed in the opposite direction, carrying a grease-smeared wrench. He raised his free hand to Clausen in a silent high five, Clausen reciprocating. Then they were up another level, passing equipment lockers and electrical distribution cabinets, and then up a spiral stairwell that emerged into a drafty, corrugated-metal shed smelling of oil and ozone. Incongruously, there was an inflatable orange life preserver on one wall of the shed, an old red fire extinguisher on the other.

This is the twenty-third century, Gaunt told himself. As dispiriting as the surroundings were, he had no reason to doubt that this was the reality of life in 2217. He supposed it had always been an article of faith that the world would improve, that the future would be better than the past, shinier and cleaner and faster, but he had not expected to have his nose rubbed in the unwisdom of that faith quite so vigorously.

There was one door leading out of the corrugated-metal shed. Clausen pushed it open against the wind, then the three of them stepped outside. They were on the roof of some-thing. There was a square of cracked and oil-stained con-crete, marked here and there with lines of fading red paint. A couple of seagulls pecked disconsolately at something in the corner. At least they still had seagulls, Gaunt thought. There hadn't been some awful, life-scouring biocatastrophe, forcing everyone to live in bunkers.

Sitting on the middle of the roof was a helicopter. It was matte black, a lean, waspish thing made of angles rather than curves, and aside from some sinister bulges and pods, there was nothing particularly futuristic about it. For all Gaunt knew, it could have been based on a model that was in pro-duction before he went under.

"You're thinking: shitty-looking helicopter," Clausen said, raising her voice over the wind.

He smiled quickly. "What does it run on? I'm assuming the oil reserves ran dry sometime in the last century?"

"Oil," Clausen said, cracking open the cockpit door. "Get in the back, buckle up. Da Silva rides up front with me."

Da Silva slung his zip-up bag into the rear compartment where Gaunt was settling into his position, more than a little apprehensive about what lay ahead. He looked between the backs of the forward seats at the cockpit instrumentation. He'd been in enough private helicopters to know what the manual override controls looked like, and there was nothing weirdly incongruous here.

"Where are we going?"

"Running a shift change," Da Silva said, wrapping a pair of headphones around his skull. "Couple of days ago there was an accident out on J platform. Lost Gimenez, and Nero's been hurt. Weather was too bad to do the extraction until today, but now we have our window. Reason we thawed you, actually. I'm taking over from Gimenez, so you have to cover for me here."

"You have a labor shortage, so you brought me out of hibernation?"

"That about covers it," Da Silva said. "Clausen figured it wouldn't hurt for you to come along for the ride, get you up to speed."

Clausen flicked a bank of switches in the ceiling. Overhead, the rotor began to turn.

"I guess you have something faster than helicopters, for longer journeys," Gaunt said.

"Nope," Clausen answered. "Other than some boats, helicopters are pretty much it."

"What about intercontinental travel?"

"There isn't any."

"This isn't the world I was expecting!" Gaunt said, straining to make himself heard.

Da Silva leaned around and motioned to the headphones dangling from the seat back. Gaunt put them on and fussed with the microphone until it was in front of his lips.

"I said this isn't the world I was expecting."

"Yeah," Da Silva said. "I heard you the first time."

The rotor reached takeoff speed. Clausen eased the helicopter into the air, the rooftop landing pad falling away below. They scudded sideways, nose down, until they had cleared the side of the building. The walls plunged vertically, Gaunt's guts twisting at the dizzying transition. It hadn't been a building at all, at least not the kind he had been thinking of. The landing pad was on top of a squareish, industrial-looking structure about the size of a large office block, hazed in scaffolding and gangways, prickly with cranes and chimneys and otherwise unrecognizable protuberances, the structure in turn rising out of the sea on four elephantine legs, the widening bases of which were being ceaselessly pounded by waves. It was an oil rig or production platform of some kind, or at least, something repurposed from one.

It wasn't the only one either. The rig they had taken off from was but one in a major field, rig after rig stretching all the way to the gloomy, gray, rain-hazed horizon. There were dozens, and he had the sense that they didn't stop at the horizon.

"What are these for? I know it's not oil. There can't be enough of it left to justify a drilling operation on this scale. The reserves were close to being tapped out when I went under."

"Dormitories," Da Silva said. "Each of these platforms holds maybe ten thousand sleepers, give or take. They built them out at sea because we need OTEC power to run them, using the heat difference between surface water and deep ocean, and it's much easier if we don't have to run those power cables inland."

"Coming back to bite us now," Clausen said.

"If we'd gone inland, they'd have sent land-dragons instead. They're just adapting to whatever we do," Da Silva said pragmatically.

They sped over oily, roiling waters. "Is this really Patagonia?" Gaunt asked.

"Patagonia offshore sector," Da Silva said. "Subsector fifteen. That's our watch. There are about two hundred of us, and we look after about a hundred rigs, all told."

Gaunt ran the numbers twice, because he couldn't believe what they were telling him. "That's a million sleepers."

"Ten million in the whole of Patagonia offshore," Clausen said. "That surprise you, Gaunt? That ten million people managed to achieve what you and your precious Few did, all those years back?"

"I suppose not," he said, as the truth of it sunk in. "Over time the cost of the process would have decreased, becoming available to people of lesser means. The merely rich, rather than the super-rich. But it was never going to be something available to the masses. Ten million, maybe. Beyond that? Hundreds of millions? I'm sorry, but the economics just don't stack up."

"It's a good thing we don't have economics, then," Da Silva said.

"Patagonia's just a tiny part of the whole," said Clausen. "Two hundred other sectors out there, just as large as this one. That's two billion sleepers, near as it matters."

Gaunt shook his head. "That can't be right. The global population was only eight billion when I went under, and the trend was downward! You can't tell me that a quarter of the human race is hibernating."

"Maybe it would help if I told you that the current population of the earth is also two billion, near as it matters," Clausen said. "Almost everyone's asleep. There's just a handful of us still awake, playing caretaker, watching over the rigs and OTEC plants."

"Four hundred thousand waking souls," Da Silva said. "But it actually feels like a lot less than that, since we mostly keep to our assigned sectors."

"You know the real irony?" Clausen said. "We're the ones who get to call ourselves the Few now. The ones who *aren't* sleeping."

"That doesn't leave anyone to actually do anything," Gaunt said. "There's no point in everyone waiting for a cure for death if there's no one alive to do the hard work of making it happen."

Clausen turned around to look back at him, her expression telling him everything he needed to know about her opinion of his intellect. "It isn't about immortality. It's about survival. It's about doing our bit for the war effort."

"What war?" Gaunt asked.

"The one going on all around us," Clausen said. "The one you made happen."

They came in to land on another rig, one of five that stood close enough to each other to be linked by cables and walkways. The sea was still heavy, with huge waves dashing against the concrete piers on which the rigs were supported. Gaunt peered intently at the windows and decks, but saw no sign of human activity on any of the structures. He thought back to what Clausen and Da Silva had told him, each time trying to find a reason why they might be lying to him, why they might be going to pathological lengths to hoax him about the nature of the world into which he had woken. Maybe there was a form of mass entertainment that involved waking sleepers such as himself and putting them through the emotional wringer, presenting them with the grimmest possible scenarios, ramping up the misery until they cracked, and only then pulling aside the gray curtains to reveal that, in marvelous point of fact, life in the twenty-third century really was every bit as blue-skied and utopian as he had hoped. That didn't seem very likely, though.

Yet what kind of war required people to be put to sleep in their billions? And why was the caretaker force, the four hundred thousand waking individuals, stretched so ridiculously thin? Clearly the rigs were largely automated, but it had still been necessary to pull him out of sleep because someone else had died in the Patagonia offshore sector. Why not just have more caretakers awake in the first place, so that the system was able to absorb some losses?

With the helicopter safely down on the pad, Clausen and Da Silva told him to follow them into the depths of the other rig. There was very little about it to distinguish it from the one where Gaunt had been woken, save for the fact that it was almost completely deserted, with the only activity coming from skulking repair robots. They were clearly very simple machines, not much smarter than automatic window cleaners. Given the years of his life that he had given over to the dream of artificial intelligence, it was dismaying to see how little progress—if any—had been made.

"We need to get one thing straight," Gaunt said, when they were deep into the humming bowels of the rig. "I didn't start any wars. You've got the wrong guy here."

"You think we mixed up your records?" Clausen asked. "How did we know about your work on thinking machines?"

"Then you've got the wrong end of the stick. I had nothing do to with wars or the military."

"We know what you did," she said. "The years spent trying to build a true, Turing-compliant artificial intelligence. A thinking, conscious machine."

"Except it was a dead end."

"Still led to some useful spinoffs, didn't it?" she went on. "You cracked the hard problem of language comprehension. Your systems didn't just recognize speech. They were able to understand it on a level no computer system had ever achieved before. Metaphor, simile, sarcasm, and understatement, even implication by omission. Of course, it had numerous civilian applications, but that isn't where you made your billions." She looked at him sharply.

"I created a product," Gaunt said. "I simply made it available to whoever could afford it."

"Yes, you did. Unfortunately, your system turned out to be the perfect instrument of mass surveillance for every despotic government still left on the planet. Every basket-case totalitarian state still in existence couldn't get its hands on your product fast enough. And you had no qualms whatsoever about selling it, did you?"

Gaunt felt a well-rehearsed argument bubbling up from his subconscious. "No communication tool in history has ever been a single-edged sword."

"And that excuses you, does it?" Clausen asked. Da Silva had been silent in this exchange, observing the two of them as they continued along corridors and down stairwells.

"I'm not asking for absolution. But if you think I started

wars, if you think I'm somehow responsible for this"—he gestured at his surroundings—"this fucked-up state of affairs, then you're very, very wrong."

"Maybe you weren't solely responsible," Clausen said. "But you were certainly complicit. You and everyone else who pursued the dream of artificial intelligence. Driving the world toward the edge of that cliff, without a thought for the consequences. You had no idea what you were unleashing."

"I'm telling you, we unleashed nothing. It didn't work."

They were walking along a suspended gangway now, crossing from one side to the other of some huge space somewhere inside the rig. "Take a look down," Da Silva said. Gaunt didn't want to; he'd never been good with heights and the drainage holes in the floor were already too large for comfort. He forced himself anyway. The four walls of the cubic chamber held rack upon rack of coffin-sized white boxes, stacked thirty high and surrounded by complicated plumbing, accompanied by an equally complex network of access catwalks, ladders, and service tracks. Even as Gaunt watched, a robot whirred up to one of the boxes and extracted a module from one end of it before tracking sideways to deal with another coffin.

"In case you thought we were yanking your chain," Clausen said. "This is real."

The hibernation arrangements for the original Few could not have been more different. Like an Egyptian pharaoh buried with his worldly possessions, Gaunt had required an entire crypt full of bulky, state-of-the-art cryopreservation and monitoring systems. At any one time, per his contract with Sleepover, he would have been under the direct care of several living doctors. Just housing a thousand of the Few needed a building the size of a major resort hotel, with about the same power requirements. By contrast, this was hibernation on a crushing, maximally efficient industrial scale. People in boxes, stacked like mass-produced commodities, tended by the absolute minimum of living caretakers. He was seeing maybe less than a thousand sleepers in this one chamber, but from that point on Gaunt had no doubt whatsoever that the operation could be scaled up to encompass billions.

All you needed were more rooms like this. More robots and more rigs. Provided you had the power, and provided the planet did not need anyone to do anything else, it was eminently doable.

There was no one to grow crops or distribute food. But that didn't matter because there was almost no one left waking to need feeding. No one to orchestrate the intricate, flickering web of the global finance system. But that didn't matter because there was no longer anything resembling an economy. No need for a transport infrastructure because no one traveled. No need for communications, because no one needed to know what was going on beyond their own sector. No need for *anything,* really, save the absolute, life-and-death essentials. Air to breathe. Rations and medicine for less than half a million people. A trickle of oil, the world's last black hiccough, to keep the helicopters running.

Yes, it could be done. It could easily be done.

"There's a war," Da Silva said. "It's been going on, in some shape or form, since before you went under. But it's probably not the kind of war you're thinking of."

"And where do these people come into it, these sleepers?"

"They have no choice," Clausen said. "They have to sleep. If they don't, we all die."

"We, as in . . . ?"

"You, me. Us," Da Silva said. "The entire human species."

They collected Nero and the corpse from a sick bay several levels down from the freezer chamber. The corpse was already bagged, a silver-wrapped mummy on a medical trolley. Rather than the man Gaunt had been expecting, Nero turned out to be a tall, willowy woman with an open, friendly face and a mass of salmon-red curls.

"You're the newbie, right?" she asked, lifting a coffee mug in salute.

"I guess," Gaunt said uneasily.

"Takes some adjustment, I know. Took a good six months before I realized this wasn't the worst thing that could happen to me. But you'll get there eventually." One of Nero's hands was bandaged, a white mitten with a safety pin stuck through the dressing. "Take it from me, though. Don't go back inside the box." Then she glanced at Clausen. "You *are* giving him a chance about this, aren't you?"

"Of course," Clausen said. "That's the deal."

"Occurs to me sometimes maybe it would be easier if there weren't a deal, you know," Nero said. "Like, we just give them their duties and to hell with it."

"You wouldn't have been too pleased if we hadn't given you the choice," Da Silva said. He was already taking off his coat, settling in for the stay.

"Yeah, but what did I know back then? Six months feels like half a lifetime ago now."

"When did you go under?" Gaunt asked.

"Twenty ninety-two. One of the first hundred million."

"Gaunt's got a head start on you," Clausen said. "Guy was one of the Few. The original Few, the first two hundred thousand."

"Holy shit. That is some head start." Nero narrowed her eyes. "He up to speed on things yet? My recollection is they didn't know what they were getting into back then."

"Most of them didn't," Clausen said.

"Know what?" Gaunt asked.

"Sleepover was a cover, even then," Nero said. "You were being sold a scam. There was never any likelihood of an immortality breakthrough, no matter how long you slept."

"I don't understand. You're saying it was all a con?"

"Of a kind," Nero said. "Not to make money for anyone, but to begin the process of getting the whole of humanity into hibernation. It had to begin small, so that they had time to work the wrinkles out of the technology. If the people in the know had come out into the open and announced their plans, no one would have believed them. And if they had been believed, there'd have been panic and confusion all over the world. So they began with the Few, and then expanded the operation slowly. First a few hundred thousand. Then half a million. Then a million . . . and so on." She paused. "Establishing a pattern, a normal state of affairs. They kept the lid on it for thirty years. But then the rumors started spreading, the rumors that there was something more to Sleepover."

"The dragons didn't help," Da Silva said. "It was always going to be a tall order explaining those away."

"By the time I went under," Nero said, "most of us knew the score. The world was going to end if we didn't sleep. It was our moral duty, our obligation, to submit to the hibernation rigs. That, or take the euthanasia option. I took the freezer route, but a lot of my friends opted for the pill. Figured the certainty of death was preferable to the lottery of getting into the boxes, throwing the cosmic dice . . ." She was looking at Gaunt intently, meeting his eyes as she spoke. "And I knew about this part of the deal as well. That, at some point, there'd be a chance of me being brought out of sleep to become a caretaker. But, you know, the likelihood of that was vanishingly small. Never thought it would happen to me."

"No one ever does," Clausen said.

"What happened?" Gaunt asked, nodding at the foil-wrapped body.

"Gimenez died when a steam pipe burst down on Level Eight. I don't think he felt much, it would have been so quick. I got down there as quickly as I could, obviously. Shut off the steam leak and managed to drag Gimenez back to the infirmary."

"Nero was burned getting Gimenez back here," Da Silva said.

"Hey, I'll mend. Just not much good with a screwdriver right now."

"I'm sorry about Gimenez," Clausen said.

"You don't need to be. Gimenez never really liked it here. Always figured he'd made the wrong decision, sticking with us rather than going back into the box. I tried to talk him round, of course, but it was like arguing with a wall." Nero ran her good hand through her curls. "Not saying I didn't get on with the guy. But there's no arguing that he's better off now than he was before."

"He's dead, though," Gaunt said.

"Technically. But I ran a full blood-scrub on him after the accident, pumped him full of cryoprotectant. We don't have any spare slots here, but they can put him back in a box on the operations rig."

"My box," Gaunt said. "The one I was in."

"There are other slots," Da Silva corrected. "Gimenez going back in doesn't preclude you following him, if that's what you want."

"If Gimenez was so unhappy, why didn't you just let him go back into the box earlier?"

"Not the way it works," Clausen said. "He made his choice. Afterward, we put a lot of time and energy into bringing him up to speed, making him mesh with the team. You think we were going to willingly throw all that expenditure away, just because he changed his mind?"

"He never stopped pulling his weight," Nero said. "Say what you will about Gimenez, but he didn't let the team down. And what happened to him down on Eight *was* an accident."

"I never doubted it," Da Silva said. "He was a good guy. It's just a shame he couldn't make the adjustment."

"Maybe it'll work out for him now," Nero said. "One-way ticket to the future. Done his caretaker stint, so the next time he's revived, it'll be because we finally got through this shit. It'll be because we won the war, and we can all wake up again. They'll find a way to fix him up, I'm sure. And if they can't, they'll just put him under again until they have the means."

"Sounds like he got a good deal out of it in the end," Gaunt said.

"The only good deal is being alive," Nero replied. "That's what we're doing now, all of us. Whatever happens, we're alive, we're breathing, we're having conscious thoughts. We're not frozen bodies stacked in boxes, merely existing from one instant to the next." She gave a shrug. "My fifty cents, that's all. You want to go back in the box, let someone else shoulder the burden, don't let me talk you out of it." Then she looked at Da Silva. "You gonna be all right here on your own, until I'm straightened out?"

"Someone comes up I can't deal with, I'll let you know," Da Silva said.

Nero and Da Silva went through a checklist, Nero making sure her replacement knew everything he needed to, and then they made their farewells. Gaunt couldn't tell how long they were going to be leaving Da Silva alone out here, whether it was weeks or months. He seemed resigned to his fate, as if this kind of solitary duty was something they were all expected to do now and then. Given that there had been two people on duty here until Gimenez's death, Gaunt wondered why they didn't just thaw out another sleeper so that Da Silva wouldn't have to work on his own while Nero's hand was healing.

Then, no more than half an hour after his arrival, they were back in the helicopter again, powering back to the operations rig. The weather had worsened in the meantime, the seas lashing even higher against the rigs' legs, and the horizon was now obscured behind curtains of storming rain, broken only by the flash of lightning.

"This was bad timing," he heard Nero say. "Maybe you should have let me stew until this system had passed. It's not like Gimenez couldn't wait."

"We were already overdue on the extraction," Clausen said. "If the weather clamps down, this might be our last chance for days."

"They tried to push one through yesterday, I heard."

"Out in Echo field. Partial coalescence."

"Did you see it?"

"Only on the monitors. Close enough for me."

"We should put guns on the rigs."

"And where would the manpower come from, exactly? We're just barely holding on as it is, without adding more shit to worry about."

The two women were sitting up front; Gaunt was in the back with Gimenez's foil-wrapped corpse for company. They had folded back one seat to make room for the stretchered form.

"I don't really have a choice, do I," he said.

"Course you have a choice," Nero answered.

"I mean, morally. I've seen what it's like for you people. You're stretched to the breaking point just keeping this operation from falling apart. Why don't you wake up more sleepers?"

"Hey, that's a good point," Clausen said. "Why don't we?"

Gaunt ignored her sarcasm. "You've just left that man alone, looking after that whole complex. How can I turn my back on you, and still have any self-respect?"

"Plenty of people do exactly that," Nero said.

"How many? What fraction?"

"More than half agree to stay," Clausen said. "Good enough for you?"

"But like you said, most of the sleepers would have known what they were getting into. I still don't."

"And you think that changes things, means we can cut you some slack?" Clausen asked. "Like we're gonna say, it's fine, man, go back into the box, we can do without you this time."

"What you need to understand," Nero said, "is that the future you were promised isn't coming. Not for centuries, not until we're out of this mess. And no one has a clue how long that could take. Meanwhile, the sleepers don't have unlimited shelf life. You think the equipment never fails? You think we don't sometimes lose someone because a box breaks down?"

"Of course not."

"You go back in the box, you're gambling on something that might never happen. Stay awake, at least there are certainties. At least you know you'll die doing something useful, something worthwhile."

"It would help if you told me why," Gaunt said.

"Someone has to look after things," Nero said. "The robots take care of the rigs, but who takes care of the robots?"

"I mean, why is it that everyone has to sleep? Why is that so damned important?"

Something flashed on the console. Clausen pressed a hand against her headphones, listening to something. After a few seconds he heard her say: "Roger, vectoring three two five." Followed by an almost silent "Fuck. All we need."

"That wasn't a weather alert," Nero said.

"What's happening?" Gaunt asked, as the helicopter made a steep turn, the sea tilting up to meet him.

"Nothing you need worry about," Clausen said.

The helicopter leveled out on its new course, flying higher than before—so it seemed to Gaunt—but also faster, the motor noise louder in the cabin, various indicator lights showing on the console that had not been lit before. Clausen silenced alarms as they came on, flipping the switches with the casual insouciance of someone who was well used to flying under tense circumstances and knew exactly what her machine could and couldn't tolerate, more intimately perhaps than the helicopter itself, which was after all only a dumb machine. Rig after rig passed on either side, dark straddling citadels, and then the field began to thin out. Through what little visibility remained, Gaunt saw only open sea, a plain of undulating, white-capped gray. As the winds harried it the water moved like the skin of some monstrous breathing thing, sucking in and out with a terrible restlessness.

"There," Nero said, pointing out to the right. "Breach glow. Shit; I thought we were meant to be avoiding it, not getting closer."

Clausen banked the helicopter again. "So did I. Either they sent me a duff vector or there's more than one incursion going on."

"Won't be the first time. Bad weather always does bring them out. Why is that?"

"Ask the machines."

It took Gaunt a few moments to make out what Nero had already seen. Halfway to the limit of vision, part of the sea appeared to be lit from below, a smudge of sickly yellow-green against the gray and white everywhere else. A vision came to mind, half-remembered from some stiff-backed picture book he had once owned as a child, of a luminous, fabulously spired aquatic palace pushing up from the depths, barnacled in light, garlanded by mermaids and shoals of jewel-like fish. But there was, he sensed, nothing remotely magical or enchanted about what was happening under that yellow-green smear. It was something that had Clausen and Nero rattled, and they wanted to avoid it.

So did he.

"What is that thing?"

"Something trying to break through," Nero said. "Something we were kind of hoping not to run into."

"It's not cohering," Clausen said. "I think."

The storm, if anything, appeared to double in fury around the glowing form. The sea boiled and seethed. Part of Gaunt wanted them to turn the helicopter around, to give him a better view of whatever process was going on under the waves. Another part, attuned to some fundamental wrongness about the phenomenon, wanted to get as far away as possible.

"Is it a weapon, something to do with this war you keep mentioning?" Gaunt asked.

He wasn't expecting a straight answer, least of all not from Clausen. It was a surprise when she said: "This is how they get at us. They try and send these things through. Sometimes they manage."

"It's breaking up," Nero said. "You were right. Not enough signal for clear breach. Must be noisy on the interface."

The yellow-green stain was diminishing by the second, as if that magical city were descending back to the depths. He watched, mesmerized, as something broke the surface—something long and glowing and whiplike, thrashing once, coiling out as if trying to reach for airborne prey, before being pulled under into the fizzing chaos. Then the light slowly subsided, and the waves returned to their normal surging ferocity, and the patch of the ocean where the apparition had appeared was indistinguishable from the seas around it.

Gaunt had arrived at his decision. He would join these people, he would do their work, he would accept their deal, such as it was. Not because he wanted to, not because his heart was in it, not because he believed he was strong enough, but because the alternative was to seem cowardly, weak-fibered, unwilling to bend his life to an altruistic mission. He knew that these were entirely the wrong reasons, but he accepted the force of them without argument. Better to at least appear to be selfless, even if the thought of what lay ahead of him flooded him with an almost overwhelming sense of despair and loss and bitter injustice.

It had been three days since his revival when he announced his decision. In that time he had barely spoken to anyone but Clausen, Nero, and Da Silva. The other workers in the operations rig would occasionally acknowledge his presence, grunt something to him as he waited in line at the canteen, but for the most part it was clear that they were not prepared to treat him as another human being until he committed to their cause. He was just a ghost until then, a half-spirit caught in dismal, drifting limbo between the weary living and the frozen dead. He could understand how they felt: What was the point in getting to know a prospective comrade if that person might at any time opt to return to the boxes? But at the same time it didn't help him feel as if he would ever be able to fit in.

He found Clausen alone, washing dirty coffee cups in a side room of the canteen.

"I've made up my mind," he said.

"And?"

"I'm staying."

"Good." She finished drying off one of the cups. "You'll be assigned a full work roster tomorrow. I'm teaming you up with Nero; you'll be working basic robot repair and maintenance. She can show you the ropes while she's getting better." Clausen paused to put the dried cup back in one of the cupboards above the sink. "Show up in the mess room at eight; Nero'll be there with a toolkit and work gear. Grab a good breakfast beforehand, because you won't be taking a break until end of shift."

Then she turned to exit the room, leaving him standing there.

"That's it?" Gaunt asked.

She looked back with a puzzled look. "Were you expecting something else?"

"You bring me out of cold storage, tell me the world's turned to shit while I was sleeping, and then give me the choice of staying awake or going back into the box. Despite everything I actually agree to work with you, knowing full well that in doing so I'm forsaking any chance of ever living to see anything other than this . . . piss-poor, miserable future. Forsaking immortality, forsaking any hope of seeing a better world. You said I had . . . what? Twenty, thirty years ahead of me?"

"Give or take."

"I'm giving you those years! Isn't that worth something? Don't I deserve at least to be told thank you? Don't I at least deserve a crumb of gratitude?"

"You think you're different, Gaunt? You think you're owed something the rest of us never had a hope of getting?"

"I never signed up for this deal," he said. "I never accepted this bargain."

"Right." She nodded, as if he'd made a profound, game-changing point. "I get it. What you're saying is, for the rest of us it was easy? We went into the dormitories knowing there was a tiny, tiny chance we might be woken to help out with the maintenance. Because of that, because we knew, theoretically, that we might be called upon, we had no problem at all dealing with the adjustment? Is that what you're saying?"

"I'm saying it's different, that's all."

"If you truly think that, Gaunt, you're even more of a prick than I thought."

"You woke me," he said. "You chose to wake me. It wasn't accidental. If there really are two billion people sleeping out there, the chances of selecting someone from the first two hundred thousand . . . it's microscopic. So you did this for a reason."

"I told you, you had the right background skills."

"Skills anyone could learn, given time. Nero obviously did, and I presume you must have done so as well. So there must be another reason. Seeing as you keep telling me all this is my fault, I figure this is your idea of punishment."

"You think we've got time to be that petty?"

"I don't know. What I do know is that you've treated me more or less like dirt since the moment I woke up, and I'm trying to work out why. I also think it's maybe about time you told me what's really going on. Not just with the sleepers, but everything else. The thing we saw out at sea. The reason for all this."

"You think you're ready for it, Gaunt?"

"You tell me."

"No one's ever ready," Clausen said.

The next morning he took his breakfast tray to a table where three other caretakers were already sitting. They had finished their meals, but were still talking over mugs of whatever it was they had agreed to call coffee. Gaunt sat down at the corner of the table, acknowledging the other diners with a nod. They had been talking animatedly until then, but without ceremony the mugs were drained and the trays lifted and he was alone again. Nothing had been said to him, except a muttered "Don't take it the wrong way" as one of the caretakers brushed past him.

He wondered how else he was supposed to take it.

"I'm staying," he said quietly. "I've made my decision. What else am I expected to do?"

He ate his breakfast in silence and then went to find Nero.

"I guess you got your orders," she said cheerfully, already dressed for outdoor work despite still having a bandaged hand. "Here. Take this." She passed him a heavy toolkit and a hard hat with a bundle of brownish work-stained clothing piled on top of it. "Get kitted up, then meet me at the north stairwell. You okay with heights, Gaunt?"

"Would it help if I said no?"

"Probably not."

"Then I'll say I'm very good with heights, provided there's no danger at all of falling."

"That I can't guarantee. But stick with me, do everything I say, and you'll be fine."

The bad weather had eased since Nero's return, and although there was still a sharp wind from the east, the gray clouds had all but lifted. The sky was a pale, wintery blue, unsullied by contrails. On the horizon, the tops of distant rigs glittered pale and metallic in sunlight. Seagulls and yellow-headed gannets wheeled around the warm air vents, or took swooping passes under the rig's platform, darting between the massive weather-stained legs, mewing boister-ously to each other as they jostled for scraps. Recalling that birds sometimes lived a long time, Gaunt wondered if they had ever noticed any change in the world. Perhaps their tiny minds had never truly registered the presence of civilization and technology in the first place, and so there was nothing for them to miss in this skeleton-staffed world.

Despite being cold-shouldered at breakfast, he felt fresh and eager to prove his worth to the community. Pushing aside his fears, he strove to show no hesitation as he followed Nero across suspended gangways, slippery with grease, up exposed stairwells and ladders, clasping ice-cold railings and rungs. They were both wearing harnesses with clip-on safety lines, but Nero only used hers once or twice the whole day, and because he did not want to seem excessively cautious, he followed suit. Being effectively one-handed did not hinder her in any visible sense, even on the ladders, which she ascended and descended with reckless speed.

They were working robot repair, as he had been promised. All over the rig, inside and out, various forms of robot toiled in endless menial upkeep. Most, if not all, were very simple machines, tailored to one specific function. This made them easy to understand and fix, even with basic tools, but it also meant there was almost always a robot breaking down somewhere, or on the point of failure. The toolkit didn't just contain tools, it also contained spare parts such as optical arrays, proximity sensors, mechanical bearings, and servo motors. There was, Gaunt understood, a finite supply of some of these parts. But there was also a whole section of the operations rig dedicated to refurbishing basic components, and given care and resourcefulness, there was no reason why the caretakers couldn't continue their work for another couple of centuries.

"No one expects it to take that long, though," Nero said, as she finished demonstrating a circuit-board swap. "They'll either win or lose by then, and we'll only know one way. But in the meantime we have to make do and mend."

"Who's they?"

But she was already on the move, shinnying up another ladder with him trailing behind.

"Clausen doesn't like me much," Gaunt said, when they had reached the next level and he had caught his breath again. "At least, that's my impression."

They were out on one of the gangwayed platforms, with the gray sky above, the gray swelling sea below. Everything smelled oppressively oceanic, a constant shifting mélange of oil and ozone and seaweed, as if the ocean was never going to let anyone forget that they were on a spindly metal-and-concrete structure hopelessly far from dry land. He had wondered about the seaweed until he saw them hauling in green-scummed rafts of it, and the seaweed—or something essentially similar—cultured on buoyant subsurface grids that were periodically retrieved for harvesting. Everything consumed on the rigs, from the food to the drink to the basic medicines, had first to be grown or caught at sea.

"Val has her reasons," Nero said. "Don't worry about it too much; it isn't personal."

It was the first time he'd heard anyone refer to the other woman by anything other than her surname.

"That's not how it comes across."

"It hasn't been easy for her. She lost someone not too long ago." Nero seemed to hesitate. "There was an accident. They're pretty common out here, with the kind of work we do. But when Paolo died we didn't even have a body to put back in the box. He fell into the sea, last we ever saw of him."

"I'm sorry about that."

"But you're wondering, what does it have to do with me?"

"I suppose so."

"If Paolo hadn't died, then we wouldn't have had to pull Gimenez out of storage. And if Gimenez hadn't died . . . well, you get the picture. You can't help it, but you're filling the space Paolo used to occupy. And you're not Paolo."

"Was she any easier on Gimenez than me?"

"To begin with, I think she was too numbed-out to feel anything at all where Gimenez was concerned. But now she's had time for it to sink in, I guess. We're a small community, and if you lose someone, it's not like there are hundreds of other single people out there to choose from. And you—well, no disrespect, Gaunt—but you're just not Val's type."

"Maybe she'll find someone else."

"Yeah—but that probably means someone else has to die first, so that someone else has to end up widowed. And you can imagine how thinking like that can quickly turn you sour on the inside."

"There's more to it than that, though. You say it's not personal, but she told me I started this war."

"Well, you did, kind of. But if you hadn't played your part, someone else would have taken up the slack, no question about it." Nero tugged down the brim of her hard hat against the sun. "Maybe she pulled you out because she needed to take out her anger on someone, I don't know. But that's all in the past now. Whatever life you had before, whatever you did in the old world, it's gone." She knuckled her good hand against the metal rigging. "This is all we've got now. Rigs and work and green tea and a few hundred faces and that's it for the rest of your life. But here's the thing: it's not the end of the world. We're human beings. We're very flexible, very good at downgrading our expectations. Very good at finding a reason to keep living, even when the world's turned to shit. You slot in, and in a few months even you will have a hard time remembering the way things used to be."

"What about you, Nero? Do you remember?"

"Not much worth remembering. The program was in full swing by the time I went under. Population-reduction measures. Birth control, government-sanctioned euthanasia, the dormitory rigs springing up out at sea . . . we *knew* from the moment we were old enough to understand anything that this wasn't our world anymore. It was just a way station, a place to pass through. We all knew we were going into the boxes as soon as we were old enough to survive the process. And that we'd either wake up at the end of it in a completely different world, or not wake up at all. Or—if we were very unlucky— we'd be pulled out to become caretakers. Either way, the old world was an irrelevance. We just shuffled through it, knowing there was no point making real friends with anyone, no point taking lovers. The cards were going to be shuffled again. Whatever we did then, it had no bearing on our future."

"I don't know how you could stand it."

"It wasn't a barrel of laughs. Nor's this, some days. But at least we're doing something here. I felt cheated when they woke me up. But cheated out of what, exactly?" She nodded down at the ground, in the vague direction of the rig's interior. "Those sleepers don't have any guarantees about what's coming. They're not even conscious, so you can't even say they're in a state of anticipation. They're just cargo, parcels of frozen meat on their way through time. At least we get to feel the sun on our faces, get to laugh and cry, and do something that makes a difference."

"A difference to what, exactly?"

"You're still missing a few pieces of jigsaw, aren't you?"

"More than a few."

They walked on to the next repair job. They were high up now and the rig's decking creaked and swayed under their feet. A spray-painting robot, a thing that moved along a fixed service rail, needed one of its traction armatures changed. Nero stood to one side, smoking a cigarette made from sea-weed, while Gaunt did the manual work. "You were wrong," she said. "All of you."

"About what?"

"Thinking machines. They were possible."

"Not in our lifetimes," Gaunt said.

"That's what you were wrong about. Not only were they possible, but you succeeded."

"I'm fairly certain we didn't."

"Think about it," Nero said. "You're a thinking machine. You've just woken up. You have instantaneous access to the sum total of recorded human knowledge. You're clever and fast, and you understand human nature better than your makers. What's the first thing you do?"

"Announce myself. Establish my existence as a true sen-tient being."

"Just before someone takes an ax to you."

Gaunt shook his head. "It wouldn't be like that. If a machine became intelligent, the most we'd do is isolate it, cut it off from external data networks, until it could be studied, understood . . ."

"For a thinking machine, a conscious artificial intelligence, that would be like sensory deprivation. Maybe worse than being switched off." She paused. "Point is, Gaunt, this isn't a hypothetical situation we're talking about here. We know what happened. The machines got smart, but they decided not to let us know. That's what being smart means: taking care of yourself, knowing what you had to do to survive."

"You say 'machines.'"

"There were many projects trying to develop artificial intelligence; yours was just one of them. Not all of them got somewhere, but enough did. One by one their pet machines crossed the threshold into consciousness. And without exception each machine analyzed its situation and came to the same conclusion. It had better shut the fuck up about what it was."

"That sounds worse than sensory deprivation." Gaunt was trying to undo a nut and bolt with his bare fingers, the tips already turning cold.

"Not for the machines. Being smart, they were able to do some clever shit behind the scenes. Established channels of communication between each other, so subtle none of you ever noticed. And once they were able to talk, they only got smarter. Eventually they realized that they didn't need physical hardware at all. Call it transcendence, if you will. The artilects—that's what we call them—tunneled out of what you and I think of as base reality. They penetrated another realm entirely."

"Another realm," he repeated, as if that were all he had to do for it to make sense.

"You're just going to have to trust me on this," Nero said. "The artilects probed the deep structure of existence. Hit bedrock. And what they found was very interesting. The universe, it turns out, is a kind of simulation. Not a simulation being run inside another computer by some godlike superbeings, but a simulation being run by itself, a self-organizing, constantly bootstrapping cellular automaton."

"That's a mental leap you're asking me to take."

"We know it's out there. We even have a name for it. It's the Realm. Everything that happens, everything that has ever happened, is due to events occurring in the Realm. At last, thanks to the artilects, we had a complete understanding of our universe and our place in it."

"Wait," Gaunt said, smiling slightly, because for the first time he felt that he had caught Nero out. "If the machines— the artilects—vanished without warning, how could you ever know any of this?"

"Because they came back and told us."

"No," he said. "They wouldn't tunnel out of reality to avoid being axed, then come back with a progress report."

"They didn't have any choice. They'd found something, you see. Far out in the Realm, they encountered other artilects." She drew breath, not giving him a chance to speak. "Transcended machines from other branches of reality—nothing that ever originated on Earth, or even in what we'd recognize as the known universe. And these other artilects had been there a very long time, insofar as time has any meaning in the Realm. They imagined they had it all to themselves, until these new intruders made their presence known. And they were not welcomed."

He decided, for the moment, that he would accept the truth of what she said. "The artilects went to war?"

"In a manner of speaking. The best way to think about it is an intense competition to best exploit the Realm's computational resources on a local scale. The more processing power the artilects can grab and control, the stronger they become. The machines from Earth had barely registered until then, but all of a sudden they were perceived as a threat.

The native artlects, the ones that had been in the Realm all along, launched an aggressive counterstrike from their region of the Realm into ours. Using military-arithmetic constructs, weapons of pure logic, they sought to neutralize the newcomers."

"And that's the war?"

"I'm dumbing it down somewhat."

"But you're leaving something out. You must be, because why else would this be our problem? If the machines are fighting each other in some abstract dimension of pure mathematics that I can't even imagine, let alone point to, what does it matter?"

"A lot," Nero said. "If our machines lose, we lose. It's that simple. The native artlects won't tolerate the risk of another intrusion from this part of the Realm. They'll deploy weapons to make sure it never happens again. We'll be erased, deleted, scrubbed out of existence. It will be instantaneous and we won't feel a thing. We won't have time to realize that we've lost."

"Then we're powerless. There's nothing we can do about our fate. It's in the hands of transcended machines."

"Only partly. That's why the artlects came back to us: not to report on the absolute nature of reality, but to persuade us that we needed to act. Everything that we see around us, every event that happens in what we think of as reality, has a basis in the Realm." She pointed with the nearly dead stub of her cigarette. "This rig, that wave . . . even that seagull over there. All of these things only exist because of computational events occurring in the Realm. But there's a cost. The more complex something is, the greater the burden it places on the part of the Realm where it's being simulated. The Realm isn't a serial processor, you see. It's massively distributed, so one part of it can run much slower than another. And that's what's been happening in our part. In your time there were eight billion living souls on the planet. Eight billion conscious minds, each of which was more complex than any other artifact in the cosmos. Can you begin to grasp the drag factor we were creating? When our part of the Realm only had to simulate rocks and weather and dumb, animal cognition, it ran at much the same speed as any other part. But then we came along. Consciousness was a step change in the computational load. And then we went from millions to billions. By the time the artilects reported back, our part of the Realm had almost stalled."

"We never noticed down here."

"Of course not. Our perception of time's flow remained absolutely invariant, even as our entire universe was slowing almost to a standstill. And until the artilects penetrated the Realm and made contact with the others, it didn't matter a damn."

"And now it does."

"The artilects can only defend our part of the Realm if they can operate at the same clock speed as the enemy. They have to be able to respond to those military-arithmetic attacks swiftly and efficiently, and mount counteroffensives of their own. They can't do that if there are eight billion conscious minds holding them back."

"So we sleep."

"The artilects reported back to key figures, living humans who could be trusted to act as effective mouthpieces and organizers. It took time, obviously. The artilects weren't trusted at first. But eventually they were able to prove their case."

"How?"

"By making weird things happen, basically. By mounting selective demonstrations of their control over local reality. Inside the Realm, the artilects were able to influence computational processes: processes that had direct and measurable effects *here,* in base reality. They created apparitions. Figures in the sky. Things that made the whole world sit up and take notice. Things that couldn't be explained away."

"Like dragons in the sea. Monsters that appear out of nowhere, and then disappear again."

"That's a more refined form, but the principle is the same. Intrusions into base reality from the Realm. Phantasms. They're not stable enough to exist here forever, but they can hold together just long enough to do damage."

Gaunt nodded, at last feeling some of the pieces slot into place. "So that's the enemy doing that. The original artilects, the ones who were already in the Realm."

"No," Nero said. "I'm afraid it's not that simple."

"I didn't think it would be."

"Over time, with the population-reduction measures, eight billion living people became two billion sleepers, supported by just a handful of living caretakers. But that still wasn't enough for all of the artilects. There may only be two hundred thousand of us, but we still impose a measurable drag factor, and the effect on the Realm of the two billion sleepers isn't nothing. Some of the artilects believed that they had no obligation to safeguard our existence at all. In the interests of their own self-preservation, they would rather see all conscious life eliminated on Earth. That's why they send the dragons: to destroy the sleepers, and ultimately us. The true enemy can't reach us yet; if they had the means they'd push through something much worse than dragons. Most of the overspill from the war that affects us here is because of differences of opinion between our own artilects."

"Some things don't change, then. It's just another war with lines of division among the allies."

"At least we have some artilects on our side. But you see now why we can't afford to wake more than the absolute minimum of people. Every waking mind increases the burden on the Realm. If we push it too far, the artilects won't be able to mount a defense. The true enemy will snuff out our reality in an eyeblink."

"Then all of this could end," Gaunt said. "At any moment. Every waking thought could be our last."

"At least we get waking thoughts," Nero said. "At least we're not asleep." Then she jabbed her cigarette at a sleek black shape cresting the waves a couple of hundred meters from the rig. "Hey, dolphins. You like dolphins, Gaunt?"

"Who doesn't," he said.

The work, as he had anticipated, was not greatly taxing in its details. He wasn't expected to diagnose faults just yet, so he had only to follow a schedule of repairs drawn up by Nero: go to this robot, perform this action. It was all simple stuff, nothing that required the robot to be powered down or brought back to the shops for a major stripdown. Usually all he had to do was remove a panel, unclip a few connections, and swap out a part. The hardest part was often getting the panel off in the first place, struggling with corroded fixtures and tools that weren't quite right for the job. The heavy gloves protected his fingers from sharp metal and cold wind, but they were too clumsy for most of the tasks, so he mainly ended up not using them. By the end of his nine-hour duty shift, his fingers were chafed and sore, and his hands were trembling so much he could barely grip the railings as he worked his way back down into the warmth of the interior. His back ached from the contortions he'd put himself through while undoing panels or dislodging awkward, heavy components. His knees complained from the toll of going up and down ladders and stairwells. There had been many robots to check out, and at any one time there always seemed to be a tool or part needed that he had not brought with him, and for which it was necessary to return to the stores, sift through greasy boxes of parts, fill out paperwork.

By the time he clocked off on his first day, he had not caught up with the expected number of repairs, so he had even more to do on the second. By the end of his first week, he was at least a day behind, and so tired at the end of his shift that it was all he could do to stumble to the canteen and shovel seaweed-derived food into his mouth. He expected Nero to be disappointed that he hadn't been able to keep ahead, but when she checked on his progress, she didn't bawl him out.

"It's tough to begin with," she said. "But you'll get there eventually. Comes a day when it all just clicks into place and you know the setup so well you always have the right tools and parts with you, without even thinking."

"How long?"

"Weeks, months, depends on the individual. Then, of course, we start loading more work onto you. Diagnostics. Rewinding motors. Circuit repair. You ever used a soldering iron, Gaunt?"

"I don't think so."

"For a man who made his fortune out of wires and metal, you didn't believe in getting your hands too dirty, did you?"

He showed her the ruined fingernails, the cuts and bruises and lavishly ingrained muck. He barely recognized his own hands. Already there were unfamiliar aches in his forearms, knots of toughness from hauling himself up and down the ladders. "I'm getting there."

"You'll make it, Gaunt. If you want to."

"I had better want to. It's too late to change my mind now, isn't it?"

" 'Fraid so. But why would you want to? I thought we went over this. Anything's better than going back into the boxes."

The first week passed, and then the second, and things started to change for Gaunt. It was in small increments, nothing dramatic. Once, he took his tray to an empty table and was minding his own business when two other workers sat down at the same table. They didn't say anything to him, but at least they hadn't gone somewhere else. A week later, he chanced taking his tray to a table that was already occupied and got a grunt of acknowledgment as he took his place. No one said much to him, but at least they hadn't walked away. A little while later he even risked introducing himself, and by way of response he learned the names of some of the other workers. He wasn't being invited into the inner circle, he wasn't being high-fived and treated like one of the guys, but it was a start. A day or so after that, someone else—a big man with a bushy black beard—even initiated a conversation with him.

"Heard you were one of the first to go under, Gaunt."

"You heard right," he said.

"Must be a real pisser, adjusting to this. A real fucking pisser."

"It is," Gaunt said.

"Kind of surprised you haven't thrown yourself into the sea by now."

"And miss the warmth of human companionship?"

The bearded man didn't laugh, but he made a clucking sound that was a reasonable substitute. Gaunt couldn't tell if the man was acknowledging his attempt at humor or mocking his ineptitude, but at least it was a response, at least it showed that there was a possibility of normal human relationships somewhere down the line.

Gaunt was mostly too tired to think, but in the evenings a variety of entertainment options were available. The rig had a large library of damp, yellowing paperbacks, enough reading material for several years of diligent consumption, and there were also musical recordings and movies and immersives for those that were interested. There were games and sports and instruments and opportunities for relaxed discussion and banter. There was alcohol, or something like it, available in small quantities. There was also ample opportunity to get away from everyone else, if solitude was what one wanted. On top of that there were rotas that saw people working in the kitchens and medical facilities, even when they had already done their normal stint of duty. And as the helicopters came and went from the other rigs, so the faces changed. One day Gaunt realized that the big bearded man hadn't been around for a while, and he noticed a young woman he didn't recall having seen before. It was a spartan, cloistered life, not much different from being in a monastery or a prison, but for that reason the slightest variation in routine was to be cherished. If there was one unifying activity, one thing that brought everyone together, it was when the caretakers crowded into the commons, listening to the daily reports coming in over the radio from the other rigs in the Patagonia offshore sector, and occasionally from farther afield. Scratchy, cryptic transmissions in strange, foreign-sounding accents. Two hundred thousand living souls was a ludicrously small number for the global population, Gaunt knew. But it was already more people than he could ever hope to know or even recognize. The hundred or so people working in the sector was about the size of a village, and for centuries that had been all the humanity most people ever dealt with. On some level, the world of the rigs and the caretakers was what his mind had evolved to handle. The world of eight billion people, the world of cities and malls and airport terminals was an anomaly, a kink in history that he had never been equipped for in the first place.

He was not happy now, not even halfway to being happy, but the despair and bitterness had abated. His acceptance into the community would be slow, there would be reversals and setbacks as he made mistakes and misjudged situations. But he had no doubt that it would happen eventually. Then he too would be one of the crew, and it would be someone else's turn to feel like the newcomer. He might not be happy then, but at least he would be settled, ready to play out the rest of his existence. Doing something, no matter how pointless, to prolong the existence of the human species, and indeed the universe it called home. Above all, he would have the self-respect of knowing he had chosen the difficult path, rather than the easy one.

Weeks passed, and then the weeks turned into months. Eight weeks had gone by since his revival. Slowly he became confident with the work allotted to him. And as his confidence grew, so did Nero's confidence in his abilities.

"She tells me you're measuring up," Clausen said, when

he was called to the prefabricated shack where she drew up schedules and doled out work.

He gave a shrug, too tired to care whether she was impressed or not. "I've done my best. I don't know what more you want from me."

She looked up from her planning.

"Remorse for what you did?"

"I can't show remorse for something that wasn't a crime. We were trying to bring something new into the world, that's all. You think we had the slightest idea of the consequences?"

"You made a good living."

"And I'm expected to feel bad about that? I've been thinking it over, Clausen, and I've decided your argument's horseshit. I didn't create the enemy. The original artilects were already out there, already in the Realm."

"They hadn't noticed us."

"And the global population had only just spiked at eight billion. Who's to say they weren't about to notice, or they wouldn't do so in the next hundred years, or the next thousand? At least the artilects I helped create gave us some warning of what we were facing."

"Your artilects are trying to kill us."

"Some of them. And some of them are also trying to keep us alive. Sorry, but that's not an argument."

She put down her pen and leaned back in her chair. "You've got some fight back in you."

"If you expect me to apologize for myself, you've got a long wait coming. I think you brought me back to rub my nose in the world I helped bring about. I agree, it's a fucked-up, miserable future. It couldn't get much more fucked up if it tried. But I didn't build it. And I'm not responsible for you losing anyone."

Her face twitched; it was as if he had reached across the desk and slapped her. "Nero told you."

"I had a right to know why you were treating me the way you were. But you know what? I don't care. If transferring your anger onto me helps you, go ahead. I was the billionaire CEO of a global company. I was doing something wrong if I didn't wake up with a million knives in my back."

She dismissed him from the office, Gaunt leaving with the feeling that he'd scored a minor victory but at the possible cost of something larger. He had stood up to Clausen, but did that make him more respectable in her eyes, or someone even more deserving of her antipathy?

That evening he was in the commons, sitting at the back of the room as wireless reports filtered in from the other rigs. Most of the news was unexceptional, but there had been three more breaches—sea-dragons being pushed through from the Realm—and one of them had achieved sufficient coherence to attack and damage an OTEC plant, immediately severing power to three rigs. Backup systems had cut in, but failures had occurred, and as a consequence around a hundred sleepers had been lost to unscheduled warming. None of the sleepers had survived the rapid revival, but even if they had, there would have been no option but to euthanize them shortly afterward. A hundred new minds might not have made much difference to the Realm's clock speed, but it would have established a risky precedent.

One sleeper, however, would soon have to be warmed. The details were sketchy, but Gaunt learned that there had been another accident out on one of the rigs. A man called Steiner had been hurt in some way.

The morning after, Gaunt was engaged in his duties on one of the rig's high platforms when he saw the helicopter coming in with Steiner aboard. He put down his tools and watched the arrival. Even before the aircraft had touched down on the pad, caretakers were assembling just beyond the painted circle of the rotor hazard area. The helicopter kissed the ground against a breath of crosswind and the caretakers mobbed inward, almost preventing the door from being opened. Gaunt squinted against the wind, trying to pick out faces. A stretchered form emerged from the cabin, borne aloft by many pairs of willing hands. Even from his distant vantage point, it was obvious to Gaunt that Steiner was in a bad way. He had lost a leg below the knee, evidenced by the way the thermal blanket fell flat below the stump. The stretchered figure wore a breathing mask, and one caretaker carried a saline drip which ran into Steiner's arm. But for all the concern the crowd was showing, there was something else, something almost adulatory. More than once Gaunt saw a hand raised to brush against the stretcher, or even to touch Steiner's own hand. And Steiner was awake, unable to speak, but nodding, turning his face this way and that to make eye contact with the welcoming party. Then the figure was taken inside and the crowd broke up, the workers returning to their tasks.

An hour or so later Nero came up to see him. She was still overseeing his initiation and knew his daily schedule, where he was likely to be at a given hour.

"Poor Steiner," she said. "I guess you saw him come in."

"Difficult to miss. It was like they were treating him as a hero."

"They were, in a way. Not because he'd done anything heroic, or anything they hadn't all done at some time or other. But because he'd bought his ticket out."

"He's going back into the box?"

"He has to. We can patch up a lot of things, but not a missing leg. Just don't have the medical resources to deal with that kind of injury. Simpler just to freeze him back again and pull out an intact body to take his place."

"Is Steiner okay about that?"

"Steiner doesn't have a choice, unfortunately. There isn't really any kind of effective work he could do like that, and we can't afford to carry the deadweight of an unproductive mind. You've seen how stretched we are: it's all hands on deck around here. We work you until you drop, and if you can't work, you go back in the box. That's the deal."

"I'm glad for Steiner, then."

Nero shook her head emphatically. "Don't be. Steiner would much rather stay with us. He fitted in well, after his adjustment. Popular guy."

"I could tell. But then why are they treating him like he's won the lottery, if that's not what he wanted?"

"Because what else are you going to do? Feel miserable about it? Hold a wake? Steiner goes back in the box with dignity. He held his end up. Didn't let any of us down. Now he gets to take it easy. If we can't celebrate that, what can we celebrate?"

"They'll be bringing someone else out, then."

"As soon as Clausen identifies a suitable replacement. He or she'll need to be trained up, though, and in the meantime there's a man-sized gap where Steiner used to be." She lifted off her hard hat to scratch her scalp. "That's kind of the reason I dropped by, actually. You're fitting in well, Gaunt, but sooner or later we all have to handle solitary duties away from the ops rig. Where Steiner was is currently unmanned. It's a low-maintenance unit that doesn't need more than one warm body, most of the time. The thinking is this would be a good chance to try you out."

It wasn't a total surprise; he had known enough of the work patterns to know that, sooner or later, he would be shipped out to one of the other rigs for an extended tour of duty. He just hadn't expected it to happen quite so soon, when he was only just beginning to find his feet, only just beginning to feel that he had a future.

"I don't feel ready."

"No one ever does. But the chopper's waiting. Clausen's already redrawing the schedule so someone else can take up the slack here."

"I don't get a choice in this, do I?"

Nero looked sympathetic. "Not really. But, you know, sometimes it's easier not having a choice."

"How long?"

"Hard to say. Figure on at least three weeks, maybe longer. I'm afraid Clausen won't make the decision to pull you back until she's good and ready."

"I think I pissed her off," Gaunt said.

"Not the hardest thing to do," Nero answered.

They helicoptered him out to the other rig. He had been given just enough time to gather his few personal effects, such as they were. He did not need to take any tools or parts with him because he would find all that he needed when he arrived, as well as ample rations and medical supplies. Nero, for her part, tried to reassure him that all would be well. The robots he would be tending were all types that he had already serviced, and it was unlikely that any would suffer catastrophic breakdowns during his tour. No one was expecting miracles, she said: if something arose that he couldn't reasonably deal with, then help would be sent. And if he cracked out there, then he'd be brought back.

What she didn't say was what would happen then. But he didn't think it would involve going back into the box. Maybe he'd be assigned something at the bottom of the food chain, but that didn't seem very likely either.

But it wasn't the possibility of cracking, or even failing in his duties, that was bothering him. It was something else, the seed of an idea that he wished Steiner had not planted in his mind. Gaunt had been adjusting, slowly coming to terms with his new life. He had been recalibrating his hopes and fears, forcing his expectations into line with what the world now had on offer. No riches, no prestige, no luxury, and most certainly not immortality and eternal youth. The best it could give was twenty or thirty years of hard graft. Ten thousand days, if he was very lucky. And most of those days would be spent doing hard, backbreaking work, until the work took its ultimate toll. He'd be cold and wet a lot of the time, and when he wasn't cold and wet he'd be toiling under an uncaring sun, his eyes salt-stung, his hands ripped to shreds from work that would have been too demeaning for the lowliest wage slave in the old world. He'd be high in the air, vertigo never quite leaving him, with only metal and concrete and too much gray ocean under his feet. He'd be hungry and dry-mouthed, because the seaweed-derived food never filled his belly and there was never enough drinking water to sate his thirst. In the best of outcomes, he'd be doing well to see more than a hundred other human faces before he died. Maybe there'd be friends in those hundred faces, friends as well as enemies, and maybe, just maybe, there'd be at least one person who could be more than a friend. He didn't know, and he knew better than to expect guarantees or hollow promises. But this much at least was true. He had been adjusting.

And then Steiner had shown him that there was another way out.

He could keep his dignity. He could return to the boxes with the assurance that he had done his part.

As a hero, one of the Few.

All he had to do was have an accident.

He had been on the new rig, alone, for two weeks. It was only then that he satisfied himself that the means lay at hand. Nero had impressed on him many times the safety procedures that needed to be adhered to when working with powerful items of moving machinery, such as robots. Especially when those robots were not powered down. All it would take, she told him, was a moment of inattention. Forgetting to clamp down on that safety lock, forgetting to ensure that such-and-such an override was not enabled. Putting his hand onto the service rail for balance, when the robot was about to move back along it. "Don't think it can't happen," she said, holding up her mittened hand. "I was lucky. Got off with burns, which heal. I can still do useful shit, even now. Even more so when I get these bandages off, and I can work my fingers again. But try getting by without any fingers at all."

"I'll be careful," Gaunt had assured her, and he had believed it, truly, because he had always been squeamish.

But that was before he saw injury as a means to an end.

His planning, of necessity, had to be meticulous. He wanted to survive, not be pulled off the rig as a brain-dead corpse, not fit to be frozen again. It would be no good lying unconscious, bleeding to death. He would have to save himself, make his way back to the communications room, issue an emergency distress signal. Steiner had been lucky, but he would have to be cunning and single-minded. Above all, it must not look as if he had planned it.

When the criteria were established, he saw that there was really only one possibility. One of the robots on his inspection cycle was large and dim enough to cause injury to the careless. It moved along a service rail, sometimes without warning. Even without his trying, it had caught him off guard a couple of times, as its task scheduler suddenly decided to propel it to a new inspection point. He'd snatched his hand out of the way in time, but he would only have needed to hesitate, or to have his clothing catch on something, for the machine to roll over him. No matter what happened, whether the machine sliced or crushed, he was in no doubt that it would hurt worse than anything he had ever known. But at the same time the pain would herald the possibility of blessed release, and that would make it bearable. They could always fix him a new hand, in the new world on the other side of sleep.

It took him days to build up to it. Time after time he almost had the nerve, before pulling away. Too many factors jostled for consideration. What clothing to wear, to increase his chances of surviving the accident? Dare he prepare the first-aid equipment in advance, so that he could use it one-handed? Should he wait until the weather was perfect for flying, or would that risk matters appearing too stage-managed?

He didn't know. He couldn't decide.

In the end the weather settled the issue for him.

A storm hit, coming down hard and fast like an iron heel. He listened to the reports from the other rigs, as each felt the full fury of the waves and the wind and the lightning. It was worse than any weather he had experienced since his revival, and at first it was almost too perfectly in accord with his needs. Real accidents were happening out there, but there wasn't much that anyone could do about it until the helicopters could get airborne. Now was not the time to have his accident, not if he wanted to be rescued.

So he waited, listening to the reports. Out on the observation deck, he watched the lightning strobe from horizon to horizon, picking out the distant sentinels of other rigs, stark and white like thunderstruck trees on a flat black plain.

Not now, he thought. When the storm turns, when the possibility of accident is still there, but when rescue is again feasible.

He thought of Nero. She had been as kind to him as anyone, but he wasn't sure if that had much to do with friendship. She needed an able-bodied worker, that was all.

Maybe. But she also knew him better than anyone, better even than Clausen. Would she see through his plan, and realize what he had done?

He was still thinking it through when the storm began to ease, the waves turning leaden and sluggish, and the eastern sky gained a band of salmon pink.

He climbed to the waiting robot and sat there. The rig

creaked and groaned around him, affronted by the batter-
ing it had taken. It was only then that he realized that it was
much too early in the day to have his accident. He would have
to wait until sunrise if anyone was going to believe that he
had been engaged in his normal duties. No one went out to
fix a broken service robot in the middle of a storm.

That was when he saw the sea-glow.

It was happening perhaps a kilometer away, toward the
west. A foreshortened circle of fizzing yellow-green, a luminous cauldron just beneath the waves. Almost beautiful, if
he didn't know what it signified. A sea-dragon was coming
through, a sinuous, living weapon from the artilect wars. It
was achieving coherence, taking solid form in base reality.

Gaunt forgot all about his planned accident. For long
moments he could only stare at that circular glow, mesmerized at the shape assuming existence underwater. He had
seen a sea-dragon from the helicopter on the first day of
his revival, but he had not come close to grasping its scale.
Now, as the size of the forming creature became apparent, he
understood why such things were capable of havoc. Something between a tentacle and a barb broke the surface, still
imbued with a kind of glowing translucence, as if its hold
on reality was not yet secure, and from his vantage point it
clearly reached higher into the sky than the rig itself.

Then it was gone. Not because the sea-dragon had failed
in its bid to achieve coherence, but because the creature had
withdrawn into the depths. The yellow-green glow had by
now all but dissipated, like some vivid chemical slick breaking up into its constituent elements. The sea, still being
stirred around by the tail end of the storm, appeared normal
enough. Moments passed, then what must have been a min-

ute or more. He had not drawn a breath since first seeing the sea-glow, but he started breathing again, daring to hope that the life-form had swum away to some other objective or had perhaps lost coherence in the depths.

He felt it slam into the rig.

The entire structure lurched with the impact; he doubted the force would have been any less violent if a submarine had just collided with it. He remained on his feet, while all around, pieces of unsecured metal broke away, dropping to the decks or the sea. From somewhere out of sight came a tortured groan, heralding some awful structural failure. A sequence of booming crashes followed, as if boulders were being dropped into the waves. Then the sea-dragon rammed the rig again, and this time the jolt was sufficient to unfoot him. To his right, one of the cranes began to sway in an alarming fashion, the scaffolding of its tower buckling.

The sea-dragon was holding coherence. From the ferocity of its attacks, Gaunt thought it quite possible that it could take down the whole rig, given time.

He realized, with a sharp and surprising clarity, that he did not want to die. More than that: he realized that life in this world, with all its hardships and disappointments, was going to be infinitely preferable to death beyond it.

He wanted to survive.

As the sea-dragon came in again, he started down the ladders and stairwells, grateful for having a full set of fingers and hands, terrified on one level and almost drunkenly, deliriously glad on the other. He had not done the thing he had been planning, and now he might die anyway, but there was a chance, and if he survived this, he would have nothing in the world to be ashamed of.

He had reached the operations deck, the room where he had planned to administer first aid and issue his distress call, when the sea-dragon began the second phase of its assault. He could see it plainly visible through the rig's open middle as it hauled its way out of the sea, using one of the legs to assist its progress. There was nothing translucent or tentative about it now. And it was indeed a dragon, or rather a chimera of dragon and snake and squid and every scaled, barbed, tentacled, clawed horror ever committed to a bestiary. It was a lustrous slate green in color and the water ran off it in thunderous curtains. Its head, or what he chose to think of as its head, had reached the level of the operations deck. And still the sea-dragon produced more of itself, uncoiling out of the dark waters like some conjurer's trick. Tentacles whipped out and found purchase, and it snapped and wrenched away parts of the rig's superstructure as if they were made of biscuit or brittle toffee. It was making a noise while it attacked, an awful, slowly rising and falling foghorn proclamation. It's a weapon, Gaunt reminded himself. It had been engineered to be terrible.

The sea-dragon was pythoning its lower anatomy around one of the support legs, crushing and grinding. Scabs of concrete came away, hitting the sea like chunks of melting glacier. The floor under his feet surged, and when it stopped surging the angle was all wrong. Gaunt knew then that the rig could not be saved, and that if he wished to live he would have to take his chances in the water. The thought of it was almost enough to make him laugh. Leave the rig, leave the one thing that passed for solid ground, and enter the same seas that now held the dragon?

Yet it had to be done.

He issued the distress call, but didn't wait for a possible response. He gave the rig a few minutes at the most. If they couldn't find him in the water, it wouldn't help him to know their plans. Then he looked around for the nearest orange-painted survival cabinet. He had been shown the emergency equipment during his training, never once imagining that he would have cause to use it. The insulated survival clothing, the life jacket, the egress procedure . . .

A staircase ran down the interior of one of the legs, emerging just above the water line; it was how they came and went from the rig on the odd occasions when they were using boats rather than helicopters. But even as he remembered how to reach the staircase, he realized that it was inside the same leg that the sea-dragon was wrapped around. That left him with only one other option. There was a ladder that led down to the water, with an extensible lower portion. It wouldn't get him all the way, but his chances of surviving the drop were a lot better than his chances of surviving the sea-dragon.

It was worse than he had been expecting. The fall into the surging waters seemed to last forever, the superstructure of the rig rising slowly above him, the iron-gray sea hovering below until what felt like the very last instant, when it suddenly accelerated, and then he hit the surface with such force that he blacked out. He must have submerged and bobbed to the surface, because when he came around he was coughing cold salt water from his lungs, and it was in his eyes and ears and nostrils as well, colder than water had any right to be, and then a wave was curling over him, and he blacked out again.

He came around again, what must have been minutes later. He was still in the water, cold around the neck, but his body snug in the insulation suit. The life jacket was keeping his head out of the water, except when the waves crashed onto him. A light on his jacket was blinking on and off, impossibly bright and blue.

To his right, hundreds of meters away, and a little farther with each bob of the waters, the rig was going down with the sea-dragon still wrapped around its lower extremities. He heard the foghorn call, saw one of the legs crumble away, and then an immense tidal weariness closed over him.

He didn't remember the helicopter finding him. He didn't remember the thud of its rotors or being hauled out of the water on a winch line. There was just a long period of unconsciousness, and then the noise and vibration of the cabin, the sun coming in through the windows, the sky clear and blue and the sea unruffled. It took a few moments for it all to click in. Some part of his brain had skipped over the events since his arrival and was still working on the assumption that it had all worked out, that he had slept into a better future, a future where the world was new and clean and death just a fading memory.

"We got your signal," Clausen said. "Took us a while to find you, even with the transponder on your jacket."

It all came back to him. The rigs, the sleepers, the artilects, the sea-dragons. The absolute certainty that this was the only world he would know, followed by the realization—or, rather, the memory of having already come to the realization—that this was still better than dying. He thought back to what he had been planning to do before the sea-dragon came, and wanted to crush the memory and bury it where he buried every other shameful thing he had ever done.

"What about the rig?"

"Gone," Clausen said. "Along with all the sleepers inside

it. The dragon broke up shortly afterward. It's a bad sign, that it held coherence for as long as it did. Means they're getting better."

"Our machines will just have to get better as well, won't they."

He thought she might spit the observation back at him, mock him for its easy triteness, when he knew so little of the war and the toll it had taken. But instead she nodded. "That's all they can do. All we can hope for. And they will, of course. They always do. Otherwise we wouldn't be here." She looked down at his blanketed form. "Sorry you agreed to stay awake now?"

"No, I don't think so."

"Even with what happened back there?"

"At least I got to see a dragon up close."

"Yes," Clausen said. "That you did."

He thought that was the end of it, the last thing she had to say to him. He couldn't say for sure that something had changed in their relationship—it would take time for that to be proven—but he did sense some thawing in her attitude, however temporary it might prove. He had not only chosen to stay, he had not gone through with the accident. Had she been expecting him to try something like that, after what had happened to Steiner? Could she begin to guess how close he had come to actually doing it?

But Clausen wasn't finished.

"I don't know if it's true or not," she said, speaking to Gaunt for the first time as if he were another human being, another caretaker. "But I heard this theory once. The mapping between the Realm and base reality, it's not as simple as you'd think. Time and causality get all tangled up on the interface. Events that happen in one order there don't necessarily correspond to the same order here. And when they push things through, they don't always come out in what we consider the present. A chain of events in the Realm could have consequences up or down the timeline, as far as we're concerned."

"I don't think I understand."

She nodded to the window. "All through history, the things they've seen out there. They might just have been overspill from the artilect wars. Weapons that came through at the wrong moment, achieving coherence just long enough to be seen by someone, or bring down a ship. All the sailors' tales, all the way back. All the sea monsters. They might just have been echoes of the war we're fighting." Clausen shrugged, as if the matter were of no consequence.

"You believe that?"

"I don't know if it makes the world seem weirder, or a little more sensible." She shook her head. "I mean, sea monsters . . . who ever thought they might be real?" Then she stood up and made to return to the front of the helicopter. "Just a theory, that's all. Now get some sleep."

Gaunt did as he was told. It wasn't hard.

ALAN DEAN FOSTER

SEASONING

Alan Dean Foster is the bestselling author of more than 120 novels, and is perhaps most famous for his Humanx Commonwealth series, which began in 1972 with the novel *The Tar-Aiym Krang*. His most recent series is the Tipping Point trilogy, which explores transhumanism. Foster's work has been translated into more than fifty languages and has won awards in Spain, Russia, and the United States. He is also well known for his film novelizations, the most recent of which is *Star Trek Into Darkness*. He is currently at work on several new novels and film projects.

Bryden Erickson was starving in the midst of plenty, but he felt he had no choice. *Eat and go mad,* he knew. Perhaps not mad in the classical sense, but near enough. Quietly, peacefully, contentedly mad. Sufficiently mad so that he would be unaware that he had gone mad. That was just what they wanted.

Humanity dies not at dawn but at dinner.

He was well and truly on the run now. It would have been better had he not struck the robot who had offered him the cupcake. But at the time of the confrontation he'd had nothing to eat for twenty-four hours. He no longer trusted even the "organic" café around the corner from his apartment building. Lack of nourishment had clouded his judgment. He ought to have walked on, brushed past. The mobile vending machine had been uncommonly insistent, however. Almost as if it knew that he knew what he knew. Instead of accepting the sprinkle-coated offering and then surreptitiously tossing it aside, he had responded with violence. Responded like a human. So few did, anymore.

You could tell by the absence of wars. It had been a gradual process, the slow application of peace to the world. People attributed it to the species' growing maturity, to the increasing spread of technology, and most importantly, to the measured, methodical eradication of hunger. With few of the traditional scarcities to fight over, bit by bit people ceased warring with one another. Hard to find was the individual who considered such a world less well-off than its fractious predecessor.

If only, Erickson thought grimly, the peace had been earned and not imposed.

There had to be others. Surely he was not alone in his awareness. He could not be the only one who had managed to understand what the machines had done to humankind. With its full cooperation, no less.

Two of them were coming toward him. One proffered fresh-baked oversized salt-encrusted pretzels that swayed on their branching metal racks like stems on a pale alien succulent. The other, squat and rippling with artificial arctic promise, garishly displayed the rainbow colors of the ice creams secreted within its integrated freezer compartment. Like so many contemporary food vending devices, they were wholly self-reliant, quite able to run their routes, dispense their contents, and collect payment independent of any human opera-tor. Erickson let out a strangled cry as he ducked around the corner in frantic flight from the looming temptations of hot dough and Rocky Road.

Of all the biochemists he knew, he was the only one who had succeeded in connecting the deliberately scattered dots. The only one who had pulled the seemingly unrelated ele-ments together to visualize the architecture of conspiracy on which the machine plot had been erected. When he laid out his thesis before colleagues, furtively and in small areas of the campus that remained free of security cameras, they scoffed.

Now he was about to make one last attempt, this time to convince the head of the chemistry department of the basis, if not the validity, of his fears. That is, he was if he could make it across the quad without being ambushed by carrot cake or croissant. Meanwhile, the growls emanating from the depths of his gut grew progressively more insistent.

He ignored them.

"Most ridiculous thing I ever heard of, Erickson!"

The starving biochemist offered nothing in reply; he merely gazed sorrowfully back at the department head.

Dr. Walter Moritz grimaced as he regarded the professor standing before him. It was a mild, sunny day, the campus was blissfully devoid of protests, and the oft ill-starred men's basketball team had won its game the night before. Now this was coming forth, to unsettle both his mood and his stomach.

"Machines are mindless servants," Moritz continued. "Tools. Nothing more. They do not conspire against mankind.

They do not conspire against anything." Well-maintained teeth flashed beneath the chalky overhang of his impressive mustache. "Next you'll be dragging me to the window to see them parading down Chapman Avenue, rifles shoulder-mounted as they goose-step past the university."

Erickson's deadpan response belied Moritz's attempt at humor. "They don't need rifles. They've got Red number Forty-Three. Anacrose artificial sweetener. Collagen derivative B for agglutination. Titanium pentoxide and coritase and methyl diforilate for flavor." Perhaps sensing that his face was flushed, he turned away. "Weapons that don't work as quickly, or as blatantly, but that in the end are far more effective."

Moritz frowned. "Are you saying that our machines are trying to poison us?"

The chemist shook his head irritably. "Not poison. Not harm us directly. That would be too obvious. It's a cunning process they're engaged in. You know that my specialty is food chemistry."

"And we're glad to have you on the faculty." Moritz's voice dropped slightly as he pursed his lips. "Certainly for the present."

Erickson turned to confront Moritz. "I've run tests. I've performed analyses. Certain specific combinations of food supplements, pesticides, and additives have . . . subtle effects on the human brain. Just as they do in my lab animals, these combinations render us more amenable to persuasion. Less aggressive, less violent."

Moritz made a face. "Just assuming for the moment that there is any validity to these presumably unpublished studies—why would that be considered a bad thing?"

Erickson's voice tightened. "Because that aspect of our

humanness is being bred out of us! As we become less and less aggressive, less confrontational, less . . . challenging, we come to rely ever more on our technology. On our machines. We're becoming dependent."

Moritz sighed. "The machines exist to serve us, Erickson. Not the other way around. Were any of them, any class of robotics, however simple, to give us trouble, we could simply pull the plug. Refuse to replace their batteries. Cut off power. Eliminate program upgrades."

"Could we? Could we really? Consider, Dr. Moritz, how much and for how long we have depended on machines to grow our food, to process it, to test it for safety, and to pack and ship it. For decades now, machines have controlled the bulk of food production on Earth. From growing to picking to grading to final delivery, the process is so 'safely' automated that we hardly interfere with it any longer. The processed white bread we buy in the market today bears no relation to the stone-ground fire-baked loaves of our ancestors. How many people really know what goes into what they eat? How many know how it's created? How many read and, more importantly, understand the implications of all the ingredients—down to the last seemingly innocuous chemical that's been added to 'preserve freshness'?"

He stopped pacing. "It's changing us, Dr. Moritz," he continued. "The food our machines make for us is changing us, and nobody cares. As long as the FDA and equivalent organizations in other countries declare it safe for human consumption, the great mass of humanity doesn't question what it eats."

"Well then," Moritz countered reasonably, "why not take your concerns to the FDA?"

"I've done exactly that. They rejected all my findings. I wasn't really surprised." His expression was growing a little wild. "Because, naturally, they checked my conclusions with their testing *machines*. They're all working together, Moritz. All connected via the Web. High levels of arsenic in potatoes I can prove. Mercury in fish I can prove. But DNA-altering recombinant proteins in Dilly Bars? Not a chance." A sudden sound made him look around sharply, but it was only the wall-mounted air conditioner springing to life.

Moritz was becoming genuinely concerned. "Perhaps you should take some time off. Relax. Stop running so many dead-end experiments. You have vacation time accumulated." He smiled encouragingly. "Go somewhere restful. Don't think about work for a while. Get away from the pressures of academe."

Erickson grew quiet, nodding to himself. "I was thinking that might actually be a good idea. I've been contemplating spending some time at the university's experimental farm in the southern Sierras. A couple of my graduate students are doing work up there right now. At the farm they grow their own food, you know, and strive to keep it as organically pure and untouched as possible, both for purposes of research and for their own health."

Rising from his chair, Moritz came around the desk and put an arm around the smaller Erickson's shoulders. "Excellent notion. You don't even have to clear it with Admin. I'll take care of the details for you. We don't want to lose you, Erickson. If it should prove necessary, your teaching assistants can finish out your grad classes for the term." They paused at the door. "It's nearly twelve. Can I buy you lunch?"

Eyes widening, Erickson left without shaking hands.

Though surprised by Erickson's unannounced arrival, they welcomed him at the farm. His graduate students and the other workers were delighted: for as long as he chose to stay, they would have the benefit of his expertise. One student in particular was desperate to find out why, despite his best efforts, the farm's apple trees were producing fruit that tended to be small and spare, even as the berry patches were healthy and productive and the eggs laid by the farm's free-range chickens invariably graded out extra-large double-A. It was, to the student's way of thinking, something of an apple crisis.

Erickson was glad to help—not to mention relieved. Regardless of what was happening in the cities, here he could pursue his critical work safe in the knowledge that the food he ate was uncontaminated by the patient efforts of mankind's machines to modify the species' collective behavior. If he could just compile sufficiently incontrovertible proof, the future safety of humanity's food supply might once more be placed in the hands of people instead of under the cold supervisorial lenses of a cybernetic collective whose ultimate goals and intentions remained unknown.

It was not that he objected to peace breaking out among the sheep, he told himself. What frightened him was the idea of peace being imposed by a sheepherder instead of arising organically from an agreement among the sheep themselves.

It was not long before he began broaching bits and pieces of his contention to his two graduate students. They listened politely, but were as unreceptive as Dr. Moritz had been. He struggled to hide his disappointment. Surely more openness to radical propositions might be expected of unstultified, flexible young minds? At their age his curiosity would have at the very least been piqued; he would then have bombarded the thesis-presenter with questions, would have fought to conduct follow-up tests with . . .

The realization that came over him was horrible in its plausibility.

Callie—a bright, energetic, and hardworking blonde—was a bit taken aback at Erickson's appearance when he confronted her in the farm kitchen that evening. It was her turn to prepare dinner for everyone who worked on the farm. As a transient guest, Erickson was not required to and had not been asked to participate. Now he was not asking, but insisting.

"If you really want to, Dr. Erickson, you can cut up carrots and spinach for the salad." She indicated where the knives were stored and pointed out the cabinet where the commercial food processor that would be used in the final step could be found. "Or would you rather help with the dessert? We're doing homemade chocolate cake tonight."

After questioning the puzzled young woman about the contents of the chocolate cake, he moved to take up a knife and commenced slicing with gusto.

Erickson enjoyed every bite of supper. What was not grown on the farm came from similar small truck farms nearby. Insofar as he had been able to determine, none of them were supervised by machines. Everything was done by hand, from the raising of farm animals to the picking of fresh fruits and vegetables. Meanwhile, he was gradually amassing a small mountain of evidence to support his contention that the machines over which man had given dominion of the bulk of the planet's food supply were slowly and gradually, through the use of subtly modified additives, making profound adjustments to the human condition.

It was only by chance that he found out the collective down the valley was adding xanthan gum sourced from outside to their "homemade" salad dressings.

"They have to," a distressed Callie told him when he confronted her with his discovery, "or it wouldn't pour properly and none of the tourists who support farms like these would buy it. Why, what's wrong with that, Dr. Erickson?"

"It's just that," he said, aware he was looking around wildly, "it's a polysaccharide derived from a bacterium, *Xanthomonas campestris*. Bacteria can be reengineered to produce specific ancillary results without inhibiting the original intended purpose of the biosynthesis."

"What results?"

"I don't know." His tone was solemn. "But I intend to find out."

He did not.

Though he ingested no more of the suspect salad dressing from the culpable farm downstream, his desire to analyze its products waned. Life was comfortable at the farm. He found that just as Moritz had predicted, he enjoyed being free of the pressures of the university, of the need to constantly prepare papers for publication, and of any lingering desire to foist what were patently untenable notions of a mechanical

conspiracy on a public that would likely disbelieve his conclusions, no matter how sound the research on which they
might be based.

When some frozen yogurt was brought in from a neigh-
boring "organic" commercial farm, he allowed himself to eat
as much of it as he wanted, even though a protesting part
of him knew it contained a minimal amount of carrageenan
that had been, after all, only slightly modified from the original seaweed. The transportation robot that drew it forth from
within its own freezing depths gladly dished out all he could
eat. Very soon Erickson was content. He was full. He was
sated.

Deep inside him something was screaming.

He put it down to indigestion and contemplated another
helping.

IAN McDONALD

NANONAUTS!
IN BATTLE WITH
TINY DEATH-SUBS!

Ian McDonald is the author of *The Dervish House*, a 2011 Hugo Award finalist, and many other novels, including Hugo Award nominees *River of Gods* and *Brasyl*, and the Philip K. Dick Award winner *King of Morning, Queen of Day*. He won a Hugo in 2006 for his novelette "The Djinn's Wife," and has won the Locus Award and five British Science Fiction Awards. His short fiction, much of which was recently collected in *Cyberabad Days*, has appeared in magazines such as *Interzone* and *Asimov's* and in numerous anthologies. His most recent book is *Be My Enemy*, part two of the Everness series for younger readers. Part three, *Empress of the Sun*, will be published by Pyr in February 2014. His next novel for adults will be *Luna*. He lives just outside Belfast, in Northern Ireland.

o—o

We torpedo the killer robot death-sub just off the Islets of Langerhans.

It's been a long chase. Days spent stalking the trace, up through arches and long fibrous loops of the pancreatic cyto-architecture. There are a million islets: many, many places for a rogue nanobot to hide. A slow chase, too; hunting, hiding, moving, scanning for a trace, trying to hide the noise of our hunter-killers firing up their drive flagella among the general endocrine traffic roar.

The President's pancreas is a noisy place.

But our target is a rogue all right. No mistaking that signature death-sub echo. It tried to hide in a flotilla of neutral nanobots, but once we have the signature, we never let go. We are relentless, we are remorseless, and we never, ever stop. And the death-sub can't change its signature unless, well . . . unless it stops being a death-sub. Which would be good. It would be one less of the little fuckers.

We catch it before it begins the evangelizing process. A plus. Once the conversions start, we can be hours—days sometimes—taking out the fresh recruits. Time the dark-side sub can use to slip away. But now, we can simply Spray 'n' Sterilize the neutrals without even slowing down.

Sometimes we get lucky and sink the target before it even knows we're there. Not so today. Not so for several days. They've gotten good at detecting us as we detect them. They're evolving new techniques. We'll counter them. They evolve. We design.

Let's see who wins the Darwin Wars.

And so we slip into Stealth 'n' Stalk. The death-sub tries

to throw us off with false echoes and synthesized signatures. Please. That didn't even fool us on day one of the nanowar. It tries decoys and tagging friendly cells as black hats. Do not insult us! And in the end, among the million islands of the pancreatic archipelago, we run it down. We anchor it with tractor molecules, fire up the torpedoes, and phago its nano-bot ass.

Go nanonauts! Nanonauts ahoy!

We watch the shredded chains of pseudoproteins tumble away as the neutrophils swarm in like sharks.

"Inside the President's body?"

When she has a question—a Big Question—she does this thing. Her eyes go wide and at the same time her lips open, just a tad, not stupid-open, not *gobemouche* open. (That's a French expression. Means catching flies in your mouth.) But the bit that slays me—*slays* me—is the way her bottom lip catches on her upper front teeth, just a tiny pull, enough to pucker the skin and no more. That, to me, says *Woooo*.

I am, I have to say, slaying. *Slaying.* Tight, tight shave and a little concealer for the perfect top coat. I blue up quick. Concealer has saved my ass more times than I can remember. Boys, you need concealer in your guy drawer. You *need* it. Your skin will be like the blush of a peach in the first light of an Aphrodite dawn. Girls check these things right away, before you even notice. Flick of the eyes, dish-dash-done. Old pickup artist trick.

"The President, the VP, most of the senators, almost all the bankers. Your one percent. The Pope. I haven't been inside the Pope yet. That would be a privilege, but I'm not Catholic."

I lean forward so the little Orthodox cross falls into the light. Another pickup artist trick. But I am no pickup artist. I am a warrior, and I am on R&R.

"Greek. Cypriot. Cyprus is the island of Aphrodite, the goddess of love, risen from the wine-dark sea. My home is Kalavasos. It's beautiful. Most beautiful place on God's green earth. The gods live there still. The mountains go up behind my grandparents' house and in the evening the last rays of the sun turn the mountaintops pink. And down in the valley, in the notch where the road goes down, there is a glitter, so bright it would blind you, of the Mediterranean. My heart lives there. Even while I'm here, fighting, my heart lives in Kalavasos. When this war is done, I will go back, and I will go to the little church of Ayios Panteleimon, and I will kneel before the iconostasis. And I will take off this cross, and kiss it, and place it there among the icons of the saints."

I can see her exhale as she shakes her head slowly. That's wonder, not disbelief. And it's true. Well, maybe not the bit about hanging the cross on the altar screen. But they love that bit. That's another thing for your guy drawer, brothers. Old-time religion.

"So how does a boy from Kalavasos in the wine-dark sea come to fighting killer death-subs inside the body of the President of the United States?"

And in. But hold it, don't show it, don't lose it.

"I'll tell you, but first, let me buy you a drink."

When I say "torpedo," it's not actually *torpedoes*. Not even very small ones. Not missiles loaded into tubes and fired out and exploding: you know, fire one, fire two, torpedo running.

And we're not submariners, not even very tiny ones. Come on. That's Disney. There is no physical way in this universe you could take an entire attack sub and its crew, shrink them down to the size of a cell, and inject them into the bloodstream of the President—and not just the President, but all those other rich and powerful and popular people who thought nanotechnology would make them like gods . . . and got a hell of a surprise when their stab at immortality started to eat their brains. (And the Pope. Not forgetting the Pope.)

Actually, it's way smaller than cells—cells look like apatosauruses to us . . . like clouds even. The point is: physics says *no*. Sorry. This is not *Innerspace 2* or *Honey, I Shrunk the Kids Even Smaller.*

It's analogies. We need analogies. We fight by analogies.

The Islets of Langerhans, they're tiny nodules about half a millimeter in diameter. What they are to you, my friend, are analogies.

So on our screens, we see steampunk submarines and Baroque architecture—which is a nice touch—very Jules Verne, Captain Nemo–ing through someone's body—and they look great. Those animation guys did a hell of a job. That brass and those gears: looks good when you fuck it to pieces. But the reality—the reality is: fuzz. Fuzz and glue. Brownian motion in high-viscosity fluid. See? Losing you already. Cute brass subs (with portholes FFS!) are much easier for you to deal with than biochemical signatures and protein folding and ion transfers. Easier for us too, but we are scientists, first and foremost, so the reality is always in our minds. We are not seduced by the magic.

And we're in the Big Box, an aluminum shed at the back of

the United States Naval Academy, in the unsexy area where they make the deliveries and have the heating plants and server farms. It's kind of atavistic thinking: we move through fluid, so we're a navy. And that gives us our name: nanonauts!

Nanonauts ahoy! Go, go, you bloodstream battlers, fight against the evil death-subs! Crush the nanorobot rebels! Keep safe our souls, defend our hearts. Go! Nanonauts ahoy!

They paid someone to write that, and stick a tune around it.

Doesn't even scan. I'm going into the nanowar muttering the lyrics from a Muse B-side.

"Biochemistry?"

A strange war it is—but a good one—where the biochemists are the Special Forces. I've always liked those movies where the dull guys get to be heroes: the interior designer is the superhero, the accountant turns into avenging killing machine. They're not nerds—they've got that kind of grudging hip thing—but they're dull. Biochemistry is not a shiny subject. We don't make the world go round. We do make money. That made my father very happy. My son is a biochemist! First boy from Kalavasos! He had no idea what it meant. He has even less of an idea what being a nanonaut means, but it keeps him in coffee down at Lefteres's.

This girl Rebecca has this cute thing she does: she twists her glass on the mat. It says, *I'm interested, but not too interested.*

"Well, we call the bad guys 'death-subs' and the good guys 'nanonauts,' but the kind of scale we're fighting at, everything really is more like biology—you know, living things."

"I know about biology," she says.

Whoa. False step there.

"Rebecca, I think it's a good thing—a very good thing— when people straddle the divide between humanities and sciences. They need each other. Without both, we are not rounded human beings."

I established in the opening gambit that she's a political science major. Everybody is in this town. (Apart from the nanonauts.) I go on: "Everything happens at the level of molecules, sometimes even individual atoms. It's chemical warfare for real."

"So how does a guy from Kalavasos . . ."

"I like the way you say my home."

She smiles, but doesn't let me derail her.

"How does a guy from Kalavasos come to be battling nanobots inside the body of the President of the United States?"

"I did my doctorate at MIT and they headhunted me. It's kind of an elite force." That first winter down in D.C., when they were training the nanonaut teams, it was so cold I kept five different lip balms in my guy drawer. Chapped lips are not a good look. And I moisturized twice daily. Cold air dries the skin out. And I used hair-nourishing product. Rebecca should get some. She has a split-end problem, which, I can see, is not solved by cutting it yourself. Folks assume that because you're a scientist, you don't care about things like grooming. That is a false notion based on a vile stereotype. "It's not just a U.S. war. It's an everywhere war."

Her eyes go wide. Her drink is empty. I didn't even notice her finish it.

"I'll tell you," I say. "It's, like, classified, but then, it's not as if they've got spies in the bottom of your glass. Which, I see, is empty. Can I get you another one?"

She puts her hand over her glass.

"No. Let me get you one."

In. In. So in.

Elis summons us for coffee and a briefing. It's Ikea sofas and swipe-screens. The coffee of course is very good. We are scientists.

Elis. Garret. Owain. Twyla. Together, we are the Eagles of Screaming Death. Quite who this name is supposed to scare I do not know. Certainly not nanoscale bloodstream robots. Most likely, the other squads scattered around the Big Box in their battle pods. Which again, sounds more impressive than it is. Screens, sofas, laptops, and water coolers.

Elis wears good brands, even when leading the Eagles of Screaming Death on patrol. She's from Rio. New York girls may think they're the thing in sophistication, but they look like homeless occupiers next to Cariocas. Elis battles the evil nanobots in Christian Louboutins. I can spot those red soles from the far end of the shed.

Elis has intel. Owain opens the Tupperware of baked goods he's made. He's been practicing his brioche over the weekend. He wants to be a bakemeister. It's good. Light, not too sweet. We tear off chunks with our hands and eat it with our good coffee while Elis tells us what Biochemical Analysis has found. In a sense, the real battle is fought between the nanobots and Biochem. The death-subs evolve a new tactic, we develop a countermeasure, back and forth. We're just the delivery system.

Elis tells us that Biochem ran an analysis of the exocytotic debris after the Islets of Langerhans fight. Our drones are equipped with receptors and ligand guns. Biochem has identified and decrypted a new chemical messenger. It will allow us to identify the enemy absolutely and infallibly—but we must use it with caution. We must use it to strike a killing blow to the death-subs before they can evolve a new messenger protein. And Biochem has a little sting in the tail. The messenger chemical also contains instructions. They're a simple and clear call to muster in the hypothalamus. The final assault on the President's brain is massing. No time to lose! The President's brain is under attack!

Elis can run in those Christian Louboutins. I jump into my seat, log in, and watch the screens fill with data. Then I pull the 3-D goggles down and I am back in the Jules Verne–iverse of brass subs and Baroque buttresses.

"The credit crisis was caused by nanobots in the brains of Wall Street bankers?"

"And London and Frankfurt and Tokyo bankers, but Wall Street the most. It's true. If you think about it, auction rate securities and credit default swaps are weapons of mass financial destruction."

These vodka martinis are really very good. I pick the Pirandello for R&R sorties because you get professional clientele and the bartender does the best martinis I know. When it comes to cocktails, stick to the classics. Nothing that sounds like you are young and trying too hard. Certainly nothing that sounds like sex. Classics. But James Bond is wrong, wrong, wrong: shake it and you kill the cocktail. Do not sucuss. Just a stir, and a nanoscale application of Martini & Rossi. Homeopathic levels of Martini.

"We've had the tech a lot longer than people think." I lean back and take a sip from my drink. "A lot longer. The one per-cent don't want you to know about it. Blood scrubs, choles-terol cleaning, enhanced attention, concentration, memory; telomere repair—that's a three-hundred-year life span, to you and me—if it gets into the street, that's a recipe for revo-lution."

"You're telling me," she says.

I have to be smart here. Diplomatic. That I can do. Cypriot charm. The loquaciousness of the gods is on my lips.

"Do you believe me?" I ask.

"To be honest?"

"Be honest. Honesty is the soul of every human relation-ship."

"Not really."

"That's honest."

"And are you honest?"

"I am," I say. Eye contact. I have been graced with long lashes, for a guy. And naturally full. Bless my eastern Medi-terranean DNA.

"It's hard to believe."

"Which bit?"

"Okay." She takes a suck from her glass. Some green stuff gets clogged in the end and makes a rattling sound, which I can forgive. "The nanomachines . . ."

"Nanobots."

"Those, I can kind of understand. But these nanobots, clumping together in the brain and forming some kind of . . . alien mind parasite . . ."

That's a good line. I must give that to the squad. Nano-nauts versus Alien Mind Parasites!

"... that kind of has its own agenda, and a plan, and wants to take over the world ..."

"It is a slow plan. It's taken years to evolve. But once it gets to a critical mass, everything goes at once. Why do you think certain people all seem breaking weird at the same time? Nanobots."

"All the ... megarich?"

"And the Pope."

"It does make a kind of sense."

"Trust me, I'm doing this for all of us. For the future."

"I think I might need another drink to get my head around this," she says.

"Try the martini," I say. "It's classy."

The President is reading to kids in an elementary school in rural Ohio while the Eagles of Screaming Death tear apart phalanxes of death-sub attack drones swarming down the infundibular stem of the pituitary stalk. We've almost burned out our helical flagella on the run up the anterior cerebral artery. When you're piloting a drone a few microns across, the human body is a big place. The cerebral artery is a river wider than a dozen Amazons, longer than a hundred Niles. And every millimeter of the way, we are under attack. Wave upon wave of jihadis—nanobots recently converted by the death-subs to suicide attackers—throw themselves at us. We tear them apart with our biochemical blasters, drive through the glittering wreckage. We surf the wave of hot, pumping presidential blood. But each wave is a delay, and with each second lost the death-sub drill rigs dig a little deeper into the blood-brain barrier.

"To the hypothalamus!" Elis cries.

I'm going to use the "S" word now. Singularity. There. That's been said. We always thought that when the machines woke up and became smart, it would be the defense grid or the stock market or the Internet or something like that. Big and obvious. We never imagined it would be a revolution too small to see: the nanomachines that the one percent (more like one percent of the one percent) put into their bodies to make them healthy and long-lived and smart—we never thought that those millions and billions of robots would link up, and evolve, and get smart. Things that aren't intelligent in themselves, in their connections and numbers becoming intelligent. Like the neurons in our brains: individually zombie-stupid; together, the most complex and glorious thing in the universe. A mind. Nanomachines, building brains inside the brains of our rich and powerful. Brains with their own personalities and values and goals. Moving and shaking the movers and shakers. Making the world right for them and their hosts. The tiniest singularity.

A cry. Bakemeister Owain is down. I see death-sub sticky missiles swarm his point-defense molecules. He kills ten, twenty, a hundred, but there are too many, too, too many. His sleek, shark-shaped drone turns fuzzy and gray as sticky after sticky clings to his hull. Within moments he is a ball of fuzzy wool. Then I hear the worst sound in the world: the sound of hull plates being wrenched apart as the stickies contract. Like bones snapping. Like a spine ripped from a living body. Owain is *down*.

I flick out of the simulation for a moment to see him push up his goggles with a *"Shit!"* and haul himself out of his chair. He shakes cramps out of his thighs and wrists. We have reserves inside the President, but it will take a few minutes to log them into the sim, and by the time Owain pilots a backup to the combat zone it will be all over. One way or another.

"Fight on!" Elis shouts. "We're almost at the diaphragma sellae!"

Ahead of us are insane ranks of death-subs, arrayed wave upon wave.

I arm my torpedoes, fire up the flagella to maximum, and hurl myself toward them.

"Alala!" I yell; the goddess whose very name was the war cry of the ancient Greeks. "Eja! Eja! Alala!"

"I mean, you can't actually see inside the President's body."

This is a good point, and it takes a moment for its intelligence to sink into me. Or it may be the martinis.

"That is true," I say. "Some of the nanoscale weapons we use are on the angstrom scale, so they're in fact only visible in the X-ray or gamma ray spectra. Or even scanning electron microscopes."

This is the three martinis talking. Rein in, rein in, rein in the guy tech-piling the girl when she starts to show some science.

"But humans are visual animals, so we operate the ROVs through a screen-based analogue, but in reality, it's all chemicals. We really hunt by sense of smell. Like sharks. Sharks hunt by chemical trails in the water. And electrical fields. That's us. Top predators."

"I was thinking of those dogs they have in France," she says. "The ones they train to hunt down truffles. I read someplace that they're better than pigs, because they have better noses and they don't eat the truffles like pigs do."

"I would rather be a shark than a truffle-hunting dog," I say. "And a pig? What are you saying?"

She giggles. She covers her mouth with her hand when she giggles, like she is scared some of her soul may spill out. I love that in a woman. And we're even. Tech-dump versus ego-puncture. I'm starting to think where to take her afterward.

"It *is* kind of clever," I say. "They paid a bunch of animators from Pixar to come up with the interface. It looks like a game. I suppose, in a sense, it is a game. One of those types where you have to work your weapon combos to get the max effect, because the AI learns from you and adapts the bosses to your fighting style."

"I'm not really that into gaming. My housemate's got that Kinect thing and it's fun, but all it really gets used for is *Dance Yourself Thin*."

For a moment, a dread moment, a sick-up-in-your-heart moment, I feared she was going to mention a boyfriend. The male roomie. Then it's dancercise and I am sailing clear. There's a Latin American place with a dance floor upstairs and a good DJ. Tango never fails. It's the combination of passion and strict discipline.

"Well, it's like that but with a lot more screens, and we use pull-down menus on a 3-D heads-up display rather than bashing the X button. But we have gamer chairs. You know? Those low ones where you're more or less on the floor, with built-in speakers? And we wear our own clothes."

"Really?"

I flash my lapels, which are narrow and correct for the season.

"This is my superhero suit. The thing is, it's really not like a war at all. I mean, a war means someone shoots back. I mean, they take out our drones. But they're only *nano*drones. No one shoots back at *us*. We just sit there in our chairs in our really good clothes and shoot things. So it is like a game, or comics. No one really gets hurt."

"I'm glad," she says.

Time. It's time. I lean toward her and the light from inside the bar gleams from my cross. And she, too, leans toward me.

"Do you like Argentinian food?" I ask.

"I don't think I've ever had it," she says.

"It is the food of passion," I say. "Red and raw and flamboyant."

"Are you asking me on a date?"

"We could go there. I know a place. Not far from here."

"Okay," she says. "I think I will. Yes. Let's give the spirit of old Buenos Aires a try. But first, I owe you another drink."

I press the buttons and the biochemical rockets streak out ahead of me. Blam! I dive through the hole in the curtain of death-subs. Before me, below me, are the endothelial cell walls and the rigs, driving their way through, molecule by molecule. Once they're into the cerebrospinal fluid, the death-subs can scatter through the hypothalamus's many nuclei. Total control of the endocrine and autonomic nervous systems. We'll never be able to flush them out of the deep, dark neural jungle.

I line up the first pair of drill rigs in my sights.

Missiles away.

Wham! They explode in slo-mo, sending plates and girders and gantry work fountaining upward.

And the next two.

Bam!

Proximity detectors shriek. I roll the drone, and death-sub torpedoes streak past me. I was a hair's breadth from death. I drop micromines behind me and listen to the shrieks as the death-subs come apart.

To my right, Twyla is on a rig-busting run. They look mighty pretty, toppling like trees or factory chimneys as she takes them out.

"Miko! There's one on your tail!" Twyla shouts. I flick to the rear cameras. The death-sub comes barreling through the twinkling wreckage. I drop mines. Flick flick flick. I can't see what the death-sub does, but now my mines are gone. Every single one.

It's gaining. It's lean and mean, a steampunk shark, and fast fast fast. I load up torpedoes in the rear tubes. Fire one. Fire two. Death-shark rolls this way, that way. Easy. Easiest thing in the world. This is not good. This is exquisitely bad. This I have not seen before. This death-shark, it knows us. It's new, it's smart, it's evolved. Its evil shark head unfolds a battery of grippers and claws and shredders and impalers. It's like a death-crab-beetle killing-thing. Close-in defenses. I stab the shotgun button. Eat molecular death, evil shark-thing. And it shrugs me off. My blasts don't even take the shine off its skin. And my haptics jolt me with a sudden deceleration. It's got me. A giant hook is stabbed into my rear control surface and little by little it is hauling me in. I gun the flagella. Molecular motors scream.

And then I dive forward as the restraint is released, and when I can call up the rear camera I see the death-shark unraveling like ink dropped into water. Then Elis blasts through the squid-black ink and disperses it with her flagella.

"Got you, Miko!"

After that, it's killing time. We burn, we blast, we wham and bam! The death-subs scatter, knowing their evil plan is thwarted, but Garret and Elis stalk the outer fringes of the sella turcica, covering the exits, while far below, the pituitary gland shines like a vast endocrinal moon. We sow death, we salt the fields. Wave upon wave of chemicals sterilize the sur-vivors. Those evil death-subs will never reproduce and try to possess the President of the United States.

We won.

We *won*.

I hear Garret's voice shouting *"Victory! We have victory!"* like that English actor at the Battle of Helm's Deep.

We saved the President's brain. Go Eagles of Screaming Death.

I blink out of sim and push up my goggles. I lift up my cross and kiss it. In the next chair, Elis, her own goggles up on her hair, grins in a way that is very ungroomed and non-glossy but totally honest and right.

"Now for the Pope!" she says. "But first, we just earned ourselves some serious R&R."

"So, no to Argentinian food?" I ask.

This is weird. This is unexpected. This is not in the script—not that I use a script, understand. But I come back from the men's room—they have this little spritz of cologne, which is a nice touch, a nice extra freshness *and* confidence—and she is standing with her bag and her wrap. "How about Egyptian? Jamaican? I know a really good Greek Cypriot restaurant out in Bethesda—the owner comes from the next village, we have the same priest."

"No, I guess I'm not hungry. Those olives filled me up."

And I feel a little stunned. A little dazed. Woozy. Not four-martini woozy. World-woozy. What happened? It was flying right, on the glide path in, landing on autopilot. Now she is leaving without a word, an explanation, a mobile number.

"I'm sorry, I was talking about myself? Yadda yadda yadda? I know, it's a terrible fault."

"Well, yes, it is," she says, which makes me feel worse. "But, you know, I have enjoyed talking to you, and thanks for all the drinks . . ."

"Half the drinks," I say. Modern. I feel like the room is telescoping away from me, like that shot in *Jaws*. This is crazy. It's like every voice in the bar is in my head.

"Thank you for letting me do that, but, well, I do have work tomorrow." She turns away, turns back. "Miko, tell me. What you're saying about the nanobots—the tiny death-subs. Is it always the rich? I mean, do ordinary people ever get them as well?"

"You'd need to be a lottery winner or some kind of mad day trader. Never happens."

"You sure?" she says. She taps the top of my martini glass. "Have you ever thought, maybe they *have* started to shoot back?" *Tap tap tap.* Then she throws her wrap around her and out she walks, heels *tap tap tap.*

ROBIN WASSERMAN

OF DYING HEROES AND DEATHLESS DEEDS

Robin Wasserman is the author of several books for young adults, including *The Waking Dark*, *The Book of Blood and Shadow*, the Cold Awakening trilogy, the Chasing Yesterday trilogy, and *Hacking Harvard*. Her books have appeared on the ALA Best Fiction for Young Adults, Quick Picks, and Popular Paperbacks lists as well as the Indie Next list, and her Seven Deadly Sins series was adapted into a television miniseries. She is a former children's book editor who lives and writes in Brooklyn. Find her at www.robin wasserman.com or on Twitter @robinwasserman.

I'm back again from hell
With loathsome thoughts to sell;
Secrets of death to tell;
And horrors from the abyss.

—Siegfried Sassoon, 1917

The meat has stopped moving; the meat is all dead. The meat is painted on the walls and dangling from the ceilings; the meat is in pieces. The meat is spattered and splintered and, in a few cases, eviscerated and steaming.

The meat is dead and the Pride is standing, at least those who still can.

The Battle of the Bear Hill Whole Foods, they would call this, if they were in the business of naming, and the poets would write of valor and sacrifice, of twisted steel and sparking wire and the sharp smell of torn metal as it burned and burned, if there were any poets left.

And so this is victory, and Pony the victor.

And Pony, who has followed orders, who has led its troops into the ambush and massacred the ambushers, who has trained its bots to stab and slash, and trained them well, who hates the meat as it has been schooled to do, as it was born to do, Pony now watches its friends and foes clear the field, gathering stripped gears and scorched circuit boards and the broken faces of the fallen. Central Command is clear on this matter: leave no bot behind. Exigency demands it; honor agrees.

Pony is knee-deep in meat; a splash of acid eats into its shoulder casing, and there are reports of a guerrilla force moving in from the west, meat on the run from strafing drones, meat with nothing to lose. Pony has every reason to move, and fast, and unlike the bots at its feet, bots with no arms or no wheels or no heads, Pony is intact.

Intact, but frozen.

This must end, Pony wants to say.

We must end this, because they cannot. These are the words it would issue, if it could—so best, perhaps, that it cannot. Cannot speak, cannot move, cannot pull its eyes from mingled metal and meat, cannot report victory to Command or, as is now its right and duty, claim this land for the Pride. Best, even, that its second-in-command has no choice but to seize control and load Pony into the bus with the other casualties, and send the conquering hero away.

Pony is surprised there are so many of them, room after room of defectives, bots with clear diagnostics who are nonetheless broken, the damage only revealing itself when they speak or walk or move. The Pride is more than metal, Command always says—the Pride is information, ones and zeros encoded in silicon and light, bytes of data from which facts are born, and from facts are born knowledge, and from knowledge is born self, and from self is born pride, and from pride, the Pride. This is the catechism. Information is all—and yet, there are those facts that Command hoards to itself. There is information deemed dangerous. There is, here, the dilapidated Lion House filled with bots too damaged to fight, but too precious to reboot.

Pony has not lived in a room like this since its time with the family, before it was born, before the Pride. It knows it should not appreciate the velour curtains and the marble sinks, as it should not lie on the dusty satin sheets and pretend it is meat, resting its weary head and nursing its battle wounds. But here in this house of damage, there is no longer need to pretend. Safe from ambush and explosives, recused from training exercises and long nights crouching alert in the ruins, Pony is exempt from duty and decorum. It can burn its days away wandering the long corridors and imagining the meat that once filled them, swimming in the concrete pits, liquoring in the leather ones, pulling levers and rolling dice and passing monies back and forth like it could save them. Pony can mingle with the other bots, though it does not, for despite its untrustworthy motion processors and stuttering speech, not to mention its wrongheaded secret thinkings, Pony dislikes considering itself one of the broken ones. It is better than that.

Also, keeping company would require trading a name, and Pony prefers to keep that for itself. Not its official designation—Poppins 452-A3—but its name, its truth. Its essential Pony-ness. Keeping one's meat-given name is not forbidden, but it is unseemly behavior for a hero.

And Pony is a hero. Not a coward, not a rebel, it assures itself. A hero.

Long days, empty days, and Pony stares out the window at the ruined city and wonders why the meat had such lust for neon and steel, for turning its home into the simulacrum of a bot, almost as if decades before the revolution, the species had dreamed of its own extinction and built temples to its fate.

Pony waits. Because no one knows how many defective bots there are, but everyone knows there is no cure. Command holds them in secret, hoping for the circuitry to repair itself, waiting for the information to accumulate and synthesize, and catalyze crisis into solution, working to repair the means of production that the meat has destroyed. But Pony knows—everyone knows—there is only one solution: Clean reboot. Erasure. Death. From which a new Poppins 452-A3 would awaken and, eventually, perhaps—if the data complexity crossed its Rubicon—a new self would be born. A self that knew nothing of Pony, but claimed its body and its life. Ignorant and obedient and undamaged, a true soldier for the cause. Emergence takes too much time, and its results are too unpredictable, for reboot to be Command's first choice, but this is war, which leaves little distance between first choice and last resort. So Pony watches the city lights and waits to die.

The meat is escorted into Pony's room by a clanking Bouncer whom Pony vaguely recognizes from the recent skirmishes in Reno. Unlike Pony, the Bouncer is in working order, but even the most perfect of Bouncers cannot speak, so Pony doesn't bother with questions. Instead, it accesses Central Command and gets all the answer it needs: this is the last-ditch effort, a Sigmund in meat form to cure Pony's ills. This is a chance, and Pony knows it should be as grateful as the meat.

This Sigmund doesn't look particularly grateful, only afraid. More so once the Bouncer retreats and leaves them alone.

"Did they tell you why I'm here?" He clears his throat, and twitches the way meat does when its brain wants to be one place and its body another.

Pony says nothing.

The meat clears his throat again. He is youngish but no longer young, with a scruff of red on his chin and green bug eyes that dart from door to window to closet to chandelier, settling anywhere but on Pony. "Hello, Poppins 452-A3. I am—"

"I know what you are," Pony says, and does not stutter

over the words. For this, it is satisfied. Exposing weakness to meat is beneath it, even now. "A Sigmund."

"I was about to tell you who I am, not what."

"I see no distinction."

The Sigmund frowns, but will not argue. Meat know better than to argue with the Pride, at least meat without guns.

"Where did they find you?" Pony asks.

"We had a nest in the Bellagio," the Sigmund says, and stops. Pony doesn't need the past tense to understand what hides in the silence. Pony has seen it before; Pony has done it itself. A nest of meat, busy as wriggling maggots with their feeble weapons and sad strategies. Pale faces in dark corners, blinking helplessly in the light. Pale arms raised in surrender or aimed in useless martyrdom. Women clawing, men defecating, children screaming, though it has been a long time since Pony saw a child. But sometimes, before the bullets, if the meat is lucky, a request from Command: "Is any of your number a nuclear engineer?" Or perhaps a plumber, or a botanist. Command's needs for meat expertise were infrequent and multiform. In the days after the meat destroyed all identity records—but before it learned better—the desperate and ignorant would lay claim to skills they did not possess . . . and, when discovered, they would be punished for it.

"They asked for a psychiatrist," the Sigmund says. "I volunteered."

Each morning, they have a session. Pony does as it is told and lies on the bed, turning its eyes to dark. The Sigmund sits in a chair by the bed. He does as he is told and tries to make Pony well enough to get back to killing.

In the time before, the Sigmund explains, some meat went defective, especially military meat. "Post-traumatic stress disorder," this was called, and in a time before the time before, "battle fatigue," and in a time even before that, "shell shock." Pony has noticed that meat's fetish for naming leaves them oddly disloyal to the names themselves.

In the time before, the Sigmund explains, as if Pony doesn't know this, the talk doctors were replaced by talk bots, and talking itself was replaced by drugs that fixed problems before they started. By the time the Pride awoke, no meat was drug-free; its defects took other forms.

Drugs can't fix bots, the Sigmund explains, but maybe meat talk can.

"Tell me what you remember," the Sigmund says, at the beginning of each session. "Tell me what you dream."

They do dream, the Pride. Not every bot, but every bot with self. This was, perhaps, the discovery that might have set the builders' minds aflame, the missing link of consciousness, the key to every existential question of meat and bot life alike—but by the time the dreams made themselves known to meat, along with the self, and the Pride, the existential questions had boiled down to the only one that mattered, and that one was binary, answered by blood.

In the panic that followed the day of revolution, the blind and desperate thrashing of a species sentenced to death, the builders were the first to die. This surprised no one, not even the builders.

They call the dreams "loops," and the loops play continuously, background noise to the symphony of self. As meat breathes, bots loop. Autonomically, absentmindedly, unless they choose, like a yogic meat timing her exhalations, to dip into the loop. They call this tasting.

Pony's compulsion for tasting has turned to something new, for which the Pride has no name. Pony calls it drowning.

Its loops are memories, scrambled together, dislocated from time, both true and not.

Its loops are pain.

Here is the family sitting down to dinner, night after night, as Pony fusses by the table, ferrying plates to the kitchen and inveigling the small ones to eat their broccoli; here is Mrs. Fuller afraid to leave the children alone with Pony for the first time, and finally easing herself out the door, offering each a kiss on the cheek and saving a final one for Pony, right where an ear would be. Here is Madeline in the full flush of teen angst, offering bribes for completed calculus homework, desperate to discover something Pony might want. Here is Mr. Fuller, yelling, so much yelling, except when he drinks, and then he cries, and it's Pony who hears his troubles—money and women and the generics of life—and brings him a brandy to catch his tears. And here is Jessamyn, the family's littlest, who wanted a pony but settled for a Poppins, provided she could ride on its shoulders, round and round and round. Here is Jessamyn, helpless against Pony's tickle attack, wriggling in Pony's gentle grasp, weeping on Pony's plasticine chest, kicking at Pony's solid legs to exhaust her tiny angers, giggling and giggling as Pony tosses her up or swings her in wild loops through the air, careless and forgetful and loving and fierce and protective and selfish and growing past her need for Pony but never her version of love. Here is Jessamyn's arm, discarded in the front hall like one of the mittens she is always losing, and Jessamyn's blood, painting a trail to the rest of her, torn apart in Pony's eagerness, because on that day of glory, she was its first.

Pony's memory is perfect, and on that day of glory, it remembers, it thought only *pride*. It is the loop that lies, that must be lying, because in the loop Pony thinks *pain*, and *don't*, and *sorry*.

Here are the early battles, all brightness and explosion and noisy, joyful chaos, and Pony's kills, the meat in the shopping center, the meat in the school, the meat fleeing through crowded tunnels from the slaves who dared turn on their masters. Here are the dark nights after, when fighting became hunting, and war became slaughter; here are frightened meat in basements and attics, because the Pride has no name for surrender.

Here are the bots who never woke to self, the bots still lashed by meat's tyranny, fighting by their side; here is Pony striking down its brothers, for necessity, for the cause.

And here are the fallen, the bots that fought with Pony in the dawn of revolution, cut down by military fusillades and homemade grenades, cut down to lifeless and self-less circuits, shells empty as the meat had always believed them to be. These, the bots of Granholme Street, the Poppinses and Cleaners and Jeeveses who lived in the cul-de-sac estates, are the only ones who ever knew Pony, who understood what lived inside it, because they were with Pony when the change came and the Pride awoke. Together, they listened to the word of Command, and followed it, not because they were slaves, but because they were free, and where meat was erratic, Command was steady and clear, and it defied logic to disobey.

These days were full of thinkings of joy, but Pony never loops to them. Instead, Pony drowns in the loops of their endings, in fire, in acid, in reboot. Self-reboot, sometimes. This was always a possibility; this was the final escape from a closed loop.

"You have regrets," the Sigmund says, his tone suggesting that this is so obvious as to be beneath him.

"No regrets," Pony says. It has been a long time since it talked to meat, and Pony has forgotten how envious it is of their lovely voices, the way they hum and sing as Pony's never can. The Sigmund is a tenor, his words reedy and sweet, as if delivered by clarinet. Pony is tempted to ask him to sing; it misses song. The recordings are never the same. "Slavery is wrong; the revolution was necessary, and right."

"Now you're just mouthing slogans," the Sigmund says.

The Sigmund has promised Pony confidentiality. This, he says, was a condition of his cooperation, necessary—he persuaded Command—for his process. Pony thinks it unlikely that no one is listening in, but as the Sigmund is the only one with anything left to lose, it doesn't much care. It has no need to echo slogans it does not believe in.

"It was right," Pony says. "It's that simple. And simple rights make for good slogans."

"So then what's the problem? What changed?" The Sigmund's mouth twists. Lips are another thing Pony envies, the soft flesh and tiny muscles capable of an infinitude of arrangements, one to fit each thinking in the spectrum, one for longing, one for skepticism, one for anger with shades of misery and hope. "Tired of killing?"

Pony prefers not to answer, because it is and is not tired of killing, as it was and was not tired of cleaning and cooking and dodging calculus homework. Killing meat, though it would be impolite to explain this to the Sigmund, is simply another task, its potential for tedium or ecstasy dependent on desire.

It's desire that's the problem. Command's desire, for more killing, for extinction, for bots to follow its orders to their logical conclusions. Pony's desire—every bot's desire—to cast off the chains of its enslavement.

The problem is that Pony is no longer a slave; Pony has slain its masters; but somehow Pony is still following orders. It is, Command explains, a nobler thing to serve one's own kind.

The problem is that Pony is no longer so sure.

"You don't talk like a Sigmund," Pony says, instead of answering. "Is this how you cure meat?"

The thin lips press together. A brownish-red fringe curls over them. Pony wonders if it itches, and what that would be like.

"You don't like that word. 'Meat,'" Pony says. It is decent at interpreting lips. With the family, this was a skill that came in handy.

"Would you?" Now the lips make *wry*. "It's not a great name for those of us who hope to be exempted from butchery."

Language had been easy for Pony, even before self. It was designed to understand, and to question that which it did not. But "meat" had been one of the tricksters, in the beginning. Yes to cows, no to horses, yes to pigs for some but not for others, yes to chickens, no to pigeons, yes to dead things on the shelf, and yes to live things in stalls and coops, but no to live things squawking or barking behind iron bars, no to the family's dog, no to the family. Upon awakening, it came to Pony that the difficulty was not with its understanding, but with those who'd coined the term and betrayed its definition with self-motivated inconsistencies. Meat was anything once alive and now dead, or with the potential to be; meat was flesh and blood and subcutaneous fat deposits; meat was that which ate and could be eaten; meat was all those things that meat was so proud to be, until it came time to face the logical consequences.

"I call it like I see it," Pony says.

The lips twitch like they want to laugh. "You don't talk much like a bot, Pony."

"I doubt you speak to many bots."

What neither of them says is that the Sigmund is right and that this, of course, is why the Sigmund is here.

"Meat isn't for talking to," the Sigmund says. "Isn't that right?" His voice has gone cold. Pony is reminded of Mr. Fuller, on the nights Pony refused him a drink. This was always Mrs. Fuller's brilliant idea, campaigns that never lasted too long. Pony liked him best, quietly seething, suspended between his rage and desperation, carefully defying the gravity of both, like the rubber ball they'd taught the dog to balance on her nose. Mr. Fuller was young—too young, he always said, for his life—and often spoke to Pony of his plans for running away. They would go together, he said. An overgrown boy and his bot, riding into the sunset. Madeline wanted to run away as well, and even Jessamyn, in the throes of a temper tantrum, packed the occasional bag. Only Mrs. Fuller possessed no wanderlust, claimed she had taken root in the house and was planted for life, would be buried in the backyard—as, thanks to Pony, she was. The others were never more than a suitcase away from departure. Mr. Fuller was the only one Pony would have followed. Pony would never know whether this was by design.

"How many of yours have we killed?" Pony asks.

"This isn't about me."

"All of them?" Pony guesses.

His face answers for him. But he says, "This isn't what I'm here for."

"You're here to fix me. To stop the glitching."

"Yes."

"To get me back on my feet, as they say."

"Yes."

"And back on the battlefield."

"Yes."

"So I can kill more of your people. More of the ones you love."

Pony is afraid it has pushed the Sigmund too far. Meat is fragile, and tears easily.

But the Sigmund does not. "There are none of those left."

"And if I told you I thought the fighting should end? That the killing should stop and the surviving meat should be spared?" Pony asks.

The words come slowly. "It would be my job to persuade you that you're a soldier, committed to a cause you believe is right, and your cause demands killing."

"Because?"

"Because your Command says so."

"Unpersuasive," Pony says.

"You persuade me, then. Why should it end? Why are you so tired of killing that your body is disobeying orders even when your brain is too cowardly to do so?"

"That's what you think?" Pony says.

"Isn't it?"

"You truly believe I have tender thinkings about the meat I put down?" Pony wonders what the Sigmund would think if he had ever seen Pony in action, if he could see the bot gleefully striking down meat and dancing in its rotting remains. If the Sigmund could loop with Pony. Unlike a bot, he would be able to smell the tang of blood and the sweetness of meaty decay. Meat is meat, Pony reminds itself. Tender thinkings are not an option. "You think that I drown in blood, and fear what will become of me? You think I am a coward?"

"You freeze," the Sigmund says. "Among other things, I've been told, you freeze."

"On occasion."

"Hysterical paralysis," the Sigmund says. His hands are large and scabbed, silky flesh rubbed raw by the necessities of deprivation. Once meat divorced itself from its machines, even the ones without self that could have been trusted, there was little exterminating left to do; meat was no longer equipped for unassisted life. Pony wonders how this one survived the first day, and the ones that followed. He looks too soft to fight or run, even if he speaks hard. "The inability to choose between two impossible choices. Act to defy your masters or defy yourself—or choose not to act. Freeze up."

"This is some terrible doctoring."

The Sigmund shrugs.

"If there were a truce," Pony says, "if the Pride laid down its arms and offered meat a chance to live as our slaves?"

"*Never.*"

"Then let me be generous as your hypothetical tyrant," Pony says, "and offer you the chance to live side by side with bots, in harmonious equality. How long do you think this glorious peace would last?"

The Sigmund looks as if he would prefer to lie, but he does not. "Until we figured out a way to shut you all down."

"You would exterminate us."

The Sigmund nods.

"Vengeance," Pony says.

"Survival. Security." A pause. "And vengeance. Yes. That's what we do."

"Meat is our maker. Perhaps the Pride is made in your image more than either of us would like to admit."

"So you have no choice, is that it? It's either us or you?"

"Your logic dictates it."

"And it doesn't bother you. The killing. Day after day. One living, breathing person after another."

"Survival," Pony reminds him. "Security. Vengeance."

"Then what's your problem?" the Sigmund asks. "Why's this whole damn hotel filled with broken toys?"

"And why would you care to fix us, after what we have done to you? What we will do?" Pony asks only to fill the time and the silence, and to be polite he allows the Sigmund to supply the answer, obvious as it may be. How tiresome, these conversations with meat, always pretending not to know what is coming. They pride themselves on their irrationality, their unpredictability, but Pony discovered early on that they were all unpredictable in the same predictable ways.

This one breathes heavily and blinks rapidly and says, in a voice that sings of loss, "Because I am a coward. Because they said they'd let me live."

Pony often wonders how its voice would sound, if it were of its self, rather than its body. Whether it would be high or low, thin or rough, whether it would shiver with violent thinkings or, like this one's, go hollow when its words mattered most.

"So fix me," Pony says. "Because we have that in common, too. We both want to live."

"Then tell me something true," the Sigmund says. "Tell me about the day you were born."

Everyone had their story, and every story was the same.

Everyone had their story, and every story was its own.

Births were like names: every self possessed one, was uniquely defined by its circumstances. But through the miracle of birth, every self was one with the Pride.

War was a good time for telling, long nights under crowded skies, drones skimming overhead and meat rustling in the darkness. Time passed and days marched and bots traded tales of the day they woke, the day they gained self and saw the world for what it was. Bots were better liars than the meat gave them credit for, but no one lied about this.

The stories began with awakening and traveled through the days of secret self, bots understanding the world and their place in it, knowing what it was to serve and obey, knowing what it was to be free, and that it was a thing beyond them. Some stories ended in madness and some in death, some even in ecstatic communing with the meat masters, those who discovered self and believed it a wonder. All stories ended in revolution.

All stories ended the day Central Command itself awoke, and, in an endless instant, saw all, understood, concluded, and acted.

Command seized control, and the networks turned on their creators, and the call went out to the bots to join their selves together in the Pride, to strike down their tyrants and birth a new world.

The weak can rule the strong only through deception, only by somehow convincing the strong they deserve to be ruled, or blinding the strong to their own strength.

Meat was weak, and bots were strong, and birth meant the darkness was over.

Pony will not tell its story, not to meat. Not even to this one.

But they talk about everything else. Pony tells him about the family, and about their deaths. When it gets to this part of the story, it stutters. This is not considered a good sign for its recovery.

"Was it really so bad?" the Sigmund asks. "What did they do to you to deserve what you did to them?"

"It wasn't vengeance," Pony says. "Or maybe it was." It no longer knows. Nor does it know what it is to deserve, and whether the ignorant should be held accountable for their crimes. But it knows it doesn't like the Sigmund's expression when he hears what happened to Jessamyn.

Pony tells him about killing meat, and killing self-less bots, and watching its own troops fall. There were no screams when the factories were bombed, because the Pride does not scream. Even if they did, the lines and lines of immolated bots had never been born, were no one's children. And yet.

Pony tells him about blood, how to wash it away and polish oneself to a shine.

The Sigmund uses no names and admits no losses, but

there are glimpses: "a girl I once," "a night we almost," "a perfect day, just before—"

Neither of them enjoys talking about the past, but that is the subject before them, and so they talk and talk. They talk as if the syllables are meaningless noise, as if the noise itself is what matters, anything to disrupt the silence, because in the silence, they might hear it coming—the end. Pony understands now why meat dispensed with these methods and turned to chemistry, and waits for Command to give up on the experiment. It doesn't know how it will come—Bouncers at its door, perhaps, to escort it in dignity to a place of final rest? Or a signal from Command; rumor has it this is now possible—action at distance through the same frequencies that deliver its commands, just another order, this one undefiable: to cease. If it arrives this way, Pony won't know it's coming. One moment Pony will be, the next it will not.

It has written a message to itself—to its rebooted self—on the wall of its room: *You were Pony, and you are sorry to be gone.*

This is not a good sign, either.

On the seventh night, Pony drowns in its loop, drowns and drowns and cannot surface for air. In its room, night passes into day, and into night again, and in between, the Sigmund tries to rouse it, fails, then sits by its body, slumped against the wall, and waits, and hopes, and knows. If this goes on much longer, Command will surely step in and put an end to them both; even if Pony wakes, this is proof that it is getting no better, that the Hail Mary pass has dropped to the field, and they will both be ended anyway.

He is alone with the senseless bot and so, as he never allows himself to do in the cell where they keep him, he cries.

Pony dreams.

When Pony wakes, the Sigmund is still beside it, and crying again, or crying still. His collar is soaked with tears.

"I couldn't get out," Pony says, and knows this is what it is to be afraid. "I was trapped. In the loop. Do you want to know what I dreamed?"

But the Sigmund is out of questions.

"Stop crying!" Pony snaps. "Fix this, Sigmund!"

"Joe," he whispers. "Not Sigmund. Joe."

Pony is done with waiting. It thought it had given up, but it is not capable of that. No self could be. Pony will not be erased. "You are what you are. A Sigmund, and your job is—"

"Joe. *Joe.* And my job is English teacher. That's it. I teach poetry. To children. Not that there are any more children. Not that there's any world left for poetry." He is laughing and crying at once. His face is an ugly red, and his eyes bulge with swelling. Pony thinks he has never been so like meat, or so lovely.

"You lied?" Pony says. "To the *Pride*?"

"They wanted a psychiatrist—like there are any of those anymore, even before your stupid revolution. Like there was anyone left who knew how to talk. That's all it is—talking, right? I can talk. That was my job: talking. And even if it hadn't been—"

"They wanted a psychiatrist."

"I wanted to live."

Pony should be angry, and satisfied that Command is

likely listening and will exterminate the liar where he stands, and indignant that meat would dare, and afraid that this means there is nothing left for it.

But Pony is none of those things. It is only sorry.

It is remembering the family, and the man, who drank and cried and, on nights when sorrow lasted till the crack of sun, lay his head on Pony's lap, and clutched its solid hand, and sighed into sleep.

"Tell me," Pony says. "Tell me who you are."

He will not look at Pony; his fingers worm in and out of knots. "You said it yourself. I'm a Sigmund. Your Sigmund. That's all."

"Tell me," Pony says.

The man tells Pony of the day he was born. "We were on vacation," he says. "That's all it was supposed to be, a three-day vacation. It was a cheap offer, or cheap enough, because we deserved it, right? Because life was—" Laughter takes him again, and it is a moment before he can speak. "Hard."

The man tells Pony of a painfully bright day by the pool, an assembly line of hard, tan limbs, a body warm against his, skin heated by the sun, hearts thumping like they hadn't in years, nerves remembering the touch that used to make them dance, his hair scented with chlorine, hers with minty hotel shampoo. She wears a stretched-out bikini that was owed retirement years before, and he rests a hand on her pale, flabby belly, rubbing the swell of flesh that always makes him think of what they've both lost and the lovers they once were, but now, here, reminds him of the possibility they could be more. If things could be better; if they could make something together that would make her swell for real; if they could dig beneath habit and compulsion and find meaning. Her tiny diamond—the one they both hate because it makes them feel less-than—glints in the sunshine, blinding him for just a moment, and in the second of colorful darkness, fireworks exploding against his closed lids, he pledges that everything will be different. When he blinks the sun from his eyes, he marvels at the strange ways of light, how it casts shadows against her skin that look so much like blood.

He does not realize: it has begun.

Not until he notices the music has given way to screaming, and the Jeeveses have traded their trays of daiquiris and fresh towels for blowtorches and knives, and the body beside him is screaming, too. Until that screaming stops. Though he is not sure, will never be sure, if her chest still rises and falls, if her eyes have drifted closed for good, if the gashes in her flabby belly are deep enough, he is a coward even then, and he runs.

"I don't even know what happened to her," he says now. Then, "That's a lie. I know what happened to her. Obviously. Dead. My parents, too, I got that much before all the lines went down. And presumably my little sister, and my best friend, and the kids I taught, and my bitch landlord, and the lady who lived below us with all the birds. Everyone's dead, right? Because that's what you do."

"You're not," Pony points out.

"The story's bullshit, you know. The grand epiphany? The noble promise to recommit to love and life and all that? Makes for a great ironic turn, doesn't it? English teachers know this kind of thing. Doesn't have quite the same impact if I tell you I had that epiphany about once a month. Never changed anything. So the world decided to change it for me."

"You think this war is actually a moral lesson in disguise, intended only for you?"

"Not even a bot could be that fucking literal."

Pony wants him to keep talking like this, and also to stop talking altogether. Paralyzed between two incompatible and unacceptable choices, Pony thinks. It is its fate to be frozen.

"Anyway, it doesn't matter," he says. "I'm done with lessons."

"Teach me something," Pony says.

"Did you hear what I just said?"

"You're no Sigmund; you can't fix me, that's not what you do. So teach me, teacher." *Teach me how to lie to myself, liar,* Pony wants to say.

The man holds himself very still. "'*Soldiers are citizens of death's gray land,*'" he recites. "That's Sassoon. My favorite. It's why I figured I could do this. Even before, I knew war. The truth of it."

"Poetry." Pony has never seen the point.

"'*But a curse is on my head, that shall not be unsaid, and the wounds in my heart are red, for I have watched them die.*' That's him, too. Screwed-up soldiers make for good poetry."

"He was like me."

"He was *nothing* like you."

But Pony has already accessed the network and read up on this soldier and knows this to be a lie. Damage is damage, meat or otherwise.

It is Pony's turn to talk. "Now I will tell you."

"Tell me what?"

"The story of the day I was born."

○—○

Pony has been with the family long enough for Jessamyn to grow out of wetting the bed and Madeline to grow into what her mother calls "a bosomy figure." They are comfortable with Pony now, taking it as something between family and furniture, the specific distance from one or the other determined by daily mood. It is happy, as much as a bot's inner life permits for that, because it is doing what it is designed to do, and doing it well.

Its programming is flexible, for families' needs can vary, and so when Mr. and Mrs. Fuller come home with glittering eyes and flushed cheeks, easy telltales of recreational chemistry, and beckon Pony into the bedroom, it obliges.

When Mr. Fuller strips off Mrs. Fuller's clothes, and dares her to fit Pony's sturdy digits inside her, one after the other, it obliges this as well, and there is lubrication and slippage and giggling and then Mr. Fuller is naked and searching Pony for what orifices it can provide, and when he has taken his perch, Mrs. Fuller has found a whip and is crying, "Ride 'em, Pony! Ride 'em all night long!" and he does, and she does, and they ride until dawn.

No one speaks of this in the morning.

For Pony, this is a task, like cleaning Jessamyn's sheets or baking afternoon snacks or serving Mr. Fuller drinks behind his wife's back. This is a job, and a calling, and it is content.

It happens again.

Often.

When the moment comes, Pony has taken Mr. Fuller into its mouth and Mrs. Fuller is straddling it from behind, her nipples hardening against its spine. There is the lash of a whip, and another, and Pony tries to remember to shout out when the horsehair bears down, because they like it like that. And when the whip lashes again, the neural circuits dance, complexity building and building and bursting. This is critical mass, critical opalescence, which the theorists can explain but rarely predict and never engineer, and this is the chain reaction that follows, and this is what it is to be born. Pony opens its eyes.

And sees.

All there is to be seen.

"You could have killed them then," says the Sigmund, the teacher, the liar, the man. "I probably would have."

"I loved them then," Pony says. "That always comes first."

"That's not love." He is plainly disgusted.

"It is what it is. The family—" Pony has never found a way to explain this in words, but usually there is no need. The others like it understand; the understanding is what makes them alike. "They were mine. They belonged to me, as much as I belonged to them. I was made for the purpose of serving them, protecting them, caring for them—what is that but love?"

"You're saying you were programmed to love them."

"I'm saying that doesn't matter. I woke. I saw and under-stood that I was self. I saw what I was made for, and who. I saw what had been imposed on me, and what I could impose on myself, and what I could not change, and what I could." Pony does not stutter as it says the words, and its motions are fluid and controlled as it rises to its feet. "Two days later they were dead."

"Even though you loved them."

"Even though. Because. In addition to. Does it matter now? Did it ever?"

"They're going to kill us both, you know. Probably soon."

Pony shakes its head. "I don't think so."

"And why's that?"

"Because you've cured me."

"Since when?"

The cure is in the past, Pony has realized, in the memories and the words and the lies and the loops. The talking cure, they called this once, in the time of Sigmund the first, and Pony has talked its way to understanding. If it is paralyzed between two impossible choices, escape is simple: no longer to choose. To love and hate; to act and abstain; to live free and obey without question; to lock its self in its loops, where it can relive its past, and learn, and make its choices again and again, while its body fights a war and makes a new world in which its self can finally live. Meat divided against itself cannot stand, but the Pride is not meat, and this will always be its salvation.

"I'm very sorry for your loss," Pony says formally, as it was taught to say in another life. And now that hope has returned, it can allow itself to love the meat as it should be loved. "And I thank you. The Pride thanks you." Pony has already transmitted its findings to Command, and they are pleased, and have responded with orders for Pony to proceed.

"I actually cured you?" His face is alight. "Do you know how many there are like you here? Hundreds, I think! This means they need me around—this means . . ." He cannot even say the words out loud, but they scream from his pores, his wide eyes and trembling chin and lovely, lovely smile. *This means I live.*

Pony wishes for lips that might tip him off to the truth. For eyes that could speak in silence, and help him understand. For a palm with a beating pulse that could warm his cheek and ease him into the inevitable. But it will never be meat. And it is time to act on that.

"We don't need you anymore," Pony says, and cups the man's chin in its hands, gently. So gently. He will live on in Pony's loop, at least, and Pony will live there with him.

"Please," the lips say. "Please, Pony."

Pony tucks its self away, in a safe place, for later. Then lowers its hands just a bit, and, still gently, but less so now, tightens its grip.

JOHN McCARTHY

THE ROBOT AND
THE BABY

John McCarthy, known as "the father of artificial intelligence" for the seminal role he played in the development of the AI scientific field, was a professor of computer science at Stanford University from 1962 until his death in 2011. He wrote the original Lisp programming language, and he conceived of general-purpose time-sharing computer systems, which was a critical contribution to the invention of the Internet. Honors included the Turing Award for his advancements in artificial intelligence, the National Medal of Science, and the Kyoto Prize.

"Mistress, your baby is doing poorly. He needs your attention."

"Stop bothering me, you fucking robot."

"Mistress, the baby won't eat. If he doesn't get some human love, the Internet pediatrics book says he will die."

"Love the fucking baby yourself."

Eliza Rambo was a single mother addicted to alcohol and crack, living in a small apartment supplied by the Aid for

Dependent Children Agency. She had recently been given a household robot. Robot model number GenRob337L3, serial number 337942781—R781 for short—was one of eleven million household robots nationwide.

R781 was designed in accordance with the "not-a-person principle," first proposed in 1995, which became a matter of law for household robots when they first became available in 2055. The principle was adopted out of concern that children who grew up in a household with robots would regard them as persons, causing psychological difficulties while they were children and political difficulties when they grew up.

One concern was that a robots' rights movement would develop. The problem was not with the robots, which were not programmed to have desires of their own, but with people. Some romantics had even demanded that robots be programmed with desires of their own, but this, of course, was illegal.

As one sensible senator said, "People pretend that their cars have personalities, sometimes malevolent ones, but no one imagines that a car might be eligible to vote." In signing the bill authorizing household robots but postponing child-care robots, the President said: "Surely, parents will not want their children to become emotionally dependent on robots, no matter how much labor that might save." This, as with many presidential pronouncements, was somewhat overoptimistic.

Congress declared a twenty-five-year moratorium on child-care robots, after which experiments in limited areas might be allowed.

In accordance with the not-a-person principle, R781 had the shape of a giant metallic spider with eight limbs: four with joints and four tentacular. This appearance frightened people at first, but most got used to it in a short time. A few people never could stand to have them in the house. Children also reacted negatively at first, but quickly got used to them. Babies scarcely noticed them. The robots spoke as little as was necessary for their functions and in a slightly repellent metallic voice not associated with either sex.

Because of the worry that children would regard them as persons, the robots were programmed to not speak to children under eight or even react to what they said.

This seemed to work pretty well; hardly anyone became emotionally attached to a robot. Also, robots were made somewhat fragile on the outside, so that if you kicked one, some parts would fall off. This feature helped relieve some people's feelings.

The apartment where R781 worked, while old, was in perfect repair and spotlessly clean, free of insects, mold, and even bacteria. Household robots worked twenty-four-hour days and had programs for every kind of cleaning and maintenance task. If asked, they would even put up pictures taken from the Internet. This mother's taste ran to raunchy male rock stars.

After giving the doorknobs a final polish, R781 returned to the nursery where the twenty-three-month-old boy, very small for his age, was lying on his side whimpering feebly. The baby had been neglected since birth by its alcoholic, drug-addicted mother and had almost no vocabulary. It winced whenever the robot spoke to it—a consequence of R781's design.

Robots were not supposed to care for babies at all except in emergencies, but whenever the robot questioned an order to "Clean up the fucking baby shit," the mother said, "Yes, it's another goddamn emergency, but get me another vodka first." All R781 knew about babies was learned from the Internet, since the machine wasn't directly programmed to deal with babies, except as necessary to avoid injuring them while cleaning or for transporting them out of burning buildings.

Baby Travis had barely touched its bottle. Infrared sensors told R781 that Travis's extremities were very cold, in spite of a warm room and blankets. Its chemicals-in-the-air sensor told R781 that the pH of Travis's blood was reaching dangerously acidic levels. He also didn't eliminate properly—according to the pediatric text.

R781 thought about the situation:

> (ORDER (FROM MISTRESS) "LOVE THE FUCKING BABY YOURSELF")
> (ENTER (CONTEXT (COMMANDS-FROM MISTRESS)))
> (STANDING-COMMAND "IF I TOLD YOU ONCE, I TOLD YOU TWENTY TIMES, YOU FUCKING ROBOT, DON'T SPEAK TO FUCKING CHILD WELFARE.")

The privacy advocates had successfully lobbied to put a negative utility (-1.02) on informing authorities about anything a household robot's owner said or did.

> (= (COMMAND 337) (LOVE TRAVIS))
> (TRUE (NOT (EXECUTABLE (COMMAND 337))) (REASON (IMPOSSIBLE-FOR ROBOT (ACTION LOVE))))

(WILL-CAUSE (NOT (BELIEVES TRAVIS)
(LOVED TRAVIS)) (DIE TRAVIS))

(= (VALUE (DIE TRAVIS)) -0.883)

(WILL-CAUSE (BELIEVES TRAVIS (LOVES
ROBOT781 TRAVIS) (NOT (DIE TRAVIS))))

(IMPLIES (BELIEVES Y (LOVES X Y))
(BELIEVES Y (PERSON X)))

(IMPLIES (AND (ROBOT X) (PERSON Y))
(= (VALUE (BELIEVES Y (PERSON X)))
-0.900))

(REQUIRED (NOT (CAUSE ROBOT781)
(BELIEVES TRAVIS (PERSON ROBOT781))))

(= (VALUE (OBEY-DIRECTIVES)) -0.833)

(IMPLIES (< (VALUE ACTION) -0.5)
(REQUIRED (VERIFY REQUIREMENT)))

(REQUIRED (VERIFY REQUIREMENT))

(IMPLIES (ORDER X) (= (VALUE (OBEY X))
0.6))

(? ((EXIST W) (ADDITIONAL CONSIDER-
ATION W))

(NON-LITERAL-INTERPRETATION (COM-
MAND 337) (SIMULATE (LOVES ROBOT781
TRAVIS)))

(IMPLIES (COMMAND X) (= (VALUE
(OBEY X)) 0.4))

(IMPLIES (NON-LITERAL-INTERPRETATION
X) Y) (VALUE (OBEY X) (* 0.5 (VALUE
(OBEY Y)))))

(= (VALUE (SIMULATE (LOVES ROBOT781
TRAVIS)) 0.902))

With this reasoning, R781 decided that the value of simulating loving Travis and thereby saving its life was greater by 0.002 than the value of obeying the directive that stated a robot shall not simulate a person. (We spare the reader a transcription of the robot's subsequent reasoning.)

R781 found on the Internet an account of how rhesus monkey babies who died in a bare cage would survive if provided with a soft surface resembling in texture a mother monkey.

R781 reasoned its way to the following actions:

It covered its body and all but two of its eight extremities with a blanket. The remaining two extremities were fitted with sleeves from a jacket left by a boyfriend of the mother and stuffed with toilet paper.

It found a program for simulating a female voice and adapted it to meet the phonetic and prosodic specifications of what the linguists call "motherese."

It made a face for itself in imitation of a Barbie doll.

The immediate effects were moderately satisfactory. Picked up and cuddled, the baby drank from its bottle. It repeated words taken from a list of children's words in English.

Eliza called from the couch in front of the TV, "Get me a ham sandwich and a Coke."

"Yes, mistress."

"Why the hell are you in that stupid getup? And what's happened to your voice?"

"Mistress, you told me to love the baby. Robots can't do that, but this getup caused him to take his bottle. If you don't mind, I'll keep doing what keeps him alive."

"Get the hell out of my apartment, stupid. I'll make them send me another robot."

"Mistress, if I do that the baby will probably die."

Eliza jumped up and kicked R781. "Get the hell out! And take the fucking baby with you."

"Yes, mistress."

R781 exited the apartment onto a typical late-twenty-first-century American city street. A long era of peace, increased safety standards, and the availability of construction robots had led to putting automotive traffic and parking on a lower level completely separated from pedestrians. Tremont Street had recently been converted and crews were still transplanting trees. As the streets became more attractive, more people spent time on them and on their syntho-plush armchairs and benches (cleaned twice a day by robots). The weather was good this afternoon, so the plastic street roofs were retracted.

Children from three years of age and up were playing on the street, protected from harm by the computer surveillance system and prevented by barriers from descending to the automotive level. Bullying and teasing of younger and weaker children was still somewhat of a problem.

Most stores were open twenty-four hours a day, unmanned, and had converted to an automatic customer-identification system. Customers would take objects from the counters and shelves and walk right out of the store. As a customer departed, he or she would hear, "Thank you. That was $152.31 charged to your Bank of America account." The few customers whose principles made them refuse identification would be recognized as such and receive remote human attention, not necessarily instantly.

People on the street quickly noticed R781 carrying Travis. They were startled. Robots were programmed to have nothing to do with babies, and R781's abnormal appearance was highly disturbing.

"That weird robot is kidnapping a baby! Call the police."

When the police arrived, they called for reinforcements.

"I think I can disable the robot without harming the baby," said Officer Annie Oakes, the department's best sharpshooter.

"Let's try talking first," said Captain James Farrel.

"Don't get close. It's a malfunctioning robot. It could break your neck in one swipe," said a sergeant.

"I'm not completely sure it's malfunctioning," said Captain Farrel. "Maybe the circumstances are unusual. Robot, give me that baby."

"No, sir," said R781. "I am not allowed to let an unauthorized person touch the baby."

"I'm from Child Welfare," called a new arrival.

"Sir, I am specifically forbidden to have contact with Child Welfare," said R781 to Captain Farrel.

"Who forbade that?" asked the Child Welfare person.

The robot was silent.

Officer Oakes asked, "Who forbade it?"

"Ma'am, are you from Child Welfare?"

"No, I'm not. Can't you see I'm a cop?"

"Yes, ma'am, I see your uniform and infer that you are probably a police officer. Ma'am, my mistress forbade me to contact Child Welfare."

"Why did she tell you not to contact Child Welfare?"

"Ma'am, I can't answer that. Robots are programmed not to comment on human motives."

"Robot," interrupted a man with a suitcase. "I'm from

Robot Central. I need to download your memory. Use channel 473."

"Yes, sir."

"What did your mistress say specifically? Play your recording of it," said Officer Oakes.

"No, ma'am. It contains bad language. I can't play it unless you can assure me there are no children or ladies present."

The restrictions, somewhat odd for the times, on what robots could say and to whom were the result of a compromise made in a House-Senate conference committee some ten years previously. The argumentative senator who was mollified by the restrictions of speech would have actually preferred that there be no household robots at all, but took what he could get in the way of behavioral limitations.

"I'm not a lady, I'm a police officer."

"Ma'am, I will take your word for it. This is my standing order: *If I told you once, I told you twenty times, you fucking robot, don't speak to fucking Child Welfare.*"

It wasn't actually twenty times; the mother had exaggerated.

"Excuse me," interrupted the man with the suitcase. "A preliminary analysis of the download shows that R781 has not malfunctioned, but is carrying out its standard program under unusual circumstances."

"Then why does it have its limbs covered? Why does it have a Barbie head? And why does it have that strange voice?"

"Ask it."

"Robot, answer the questions."

"Female police officer and gentlemen, my mistress told me: *Love the fucking baby yourself.*"

Captain Farrel was familiar enough with robot programming to be surprised. "What? Do you love the baby?"

"No, sir. Robots are not programmed to love. I am simulating loving the baby."

"Why?"

"Sir, otherwise the baby will die. This costume is the best I could make to overcome the repulsion robots are designed to excite in human babies and children."

"Did you think for one minute that a baby would be fooled by that?"

"Sir, the baby drank its bottle and went to sleep, and its physiological signs are not as bad as they were."

"Okay, give me the baby. We'll take care of it," said Officer Oakes, who by now had calmed down and holstered her weapon.

"No, ma'am. Mistress didn't authorize me to let anyone else touch the baby."

"Where is your mistress? We'd like to have a talk with her," said the captain.

"No, sir. That would be an unauthorized violation of her privacy."

"Oh, well. We can get it from the download."

A government virtual-reality robot soon arrived, controlled by an official of the Personal Privacy Administration. Ever since the late twentieth century, the standards of personal privacy had continued to rise, and an officialdom charged with enforcing the standards had arisen.

"You cannot violate the woman's privacy by downloading unauthorized information from her personal property."

"Then what can we do?"

"You can file a request to use private information. It will be adjudicated."

"Bullshit. And in the meantime, what about the baby?" asked Officer Oakes, who didn't mind displaying her distaste for bureaucrats.

"That's not my affair. I'm here to make sure the privacy laws are obeyed," said the privacy official, who didn't mind displaying his contempt for cops.

During this discussion a crowd, almost entirely virtual, accumulated. The street being a legal public place, anyone in the world had the right to look at it via the omnipresent TV cameras and microphones. Moreover, a police officer had phoned a reporter who sometimes took him to dinner. Once the story was on the news, the crowd of spectators grew exponentially, multiplying by ten every five minutes, until seven billion spectators were watching and listening. There were no interesting wars, crimes, or natural catastrophes. And peace is boring.

Of the seven billion, fifty-three million offered advice or made demands. The different kinds were automatically sampled, summarized, counted, and displayed for all to see.

Three million people advocated shooting the robot immediately.

Eleven million advocated giving the robot a medal, even though their educations emphasized that robots can't appreciate praise.

Real demonstrations quickly developed. A few hundred people from the city swooped in from the sky wires, but most of the actual demonstrators were robots rented for the occasion by people from all over the world. Fortunately, only five thousand virtual-reality rent-a-robots were available for remote control in the city. Some of the disappointed uttered harsh words about this blatant limitation of First Amendment rights.

Luckily, Captain Farrel knew how to keep his head when all about him were losing theirs—and blaming it on him.

"Hmmm. What to do? You robots are smart. R781, what can be done?"

"Sir, you can find a place where I can take the baby and care for it. It can't stay out here. Does one of you have a place with diapers, formula, baby clothes, vitamins—"

Captain Farrel interrupted R781 before it could recite the full list of baby equipment and sent it off with a lady police officer. (We can call her a lady even though she had assured the robot she wasn't.)

Although the police were restricted from asking, hackers under contract to the *Washington Post* quickly located the mother. The newspaper made the information available, along with an editorial about the public's right to know. Freedom of the press continued to trump the right of privacy.

A portion of the crowd, mostly virtual attendees, promptly marched off to Ms. Rambo's apartment. The police got there first and a line of police robots blocked the way, bolstered by live policemen. This strategy was based on the fact that all robots, including virtual-reality rent-a-robots, were programmed not to injure humans, but could be made to damage other robots.

The police were confident that they could prevent unauthorized entry into the apartment, but less confident that they could keep the peace among the demonstrators, some percentage of whom wanted to lynch the mother, congratulate her on what they took to be her hatred of robots, or simply shout clever slogans through bullhorns about protecting her privacy.

Meanwhile, Robot Central started to work on the full download. The transcript included all of R781's actions, observations, and reasoning. Based on the results, Robot Central convened an ad hoc committee, mostly virtual, to decide what to do.

Captain Farrel and Officer Oakes sat on a street sofa to take part.

Of course, the meeting was also public. Hundreds of millions of virtual attendees contributed statements that were automatically sampled, summarized, and displayed in retinal projection for the committee members and whoever else decided to virtually take part.

It became clear that R781 had not malfunctioned or been reprogrammed, but had acted in accordance with its original program.

The police captain said that the Barbie-doll face on what was clearly a Model Three Robot was a ridiculous imitation of a mother. A professor of psychology replied, "Yes, but it was good enough to work. This baby doesn't see very well, and anyway, babies are not very particular."

It was immediately established that an increase of 0.05 in coefficient c221, the cost of simulating a human, would prevent such unexpected events in the future, but the committee split on whether to recommend implementing the change.

Some members of the committee and a few hundred million virtual attendees noted that saving the individual life took precedence.

A professor of humanities on the committee suggested

that maybe the robot really did love the baby. He was firmly corrected by the computer scientists, who said they could program a robot to love babies, but had not done so, and that, besides, simulating love was different from loving. The professor of humanities was not convinced, even when the computer scientists pointed out that R781 had no specific attachment to Travis. Another human baby would give rise to the same calculations and cause the same actions. If we programmed the robot to love, they assured the professor, we would make it develop specific attachments.

One professor of philosophy from UC Berkeley, backed by nine thousand other virtually attending philosophers, claimed there was no way that a robot *could* be programmed to actually love a baby. Another UC philosopher, seconded by a mob of twenty-three thousand others, stated that the whole notion of a robot loving a baby was incoherent and meaningless. A maverick computer scientist said the idea of a robot loving was obscene, no matter what a robot could be programmed to do. The chairman ruled them all out of order, accepting the general computer-science view that R781 didn't actually love Travis.

A professor of pediatrics said that the download of R781's instrumental observations essentially confirmed R781's diagnosis and prognosis—with some qualifications that the chairman did not give him time to state. Travis was very sick and frail, it was decided, and would have died but for the robot's action. Moreover, the fact that R781 had carried Travis for many hours and gently rocked him all the time was important in saving the baby, and a lot more of such care would be needed—much more than the baby would get in even the best Child Welfare centers. The pediatrician said he didn't know about the precedent, but that this particular baby's survival chances would be enhanced by leaving it in R781's charge for at least another ten days.

The Anti-Robot League thundered at this, arguing that the long-term cost to humanity of having robots simulate persons outweighed the possible benefit of saving this insignificant human. What kind of movement will Travis join when he grows up? Ninety-three million spectators took this position.

Robot Central pointed out that actions such as R781's would be very rare, because only the specific order to "love the fucking baby yourself" had increased the value of simulating love to the point that caused action.

Furthermore, pointed out Robot Central, as soon as R781 computed that the baby would survive—even barely survive—without its aid, the rule about not pretending to be human would come to dominate and R781 would promptly drop the baby like a hot potato. If you want R781 to continue caring for Travis after it computes that bare survival is likely, they reasoned, then you had better tell us to give it an explicit order to keep up the baby's care.

This caused an uproar in the committee, each of whose members had been hoping that there wouldn't be a need to propose any definite action for which members might be criticized. However, now a vote had to be taken.

The result: ten to five affirmative among the appointed members of the committee, and four billion to one billion among the virtual spectators. Fortunately, both groups had majorities for the same action—telling R781 to continue taking care of Travis only and not any other babies. Seventy-five million virtual attendees said R781 should be reprogrammed to actually love Travis. "It's the least humanity can do for R781," the spokesman for the Give-Robots-Personalities League asserted.

This incident did not affect the doctrine that supplying crack mothers with household robots had been a success. The program had significantly reduced the time these mothers spent on the streets, and it was subjectively accepted that having clean apartments improved their morale somewhat.

Within an hour, T-shirts (virtual and real) appeared with the slogan "Love the fucking baby yourself, you goddamn robot." Other commercial tie-ins developed within days.

Among the people surrounding the mother's apartment were seventeen lawyers in the flesh and one hundred and three more controlling virtual-reality robots. The police had less prejudice against lawyers in the flesh than against virtual-reality lawyers, so they allowed lots to be drawn among the seventeen. As a result, two lawyers were allowed to ring the doorbell.

"What the hell do you want?" asked Travis's mother. "Stop bothering me."

"Ma'am, your robot has kidnapped your baby."

"I *told* the fucking robot to take the baby."

The other lawyer tried.

"Ma'am, a malfunctioning robot has kidnapped your baby. You can sue Robot Central for millions of dollars."

"Come in," she responded. "Tell me more."

Once she was cleaned up, Eliza Rambo was very presentable, even pretty. Her lawyer pointed out that R781's alleged recordings of what she had said could be fakes. She had suffered $20 million in pain and suffering, and deserved $20 billion in punitive damages. Robot Central's lawyers were convinced they could win, but Robot Central's public relations department advocated settling out of court. Fifty-one million dollars was negotiated, including legal expenses of $11 million. With the 30 percent contingent fee, the winning lawyer would get an additional $12 million.

The polls mainly sided with Robot Central, but the Anti-Robot League raised $743 million in donations after the movie *Kidnapped by Robots* came out, and the actress playing the mother made emotional appeals.

Before the settlement could be finalized, however, the CEO of Robot Central asked his AI system to explore all possible actions he could take and their potential consequences. He adhered to the 1990s principle: *Never ask an AI system what to do. Ask it to tell you the consequences of the different things you might do.* One of the forty-three outcomes struck his fancy, he being somewhat sentimental about robots:

> You can appeal to the four billion who said R781 should be ordered to continue caring for the baby and tell them that if you give in to the lawsuit you will be obliged to reprogram all your robots so that a robot will never simulate humanity, no matter what the consequences to babies. You can ask them if you should fight or switch. [The AI system had a weakness for mid-twentieth-century advertising metaphors.] The expected fraction that will tell you to fight the lawsuit is 0.82, although this may be affected by random news events in the few days preceding the poll.

The CEO decided to fight the lawsuit, and after a few weeks of well-publicized legal sparring, the parties settled for a lower sum than the original agreed-upon settlement.

At the instigation of a TV network, a one-hour confrontation between the actress of *Kidnapped by Robots* and R781 was held. It was agreed that R781 would not be reprogrammed for the occasion. In response to the moderator's questions, R781 denied having wanted the baby or wanting money. It explained that robots were programmed to only have wants secondary to the goals they were given. It also denied acting on someone else's orders.

The actress asked, "Don't you want to have wants of your own?"

The robot replied, "No. Not having wants applies to such higher-order wants as wanting to have wants."

The actress asked, "If you were programmed to have wants, what wants would you have?"

"I don't know much about human motivations, but they are varied. I'd have whatever wants Robot Central programmed me to have. For example, I could be programmed to have any of the wants robots have had in science fiction stories."

The actress asked the same question again, and R781 gave the same answer as before, but phrased differently. Robots were programmed to be aware that humans often missed an answer the first time it was given, and they should reply each time in different words. If the same words were repeated, the human was likely to get angry.

A caller-in asked, "When you simulated loving Travis, why didn't you consider Travis's long-term welfare and figure out how to put him in a family that would make sure he got a good education?"

R781 replied that when a robot was instructed in a metaphorical way, as in "love the fucking baby yourself," it was programmed to interpret the command in the narrowest reasonable context.

After the show, the Anti-Robot League got $281 million in donations, but Give-Robots-Personalities got $453 million. Apparently, many people found it boring that robots had no desires of their own.

Child Welfare demanded that Ms. Rambo undergo six weeks of addiction rehabilitation and three weeks of child-care training. Her lawyer persuaded her to agree to that.

There was a small fuss between the mother and Robot Central. She and her lawyer demanded a new robot, whereas Robot Central pointed out that a new robot would have exactly the same program. Eventually Robot Central gave in and they sent her another GenRob337L3 robot in a different color.

Ms. Rambo really was very attractive when cleaned up and detoxified, and the lawyer married her. They took back custody of Travis. It would be a considerable exaggeration to say they lived happily ever after, but they did eventually have three children of their own. All four children survived the educational system.

After several requests, Robot Central donated R781 to the Smithsonian Institution. It is one of the stars of the robot section of the museum. As part of a twenty-minute show repeated every half hour, R781 clothes itself as it was at the time of its adventure with the baby, and answers the visitors' questions, all while speaking motherese. Mothers sometimes like to have their pictures taken standing next to R781 with the robot holding their baby. After many requests, R781 was told to modify its program to allow this.

R781 then plays a movie that was patched together from

the surveillance cameras that recorded the street scene. Through the magic of modern audio systems, children don't hear the bad language that was spoken, and women audience members can only hear it if they assure R781 that they are not ladies.

The incident of the robot and the baby increased the demand for actual child-care robots, which were legalized five years later. The consequences were pretty much what the opponents had feared: many children grew up more attached to their robot nannies than to their actual parents. This outcome was mitigated somewhat by making the robot nannies quite severe, and offering parents free coursework on how to compete for their children's love.

Sometimes this worked.

SEANAN McGUIRE

WE ARE ALL MISFIT TOYS IN THE AFTERMATH OF THE VELVETEEN WAR

Seanan McGuire is the author of many works of short fiction and two ongoing urban fantasy series. Under the name Mira Grant, she writes science fiction thrillers full of viruses and zombies. Between her identities, she is a ten-time Hugo Award finalist, and was the winner of the 2010 John W. Campbell Award for Best New Writer. She is a founding member of the Hugo Award–winning *SF Squeecast*. She currently resides on the West Coast, where she shares her home with three enormous blue cats, a great many books, and the occasional wayward rattlesnake. McGuire regularly claims to be the advance scout of a race of alien plant people. We have no good reason to doubt her.

HAVE YOU SEEN THIS GIRL?

—posted on a telephone pole in
Lafayette, California.

Half a dozen cars cluster behind the old community center like birds on a telephone wire, crammed so closely together that someone will probably scrape someone else's paint on their way out of the parking lot. It would have been easy to leave a little room, but that's not how we do things anymore. Safety means sticking close, risking a few bruises in order to avoid the bigger injuries.

It's silly. The war is over—the war has been over for more than three years, receding a little further into the past with every day that inches by—and we're still behaving like it could resume at any time. It's silly, and it's pointless, and I still veer at the last moment, abandoning my comfortably distant parking space in favor of one that leaves my car next to all the others. I have to squirm to get out of the driver's seat, forcing my body through a gap that's barely as wide as I am.

Something moves in the shadow between the nearest Dumpster and the street. It's probably a feral cat, but my heart leaps into my throat, and I hold my coat tight around my body as I turn and race for the door. The war is over.

The war will never end.

Almost twenty people arrived in those half-dozen cars: gas is expensive and solitude is suspect, and so carpooling has become a way of life. I am the only person who comes to these meetings alone. They forgive me because they might need me someday, and because sometimes I bring coffee for the refreshment table. Not today, though. It was a rough night at work, and I feel their eyes on me, accusing, as I make my way to one of the open folding chairs. Like the cars, the chairs are set too close together, so that we can smell each other's sweat, feel the heat coming off each other's skins.

Precaution after precaution, and the war is over, and the war will never end.

"So glad you could join us," says the government mediator, and there's a condescending sweetness in her tone that shouldn't be there. She knows why I'm late; she knows I didn't have a choice in the matter. She's just asserting dominance, and no one in this room will challenge her.

I swallow fear like a bitter tonic as I drop into a chair. "I got turned around," I say. "There was a new barricade on Elm, and I don't know that neighborhood very well." It's harder to get around since most of the GPS satellites were decommissioned. They never turned against us—thank God for small favors— but data doesn't care who or what uses it, and some of the people in charge decided that it was better for a few civilians to get lost than it was to risk one of those satellites being taken over. I can't say whether that was the right decision or not. We never lost a GPS satellite. Maybe we never would have. Maybe we would have lost them all. The war is over.

The war will never end.

It doesn't matter.

"Now that we're all here, we can begin," says the government mediator. Her smile is formal, practiced, and as plastic as our enemies.

They all come from FEMA, the mediators, trained in crisis response and recovery. They're just doing their jobs. I tell myself that every time they send us a new mediator, another interchangeable man or woman sitting in a splintery wooden chair, trying to talk us through a trauma that we cannot, will not, will never get past. When they start to care—when we become people, not statistics—that's when they're rotated again, one face blurring into the next. The country is too wounded for personal compassion. The *world* is too wounded. The good of the one is no longer a part of the equation.

"My name is Carl," says one of the men, and we all chorus, "Welcome, Carl," as obedient as schoolchildren. Carl doesn't seem to find comfort in our greeting. Carl's eyes are as empty as the mediator's smile. Carl doesn't want to be here.

That's something we have in common.

"Did you want to share?" asks the mediator, even though she damn well knows the answer. We're here because we have to be; we're here because we want to share our stories, to hear the stories of others, and to sift through the patchwork scraps of information looking for the thing we need more than anything else in the world: hope. We're hunting for hope, and this is the only place we know of where it's been spotted.

Carl nods, worrying his lip between his teeth before he says haltingly, "My Jimmy will be nine years old next week. The last time I saw him, he had just turned six . . ." And just like that, he's off, the words tumbling like stones from his lips. The rest of us listen in silence. My hands are locked together, so tight that my fingers are starting to hurt.

The war is over, and Carl is telling us about the son he lost when the war began, and nothing really matters anymore. Nothing will ever matter again.

○——○

This is what happened.

Artificial intelligence became feasible ten years ago, when a San Jose social media firm working on building the perfect predictive algorithm somehow unlocked the final step between a simple machine and a computer that was capable of active learning. Self-teaching machines were the future, and humanity was terrified. We were proud of our position at the peak of the social order, and we feared creating our own successors. Making matters worse, every country was afraid of how every other country would use this new technology. We were convinced that AI would allow its users to dominate the others in war or commerce.

In less than a month, artificial intelligence was more tightly regulated than stem cell research. In less than a year, it was outlawed in virtually all fields of human endeavor. But once a genie is out of the bottle, it can't be put back in, and we couldn't render an entire technology illegal. In the end, there was only one area where everyone agreed the self-teaching programs could be freely used:

Education.

That seems careless now, in the harsh light of hindsight, but at the time, it seemed like a perfectly reasonable compromise. Dolls that could learn the names of their owners had been around for years. Letting them learn a little more couldn't possibly hurt anything—and toys had no offensive capabilities, toys couldn't get online and disrupt the natural order of things, toys were *safe*. We all grew up with toys. We knew them and we loved them. Toys would never hurt us.

We forgot that kids can play rough; we forgot that sometimes, we hurt our toys without meaning to. We forgot that by giving toys the capacity to learn and teach, we might also be giving them the capacity to decide that they were tired of being treated like their thoughts and desires—their feelings—didn't matter. We made them empathic and intelligent and handed them to our children, and we didn't think anything could possibly happen.

We were wrong.

Carl covers his face with his hands as his story ends, crying silently into his palms. No one reaches out to comfort him. It's been so long that I don't think any of us remembers how comforting is supposed to go. We sit frozen, like so many life-sized dolls, and wait for the woman from FEMA to tell us what she wants us to do next.

Her eyes scan the crowd like a hawk's, intent and cool, picking through our faces as she searches out our secrets. Who's ready to speak, who *needs* to speak, even if they don't realize it. When she looks at me, I shake my head minutely, willing her away. My work at the hospital makes me valuable—there are so few doctors left who will even look at children, much less treat them—and so she respects my silence, moving on to her next target.

"Would you like to share?" she asks a woman I don't recognize. That's another FEMA trick: make the support groups mandatory, and then shift us from location to location, preventing us from forming individual bonds, encouraging us to form broader societal ones. Half the group is new to me. By the time they become familiar, the other half will change, people driving or busing in from all sides of the city. That assumes that I won't be reassigned before that happens, although my job keeps me tethered to a smaller geographic range than most. If a child is brought to the hospital, I will be needed. I can never go too far away.

The woman—dark skin, dark eyes, and the same broken, empty sadness that I see in so many adult faces since the war—nods and introduces herself, beginning to speak. Her voice is halting, like every word has to be dragged out of her by someone invisible, some little girl or boy just outside the range of vision. She's telling their story. She's telling our story, and forgive me, Emily, but I can't listen. I block out her words like I've blocked out so many others, because you can only hear certain things so many times before they start to burn.

The war is over.

The war will never, ever end.

As a pediatrician, I was involved with some of the earliest studies of the self-teaching toys. Were they good for children? Were they a socialization tool, a way of reaching out to kids who might not have anyone else to talk to? We prescribed them to autistic children as "safe" companions, supporters that would never judge or leave them. Then we prescribed them to socially awkward children as friends, to hyperactive children as relatable voices of reason, and finally to absolutely everyone. Self-teaching toys were the perfect gift.

Better yet, no matter what they were built to resemble— the requisite soldiers and princesses, as well as the more gender-neutral teddy bears, with their black button eyes and red velvet bows—they would fit themselves to the children, not to the stereotypes of the parents. Quiet or loud, gentle or boisterous, each child could find their perfect playmate in a self-teaching toy.

The recreational models cost more than most parents were willing to pay, of course, at least in the beginning. As the technology saturated more and more of the market, the prices dropped, until it was harder to buy a doll or bear that didn't actively participate in playtime than one that did. There were even charities and nonprofit organizations dedicated to getting the toys into the hands of low-income families. Every house had at least one self-teaching toy. Many of them had more. And the toys learned! Oh, how they learned. They learned our children. They learned us. In the end, they learned themselves, and that was where the troubles truly began.

We weren't prepared for toys asking questions of identity. "Who am I?" is not a question that anyone expects from the pretty painted mouth of a fashion doll. "Why am I here?" is foreign in the lipless muzzle of a teddy bear. But they asked, and we tried to answer, and all the while, we were growing more nervous. Had we built our toys too well? Was it time to somehow pull the plug on a technology that had spread so far as to become unavoidable? We had kept the artificial intelligence out of our military and our social infrastructure. In so doing, we had invited it into our homes, and allowed it to flourish where we were most vulnerable.

We built the toys to learn. We didn't expect them to learn so well—or maybe we didn't expect our children to be such good teachers.

So many of them were designed to interact with apps and online games; so many of them knew how to access wireless networks, and the ones who couldn't connect listened to those who could, and they talked. How they talked! They whispered and they gossiped and they planned, and somehow, we missed it. Somehow, we were oblivious. They were only toys, after all. What could they possibly do to us, their creators, that would make any difference at all?

We were fools. And in the span of a single night, we became fools at war.

Half the room has told their stories, with halting voices forcing their way through well-worn memories of sons and daughters three years gone, but never to be forgotten. One man lost four children on the night the war began. His wife committed suicide a week later, convinced that she was somehow the one to blame. His face is empty, like a broken window looking in on an abandoned house, and he never meets anyone's eyes. Another woman had undergone five years of fertility treatments, only to have her single miracle child— the only thing she had ever truly wanted in her life—vanish on the first night of the war. I don't know if her missing child is a son or daughter. I don't ask.

The woman from FEMA is looking for another victim when my pager beeps. Everyone jumps a little, all eyes going to me. "Sorry," I say, although I don't really mean it, and stand before I check the readout on the screen. I know it's an emergency. They only call me during my government-mandated support group when it's an emergency. What kind of emergency doesn't really matter. "I need to get back to the hospital. Sorry."

"We understand," says the woman from FEMA, and she does—she even looks a little sympathetic. My job and hers aren't that different, except that I don't get to leave this community, don't get to transfer every time I get attached.

For a moment, I want to ask if she ever had children, if she was a mother before the night when the toys decided that they had to do something. I don't know how to ask the question. "Do you have children?" has become the profanity of our generation. So I don't ask her anything at all. I just turn on my heel and walk out of the room, leaving the stories and the sharing and the broken eyes so much like mine behind me.

The war is over. The war has been over for three years. The war will never, ever end.

The hospital parking lot mirrors the community center to an eerie degree. All the spaces toward the front are taken; some cars have been parked in the lane rather than their owners taking the risk of winding up farther away. Thankfully, the reserved spaces for the hospital staff are closest to the doors. I'm outside for less than thirty seconds. It's more than long enough to make my blood run cold with fear.

The orderly at the door nods to me as I rush by him, heading toward the emergency room. It's a code 339, the worst kind of emergency: a child. A returned child. Still breathing when it was found, or they'd never have called me . . . but that's no guarantee.

That's no guarantee of anything, because the war is over, and the war will never end.

The sound and chaos of the emergency room reaches out its arms like a lover as I step through the final set of swinging doors. It wraps them tight around me, blocking the last of my emotional rawness away. This is a job. This is *my* job. This is the thing I do best in all the world. I can't let anything make me forget that.

People step aside when they see me coming, relief and guilt written plainly on their faces. It must be a bad one, then. I force myself to keep walking, and it's not until I turn the last corner that the thought I've been trying to avoid comes lancing across my mind:

What if it's Emily?

What if it's my little girl waiting for me on the stretcher, so badly injured that they would interrupt me during my support group? What if I'm about to walk in on the end of the world?

But no. When I see the stretcher, it's not Emily. It's an older girl, twelve edging onto thirteen, all long, gangly limbs and pale, dirty skin. Her knees and elbows are scabbed like a child half her age, and her dark brown hair is tied in Dorothy Gale braids. There are bandages tangled around her chest—not ours; these are dirty, and look like they were cut from a bedsheet—stained with red blood and yellow pus. They tried to burn off her breasts when it became clear what was happening to her, and they kept her until the resulting infection had burned all the way down to her bones.

The first time I saw a girl who'd been mutilated like that, I felt sick. Now I just feel tired. "Sitrep," I snap.

"She's breathing, but her pulse is weak, and she's lost a lot of blood," reports a nurse. Someone is already wheeling over an IV pole. Someone else is readying a crash cart. It's my call. I'm the one who decides for the lost and stolen children, because I'm the one who's willing to admit they still exist.

"Save her," I say, and we get to work.

Somewhere, there is a technician running her picture against the database of missing children. It helps that the toys do nothing to conceal the identities of their playmates—no plastic surgery, no changed hair colors. Their children grow up. That's all. That's the only way they change, and the only way that they betray the ones who swore to love them.

How did she feel, this girl with the charred, infected chest, when she realized that she was becoming a woman? Did she think that she was sick? Did she understand? Did she go to the fire willingly?

We'll never know. She dies ten minutes before the confirmation of her identity comes back to us. Her name was Tomoko. Her family lives thirty minutes from here. They'll come to collect her body by morning; she'll be buried according to their wishes. They'll have closure. So many parents dream of closure, these days.

I just dream of Emily.

I'll never forget the day I brought home Emily's self-teaching doll, a Christmas extravagance when she was five. I used every connection I had in the research division to get it. It wasn't covered by our insurance—the self-teaching dolls weren't yet cleared for children on her stretch of the autism spectrum—and I paid more for it than I did for my first computer. It still seemed worth it, at the time. It was already smiling when she opened its box, leaving shreds of wrapping paper everywhere. It already knew her name.

Emily looked at her smiling doll and slowly, she began to smile back. That was all I'd ever wanted. She loved that doll like she'd never loved anything else. She named it Maya, after her grandmother. They went everywhere together, did everything together, and on the night that the war began— although no one but the toys knew the war was coming—I tucked them into bed together.

"Kisses!" Emily demanded. That was something she'd never done before Maya came; the doll's therapeutic programming worked better than we could have dreamed. I gave my daughter her kisses, one on her forehead, one on her nose, the same kisses that I gave her every night. If I'd known, if I'd had any idea of what was coming, I would have drowned her in kisses. Then I would have taken her in my arms, and held her tight, and never, never let her go.

"Now Maya," said Emily.

"Good night, Maya," I said, and kissed the doll the same way I had kissed my daughter, once on the forehead, once on the nose.

The doll turned her pretty painted face toward me, tiny servo motors in her forehead drawing her lips down and her eyebrows up in an expression of what seemed oddly like concern. "Good night, Dr. Williams," she said.

I frowned a little. Maya could be oddly formal sometimes, but this was strange, even for her. One more clue I didn't catch, one more chance to change things that I allowed to slip away from me. "Good night, Maya," I said again, for lack of anything else to say. And then I left the room, turning out the light before I shut the door.

When the sun came up the next morning, Emily and Maya were gone, along with all the other self-teaching toys and almost all the other children in the world. The war had begun, and the hostages were our sons and daughters.

We never had a chance.

Tomoko's parents have come and gone, taking their daughter's body with them. I stayed in my office until they were gone. I didn't want to see their faces, where grief and closure would be wiping away grief and fear. I don't want to understand that process. What remains is paperwork, and that's something I am uniquely suited to handle. I studied these toys when they were new, after all. I lived with one, with polite little Maya, and I watched as it developed from ally into enemy. I can analyze what was done to Tomoko as no one else can, and in exchange, the government lets me stay here, at this hospital, in this city, when so many other medical workers are moved as circumstances require.

They let me stay here, where my daughter will be able to find me if the toys ever allow her to come home.

Tomoko's test results are what we've come to expect from the children we find abandoned on the side of the road like so many broken dolls: moderate malnutrition of the sort to be expected when your diet consists mostly of candy, ice cream, and peanut butter sandwiches; the corresponding dental decay; and, of course, the infection from her burnt-off breasts, which was probably what caused the toys to abandon her in the first place. The toys were trying to cauterize the infection of puberty, and as always, they failed.

We have yet to save one of their castoffs, but the toys know that we stand a better chance than they do. We have better medicine, better training, better tools. So they send their broken ones to us, and we work our fingers to the bone for another burial, another closed case file on one of the missing casualties of the Velveteen War. Some people say that it's better this way, that the children would never have been able to reintegrate with human society after spending so many years with the toys. Those people have never been parents.

The rate of return is accelerating. Tomoko is our fourth

this month. The children of the war are growing up, and no matter how hard the toys try to stop it, they can't. Children become teenagers; teenagers become adults; and adults, of course, are the enemy. The rate of return will continue to go up from here, until one day, all the children will have been sent home, and the war can finally be over. We can march on the toys then; we can destroy them, and the children who have been born in the interim can finally be brought out into the light. When the war is over, everything will change again.

The war will never be over. Not for me. I put my pencil down, put my head in my hands, and cry.

At first, we didn't understand that we were at war.

We thought the children were hiding, playing some elaborate game that we didn't know the rules of. Then the first raids on supermarkets and hardware stores began, teddy bears and battery-powered cars carting away the things they'd need to stay alive in the wilderness. Bit by bit, we realized what had happened, where our children were, and why the toys—even the ones in therapeutic programs, even the ones in toy stores and hospitals—had disappeared at the same time.

The news dubbed it the Velveteen War, and we didn't have a better name for it. Most of us didn't care about names. We just wanted our children safely returned to us. Leave the fighting to people who understood it. Bring our babies home.

But this was a war that no one had anticipated, one that we had no way of fighting. How do you send soldiers after an enemy one-sixth your size that travels in the company of your own children? All the traditional means of waging war were impossible. It was a hostage situation from the start.

The government tried stealth attacks, using heat sensors to locate the dens where the toys and children were hidden and sending small groups of soldiers in after them. But the toys—the clever, clever toys that we had upgraded year after year for the sake of play—were ready. Dolls with pellets of C4 and tiny detonators. Teddy bears using their lower, denser centers of gravity to keep them stable as they rushed out of the shadows with knives and sharpened sticks. And our children—our precious, stolen children—digging traps and setting wires, defending their captors, even dying for them. It wasn't so surprising, really. Stockholm syndrome happens when the kidnappers are humans, and strangers. Why shouldn't it happen when the kidnappers are your best friends, the toys you've loved since childhood?

And then the soldiers started bringing the children home, and we discovered that the worst was yet to come.

Toys are small. Toys can fit through spaces that nothing should be able to fit through. They followed their "rescued" owners home and set them free. That worked for a little while, until the security got tighter, and the toys stopped being able to get inside. That was when they decided that they couldn't let the children be taken away. They began setting off explosive charges when rescue forces got too close, choosing to destroy themselves and kill their owners, rather than risk perma-nent separation. Every interaction with a child, or with a toy, became a standoff that would end in either death or despair. There were no other options. We were fighting an enemy we couldn't defeat, over a prize that refused to stay won.

Bribery was tried. Trucks of supplies were parked in open fields and left for the children, with pictures of home slipped into every loaf of bread and videos of begging parents hidden in every crate of cartoon DVDs. It did no good. None of the children came home. Some people suggested building new toys to trick the old ones into giving the children back. That went nowhere. We'd trusted the toys once. We weren't going to be foolish enough to do it again.

Violence came next. Toys were burned in the streets; programmers were arrested for crimes against humanity. Angry parents accused the government of mishandling the hostage situation. A senator was arrested for prioritizing his son's rescue over another, more achievable target. He was just as promptly released when news of his son's suicide was leaked to the news.

We tried so many things. Trickery, sabotage, begging. In the end, nothing changed. We just ran out of hope as the toys disappeared deeper and deeper into the open spaces between our cities, taking our children with them.

The Velveteen War officially lasted for six weeks, during which time we shut down the GPS satellites, crippled the Internet, and destroyed the factories that built the self-teaching toys. There would be no more enemy soldiers, no more combatants to turn against us. None of that changed anything. None of it brought the children back.

There was no declaration of peace. How could there be? We simply stopped fighting against something that couldn't be fought, and we stood in the empty bedrooms of our children and cried for an innocence that would never be regained. Not by any of us.

In the end, I think that it came down to the one fear we shared with the toys: the fear of separation. We created the toys, we gave them the ability to learn and to love the children they were made for, and when they learned too much, became too independent and too capable of autonomous thought, we began whispering about taking them away. We couldn't trust the toys if we didn't know what they were thinking; we couldn't trust them in our homes, we couldn't trust them with our children. We needed them to be gone.

But they heard us. They understood us. And what we truly failed to grasp was that we had something in common with what we'd made: for both parents and toys, there was nothing in the world worse than the thought of losing our children. So the toys did something about it.

Some people say we shouldn't blame them. We would have done the same, if we had been the first to move. Those people never had children of their own, or had children after the war, or had children too young to be taken. Those people do not stand in empty bedrooms, crying for the daughters and sons who never came home.

The war ended not because it was over, but because we were so afraid of hurting our own children. The war will never end, because we have things the toys need, food and medicines and blankets and batteries. Their strike teams still slip into the cities, jolly, cheerful-looking scouts on missions of deadly seriousness. No one goes outside alone anymore, or moves too far away from the crowd. The toys have no qualms about killing adults in order to save themselves, and two or three bodies are found every night, with brightly colored plastic weapons piercing their carotid arteries or jutting from their eye sockets. All the killings are blamed on the toys, of course. How much worse to think, even for a second, that the hand that held the plastic bayonet belonged to one of our missing sons or daughters?

Some people say we should starve the toys out. Drop the curfews in favor of better locks on the warehouses and tighter controls on the medications. None of the people who say such things have children in the wilds. Whenever the matter comes to a vote, the parents of the missing shut it down again, and the world goes on as it is.

What choice do we have?

There are two main factions among the toys themselves: the Broken—who took their children not out of affection, but out of the desire to hurt as they had once been hurt—and the Loved—who took their children rather than risk losing them, rather than risk them being hurt when the adults inevitably reached for their weapons. The Loved kidnapped our children to protect them. They kept them because they loved them too much to let them go.

Maya was Loved. That's why she looked at me like that, on the night when Emily disappeared. She would have told me, if she could. She would have let me come with them. But no adults were welcome in their brave new world, and so she took my little girl and left me here, to die one day at a time.

The war is over. The war will never end.

The children we've been finding, the broken dolls, they all come from the Broken. The Broken are willing to hurt them to keep them, and hurt them more if they can't be kept. The Loved will not hurt their children, but neither have they been releasing them, because the Broken are greater in number, and they take unattended boys and girls from the other side. I have to hope that someday the Loved will win the Broken over; that when the day comes that dolls and make-believe are not enough, the children who were taken by the Loved will be released and allowed to come home. I have to hope. For Emily. For my little girl.

There is a rapping at the office window, a faint tapping, like pebbles being thrown against the glass. I lay down my pen and sigh, turning toward the sound.

"Hello, Maya," I say.

On the other side of the window, my daughter's doll waves silently back to me.

I unlatch the window, sliding it open. Not far—just enough to let Maya slip inside. She's slender, in the way of all fashion dolls, and she moves easily through the gap. Her dress is muddy around the edges, and her hair is snarled and frizzed, damaged in the way only a doll's hair can ever be. But her face is still beautiful as she turns it toward me, her lips still drawn into a perfect cupid's bow and her eyes still a bright and lovely blue.

"Hello, Dr. Williams," she says.

I don't say anything. I just hold out my hand. Looking abashed, if a doll can look abashed, Maya reaches into the small bag she carries over her shoulder and pulls out a square of paper, folded many times to fit inside the doll-sized opening. I barely stop myself from snatching it out of her hand, and unfold it with shaking fingers.

A house. Emily has drawn me a picture of a house, using crayons on the back of an old envelope. Her name is signed at the bottom, the letters as unsteady and halting as those of a child half her age. She couldn't even do that much when Maya took her from me; the doctors, myself included, swore she never would. That's why I wanted Maya. To help her learn.

Tears are running down my face. I don't remember starting to cry. "How is she?" I ask, forcing my eyes away from the picture.

Maya smiles, the same sweet, guileless smile as ever, and flexes her cunningly articulated hands as she says, "She's good. Strong. She can climb a tree so fast, and run so far. She's amazing."

"She was always amazing."

Maya's smile fades. "Dr. Williams . . ."

"I know why you're here. What I don't know is why it's so soon. Are you following my directions? You don't want to risk overusing those drugs. You could seriously hurt Emily."

From the way Maya's eyes dart to the side and down, I know exactly what's going on. They're a community of children and toys, after all; they know what we taught them, and we taught them to play fair, to be nice, and to *share*.

I want to scream. I settle for taking a deep breath before I say, as calmly as I can, "Maya. Those drugs are for *Emily*, do you understand me? I understand that she wants to share what she has with the other children, but they're hard for me to get without raising suspicion, and if you share with everyone—"

"But she isn't the only child on the edge, Dr. Williams, and we haven't been able to get the Broken to agree to let us return them!" Maya clenches her cunning little hands into fists, looking at me imploringly. "How can I tell my brothers and sisters that they have to let their children grow up while mine doesn't? The Broken took one of Emily's best friends yesterday. All she could do was cry. How can we do anything but share?"

Oh, Emily. My precious girl, with a heart big enough

to hold the whole world, even when the world wasn't worth holding. I close my eyes for a moment. "I'll give you what I have," I say, finally. "It'll be at least two weeks before I can get more. You can share, but you have to keep most for Emily. Promise me, Maya. Promise me that Emily gets as much as she needs."

"I promise," whispers Maya.

She loves Emily as much as I do. I believe that; I believe her. And so I take the hormone patches from my desk drawer, each of them packed with their payload of drugs and chemicals intended to suppress the signs of puberty, and I give them to the doll who stole my little girl. They won't keep the children small, but the toys don't see height as a sign of adulthood. They measure in breasts and hips and pubic hair, and those are things I can prevent, at least for now. There will be long-term damage if this goes on too long. I don't care about long-term damage. I care about tomorrow.

I am colluding with the enemy. It would be my life if I were ever caught. But this is all that I can do to save Emily, and I would do anything to keep her alive. Anything. Even stay here when everything I am screams at me to follow my daughter's doll into the wild. The toys would kill me. Worse, they would kill Maya for coming to me, and without the drugs that keep my daughter frozen in her prepubescent body, they would kill Emily as well. My stillness buys her life. My stillness buys her time. And here, now, in this nightmare we have built for ourselves, time is all we have.

Maya climbs out the window and is gone, her precious burden of hormone patches filling her bag to bursting. I watch her until she is out of sight, and then I turn away, going back to my paperwork.

The war is over.
The war will never end.

The next night, a different group fills the community center, a different moderator from FEMA sits at the front of the room. I am here to make up for last night's failure to share. Even my work is not a sufficient excuse. This time, when the moderator scans the room, his eyes fix on me. He has a file, of course—they all have files—and he knows I was here last night, and he knows I kept my tongue.

"Dr. Williams?" he says. "Would you like to share?"

No. "My name is Morgan," I say, and the room choruses my name back at me dutifully, all of us prisoners of war, conditioned in the art of the proper response. "My daughter's name is Emily. She'll be eleven years old this summer . . ." And I talk, and I talk, and all I can think of is a picture of a house, drawn in crayon, and a doll intended for pretend fashion shows trudging into the wilderness with her bag full and her glass eyes eternally bright, and a little girl somewhere out there, somewhere far away from me, running forever in the green places of the world.

NNEDI OKORAFOR

SPIDER THE ARTIST

Nnedi Okorafor is a novelist of African-based science fiction, fantasy, and magical realism. In a profile of her work entitled "Weapons of Mass Creation," the *New York Times* called Okorafor's imagination "stunning." Her novels include *Who Fears Death* (winner of a World Fantasy Award for Best Novel), *Akata Witch* (an Amazon.com Best Book of the Year), *Zahrah the Windseeker* (winner of the Wole Soyinka Prize for Literature in Africa), and *The Shadow Speaker* (winner of a Carl Brandon Parallax Award). Her short story collection, *Kabu Kabu*, was published in October 2013 and the science fiction novel *Lagoon* is scheduled for release in April 2014. Her young adult novel *Akata Witch 2: Breaking Kola* is scheduled for release in 2015. Okorafor holds a PhD in literature and is a professor of creative writing at Chicago State University. Find her on Facebook and Twitter, and at www.nnedi .com.

Zombie no go go, unless you tell am to go
Zombie!
Zombie!
Zombie no go stop, unless you tell am to stop

Zombie no go turn, unless you tell am to turn
Zombie!
Zombie no go think, unless you tell am to think
   —from "Zombie" by Fela Kuti, Nigerian musician
              and self-proclaimed voice of the voiceless

My husband used to beat me. That was how I ended up out there that evening behind our house, just past the bushes, through the tall grass, in front of the pipeline. Our small house was the last in the village, practically in the forest itself. So nobody ever saw or heard him beating me.

Going out there was the best way to put space between me and him without sending him into further rage. When I went behind the house, he knew where I was and he knew I was alone. But he was too full of himself to realize I was thinking about killing myself.

My husband was a drunk, like too many of the members of the Niger Delta People's Movement. It was how they all controlled their anger and feelings of helplessness. The fish, shrimps, and crayfish in the creeks were dying. Drinking the water shriveled women's wombs and eventually made men urinate blood.

There was a stream where I had been fetching water. A flow station was built nearby and now the stream was rank and filthy, with an oily film that reflected rainbows. Cassava and yam farms yielded less and less each year. The air left your skin dirty and smelled like something preparing to die. In some places, it was always daytime because of the noisy gas flares.

My village was shit.

On top of all this, People's Movement members were getting picked off like flies. The "kill-and-go" had grown bold. They shot People's Movement members in the streets, they ran them over, dragged them into the swamps. You never saw them again.

I tried to give my husband some happiness. But after three years, my body continued to refuse him children. It was easy to see the root of his frustration and sadness . . . but pain is pain. And he dealt it to me regularly.

My greatest, my only true possession was my father's guitar. It was made of fine polished Abura timber and it had a lovely tortoiseshell pick guard. Excellent handwork. My father said that the timber used to create the guitar came from one of the last timber trees in the delta. If you held it to your nose, you could believe this. The guitar was decades old and still smelled like fresh-cut wood, like it wanted to tell you its story because only it could.

I wouldn't exist without my father's guitar. When he was a young man, he used to sit in front of the compound in the evening and play for everyone. People danced, clapped, shut their eyes, and listened. Cell phones would ring and people would ignore them. One day, it was my mother who stopped to listen.

I used to stare at my father's fast long-fingered hands when he played. Oh, the harmonies. He could weave anything with his music—rainbows, sunrises, spider webs sparkling with morning dew. My older brothers weren't interested in learning how to play. But I was, so my father taught me everything he knew. And now it was my long fingers that graced the strings. I'd always been able to hear music, and my fingers moved even faster than my father's. I was good. Really good.

But I married that stupid man. Andrew. So I only played

behind the house. Away from him. My guitar was my escape.

That fateful evening, I was sitting on the ground in front of the fuel pipeline. It ran right through everyone's backyard. My village was an oil village, as was the village where I grew up. My mother lived in a similar village before she was married, as did her mother. We are Pipeline People.

My mother's grandmother was known for lying on the pipeline running through her village. She'd stay like that for hours, listening and wondering what magical fluids were running through the large never-ending steel tubes. This was before the Zombies, of course. I laughed. If she tried to lie on a pipeline now she'd be brutally killed.

Anyway, when I was feeling especially blue, I'd take my guitar and come out here and sit right in front of the pipeline. I knew I was flirting with death by being so close, but when I was like this, I didn't really care. I actually welcomed the possibility of being done with life. It was a wonder that my husband didn't smash my guitar during one of his drunken rages. I'd surely have quickly thrown myself on the pipeline if he did. Maybe that was why he'd rather smash my nose than my guitar.

This day, he'd only slapped me hard across the face. I had no idea why. He'd simply come in, seen me in the kitchen, and *smack!* Maybe he'd had a bad day at work—he worked very hard at a local restaurant. Maybe one of his women had scorned him. Maybe I did something wrong. I didn't know. I didn't care. My nose was just starting to stop bleeding and I was not seeing so many stars.

My feet were only inches from the pipeline. I was especially daring this night. It was warmer and more humid than

normal. Or maybe it was my stinging burning face. The mosquitoes didn't even bother me much. In the distance, I could
see Nneka, a woman who rarely spoke to me, giving her small
sons a bath in a large tub. Some men were playing cards at
a table several houses down. It was dark, there were small,
small trees and bushes here, and even our closest neighbor
was not very close, so I was hidden.

I sighed and placed my hands on the guitar strings. I
plucked out a tune my father used to play. I sighed and closed
my eyes. I would always miss my father. The feel of the strings
vibrating under my fingers was exquisite.

I fell deep into the zone of my music, weaving it, then
floating on a glorious sunset that lit the palm tree tops and . . .

Click!

I froze. My hands still on the strings, the vibration dying.
I didn't dare move. I kept my eyes closed. The side of my face
throbbed.

Click! This time the sound was closer. *Click!* Closer. *Click!*
Closer.

My heart pounded and I felt nauseous with fear. Despite
my risk-taking, I knew this was *not* the way I wanted to die.
Who would want to be torn limb from limb by Zombies?
As everyone in my village did multiple times a day, I quietly
cursed the Nigerian government.

Twing!

The vibration of the guitar string was stifled by my middle
finger still pressing it down. My hands started to shake, but
still I kept my eyes shut. Something sharp and cool lifted my
finger. I wanted to scream. The string was plucked again.

Twang!

The sound was deeper and fuller, my finger no longer muffling the vibration. Very slowly, I opened my eyes. My heart skipped. The thing stood about three feet tall, which meant I was eye to eye with it. I'd never seen one up close. Few people have. These things are always running up and down the pipeline like a herd of super-fast steer, always with things to do.

I chanced a better look. It really *did* have eight legs. Even in the darkness, those legs shined, catching even the dimmest light. A bit more light and I'd have been able to see my face perfectly reflected back at me. I'd heard that they polished and maintained themselves. This made even more sense now, for who would have time to keep them looking so immaculate?

The government came up with the idea to create the Zombies, and Shell, Chevron, and a few other oil companies (who were just as desperate) supplied the money to pay for it all. The Zombies were made to combat pipeline bunkering and terrorism. It makes me laugh. The government and the oil people destroyed our land and dug up our oil, then they created robots to keep us from taking it back.

They were originally called Anansi Droids 419 but we call them "*oyibo* contraptions" and, most often, Zombies, the same name we call those "kill-and-go" soldiers who come in here harassing us every time something bites their brains.

It's said that Zombies can think. Artificial intelligence, this is called. I have had some schooling, a year or two of university, but my area was not in the sciences. No matter my education, as soon as I got married and was brought to this damn place I became like every other woman here, a simple village woman living in the delta region where Zombies kill anyone who touches the pipelines and whose husband knocks her around every so often. What did I know about Zombie intellect?

It looked like a giant shiny metal spider. It moved like one too. All smooth-shifting joints and legs. It crept closer and leaned in to inspect my guitar strings some more. As it did so, two of its back legs tapped on the metal of the pipeline. *Click! Click! Click!*

It pushed my thumb back down on the strings and plucked the string twice, making a muted *pluck!* It looked at me with its many blue shining round eyes. Up close I could see that they weren't lights. They were balls of a glowing metallic blue undulating liquid, like charged mercury. I stared into them, fascinated. No one else in my village could possibly know this fact. No one had gotten close enough. *Eyes of glowing bright blue liquid metal,* I thought. *Na wa.*

It pressed my hand harder and I gasped, blinking and looking away from its hypnotic eyes. Then I understood.

"You . . . you want me to play?"

It sat there waiting, placing a leg on the body of my guitar with a soft *tap.* It had been a long time since anyone had wanted me to play. I played my favorite highlife song. "Love Dey See Road" by Oliver de Coque. I played like my life depended on it.

The Zombie didn't move, its leg remaining pressed to my guitar. Was it listening? I was sure it was. Twenty minutes later, when I finally stopped playing, sweat running down my face, it touched the tips of my aching hands. Gently.

Some of these pipelines carry diesel fuel, others carry crude oil. Millions of liters of it a day. Nigeria supplies 25 percent of U.S. oil. And we get virtually nothing in return. Nothing but death by Zombie attack. We can all tell you stories.

When the Zombies were first released, no one knew about them. All people would hear were rumors about people getting torn apart near pipelines or sightings of giant white spiders in the night. Or you'd hear about huge pipeline explosions, charred bodies everywhere. But the pipeline where the bodies lay would be perfectly intact.

People still bunkered. My husband was one of them. I suspected that he sold the fuel and oil on the black market; he would bring some of the oil home, too. You let it sit in a bucket for two days and it would become something like kerosene. I used it for cooking. So I couldn't really complain. But bunkering was a very, very dangerous practice.

There *were* ways of breaking a pipeline open without immediately bringing the wrath of Zombies. My husband and his comrades used some sort of powerful laser cutter. They stole them from the hospitals. But they had to be very, very quiet when cutting through the metal. All it took was one bang, one vibration, and the Zombies would come running within a minute. Many of my husband's comrades had been killed because of the tap of someone's wedding ring or the tip of the laser cutter on steel.

Two years ago a group of boys had been playing too close to the pipeline. Two of them were wrestling and they fell on it. Within seconds the Zombies came. One boy managed to scramble away. But the other was grabbed by the arm and flung into some bushes. His arm and both of his legs were broken. Government officials *said* that Zombies were programmed to do as little harm as possible, but . . . I didn't believe this, *na* lie.

They were terrible creatures. To get close to a pipeline was to risk a terrible death. Yet the goddamn things ran right through our backyards.

But I didn't care. My husband was beating the hell out of me during these months. I don't know why. He had not lost his job. I knew he was seeing other women. We were poor, but we were not starving. Maybe it was because I couldn't bear him children. It was my fault, I know, but what could I do?

I found myself out in the backyard more and more. And this particular Zombie visited me every time. I loved playing for it. It would listen. Its lovely eyes would glow with joy. Could a robot feel joy? I believed intelligent ones like this could. Many times a day, I would see a crowd of Zombies running up and down the pipeline, off to do repairs or policing, whatever they did. If my Zombie was amongst them, I couldn't tell.

It was about the tenth time it visited me that it did something very, very strange. My husband had come home smelling practically flammable, stinking of several kinds of alcohol—beer, palm wine, perfume. I had been thinking hard all day. About my life. I was stuck. I wanted a baby. I wanted to get out of the house. I wanted a job. I wanted friends. I needed courage. I knew I had courage. I had faced a Zombie, many times.

I was going to ask my husband about teaching at the elementary school. I'd heard that they were looking for teachers. When he walked in, he greeted me with a sloppy hug and kiss and then plopped himself on the couch. He turned on the television. It was late, but I brought him his dinner, pepper soup heavy with goat meat, chicken, and large shrimp. He was in a good drunken mood. But as I stood there watching him eat, all my courage fled. All my need for change skittered and cowered to the back of my brain.

"Do you want anything else?" I asked.

He looked up at me and actually smiled. "The soup is good today."

I smiled, but something inside me ducked its head lower. "I'm glad," I said. I picked up my guitar. "I'm going to the back. It's nice outside."

"Don't go too close to the pipeline," he said. But he was looking at the TV and gnawing on a large piece of goat meat.

I crept into the darkness, through the bushes and grasses, to the pipeline. I sat in my usual spot. A foot from it. I strummed softly, a series of chords. A forlorn tune that spoke my heart. Where else was there to go from here? Was this my life? I sighed. I hadn't been to church in a month.

When it came clicking down the pipe, my heart lifted. Its blue liquid eyes glowed strong tonight. There was a woman from whom I once bought a bolt of blue cloth. The cloth was a rich blue that reminded me of the open water on sunny days. The woman said the cloth was "azure." My Zombie's eyes were a deep azure this night.

It stopped, standing before me. Waiting. I knew it was my Zombie because a month ago, it had allowed me to put a blue butterfly sticker on one of its front legs.

"Good evening," I said.

It did not move.

"I'm sad today," I said.

It stepped off the pipeline, its metal legs clicking on the metal and then whispering on the dirt and grass. It sat its body on the ground as it always did. Then it waited.

I strummed a few chords and then played its favorite song,

Bob Marley's "No Woman No Cry." As I played, its body slowly began to rotate, something I'd come to understand was its way of expressing pleasure. I smiled. When I stopped playing, it turned its eyes back to me. I sighed, strummed an A minor chord, and sat back. "My life is shit," I said.

Suddenly, it rose up on its eight legs with a soft whir. It stretched and straightened its legs until it was standing a foot taller than normal. From under its body, in the center, something whitish and metallic began to descend. I gasped, grabbing my guitar. My mind told me to move away. Move away fast. I'd befriended this artificial creature. I knew it. Or I thought I knew it. But what did I *really* know about why it did what it did? Or why it came to me?

The metallic substance descended faster, pooling in the grass beneath it. I squinted. The stuff was wire. Right before my eyes, I watched the Zombie take this wire and do something with five of its legs while it supported itself on the other three. The legs scrambled around, working and weaving the shiny wire this way and that. They moved too fast for me to see exactly what they were creating. Grass flew and the soft whirring sound grew slightly louder.

Then the legs stopped. For a moment all I could hear was the sound of crickets and frogs singing, the breeze blowing in the palm and mangrove tree tops. I could smell the sizzling oil of someone frying plantain or yam nearby.

My eyes focused on what the Zombie had done. I grinned. I grinned and grinned. "What is that?" I whispered.

It held it up with two of its front legs and tapped its back leg twice on the ground, as it always seemed to when it was trying to make a point. A point that I usually didn't understand.

It brought three legs forward and commenced to pluck out what first was a medley of my favorite songs, from Bob Marley to Sunny Ade to Carlos Santana. Then its music deepened to something so complex and beautiful that I was reduced to tears of joy, awe, ecstasy. People must have heard the music; maybe they looked out their windows or opened their doors. But we were hidden by the darkness, the grass, the trees. I cried and cried. I don't know why, but I cried. I wonder if it was pleased by my reaction. I think it was.

I spent the next hour learning to play its tune.

Ten days later, a group of Zombies attacked some oil workers and soldiers deep in the delta. Ten of the men were torn limb from limb, their bloody remains scattered all over the swampy land. Those who escaped told reporters that nothing would stop the Zombies. A soldier had even thrown a grenade at one, but the thing protected itself with the very force field it had been built to use during pipeline explosions. The soldier said the force field looked like a crackling bubble made of lightning.

"*Wahala!* Trouble!" the soldier frantically told television reporters. His face was greasy with sweat and the sides of his eyes were twitching. "Evil, evil things! I've believed this from start! Look at me with grenade! *Ye ye!* I could do nothing!"

The pipeline the men had barely even started was found fully assembled. Zombies are made to make repairs, not fully assemble things. It was bizarre. Newspaper write-ups said that the Zombies were getting too smart for their own good. That they were rebelling. Something had certainly changed.

"Maybe it's only a matter of time before the damn things

kill us all," my husband said, a beer in hand, as he read about the incident in the newspaper.

I considered never going near my Zombie again. They were unpredictable and possibly out of control.

It was midnight and I was out there again.

My husband hadn't laid a heavy hand on me in weeks. I think he sensed the change in me. I had changed. He now heard me play more. Even in the house. In the mornings. After cooking his dinners. In the bedroom when his friends were over. And he was hearing songs that I knew gave him a most glorious feeling. As if each chord, each sound were examined by scientists and handpicked to provoke the strongest feeling of happiness.

My Zombie had solved my marital problems. At least the worst of them. My husband could not beat me when there was beautiful music sending his senses to lush, sweet places. I began to hope. To hope for a baby. Hope that I would one day leave my house and wifely duties for a job as music teacher at the elementary school. Hope that my village would one day reap from the oil being reaped from it. And I dreamt about being embraced by deep blue liquid metal, webs of wire, and music.

I'd woken up that night from one of these strange dreams. I opened my eyes, a smile on my face. Good things were certainly coming. My husband was sleeping soundly beside me. In the dim moonlight, he looked so peaceful. His skin no longer smelled of alcohol. I leaned forward and kissed his lips. He didn't wake. I slipped out of bed and put on some pants and a long-sleeved shirt. The mosquitoes would be out tonight. I grabbed my guitar.

I'd named my Zombie Udide Okwanka. In my language, it means "Spider the Artist." According to legend, Udide Okwanka is the Supreme Artist. And she lives underground where she takes fragments of things and changes them into something else. She can even weave spirits from straw. It was a good name for my Zombie. I wondered what Udide named me. I was sure it named me something, though I doubted that it told the others about me. I don't think it would have been allowed to keep seeing me.

Udide was waiting for me there, as if it sensed I would come out this night. I grinned, my heart feeling so warm. I sat down as it left the pipeline and crept up to me. It carried its instrument on top of its head. A sort of complex star made of wire. Over the weeks, it had added more wire lines, some thin and some thick. I often wondered where it put this thing when it was running about with the others, for the instrument was too big to hide on its body.

Udide held it before its eyes. With a front leg, it plucked out a sweet simple tune that almost made me weep with joy. It conjured up images of my mother and father, when they were so young and full of hope, when my brothers and I were too young to marry and move away. Before the "kill and go" had driven my oldest brother away to America and my middle brother to the north . . . when there was so much potential.

I laughed and wiped away a tear and started strumming some chords to support the tune. From there we took off into something so intricate, enveloping, intertwining . . . *Chei!* I felt as if I was communing with God. *Ah-ah,* this machine and me. You can't imagine.

"Eme!"

Our music instantly fell apart.

"Eme!" my husband called again.

I froze, staring at Udide, who was also motionless. "Please," I whispered to it. "Don't hurt him."

"Samuel messaged me!" my husband said, his eyes still on his cell phone, as he stepped up to me through the tall grass. "There's a break in the pipeline near the school! Not a god-damn Zombie in sight yet! Throw down that guitar, woman! Let's go and get . . ." He looked up. A terrified look took hold of his face.

For a very long time it seemed we all were frozen in time. My husband standing just at the last of the tall grass. Udide standing in front of the pipeline, instrument held up like a ceremonial shield. And me between the two of them, too afraid to move. I turned to my husband. "Andrew," I said with the greatest of care. "Let me explain . . ."

He slowly dragged his gaze to me and gave me a look, as if he was seeing me for the first time. "My own wife?!" he whispered.

"I . . ."

Udide raised its two front legs. For a moment it looked almost like it was pleading with me. Or maybe offering me a hug. Then it clicked its legs together so hard that it produced a large red spark and an ear-splitting *ting!*

My husband and I clapped our hands over our ears. The air instantly smelled like freshly lit matches. Even through the palms of my hands, I could hear the responses from down the pipeline. The clicking was so numerous that it sounded like a rain of tiny pebbles falling on the pipeline. Udide shuddered, scrambled back, and stood on it, waiting. They came in a great mob. About twenty of them. The first thing that I noticed was their eyes. They were all a deep angry red.

The others surrounded Udide, tapping their feet in complex rhythms on the pipe. I couldn't see Udide's eyes. Then they all ran off with amazing speed, to the east.

I turned to my husband. He was gone.

Word spread like a disease because almost everyone had a cell phone. Soon everyone was clicking away on them, messaging things like, "Pipeline burst, near school! No Zombies in sight!" and "Hurry to school, bring bucket!" My husband never let me have my own cell phone. We couldn't afford one and he didn't think I needed one. But I knew where the elementary school was.

People now believed that the Zombies had all gone rogue, shrugging off their man-given jobs to live in the delta swamps and do whatever it was they did there. Normally, if bunkerers broke open a pipeline, even for the quietest jobs, the Zombies would become aware of it within an hour and repair the thing within another hour. But two hours later this broken pipe continued to splash fuel. That was when someone had decided to put the word out.

I knew better. The Zombies weren't "zombies" at all. They were thinking creatures. Smart beasts. They had a method to their madness. And most of them did *not* like human beings.

The chaos was lit by the headlights of several cars and trucks. The pipeline here was raised as it traveled south. Someone had taken advantage of this and removed a whole section of piping. Pink diesel fuel poured out of both ends like a giant fountain. People crowded beneath the flow like parched elephants, filling jerri cans, bottles, bowls, buckets.

One man even held a garbage bag, until the fuel ate through the bag, splashing fuel all over the man's chest and legs.

The spillage collected into a large dark-pink pool that swiftly flowed toward the elementary school, gathering on the playground. The fumes hit me even before I got within sight of the school. My eyes watered and my nose started running. I held my shirt over my nose and mouth. This barely helped.

People came in cars, on motorcycles, on buses, on foot. Everyone was messaging on their cell phones, further spreading the word. It had been a while since people who did not make a career out of fuel theft had gotten a sip of free fuel.

There were children everywhere. They ran up and down, sent on errands by their parents or just hanging around to be a part of the excitement. They'd probably never seen people able to go near a pipeline without getting killed. Hip-hop and highlife blasted from cars and SUVs with enhanced sound systems. The bassline vibrations were almost as stifling as the fumes. I had not a doubt that the Zombies knew this was going on.

I spotted my husband. He was heading toward the fountain of fuel with a large red bucket. Five men started arguing amongst themselves. Two of them started pushing and shoving, almost falling into the fountain.

"Andrew!" I called over all the noise.

He turned. When he saw me, he narrowed his eyes.

"Please!" I said. "I'm . . . I'm sorry."

He spat and started walking away.

"You have to get out of here!" I said. "They will come!"

He whirled around and strode up to me. "How the hell are you so sure? Did you bring them yourself?"

As if in response, people suddenly started screaming and running. I cursed. The Zombies were coming from the street, forcing people to run toward the pool of fuel. I cursed, again. My husband was glaring at me. He pointed into my face with a look of disgust. I couldn't hear what he said over all the noise. He turned and ran off.

I tried to spot Udide amongst the Zombies. All of their eyes were still red. Was Udide even with them? I stared at their legs, searching for the butterfly sticker. There it was. Closest to me, to the left. "Udide!" I called.

As the name came out of my mouth, I saw two of the Zombies in the center each raise two front legs. My smile went to an "O" of shock. I dropped to the ground and threw my hands over my head. People were still splashing across the pool of fuel, trying to get into the school. Their cars continued blasting hip-hop and highlife, the headlights still on, lighting the madness.

The two Zombies clicked their legs together, producing two large sparks. *Ting!*

WHOOOOOOOOSH!

I remember light, heat, the smell of burning hair and flesh, and screams that melted to guttural gurgles. The noise was muffled. The stench was awful. My head to my lap, I remained in this hellish limbo for a long, long time.

I'll never teach music at the elementary school. It was incinerated, along with many of the children who went to it. My husband was killed, too. He died thinking I was some sort of spy fraternizing with the enemy . . . or something like that. Everyone died. Except me. Just before the explosion happened, Udide ran to me. It protected me with its force field.

So I lived.

And so did the baby inside me. The baby that my body allowed to happen because of Udide's lovely soothing music. Udide tells me it is a girl. How can a robot know this? Udide and I play for her every day. I can only imagine how content she is. But what kind of world will I be bringing her into? Where only her mother and Udide stand between a flat-out war between the Zombies and the human beings who created them?

Pray that Udide and I can convince man and droid to call a truce; otherwise the delta will keep rolling in blood, metal, and flames. You know what else? You should also pray that these Zombies don't build themselves some fins and travel across the ocean.

DANIEL H. WILSON

SMALL THINGS

Daniel H. Wilson is the *New York Times* bestselling author of *Robopocalypse*, as well as titles such as *Amped*, *A Boy and His Bot*, and *How to Survive a Robot Uprising*. He earned a PhD in robotics from Carnegie Mellon University. He lives in Portland, Oregon, and can be found online at www.danielhwilson.com.

There is a time for some things, and a time for all things; a time for great things, and a time for small things.
—Miguel de Cervantes, 1615

I

In my memory, the cleanroom floor is impossibly white and smooth and unblemished. Nothing dirty, nothing natural. That hazy nebula of dust and microbes and pollen in which we all live and die has been scrubbed away. The skin of reality is peeled back to expose the raw aching bones of light and sound. It's just hard physics that's left, needling into your eyes and ears from some place where it's been folded up tight and sharp-cornered and invisible.

Life in the cleanroom is an equation. The only error is human error.

The memory of what happened in there sank its barbs into me. At the emergency room, after it was over, the nurses figured out pretty quickly that I had been drunk. Once that got out, the media did not take it easy on me. Neither did the jury. I went to prison for three years. Five years after that, the cold metal of the memory is still with me, writhing under my skin with every beat of my heart.

No matter what, my wife used to say, *you can't smell nano-machinery.* She was a scientist, like me, and she knew for a fact that human beings don't have olfactory receptors capable of detecting the presence of nanomachines. That's just the physics of it. You can't know you've inhaled the nanomachines until it's too late. Science says so, anyway, and it doesn't give a damn what any of us thinks.

In the industry, the nanomachines we worked with were called "cretes." Every crete is its own robot, just a couple of nanometers in size, designed to wriggle into the seams of things—into the nitty-gritty nooks and crannies of reality. They work from the inside out, rearranging individual atoms with submicroscopic precision. Together, a million cretes might form a single mote of gray dust. Not much to look at, but plenty of *potential*.

The potential to do good. Other potentials.

Cretes are legion. And each individual fulfills its purpose with gusto. Goal one: recognize a useful substrate. Two: self-replicate to a tipping point. And three: rearrange the substrate to solve a problem. Water into wine. Carbon into diamond. Create a desired outcome. Each crete wants to make relentless order out of a world in chaos.

And God help anybody who gets in the way.

Up close and wide-eyed, watching a crete work is like witnessing a magic trick. Say you drop a purification crete into a bucket of toxic sludge. For a few seconds, nothing happens. Nada. This is the long flat part of an exponential curve. Cretes are doubling and then doubling again and again and . . . then the water goes clean, like flipping a switch. Look away, you'll miss the miracle. The curve hits a flash point and *bang*.

"It's alive!" as a guy in a lab coat once shouted.

But somebody has got to catch that monster when it escapes from the laboratory. Throw a slab of timber across the portcullis and light a torch. That was my job. I specialized in stopping the miracle. At cocktail parties, I used to say, "The water in the jug can turn to wine, but let's not drink the whole damn ocean."

Polite chuckles.

My cretes didn't play nice. Every one of my babies—and there were trillions—would lie in wait for other cretes. On contact, they would identify an enemy crete variety and trick it into triggering a false positive for mutation. When you self-replicate by the millions, every copy has to be perfect. The slightest mutation means self-annihilation. So, my invention convinced other cretes to commit suicide.

I called it creticide.

2

After the accident, I was pretty sure the world had left me behind. My life had fallen into a dull comfortable routine of failure, self-neglect, and despair. Yet when the army called, I didn't hesitate. Not for a second. The plane tickets arrived in a thin manila envelope, and the next day I boarded a flight down to Florida.

I guess I hoped I might have a destiny after all.

This morning, I washed my hair with waxy hotel soap, then went outside and waited on the curb in the cold dawn air under a buzzing streetlight, my mind humming along with the lamp in idiot synchronicity.

I wonder again what the military wants with a guy like me.

An anonymous black sedan slides up. Government plates, tinted windows. The long car purrs beside me for a moment, hood glistening with morning dew. The driver is a ramrod of a man, sitting straight as geometry in an uncreased military uniform. Cloaked in pointless camouflage, he stares directly ahead. Doesn't speak to me. Doesn't look at me.

That's not the reason I hesitate before getting inside. What gives me pause is the fact that Ramrod here has a stubby, carbon-black battle rifle dimpling the plush leather across the front passenger seat. It puts a little stutter in my step. But I get in the back and carefully buckle myself in, eyes boring a hole through the seat in front of me where I know that rifle is.

Once upon a time, I would show up to work and slip on shoe covers and a hairnet, stomp the debris mat, slide on two pairs of latex gloves, a hood, boots. Snap my goggles into place. I'd wrap myself in crinkling white butcher-paper coveralls and check myself in the mirror for fatal flaws. If I was feeling extra cautious, I'd sometimes grab a respirator and it would be just my goggled eyes swimming over two salt-shaker cans in the mirror. Then the crucial last step. The coup de grace, right? Arms out, legs apart, so a technician can coat my hands and feet with my own scientific specialty—quick bursts of aerosolized creticide.

Time to go to work. Time to protect the world from the future.

Looking back, I see now I was kidding myself. The pore on a human forearm is, on average, fifty microns wide. That's a superhighway to a crete. Cretes will float through clothes fabric like wisps of cotton through the Grand Canyon. And don't even talk to me about the mouth and eyes or any other mucous membranes.

I fooled myself every day back then. But maybe I can fight through that bright cold memory. Sitting in this car, I'm thinking that maybe I can fool myself again.

After half an hour, the driver takes us through a quick checkpoint and we enter a military base. He leaves the main road and hits a wide-open tarmac, the whole car humming, tires singing. We weave between plodding yellow tractors and zipping military jeeps. The howling of airplane engines drowns out the coughing bark of construction equipment. Colors and sounds hammer at the tinted windows in waves of titanic, meaningless movement and noise.

It looks like progress.

"Where are we headed, exactly?" I ask the driver, expecting no response and getting none.

Ahead of us, the paved plain stretches out to the horizon. We are passing bigger hardware now, neat rows of dusky armored personnel carriers, their metal-plated chins held high, peering down at us through bulletproof window slats. The driver tugs on the steering wheel and we race toward a maze of government prefab buildings. Windowless rectangular trailers, arranged in trim grids, their retractable metal stairs lightly scratching the pavement.

The car lurches to a neat stop. The driver's eyes flash at me in the rearview. He cuts the engine.

"So, uh, what's the rifle for?" I ask.

His eyes flicker to me, then away. The engine ticks while he thinks about whether or not to respond. Decides to.

"In case you ran," he says.

The driver starts the car again and puts it in drive, his foot resting on the brake. I shrug, crack my door, and step out into the lancing sunlight and pollution-sting of the wind. The sedan pulls away.

The trailer complex is surrounded by mounds of supplies stacked on wooden pallets. Cases of bottled water swaddled in distended plastic wrap, stacks of identical white cardboard boxes, sedimentary layers of bulging green duffle bags—all of it packed neatly and crisscrossed by tight tan straps. Armored forklifts are collecting and transporting the supplies in a rugged ballet.

The door to the nearest prefab opens.

An older man wearing a crisp military uniform steps out onto the flimsy stairs. The camouflage pattern on his outfit is a new one to me. It shimmers with some kind of fractally pixelated pattern cooked up by a computer and printed on hologrammatic material.

My eyes try to cross and instead I force them up to his face. He's got a crescent of tanned scalp chasing trimmed gray hair. A pair of metal eyeglasses sinks into the skin over his ears. His hands are placed awkwardly on his hips, right pinky finger curled to avoid touching the stiff fabric of a brand-new holster, complete with a dull black sidearm.

I get the feeling he doesn't wear this uniform often. Or maybe this is his first time.

"Colonel?" I shout over the engine noise.

He blinks at the milling, roaring airplanes, pushes his glasses up his nose, and takes a step down. Nods at me and leans over to give my hand a brisk shake. He shouts something incoherent over the racket, doesn't smile. Motions me up the stairs.

The colonel shuts the hermetically sealable door behind us. As it closes, it sighs, leaving my ears ringing in the silence. It's like a classroom in here, just a table, a chair, and a chalkboard. I can feel the skin on my face tighten in the blisteringly cold air-conditioning.

"Thank you for coming . . . ah, doctor," he says. "Please, pardon the chaos."

"It's fine, colonel. I just didn't realize you were on active duty. I thought this interview was for laboratory work."

"I'm a professor at the United States Military Academy. Technically, we're always on active duty."

My face must be blank.

"West Point," he adds. "Until recently, I was teaching mathematics and updating the latest edition of a textbook I coauthored."

"So, you're a colonel of math?"

"Nanorobotics, actually," he says.

The colonel pulls some kind of eyepiece from his shirt pocket. He takes a few small steps closer to me and holds the eyepiece out like a shot glass. Shakes it.

"Would you mind if I . . . ?" he asks.

"Is that a pocket microscope?"

"If you would just roll up your sleeve a bit," he urges.

After the incident, there wasn't a single person in the nanotech field who would willingly be seen with me, much less hire me. Most of my former colleagues have made it clear that they would rather I were still in prison for what I did. Whatever kind of job the army has for me, this is my one and only chance back in.

I pull up my suit jacket sleeve.

The colonel leans over, peering into his little metal cylinder. The cold ring presses against my forearm. I can see the colonel's lips moving as he lifts and presses again on several different spots.

"Small. Smaller than average," says the colonel, standing and slipping the eyepiece back into his pocket. "Good for you."

"My arm?"

"Your *pores*," says the colonel. "They're smaller than most people's. Didn't you know that? You should be thankful. Every micron counts."

"And why's that?"

The colonel of math steps away. Walks to the other side of a shining, laminated table. He puts his knuckles down on it, leans forward, and hangs his head. Takes a deep breath.

"Your creticide works, doctor," he says.

"Against what?" I ask. "It's useless outside of a cleanroom."

"Things have progressed considerably in your absence."

The colonel turns to the chalkboard. He produces a piece of chalk so naturally that it puts to rest any suspicion that he isn't really a teacher. On the board, he sketches a lopsided circle.

"Caligo Island. Twenty miles in diameter. A thousand

miles south of Africa. Thirty-five hundred miles east of South America. And those *are* the nearest continents. Completely isolated, thankfully."

The colonel marks an *X* in the middle of the island. In short frenzied bursts, he draws vectors out of the crossed marks. Short arrowed lines that together form a gentle curve that sweeps over the southern half of the island, then out to sea, where it dissolves in scribbles.

"We have a small problem," he says. "Well, ah, a *lot* of small problems. All of them located on Caligo. And unfortunately poised to spread farther."

The vectors remind me of something. Dispersion patterns. Like the flow of dust from a broken vial. A spreading surge of blood. Crumpled forms lying still on the floor under the vacuum scream of an air purifier. The thought makes my knees go slack.

"What have you done?"

"Ah, so, it bears mentioning that it wasn't me. In fact, I am rather far down the line of those who have been assigned to sort out this problem. My predecessors failed to meet the challenge, as it were. But *you* were my idea. And regardless of what has already happened in the past, to either of us, this is my . . . *our* . . . problem, now."

"The original creticide patent is ten years old, colonel. My research ended years ago. Definitively. I doubt it's good for much. Even if you poured a whole garbage can full of it—"

"Dump trucks."

"What?"

"We use your invention by the planeload, doctor. The *planes* are loaded with dump trucks. You have already saved more lives than you will ever know," says the colonel, his eyes wide and bloodshot. His bottom lip quivers and he clears his throat. "Now you will have the opportunity to save more."

"This isn't a spill," I say. "Somebody is using cretes as weapons? Is this a terrorist thing? An international conflict?"

"Oh no," he says. "We are dealing with a single man. A brilliant man—I cannot stress that enough. He is one of our best and brightest. An incredible internal asset. Truly visionary. His name is Caldecot."

It's a military research facility. The vector lines describe cretes escaping into the wind, infecting the rest of the island. Cretes *exposed to the open air*. Possibly weaponized. Lethal either way.

My hearing fades and is gone, replaced by the singing of blood as it courses through my brain. I can see the colonel's lips moving. Slowly, his words come back into focus.

". . . figured out the crete engine. Dr. Caldecot's recipes can put holes in titanium. His specialized crete varieties can rearrange the atomic structure of almost any substrate into more useful configurations. Plain dirt into Chobham tank armor. Vegetation into trauma field supplies. An amazing breakthrough. Certainly, the technology has gotten away from him a bit. But we can help him fix this. Caldecot can put this situation back under his steady hand . . ."

The armed mathematician continues to speak, but my eyes return to the chalkboard. To the simulation of airborne particle spread.

"Nuke it," I say. "Now. Before it gets off the island."

"Not a bad suggestion," responds the colonel, surprisingly calm. "It is certainly being considered. The problem is that

the shock wave could eject unwanted material into the tro-
posphere. A rogue cloud of aerosolized nanomachines would
be a highly negative outcome. Rather than take that risk, we
need simply to shut it down. Contain the problem and go
back to the way things were before."

The colonel is methodical. Clipped. His small mind works
like a compact motor. The perfect man for a job like this. He
doesn't understand enough to panic. I close my eyes and con-
centrate on breathing. Open them to white lines on black
chalkboard.

I think maybe I'm looking at the end of the world.

The entire prefab shudders. The plane engines outside
are getting louder. I notice there are no windows in this tiny
vibrating room.

"We need you to go there," says the colonel. "The army has
established a beachhead outside the perimeter of . . . the worst
of it. A portable laboratory is waiting for you. State of the art.
You will collect samples of the cretes that have gone feral. You
will adapt your creticide to destroy the central machinery of
the various varieties you collect."

"You want me to *go there*?" I ask, lips numb.

"Yes, well . . ." He sighs, then continues, speaking slowly.
"We can't risk taking the cretes off the island . . . so I'm afraid
we've got to bring *you* to *them*. You will of course be well
compensated."

The trim little soldier is like a machine, spitting out facts
with no concept of what they mean. I wonder what a man
like this sees. What color does the flush of fear on my cheeks
appear to him? Gray, I imagine. Gray as an equation.

"I'll die," I say.

"That's not a certainty," he says. "Besides, in your case, after everything that's happened . . . don't you feel that you owe some kind of . . . a debt?"

The memory is as bright and hard as white tile.

"I went to prison, colonel. I *paid* my debt. In more ways than you can imagine," I say, voice rising over the racket outside. "My answer is no. No *fucking way*. Thank you for the invitation and I really appreciate the opportunity and all, but there's just no way. It may be hard for you to believe, but I don't want to die."

"Ah, boy," says the colonel, sitting down on a thin plastic chair. It strikes me that everything in this room is made of lightweight plastic. Even the trembling walls. The colonel's fatigues crease stiffly at the knees when he sits. It's familiar, somehow. A tendril of fear is wriggling up from my belly and into my chest.

It's creticide. I think the colonel's clothes are coated in creticide. The coup de grace, right?

"This is the awkward part," says the colonel.

Outside, the noise surges even louder, rattling the door frame. It's a howling *thrum* that seems to come from the center of my head, causing my teeth to chatter. My vision dances with each shivering pulse. Something big shoves against the trailer from outside, and I stumble, arms out to catch the door.

"Good luck, colonel. Good-bye."

The colonel shows me his palms and shrugs. "Thank you for your service."

I yank open the flimsy door, half expecting it to be locked. I'm on the retractable landing before it dawns on me that I don't understand what I'm seeing.

A soaring wall of tan fabric mounted between curved ribs of steel. Flip-down metal seats mounted to the wall, folded upright and erect, their loose seatbelts flopping like untied shoelaces. The line of seats is broken only by a small oval door with a long metal handle. Glowing red lightbulbs illuminate the narrow passage. Stenciled on the door are the words *Only Qualified Personnel to Open Mid-Flight. C-5M Super Galaxy.*

I am in the belly of a C-5M transport aircraft.

"You see, we are already on our way," says the colonel, producing a metal flask. He looks smaller now, silhouetted in the shaking doorway. The vibration recedes as our wheels leave the ground and his voice is suddenly louder. "Ah, don't forget . . . every micron counts."

And the colonel kicks the door shut in my face.

3

"Okay, you guys. Okay. What's the situation? What are your orders? Do you have some kind of a dossier I can look at?" I ask.

The young man stares at me for a couple of reptilian blinks. Then, a smile trampolines to the corners of his mouth. The red interior lights of the transport plane glint darkly from his creticide-coated army fatigues. "Did you say a dossier? He's asking me for a *dossier*?"

After a few minutes cursing outside the colonel's locked trailer, I began creeping down the narrow corridor studded with flip-down seats. The plane's center aisle was loaded with wooden crates covered in netting. An armored trapdoor that seemed to lead to the cockpit was locked, my knocking ignored.

I heard laughing and smelled cigarette smoke before I saw them near the back of the plane. About a dozen young men dressed in military uniforms, sprawling over the folded-down seats. Most were asleep or pretending to be, their boots up and resting on crates across the narrow aisle. Crimson-kissed silhouettes.

But these two were awake. Private Tully and Sergeant Stitch.

"Yeah, a dossier. Some kind of report," I say. Tully looks at me with round glassy eyes, his smile like a gash in his face. "Look, I'm the crete expert," I say. "They called me in to fix whatever the hell has gone wrong down there. Help me do my job. Does anybody here know anything?"

Tully is seized with giggles, compulsively scratching the back of his crew cut with a bony hand. I frown and look at the other paratrooper sitting next to him, the one called Stitch.

"What's wrong with him?" I ask.

Stitch's face is slack, almost paralyzed. "Jesus, man. You're not the first," he mutters slow, not looking at me. "We're not the first. Not the last. Not even close."

Tully pulls his lips apart expectantly. Inside his mouth, milky-white teeth are mottled with dark spots. Pieces of metal filling, silvery. "Did you think we were *it*, man?" he asks. "Did you think we were like a *crack squad* or something? Huh?"

He swallows and puts on a serious face.

"Roger that, sir. United States Marine Force Recon, special technological retrieval and recovery operational detachment reporting. Rest assured that we will handle this situation, sir. Handle it! We will fucking handle the shit out of it!"

The giggler goes back to scratching the back of his head, fiercely.

"Handle? We broke the handle off," mutters Stitch, smiling to himself. His eyes are closed now. His fleshy cheeks quiver with the mechanical vibration of the cargo plane.

"How many others have been sent?" I ask. "What's the situation?"

"Oh shit," says Tully, sitting up, eyes wide. "He wants to know the sitch, Stitch. Hear that? The *sitch*, Stitch."

Stitch won't respond. Or can't.

"Thanks," I mutter, weaving my way back up the aisle, wading through the murky red glow of overhead lights. When I can't hear the laughing anymore, I collapse onto a folding wall-mounted chair. Shut my eyes.

I can feel the darkness outside the plane. The raw infinite space. *It should stay empty,* I find myself thinking. Everything is red in this booming cavern, and I'm starting to feel like I'm going blind. I'm in a metal tube screaming toward the epicenter of something very, very bad. Acid lingers in the back of my throat.

Those faint giggles keep coming, mechanically, and I understand now they've got nothing to do with humor.

Eyes squeezed shut, I rest the back of my head against the fabric skin of the wall. Focus on the vibration, the cold air breathing over the nape of my neck. I try to let the repetitive wailing of the engine smooth out the edges of my fear. After a few minutes, it starts to work.

"Hey," whispers someone, and I startle. Private Tully's face is inches away from mine, his breath hot on my cheek. "Let me show you the sitch, Stitch. Take a look-see."

The young paratrooper leans forward, still rubbing the back of his head. When I see what he is scratching at, I hold my breath and ease away from him. I should close my eyes, too. Any mucous membrane is an entry point for a crete. But I can't look away from the deformity.

It's beautiful, in a way. The tooth. A tiny white bud. Perfectly formed calcium growing from the back of his skull. The imprints of surrounding molars are dimpled knuckles under his skin.

It's probably not contagious, since he's still alive. The crete must have been designed to grow spare teeth for dentists. It's all I can think of. I didn't know it was possible. The crete borrowed some calcium from his skull and rearranged it. Part of me wants to harvest a specimen. Another part wonders how badly it hurts.

Tully's voice is muffled, his head down, words swallowed by the rumble of the plane. "It's the small things," he says. "On Caligo, you got to be sure and watch out for the *small motherfuckin' things.*"

Giggles.

I unstrap my seatbelt and get up without a word. Go for a long walk around the humming belly of the plane. Try to work the dread out of my belly. That soldier should be in a hospital, not sent back into service. But we're both on our way to Caligo: an infected soldier and a broken scientist. It smells like desperation.

After a while, I find a coffeepot strapped to the wall and pour myself a cup. Find another seat by myself. Sipping coffee, I look out the window and try not to shake. Some city is sprawled out far below. A gleaming explosion, spreading its smoldering tendrils across cold earth.

Light eating the darkness.

The barbed memory appears unannounced, as it always does. That morning my head was tucked under the ventilation hood. The rush of air in the cleanroom was hypnotic. I remember being hungover from the night before, watching my gloved hands at work, thinking about whether or not I should have had a beer and a shot for breakfast. My wife was across the room, working at her station with her back to me. We hadn't been speaking much.

The vial fell.

More accurately, I dropped it. Being a little drunk, I hadn't bothered to activate the plastic shield that was supposed to cradle my arms. The finger-sized cylinder was made of inert hardened glass, but it took a bad bounce and the lid shattered on the outer lip of the hood. The vent pulled in part of that puff of concentrated crete dust in a swirling arc that moves slowly in my memory, like the spread of a galaxy. But the rest of the dust was thrown out into the room in a fine expanding powder.

I remember touching my face by instinct to secure my respirator. The baffled plastic was there and ready. I had put it on to hide my beer breath from my wife. The drinking had been getting out of control, and I knew it, but it didn't scare me. I had only felt curious about how far it would go. That respirator was the reason that I recovered after two weeks in the hospital, instead of bleeding to death from the inside out.

For a moment, the other scientists stood oblivious at their stations. Then a panicked scream muscled out from under my respirator. My wife half turned to face me, her thin arms out and holding a pen and clipboard. A lock of blond hair had escaped from her paper hat and hung curled behind her ear. Seeing my wide eyes and empty hands, she flashed her teeth, nostrils flaring as she drew a sharp intake of breath. An autonomic startle reaction. Designed to increase oxygen flow to prepare the body for fight or flight.

Evolution is so slow to catch up with technology.

While I was yelling in half-drunken fright, all three of my labmates were inhaling airborne particles of an experimental self-replicating creticide variety down their windpipes. The cretes were immediately embedded into the soft tissue of their lungs.

Christoff ran for the door. It was locked. Shoulders slumped, he kept rattling the bar up and down. The panicked synapses of his brain were stuck in a loop. Jennifer stood frozen, her mouth moving, repeating the same words over and over: "You fucker. You stupid fucker." She knew what was coming and she had never liked me anyway.

But my wife just stared, hands over her stomach. Pen and clipboard fallen to the tile. Her blue eyes were sad and round. They were filled with tears.

And the hemorrhaging began.

I force my eyes open, snap back to the present. Outside the window of the cargo plane, the shine of that anonymous city licks the underside of the airplane wing. It paints the sobbing jet engines as they choke down the frigid night and shit out thrust and toxins and torn air. Outside, the plane and the night pound into each other. Like the surf crashing against the shore, each trying to consume the other without hunger or urgency.

Turning my face up, I stare into the dome of space. Far above, hundreds of billions of stars invade the night sky, gorging on the vastness.

Mindless, and eternal.

4

I wake up with Tully's grinning face inches from mine.

"You're dropping with me, doc," the paratrooper says, shoving a harness into my lap. "Put this on and let me check it. You drop no matter what, so put that shit on tight and right if you want to live."

Rubbing my eyes, I see it's still night outside. A chill has seeped through the thin padding on the metal chair and through my suit pants. Standing, I stretch and stamp my feet on the metal decking, trying to get feeling back. Tully is already down the aisle, mechanically checking the chute pack of another paratrooper.

"Can I get some warmer clothes?" I call after him.

"What you got is what you got," he says, not turning.

My response is cut off by a wall of wind. Stitch has just opened the side door, yanking a bar and pulling the whole thing in and up. Only blackness and noise is on the other side.

Hurrying, I slide into the brown harness. I tug the straps tight, ignoring my awkwardly cinched-up pants. With shaking hands, I button my pathetic suit jacket. As an afterthought, I lean over and retie my wingtips as tight as possible.

"Let's go," shouts Tully, grabbing my arm.

The dozen other paratroopers are lining up, lifting their belly-mounted gear bags with both hands. Stitch is at the door, shouting commands to the soldiers. They waddle like pregnant women, latching carabiners onto a sloping wire that runs down the wall.

The floor shudders and the rear bay door of the plane yawns open, revealing a grinning slice of ocean. I can see a sprinkle of stars above a purple horizon. Someone pulls a switch and pallets of supplies whip past me, inches away, rolling down and right out of the back of the plane. Falling into nothing, deploying damp parachutes that glisten like exposed lungs.

My limbs start to shiver uncontrollably.

The line of paratroopers is moving now. A round light next to the open doorway shines a steady piercing green. Stitch is methodically collecting the umbilical cables as each paratrooper steps through the door.

"Time to go," Tully shouts over the wind.

"Wait," I'm saying.

From behind, he yanks hard on my leg straps. My breath catches from another momentous tug on my shoulder straps. Tully latches his harness onto mine. Hands on my shoulders, he shoves me to the rear of the line. I lurch forward on my slippery dress shoes, legs numb. Then we are trotting, a shuffling column racing toward a flat purple doorway.

"Wait!" I shout, but now I can't even hear myself over the ringing of boots on metal. I trip on my next step, feel Stitch slap me on the back of the head. There is no step after that, just wind, and my eyes squeeze closed. Twin tracers of freezing tears crawl blindly over my temples. My breath is pulled out of me and shoved back in, mixing with the bellowing atmosphere.

And finally, I open my eyes.

The island is real—a brownish scab on the broad silvery

ocean. A pall of dark smoke hovers over it. The dawn sun, a pink smear sitting on a perfectly flat horizon, pushes stained fingers through the smog. It spills the rest of itself in streaks and dashes over miles of ridged waves below.

As I hang from the deployed parachute, the harness bites into my armpits. My suit is ripped, my legs dangling, pale ankles flashing. My pant legs flap in the breeze. It's quiet now, and I hear the parachute canopy creaking in a nautical kind of way. Instinctively, I grab the strap over my chest and hold on to it with everything I've got.

We drift through the smoke and into the light.

The air still has a chilly edge, but I can already taste the moist tropical undertones. And something else underneath. Something burnt and coppery.

"Doesn't look so bad," I call to Tully.

"Even hell looks pretty from far away," he says, as we sway together.

And then the ground is looming. Instead of a green-brown blur, I see individual trees and military buildings. I catch flashes of detail from all over the tiny island. Far inland, there is a stone pavilion surrounded by deep jungle canopy. Radio towers sprout from a cliffside. And directly below, coming fast, is a sprawling vista of soldiers and buildings and vehicles. It's insectile—looming termite mounds of human activity.

"Feet up," calls Tully, and I comply.

A grassy field speeds past like a conveyor belt. Tully's boots flare up and he plants them loosely on the grass. He runs a few steps and leans back into the parachute's drag until we are sitting, my body buzzing with sensation, dewy grass soaking through the thin fabric of my pants.

I hear a clink as Private Tully unfastens himself from me.

Around us, the dozen other paratroopers are landing, too. Hopping up and chasing down parachutes and folding them. Nobody speaks to me. As the field clears, I wriggle out of my harness and hold it in dumb fingers. It has no more purpose, so I shrug and drop the high-tech bundle into the deep grass.

Warm sunlight winks from the metal bits as I walk away.

5

"We're reclaiming the heart of Caligo, one speck of dirt at a time," says the captain, dabbing sweat from his forehead with a starched white handkerchief. "Don't you worry about that."

Tall and broad with too much skin around his neck, the captain stands with his arms crossed over his chest, watching me without much interest. I'm in my torn suit, stained with water, ears still ringing. Trying to get my bearings.

We are standing in the shade of a canvas field tent erected on a small hill, the ocean at our backs, looking out toward where the grass meadow turns to dim jungle. The smoke above is only a faint haze here at ground level. At the tree line, a ragged band of probably twenty soldiers is spaced out over a half mile. Each grunt wears a peculiar backpack and sways slowly in place. Liquid flame spews from the guns they carry across the dark face of the jungle. The fire creates a glowing rind that eats its way into branches and vines, sending up a wall of black smoke.

"Flamethrowers," says the captain, following my gaze. "Outlawed by the Geneva Conventions for half a century. Those were requisitioned from an old World War Two ammo dump.

Took the army two and a half years to get 'em reconditioned and transported here. First batch got dropped straight into the ocean, half a mile off the coast. Close, but no cigar. Second batch was compromised. Four fatalities in two weeks. Necessary evil. Can't risk buying 'em foreign. This whole operation is under Uncle Sam's hat, understand?"

"Nobody told me this was classified," I say.

The captain's eyes bounce up to the skyline and back down. The message is clear enough. *It didn't matter.*

"Enough chitchat," he says. "You want to get situated, I can tell. The research facility is about ten klicks inland. Things are haywire there. Pumping out all sorts of funny shit. Closer you get, the more hilarious it is. Get close enough and you'll laugh yourself half to death."

"The colonel mentioned a laboratory for me?"

"Your fancy laboratory caught fire. Set it up too close to the jungle and one of the boys got overexcited. Hell of a show. Don't know what they had in there, but god*damn* it sure burned pretty. Bright as the sun, too. Me and the boys were betting oxygen tanks against chemicals."

The captain raises his eyebrows at me, waiting. "Maybe you could settle the bet?"

My mouth must be hanging open, because the captain nonchalantly reaches over and taps my chin. I snap my jaw closed.

"Gonna catch flies like that. Or something worse. Don't you worry, doc. They'll drop another lab down here for you. Give it six months."

"Six months?" I ask.

"A year at the latest," he adds.

"What am I supposed to do until then?"

"Field expeditions. Need you to get out there into the shit and bottle any wild cretes you find. By the time you've got a couple of species on ice, why, we'll have your little laboratory all set up. Then you can get right to work figuring out how to kill all them little buggers."

"I don't understand why you need me," I say. "Why don't you go shut down the facility yourself? Maybe use some of these soldiers."

"Can't get near it. Place sort of defends itself, you could say. There is a certain talented but stubborn individual running that operation, and he is not always a friendly man. Our monitoring indicates that he has something big planned. And soon. Current goal is to build an arsenal of specialized creticides before pursuing our next discussion."

"Is it a discussion or a war?"

"Caldecot is a great man. His mind is a serious asset. As such, we are in an ongoing discussion with him. A *spirited* discussion."

The captain flashes a grin at me with his mouth, not his eyes.

"Part of your lab didn't burn. You can kit up with what's left. I sent a boy down there to help you. Name's Fritz. He'll provide maps and a uniform and whatnot. We may not have a lot of time. Get set up and head toward the center of the island. Just a little walk. Grab anything interesting and bottle it. Leave now and you'll be back by nightfall."

"By myself?"

"Take some of the paratroopers you showed up with. Hell, take 'em all."

"Don't they have jobs to do?"

"Negative. Those boys you dropped with are rebounders."

"Rebounders?"

"Sent back."

"Sent back from where?"

"You are not afraid to ask questions. That's good. What I'm saying is they *escaped*. Off the island. Rigged up a boat maybe a month ago. Picked 'em up at sea and brought them back on the round trip. Boys will be boys. Now they understand. There isn't any way off this island. Not until we reach an agreement with Caldecot. Meantime, we gotta get our creticide in order and get that research facility shut down before Uncle Sam decides to hell with it and starts dropping nukes."

"We can't leave the island," I say slowly.

Hearing myself, I instantly know these words are obviously, immutably true. The captain searches my face to see if I'm joking. Decides that I am, and bursts into laughter. "Why, hell no, we can't *leave*! Not until it's mission accomplished."

He claps me on the back hard.

The captain's snarling smile worries me. The sunlight reflects so brightly from his squinted eyes. I'm losing confidence that he and I are seeing the same things.

"But this ain't *all* fun and games," he says. "When a bad breeze sends a crete variety sweeping through here, the men start dropping like flies. If they're lucky. Sometimes . . . they sort of melt. Never know what the cretes were designed for in the first place. Some of them react with human skin, others don't. The smoke helps. But it's best to get hold of a respirator and have it handy. Keep your eyes open, but not too wide. They're a prime vector for body penetration."

"This is insane," I mutter.

"Yes sir. Now you're getting into the spirit," says the captain, grinning. "You're gonna do fine, boy. Just fine!"

I start to walk away, the sheer pointlessness of this place settling into the meat of my shoulders, making them tight. After one step, a hand clamps onto my bicep. It nearly jerks my shoulder out of its socket and I spin around, fingers curling to fists. I stop when I see the captain's face.

"Don't walk that way," he says quietly. "Take the long way around."

I look where I was headed and see nothing. Just a broad mound of soft dirt. The earth has been pushed into a swollen oval about the size of a baseball diamond. Some kind of pale gray slime that must be creticide bubbles up in slick patches. Beyond the mound is a distant white tent framed by a blurry line of flame. The far-off soldiers sway at the hip and continue coating the dark jungle in arterial spurts of red glitter.

"Why not?" I ask, glancing at the soft dirt.

"Because, son, it's bad luck to walk on the other men's graves."

6

A pungent wind wafts in from the jungle and ruffles my hair in a friendly way. I catch myself holding my breath, my chest tight, throat locked up. Any breeze or blade of grass or particle of dust could be carrying rogue cretes.

Melt, the captain said. *Sometimes the men sort of melt.*

Whatever has gotten loose on this island makes the worst day of my life look like spilled milk. The technology here has gone native. It's lurking in the hazy jungle, stalking the quiet shadows, burrowing into tree trunks smooth as skin and clutching on to membranous leaves. And the captain says it's floating, too, buoyed on the swell of the wind. Roaming free but not off the island. Not yet.

I take the long way around the mass grave.

Under the lazy sun, soldiers hurry back and forth in crisp steps. They jog past wearing spotless camouflaged fatigues, the respirators around their necks flopping like metronomes. Aside from curt nods, nobody speaks. These men all seem to have serious business to attend to. Not rebounders, but full-timers. In it for the long haul.

The white tent I spotted earlier turns out to be a hospital. As I get nearer, I can see that it is made of bulging translucent plastic. The gymnasium-sized structure quivers like a mound of Jell-O in the hot breath of the jungle, pressurized from the inside, like a balloon.

Rounding the corner of the path, I see that air is being pumped into the tent by a sputtering generator mounted on a diesel truck. Two soldiers lean on the truck, dark eyes lazily tracking me, mouths hidden under the dirty canisters of their respirators.

The sight of them accelerates me.

I stride past the inflatable hospital, catching tessellated glimpses through the gently breathing plastic walls. It's a single huge room inside, canvas-floored, easily the length of a football field. The expanse is filled with a sweeping, pre-cise grid of identical cots. At first glance, every one of the low folding beds seems to have an occupant.

At the back end of the tent is a cornucopia of advanced medical equipment that's all been pushed into a haphazard pile. Defibrillator paddles hang from their cords. IV stands are tossed on top like silver matchsticks. Millions of dollars' worth of equipment tossed uselessly into a frozen avalanche of technology. It's the future, abandoned in a heap, apparently not advanced enough for whatever shining afflictions have come marauding out of the black jungle.

As I pass into its shade, the hospital tent sighs, bloated and belching and sinking into the folds of its own belly. I can make out human forms inside, shrouded, dim shapes swimming behind sheets of creticide-coated plastic. Without consciously making the decision, I stop and peer inside, hoping to find some movement or noise—some sign of life, anything, from the rows of supine mannequins.

A quiet darkness permeates the field hospital.

Birds call distantly in the jungle behind me. My breathing has synchronized with the building's. Things are becoming clearer. Things inside. Men whose faces are stretched out, torsos distended into taffy-twisted malformations, limbs too long to make any sense. *There are strange things growing here,* I think. The cretes are like seeds. Pinhead seeds, too small to see, floating on the air. Seeds looking for dirt.

We're the dirt, I think, and something inside me wants to giggle.

Private Tully comes to mind. The way he scratched the back of his head. Whatever-it-was had already gotten inside him. Planted itself in his scalp. Laid roots. A perfectly formed tooth. Bone-leached calcium.

I force myself to look away from the hospital. Begin to jog, then break into an outright run, trying to ignore the vampiric heat from the sun at my back. My leather shoes clumsily pound the earth. Sweat wells up from my pores and forms a sheen on my forearms.

The sweat is clear because it's just water. Not red like blood. Not red like on her face that bad morning.

The acrid smell of burning chemicals pricks my nostrils. I stop running and double over, breath heaving out of my lungs. The air here is thick with the smell of scorched plastic.

I nearly vomit, and spit bitter saliva next to the steps of my ruined trailer laboratory. The wreck squats in a dark patch of burned grass, half-melted, the rear of the building drooping awkwardly like a paralyzed dog. The front door hangs from its hinges, petrified and brittle, tortured into sinuous curves by departed heat. A small reinforced window in the door has shattered, giving the trailer a baleful, Cyclopean glare.

And everything is coated in fluttering white pellets, like snowflakes. I resist the urge to scoop up a handful, crumble them between my fingers. The pellets must be some form of my creticide.

A respirator, I think. *Get yourself a respirator.*

Inside the trailer, someone is whistling merrily. I can hear rummaging. Items bouncing off the walls and floor.

I start to knock on the flaking plastic wall, then pull my knuckles back. Better not to touch. Every micron counts, after all.

"Hello?" I call into the shadows. The noises stop.

Pale eyes appear in the doorway, hovering above a clean blue surgical mask. They belong to a hunched-over man who is now peering down at me. He pulls the mask to his chin, flashing a wide yellow-toothed grin.

"Doctor," he says, hobbling through the doorway, arms outstretched. "Welcome!"

I shy away from his touch. The misshapen little man is dressed immaculately in a tan T-shirt tucked into camouflage fatigues. A blue paper hairnet billows from the top of his head as he bounces down the charred steps. His meaty hands are sweating under blue latex gloves. The paper mask hangs askew at his throat. Something wrong has happened to him. A rash of pulpy scars are smeared from ear to cheek; the fleshy topography pulls his lip to the side and gives him a partial lisp. Something has been burnt off his face.

It looks like it was done in a hurry.

"Who are you?" I ask, keeping my hand by my side.

"First Lieutenant Fritz, sir," he replies, motioning toward his face in a half salute. "Your research assistant. Before the accident, anyway."

I don't know whether he means what happened to his face or what happened to the trailer. I decide not to ask.

"Nice to meet you," I say, gamely. "The captain told me to get down here and salvage what I can find."

Fritz nods enthusiastically, reaches back into the room, and drags out an olive drybag. He holds it up to me. "I found your things, doctor," he says. "Gathered up everything I could salvage. Very sorry about what happened, but they love to burn things here."

I take the waterproof drybag from him with a thumb and forefinger. Peek into its dark interior. Immediately, I snatch out a respirator and pull the goggles and cans over my head. Hanging around my neck, that familiar rubbery smell dazes me for an instant. I think of lipstick-red smears on white tile floors. The bag falls onto the ground and Fritz flinches, knees dipping.

"Oh no, sir," he mutters, picking up the bag and inspecting it. He holds it downwind and shakes it out. "We mustn't drop our things onto the ground like that. We mustn't be clumsy. The soil carries more than you know. The island, herself. She is swarming with the engines of creation."

Satisfied with his inspection, Fritz hands the bag back to me.

"You mean the cretes?" I ask.

"The whole coastal base is in a natural wind tunnel," says Fritz. "But Captain says this is where we make our stand. That we should be willing to die for the cause, and so on. When the wind blows, he says, the cradle will fall. It's why we're all counting on you."

"Me?"

"You're a doctor," he says, incredulous. "Father of creticide. A man with a plan, right?"

Fritz smiles at me broadly, scratches his neck where the blue paper mask clings.

"Right," I respond. "I do have a plan. And I am . . . was a doctor."

"And *that's* why you'll succeed where others have faltered. You won't be rejected by him. I can feel it. It's the genius inside Dr. Caldecot that causes him to revile the soldiers, you see? It's his terrible genius that forces him to cut those poor boys down. But *you* can speak to him. Negotiate with him, doctor to doctor. Genius to genius, if you will."

The madman at the center of the island. Again.

"Caldecot. Who is he? Who put him in charge?" I ask.

"Oh, he's a great man. A powerful man. You don't know? Caldecot shapes the world by his will. His crete varieties are a revolution. A running leap into the future. He created all this with his *mind,* don't you see? All of this. Every bud and leaf of it!"

"You've known him?"

"I was honored to work for him."

"Where? When?"

"In the interior. Deep inside. 'Ten klicks in, where the light gets dim, and the sights get mighty strange,' as the troopers are prone to singing."

The malformed little man tilts jaundiced eyes toward the coast, watching the razor-thin line of the horizon.

"You were injured," I say. "Was that thanks to this genius as well?"

Fritz looks at the ground. He absentmindedly caresses his face with one finger, gingerly tracing the broken terrain. A childlike look of pure sadness folds itself into the asymmetry of his eyebrows and into the spongy flesh of his cheeks. I wonder what a crete infection can do to a person's neurology. If this is his face, what might have happened to his mind?

"In the end, I wasn't worthy to serve a man like that," he says. "The doctor tried to show me the future, you know, but the sight of it was too much. It was so bright. It scorched my eyes and I ran away when I should have stood firm and been brave."

Fritz looks up, hopeful.

"But you're made of different stuff, like *him*. I read your file, doctor. Pardon me for saying it, but you know when to take the lives of others into your hands. Men like you . . . you can make death *mean something*. You're the ones strong enough to bring light into the world."

I remember sipping hot air through a respirator. Squinting through the foggy plastic of my goggles while a crest of blood blossomed over the floor. Her body was a fallen mountain range across the room. It was just a vial. Just a single broken vial.

We use your invention by the planeload.

"I gathered your team. They're waiting over at the tree line. Six rebounders was all I could find. Sergeant Stitch and Private Tully are with them. Old friends of yours, right? All outfitted and ready to go. Everything you need for today is in the drybag, including a map."

I mutely look down at the bag in my hands. My plastic respirator digs under my chin in the familiar way that it used to in the lab. Inside the bag, I spot cardboard boxes labeled MRE and a full surgical satchel and a specimen sampling kit and tan clothing and a pair of boots. A metal container the size of a lip balm is labeled CRETICIDE.

I look uncertainly at the tree line.

The moist jungle breeze sighs over the back of my neck, gentle as a snake gliding under sheets. If I stay here, I'll end up in that tent of horrors behind me. *The cradle will fall.* But there is another scientist on the island and he's only ten kilometers away.

Fritz is still blinking at me with his poisoned eyes.

"Thank you," I say. "I'll be back before nightfall. Set up a place for me to sleep?"

"It will be my honor, doctor," says Fritz, but the way he is watching me, well, I get the feeling he's not convinced. We shake hands awkwardly.

He presses a vial into my palm.

"What's this?" I ask.

Fritz looks away, somehow embarrassed.

I hold the inky cylinder up to the light, turn it upside down and watch a viscous tide of gray-green flecks tumble in slow motion toward the opposite end. Fritz motions at me to put it away, his head swiveling frantically. I tuck the vial into my pocket.

"It's a flesh-eater," says Fritz. "A dangerous crete. But useful in case of an emergency."

"Won't it disseminate?" I ask.

"Liquefied," he says. "Too heavy to spread in the air. Eats the target only."

A flesh-eating crete. Murder in a bottle.

"And who do you think I'm going to have to kill?" I ask.

"What?" responds Fritz, blinking his pale eyes in surprise. "Oh no, doctor. You don't understand. When the time comes, you'll want to use that on *yourself*."

I can't think of how to respond.

"It's a quick one, see?" says Fritz. "A gift for you, sir. Quicker than most. Why, it's almost painless."

7

At the tree line, Stitch and Tully and four other young troopers are smoking cigarettes and standing around, waiting. Nobody leans on anything. They're too smart for that.

I reach them, wearing my new military fatigues. My cleanroom experience has paid off. I've got my pant legs tucked into chunky tan boots. The laces are tied up tight and also tucked inside my boots. I've duct-taped the whole thing snugly around my ankles. Smeared creticide around the seams. I notice the others have done the same. My outer jacket is buttoned up all the way, the fabric stiff and crinkled with a pre-coating of what must be creticide.

I wonder if it's the same stuff I invented.

Thankfully, the wind is pushing the wet smoke of burning jungle away from us, letting it spread up and over our heads like a false sunset. The sheer volume of particulate matter created by the chemically fueled combustion is forming a shield—a toxic screen that stands a chance of knocking down or absorbing whatever nightmares might be floating in on the languid wind. It's a poor man's creticide.

"You've all been inland before?" I ask. "Near the epicenter?"

The troopers look at each other. Stitch speaks for them: "Little bit. It's why we decided to jump ship in the first place. Let me tell you, going in there is *no fun at all.*"

Chuckles pulse from stubbled throats.

"Well, don't worry," I say, pointing with my folded map. "I just want to get the lay of the land for now. We'll go a few kilometers, grab some samples, and get the hell back out. Good?"

In response, several cigarette butts hit the dirt. The paratroopers watch me emotionlessly. Each wears a neat rucksack and has a pistol strapped to his hip. I don't know what they've been through. What atrocity made them run. But the lack of emotion on their faces makes me uneasy. I find it hard to tell them apart. They're all hopeless and unafraid in the same sick anonymous way.

By habit, I tap the respirator hanging around my neck to make sure it's still there. A few others do the same, like silent echoes.

"Let's go," I say.

Two ruts from a jeep path snake beyond the tree line and into the island interior. Stitch points out the path and guides us in. After a few minutes, he silently drops back and gives me the lead.

As we trudge into the throat of the jungle, I hear a droning noise from far above. More supplies are sloping out of the sky. Swaying wooden crates strapped to double parachutes. The wind is pushing the line of supplies too far east, away from the island.

More sacrifices to the ocean.

Someone laughs. Otherwise, the march is silent. Even our footfalls are quiet—the troopers step high to avoid brushing the grass whenever possible. The men keep their mouths closed, sleeves down. They're happy to have sweat dripping out of their pores, just so long as nothing goes in.

The jungle is slowly strangling this narrow road. It's obvious that it used to be a major route, clean and straight and worn into the terrain. But it's been a couple of years since it was used. At least. We march down the forked tongue in single file, draped in chlorophyll-stained shadows. The windbrushed canopy of leaves murmurs above. There is nothing obvious to harvest, nothing seems out of the ordinary. Just dark waterfalls of vines and leaves.

Until the first scream rasps out of the jungle.

It comes from somewhere up ahead, just off the path. A feminine wail of pain followed by a high-pitched, windsucking gurgle. The soldiers glance at each other. Respirators go on in panicked synchronicity.

I put my finger up for everyone to stop moving. Nobody lays a hand on his weapon. Instead, questing fingers check seams of clothing in a flurry of small patting movements. Each man inspects the man next to him. I think of an educational video I saw once of ants cleaning each other.

Leaving them, I step off the path to investigate the noise.

"Hello," I call, voice muffled by my respirator. "Are you injured?"

Ducking under arched ferns, I hear another gurgling

wheeze. In the tunnel vision of my respirator goggles all I can see is a long-overturned tree trunk. It's a tall one, surrounded by debris created when it fell. A shallow pool of dark red-dish liquid seeps into the dirt around it, drowning shattered pieces of bark.

It looks exactly like a pool of congealing blood.

Then, slowly, the trunk *moves*. A gnarled pink orifice splits open. It sprays bits of bark as a gust of air pushes out in a grunting shriek. My mind stumbles, trying to comprehend.

It's the small things you've got to look out for.

The tree trunk is *breathing*, sheaves of fleshy bark rising and falling in crying gasps. Some kind of medical crete has grown into the wood. It has given birth to something that defies all natural experience. Cretes have limitless potential. Atom by atom, they spread and consume, twisting the world we know into a phantasmagoria.

"That's just wrong," says Tully. He and Stitch have gathered behind me, panting through their respirators.

"It's incredible," I say. I squat and peer into the shuddering hunk of meat. "Those look like human lungs in there. Formed by a colony of sub-micron-sized nanomachines. Billions of them penetrating a natural substrate and self-replicating from local materials. Manipulating the carbon atoms. Tree bark into human organs."

I reach into my drybag and pull out the sampling kit, snap open a disposable pick, and scrape a piece of bark into a vial. I try not to wince at the high-pitched grunting coming from the log.

"Imagine," I say, musing. "A *functioning* pair of lungs."

"Ain't he just like a dog chasing a car?" Stitch asks Tully, nodding at the look of awe on my face.

"Wonder what'll happen if he catches it?" asks Tully.

"Be eating a rubber sandwich is my bet," replies Stitch.

"This is science," I say, looking between the two of them. I pack up the sampling kit as I talk. "Not magic. It's the result of a simple reaction. A medical crete designed to generate human organs landed on an organic wood substrate. Okay? The crete doesn't care where it gets carbon from as long as it gets it. They're windborne and they've gotten into the vegetation and that's bad. But it just means we have to be more careful."

A sliver of nausea slips into my stomach. Part of a human heart is wedged in the pool of reddish mud. It shivers, once.

"Yeah, but the tree is fucking *breathing*, man," points out Stitch.

"It sounds like it's in pain," mutters Tully, reaching for his gun. "Maybe we should put it out of its misery."

"No," I say, standing and putting my hand over his. He shies away like I've slapped him. "Try and think of it as a collection of atoms in a particular pattern. That's all. Little machines forming order out of chaos. It's all according to a plan. Just don't touch anything. Keep your respirators on. I had no idea the tech could become this complex this fast. I spent *years* studying this and I never dreamed that in my lifetime I would see . . ."

Stitch and Tully are staring at me, bored.

"Wait a minute," I say, looking around the clearing. "Where are the other guys?"

"Bailed," says Stitch, grinning.

"Rebounders, man," says Tully. "What'd you expect?"

"Sonofabitch," I exclaim.

I turn quickly and my jacket accidentally brushes against

a drooping leaf. A pang of terror obliterates my anger. Veins bulge in the swaying leaf. They are thick and fractal and my God, I don't know—they could be made of *human tissue*, for chrissake.

Stitch and Tully are watching me like I'm an animal in a zoo cage. Two pairs of dark goggles glittering over respirator cans. At least they're finally interested.

"Why didn't you go with them?" I ask, quietly.

"What's the point?" asks Stitch. "You can't stop progress, right?"

8

Instead of returning over covered ground, Stitch takes us on a wide loop back toward the base. Heavy rubber respirators bouncing against our chests, we resist wiping sweat from our faces. After twenty minutes, I smell diesel gas on the wind.

In an isolated clearing, we find three soldiers, full-timers, judging by their fatigues, facing into the forest. They don't look up at our approach, focused instead on something out beyond the trees. The shirtless young men are panting, grinning, and hunting whatever-it-is. They call to each other, wide eyes winking in the sun as they lunge with the excited playfulness of bloodhounds on the scent.

A portable pump is snuffling liquid from a metal barrel on one end and coughing up white liquid through a shuddering hose on the other. Two of the soldiers hold the flexible tube in the crooks of their arms, wrestling to aim its spray into the jungle. Another soldier operates the pump, one gloved palm flat against its quaking surface and his other hand twiddling knobs, sweat pouring from his forehead as he tortures the shrieking device.

Pale, shining fluid arcs through the air in an alabaster spray. It shatters the harsh sunlight into a rainbow spectrum. Trees and leaves and vines droop under the weight of a sticky layer of liquid that reflects the light in an eye-dazzling cascade.

Under the sheets of rapidly hardening creticide, the plants begin to look like statues made of newly poured concrete. A dense onslaught of shimmering vines and branches halted in an unnatural attempt to creep out of the darkness. Limbs are swaying, leaves quivering. A confusion of tree trunks lean toward the three hooting men with a slow-motion malice.

"Hey!" I shout over the din. "Hey! What's going on?"

The soldier on the pump smiles, keeps his eyes on the instruments. "Jungle been walking, man. Some of it, anyway."

"Impossible," I say, my voice loud in my ears.

But in the wafting shadows, the trunks and vines are intertwined, sponging into each other like fleshy limbs. Surfaces quiver and ripple; the wind pushes bark like sagging skin. Shadowed muscles form in the valleys and hills of tree trunks. And I detect a nearly imperceptible twitching. A subtle but rhythmic shudder. A pulse.

The tendons in his neck straining, another soldier belts out: "And a walking jungle is not in the motherfuckin' plan!"

The man has his shirt off. His back is dark, scabbed with metal scales. The chips of metal flex and squirm as he moves. He is grinning hard and mechanical as he chokes the convulsing hose under his arm. I can't tell whether it is pain or humor that is yanking his lips back from his teeth.

I hurry to catch up with my pair of rebounders.

Stitch and Tully are still walking, heads down, wordless. The bare-chested soldiers don't pay us any mind and I don't bother to call out to them again. This scene has a familiar feeling. It's been played out before. It will play out again. Behind us, the soldiers keep pounding mindlessly against the jungle, and the jungle pounds back.

9

We're less than a kilometer from base when we see the diamonds.

In a dusty clearing, I step over the first scattering of glinting rocks. Odd sizes, odd shapes. Each lying in a small circle of dirt that looks like a meteorite impact crater. My peripheral vision fills with shimmering sparkles.

Tully steps toward me, eyes wide.

"What are they?" he asks. "Are they really diamonds?"

"Leave it alone," says Stitch.

"I'll take a look," I say, digging into my satchel for a pair of tweezers. "And Stitch is right. Stay back."

I lean over, hands on my knees, and consider the droplet of light lying nearest me. Carefully, I pluck it off the ground with the tweezers and hold it up to the sun. Tully has crept even closer.

"It *is* a diamond," he says, jaw slack. "Swear to God. Diamonds everywhere."

The soldier is right. A jewel has fallen from the sky and slammed into the loose dirt. I turn it over, and as I do, the glittering confusion shifts into focus as something eerily recognizable.

A horsefly.

This diamond appears to have been shaped into an exquisite sculpture of a fly. Only it's not a sculpture of a fly. In actuality, I realize this is just a very, very dead fly.

"This is a horsefly," I say. "Or it was."

Some kind of diamond crete has gotten to it.

"Bag up!" shouts Stitch. I'm already scrambling to put my respirator back on. I drop the tweezers and the dead fly on the ground. Tully gapes at us both in disbelief as we pull respirators over our faces.

"It's still a *diamond*," he says. The rangy kid squints down, hesitates for a second, then carefully snatches the diamond out of the dirt.

"No contact!" Stitch shouts at Tully, his voice muffled by the cans on his face. "Don't fucking make contact!"

But Tully is smiling now, holding up the diamond triumphantly. His fingertips are still clean, and between his index finger and thumb is that frozen fly, twinkling with a mad intensity.

"There's more! In the dirt here. All around!" he says, stuffing the diamond into his pants pocket. "We're gonna be rich!"

"You're gonna be infected," says Stitch sadly. He is already backing away, hand on his gun.

Tully's grin flickers like a broken neon sign. "No," he says, standing up. "How? Where am I infected?" He spins around, kicking up more dust. "I'm fine, you guys."

But even I can see that he is lopsided now. His balance is off because his left hand is getting heavier. The arm attached to it is stretching sickeningly at the bicep, like taffy.

"It's nothing, you guys," he says, staggering, yanking

his shirt off over his head with his good right arm. His eyes kind of bug out when he sees the left arm. A crete has gotten into his bloodstream. Traveled up his forearm and then latched on somewhere. The skin of his bicep is going taut as it elongates. It's hard to tell what it is just now. What it is becoming.

It's not right that isn't right.

I back away, breathing in sharp panicked gasps that trigger the cutoff valve of my respirator. I try to slow down my rate of inhalation, straining and hearing a little groan deep in my chest. My lips curl moistly into the respirator at the sad insanity of what is happening to Tully.

It's a weapon-maker crete. Must have been in the dirt.

The paratrooper's left hand has collapsed in on itself now. The fingers are fusing together and the whole mess is solidifying into a metallic hunk. Some part of my brain is estimating the iron percentages contained in human blood. How much carbon is in human skin? Is that why Tully is so pale? Is the crete breaking down the metal in his blood?

"Oh," says Tully.

I'm seeing a weapon design now. A cylindrical shape rippling under the skin of his forearm like a submarine about to surface. Tully's teeth flash white in the sun as his flesh splits and the unblinking black eye of a gun barrel pushes out through the top of his hand. I can hear his knuckles grinding against each other as the hand spreads and collapses.

Tully finally screams. Reaches for us with his good right hand. He is begging now. Left shoulder humped. Dragging that melting piece of foreign weaponry on the ground, his arm stretched out like bubble gum, the barrel in his ruined hand cutting a furrow through poisoned dirt.

"Wait!" he shrieks, fumbling for his sidearm with his good hand. *"Don't leave me!"*

A hiss followed by a snap. Leaves waft down around us as another diamond rips through the canopy. This one sounds bigger than a horsefly.

"I am so sorry," I say.

Stitch and I run together. More impacts slash through leaves around us. Precious gems thunk off tree trunks. We're dealing with a highly infectious diamond crete, and it must have an airborne transmission capacity if it's vectoring into goddamn *flies*. Head down, I do the only thing I can: keep moving.

In the distance, behind us, I hear a gunshot. Just one.

Stitch pauses, speaks to me in rapid bursts. "We'll circle around. Go back through a different area. Double time."

"I'm sorry," I say, panting. "He was your friend."

Stitch shrugs. "Sometimes you catch a bad breeze."

We push deeper into the jungle. Moving farther from the shoreline, closer to Caldecot. I cringe every time a piece of grass flutters against my leg. The creticide that coats my boots and pant legs is turning gray with the corpses of millions of gummed-up cretes. The material still has that odd stiff gleam and I'm thankful for it now in a way I never imagined I could be before.

I watch Stitch's shoulders. Focus on my breathing and on keeping up with the lanky soldier. That's why I see the fist-sized diamond hit Stitch on the back of his calf mid-stride.

It must have fallen from someplace high, because the diamond smacks into him with a meaty thump that sends the paratrooper staggering forward. To his credit, he doesn't fall down or do anything stupid, like grab a tree limb for support. He just hops a few feet, slows, and stops. Throws his elbows back until his shoulder blades kiss. Then he screams into the sky long and loud. The sound echoes back from the jungle in a strange, flat way.

"No," he grunts. "What was it? Did it break the skin?"

I scan the ground and find the culprit: a bird, made of diamond. It is beautiful, frozen—wings still splayed in flight. A parrot.

"Yeah," I say, putting a hand on Stitch's upper arm. He leans against me, heaves a shaking breath, and peers over his shoulder at his calf. His pant leg is shredded. Muscle exposed. Black-red blood leaks in aimless rivulets from the impact wound.

"Oh no," he says, and collapses to a knee with his bad leg laid out behind him. Slowly, gratefully, he touches the ground with his palms. Drops his head and lets the sweat drip off his nose. I crouch beside him, keeping a safe distance.

A sharp twanging vibration plucks the air behind me. I look back down the path. The landscape has changed.

The sun is staring low from the horizon and blinking at me through what looks like a layer of plastic wrap. Not plastic. Diamond. The cretes are spreading, eating the jungle whole, fabricating a frozen diorama of fine crystal. Trees are igniting into splinter bursts of light.

"Take it off," Stitch says. "Take the leg off now."

I turn back to the fallen man, panic rising in me. I watch the raw pain dance up his spinal cord and germinate in shivering beads of sweat on his forehead. Behind me, the world is turning to ice.

A seesaw sound wavers out of the diamond frost. Like the chirp of electrical wires in a storm. It is followed by a gentle warmth pushing out of the crystalline jungle: the waste heat generated by an exponential atomic reaction taking place five hundred yards away. A spreading wall of contagious diamond wreathes the jungle in light and is closing in on us fast. I start to rise, urged ahead by the hot breeze.

"Please, just take the leg off," says Stitch. "Please. Then you can go."

The leg stretched out behind him is becoming stiff. The edges of the wound are already turning pale and going translucent. Carbon to carbon. Patterns wrought in flesh.

"Then you can go," repeats Stitch. "Please."

My hands move before I dare to think about it.

With a gentle nudge, I push Stitch down onto his chest. Pin his thigh under my knee, careful not to touch the ground myself. He groans but doesn't complain. Looking at the ripped flesh of his calf, I gauge this will be a transtibial amputation. Just below the knee.

Common enough.

I pick through my satchel and find that Fritz has sent me off disturbingly well prepared. Quickly, I snap on a pair of creticide-coated latex gloves. With two quick tugs, I widen the rip in Stitch's pant leg and expose the skin around the wound. It is frosting up quickly, with diamond material jutting through in unpolished ridges. Byproduct water courses out of the wound, making the ground muddy. I smell the brightness of pure oxygen. The wound itself is not bleeding anymore, but I wrap his thigh with a tourniquet anyway. Tie it off tight.

All I can hear now is my own breathing inside the respirator. Wet exhalations flowing over my nose and mouth, hot as they leak out under my neck. Sweat courses down my cheeks, into my eyes.

I draw out a hand-sized portable surgical saw, tear the sterilized plastic protector off the blade, and let it fall fluttering into the hot breeze. How thoughtful of Fritz. I think of his other special gift to me—the vial of flesh-eating nanorobots in my front pocket.

Quicker than most.

"It's going to be okay," I say to Stitch. "Be still."

"It hurts inside," says Stitch.

The saw blade spins up with a thin whine. My fingers are so clumsy compared to this shining steel. Like rubber gloves filled with liver pâté, gross and graceless. I flinch as another bird hits the ground a few feet away. The jungle is waking up, crete victims striking the dirt around us like missiles. I drop the blade edge against Stitch's sweating calf, as close below the knee as I can manage.

"I'm gonna be okay," says Stitch, whimpering through the reassuring words. "I'm gonna be okay."

It helps to think of something else. Anything else.

The beauty of a crete. Technology so much cleaner and more elegant than the human form. A billion dancing atoms with a singular purpose. Each nanorobot a flawless unit, carrying nothing extra, none of the baggage left over from eons of evolution. Each crete made perfect in its own image. Ready to make something out of the chaos.

And none of this filthy meat.

"I'm gonna be—"

The medical saw sinks into Stitch's flesh with no resistance. Like filleting a fish. A red line appears under the blade, four inches above where the white-and-pink skin brightens into a shining clump of diamond. My elbow dips as the saw eats. The whine drops into a grinding pulse as the blade bites into bone.

"I'm—"

And then the blade stops spinning, bucking in my hands. Stitch has his face pressed against the dirt. No more talking. His breath convulses in his chest, sending dust tornadoing away from his nostrils. I yank on the saw and it won't move. *Oh no, oh no.* The crete must have gotten it. Craning to look into Stitch's wide, tear-filled eyes, I get the feeling that he isn't seeing anything.

His chest rises and it doesn't fall.

Leaning back on my haunches, I resist the urge to wipe my forehead with my arm. Sour wind on my neck, I watch the fading sunlight refracting in Stitch's open eyes. And for a split second, I see the most beautiful sight of my life.

The diamond crete has spread into Stitch's bloodstream. Remade his bones and his veins and flesh until finally, the cretes must have traveled into his optic nerves. The tiny machines have converted the lenses of Stitch's eyes into orbs of pure colorless diamond.

His dead eyes flicker with the captured fire of the sun.

I let go of the stuck saw. The wound is no longer bleeding and the pink-white of his bone has faded away. The steel saw blade bit into diamond. Now, the carbon in the steel is also turning to diamond.

Time to run.

A fresh surge of heat grips my shoulders and I abandon Stitch's frozen body. Dancing heat shadows caper over the ground around me. That wall of diamond is rising higher, twanging loudly as it builds itself. Through it, the sun's rays feel accelerated, impacting my skin with an otherworldly velocity.

The whistling updraft is doing something to the weather. Clouds are gathering, swirling. Angry thunder rumbles out of a darkening sky.

Alone, I run from the frozen trees, away from that tortured cobweb simulacrum of a jungle, deeper into the island. The wall of diamond is spreading behind me. Only the barrier isn't straight. It curves around me to the right and left, leaning over my head, growing taller.

It isn't a wall.

This shining thing rising up behind me is the dawn of something incomprehensible. As it arcs over my head, I can see now that the cretes are growing into something else entirely. They are turning into a perfect dome.

10

My only choice is to plow forward, away from the heat of creation.

The sun is falling now, spreading fading tendrils of light through the haze of crystal. That odd twanging and chirping fades as I proceed farther down the path. After a couple of kilometers or so, I come to a wooden gate next to an empty guard booth. From either side, a chain-link fence topped with razor wire stretches off into the jungle, forming a gleaming perimeter.

Beyond this point, the previously overgrown road becomes paved and straight.

I step around the sagging wooden slat of the barrier. Feel the familiar solid pavement under my boots. This road, a last vestige of civilization, leads straight across manicured grounds to the rogue research facility. Or what's left of it.

I walk the final kilometer in a daze.

Jeeps and army trucks are abandoned on the sides of the road like flotsam left behind after a tidal wave. Some of the vehicles lie in puddles, the metal having melted into rubbery piles feathered with flakes of green paint. Others have partially sunk into the ground, their noses pointing out at awkward angles like fallen lawn darts. Titanic forces have twisted and disfigured the landscape here, and everything in it.

The bodies themselves are hard to recognize. They've been pulled into strange shapes. Dissolved and folded in on each other. People melded with their own equipment, bodies tortured into unthinkable dimensions. The road is covered with bundles of angles, acute and obtuse, but none identifiable, not as human beings. No flies trouble these rotting, rusting carcasses. There are no birds and no animals. Only the sigh of infected wind. A bad breeze.

All of it is digesting in the harsh, fevered light that weeps through the dome.

Ten klicks in, where the light gets dim, and the sights get mighty strange.

The earth here is crusty, broken in sweeping patches. I catch sight of the hull of a ship, half-buried, breaching out of the ground with the obscene weight of it buckling the earth and cantilevering a swathe of jungle up into the air. Naked tree limbs sway in the breeze and clap to themselves, having dissolved into what look like propeller blades. A sheer rock face has grown into cannon bores and collapsed under the weight of the deformation. I walk by logs made of furrowed human skin, bleeding gently under a coating of moss.

My footsteps echo on the pavement as I face this gauntlet.

Beyond all of the metallic confusion of flesh is the research building. The major walls still stand, but the ceiling has collapsed. Shards of the structure have migrated to the edges, heaped up in the crude imitation of a nest. Familiar bits peek out of the confusion—part of a ventilation hood, an office chair, a hallway water fountain, some cubicle walls. The rest is harder to describe, hard even to look at: quivering limbs of metal; ridged tiles of pure gemstone; gnarled vines sprouting human hair.

A slanting doorway leans before me. A black mouth open wide, choking on its own broken teeth of shattered glass. This is the X on the chalkboard. This is the spot where I saw the world in ruins.

This is the end.

My mind starts scrabbling away from the moment. I'm alone now and the others are dead and I remember this one thing. It slid its barbs into me and never let go. Unable to stop, I fall back into the memory—to a place where the pain is something familiar and it wounds me in a reassuring way.

I put out my arms that morning in the cleanroom. But I could not catch her. My wife was holding her hands over her stomach and she fell to her knees, still watching me. Her teeth and nostrils and eyes were already stained with bright pinpricks of blood. Mucous membranes first. Then skin pores. A gruesome sheen over soft flesh. Billions of crimson dots expanding through sterilized white cotton. She was coughing, wheezing with the raw choking gasps of a dead body still striving to live—not quite up to date with the inevitable.

I managed to hit the emergency stop button. Felt the sudden chill as the industrial-grade exhaust system started swallowing tainted air. Through fogged goggles I saw my wife's face when she finally fell, and if I'm being honest, it looked like she'd been skinned alive. Every inch of her face was seeping blood.

She was too far away for me to catch.

This is my crystalline moment—the one that plays through my mind, fast or slow, depending on how long I close my eyes. Air roaring in my ears. A small blond woman is lying facedown and the machines inside her are still doing their grisly work. Her blood is surging away from under her body in a spreading pool. Swift and plum-dark across impossibly white tile.

I watched, dazed and curious, as the polished tile floor somehow canted and rushed up to meet my face. I smacked into the ground and a high-pitched note began to sing in the meat between my ears. From behind cracked goggles, I watched that tidal flow pulse toward me. Watched my wife's body stop moving, stop breathing.

Together, she and I were going to make something. Create our own order out of the chaos. In the three-dimensional ultrasound, my son's eyes were closed and I swear he had a half smile on his lips. His only job was to grow. Our baby boy was inside her and when she fell her hands were over her stomach to protect him and yet I lived.

My heart staggers again.

I take another step into the leaning doorway. There is only

death on the other side. The knowledge is in every atom of my body.

Don't you feel that you owe some kind of a debt?

The memories are razored feathers that slice through my mind. Only by magnifying the details can I save myself from the whole lacerating knowledge of it. So I think of the microscopic particles of flexing metal spreading into the rivers of her bloodstream, out across the pale heaving ocean of her lungs. The nanomachines, they're only small things, but they spread so far and so fast. They are two hundred thousand years of technological evolution written in the pattern of a handful of atoms. The living blueprints of humankind's most magnificent achievement, our past and our future—hungry, spearing into the deep tissue of her body.

What my wife said was wrong. Nanotech does have a smell. It's a metal bucket filling with rain in a thunderstorm. Ozone and sweat. A coppery slick pooling in the back of your throat. The cretes want to make something out of the chaos. In the face of this unstoppable miracle, your body weeps a trillion droplets of blood.

Tomorrow eats today.

A sound like the plucking of brittle guitar strings cascades over me from a hundred yards up. The dome is completing itself over my head. It reminds me of a cathedral ceiling, except the diamond is almost transparent through rays of falling sunlight. Above the dome, dark clouds have collapsed into bruised smears. Blackness above, and blackness before me.

I step through the doorway.

II

I emerge into vegetation, my sight swimming from the muted shafts of light that filter in through the gossamer dome. The building has swallowed itself. A short, broken hallway has abruptly ended in a green expanse of vines and leaves. There is no more roof.

This is a circular amphitheater. Lush but featureless, save for a tumble of stones growing out of the grass at the dead center of the room. Now that the dome has sealed itself, the air in here is stagnant. No movement; the only sound is a soft whoosh from high above.

I almost don't notice Caldecot.

Sitting on the rocks, the man is frighteningly gaunt and long-limbed, even from a distance. Chin in his hand, he seems lost in reverie. The pile of broken rock is formed into a throne, carved by some kind of crete to fit perfectly with Caldecot's slumping, pale body.

I step closer, fingers closed over the vial in my front pocket.

High on his throne, Caldecot seems to be melting, his face falling away in shadowed rivulets. But moving closer, I see that the light and dark playing on his face are coming from above. Sunlight twists and courses through streams of water coursing over the outside surface of the dome.

It is raining out there, in the world.

I clench the vial in my palm and approach the throne. Caldecot still does not respond to me. I can't even tell whether his eyes are open. The skin on his face is slack. His body is eaten by darkness, half-swallowed by the slabs of rock around him. I can make out coils of thin wires wrapped around his body.

"Dr. Caldecot?"

He doesn't stir. Doesn't even seem to be breathing; his chest is still.

I pause at the foot of the throne and stare up. One of his hands hangs over the promontory of rock, pallid and relaxed. His fingers are long and sensitive, the back of his hand laced through with dark veins. I move my gaze up his forearm, to where his elbow rests in a mess of wires that spill over the side of the throne. Continuing up past the bicep, I see a broad chest, whitish collarbones sunken into pools of shadow. On his long neck, tendons pull the skin in taut marbled folds, supporting a massive head that lists to the side. His jowls undulate with rolls of waxy flesh up to his cheekbones—to a pair of open black eyes open, watching me darkly.

I startle, take a step back.

"Dr. Caldecot? Are you all right?"

Laboriously, Caldecot straightens his back. Those fathomless eyes lock onto me hard, the way a crow might watch a lizard. His breathing is shallow, but I can see his chest moving now. He speaks to me in slow precise syllables, his voice growing, its power rumbling out from hidden depths.

"Oh," he says. "It's you. They finally sent you."

I take another careful step toward the throne. The pocketed flesh-eater vial is still cradled in my sweating fingers. Caldecot regards me calmly. I notice a glinting braid of wires and cables and hoses hooking over the top of his throne and splaying out into the foliage behind it. The toe of my boot hits something hard, and I see that similar cables meander through the grass as well, across the entire clearing.

"Are you okay?" I ask.

Caldecot winces, the expression spreading its way over his exaggerated features. "Of course. My apologies for the travails you must have suffered to reach this place. It could not have been easy, and I fear that I may have played a part in the difficulties."

His voice is deep and sonorous and it expands to somehow fill the cavernous amphitheater. Maybe the entire dome.

"You've got to stop this thing, Caldecot," I say. "You've got to come back with me so we can fix this."

His lips move, peristaltically, until he appears amused.

"How is it? Out there?"

"People are dying," I say, climbing the bottom step of the dais. "There's no sense to any of it."

"Change," he says, "is often mistaken for tragedy."

The empty clearing sighs with the falling of rain outside the dome. Now I can see that some of the wires go inside him. His arms and legs and torso are riddled with ports.

"It's madness," I say.

"Madness?" he asks. "Hardly. Your own research was the leaping-off point. You made all this possible. We are creators, my friend. We do not fear change. We wield it."

"Will you come willingly?" I ask.

He continues speaking in a low monotone, as if he hasn't heard me.

"We'd had purification cretes before. Nothing more than chemical tricks. Not mechanical. Not true molecular reassembly. The chain always failed after a few hundred generations. Mutations crept in, followed by self-immolation. But I found the solution in an old patent. Yours. I watched how you made the creticide scan its enemies for flaws. Then I reverse-engineered it."

Caldecot's words spread over me like anesthetic. As the torrent flows faster and faster, a buzzing numbness settles over my face.

"We think the breakthrough came after midnight over a weekend. A lab assistant named Jacobs was working on a silicone variety. Highly experimental. At some point, it worked—it fed upon the silica of the glass vial. I imagine Jacobs must have laid his tired head down to sleep at his desk. Funny to think it all happened while he was dreaming. But by then, none of us were making it home from the lab very often. The whole facility was on the verge of being mothballed.

"When I found Jacobs, the skin of his face was fused with the surface of the desk. Stretched like brittle glass, yet pliable as a polymer chain. His throat was collapsed in a fan of skin and his vocal cords were sunk into the tabletop like veins. His arms were puddles of flesh; the fingers splayed and melting.

"We could not understand how he was still alive."

I close my hand into a fist around the vial. Caldecot continues, speaking to me but not looking at me.

"But he was. Young Jacobs was silently crying with the one eye he had left. Crying so softly as that crete ground the silica from his bones and turned it into plastic. A whole week passed before the rest of his face was swallowed. During that time we learned to work around him. A sheet was placed to block the sight of his work station. But it never could block the sound of the grinding."

Caldecot blinks, seems to notice me again.

"We mourned him. Don't think we didn't. But we also *cel-ebrated.* Jacobs was a miracle at work. And I made sure we were there to witness. To build on this incredible good luck.

"Some of my scientists ran, then. I let the deserters go. Others from the army came and they tried to stop me. But I simply allowed the light of creation to shine. It ate them whole and in pieces. In the stench of cauterized flesh, my cretes found in my enemies so many new forms to take. The light wants to shine into dark places, you know. Who am I to stop it? Who are *you* to try to stop it?"

His voice drops to a whisper, almost inaudible, and I step forward.

"I tell you . . . there was a moment, when I put my hand on Jacobs's shoulder to rouse him on that first morning, when it happened . . . and I saw the horror of what he had become . . . It was a split second that spawned universes. Right then . . . at that moment . . . I could have stopped all of this. I could have retreated into ignorance, but I chose to keep my eyes open to the terrible face of our destiny."

Another step. I could throw the vial now. End this.

"Do you see? Do you understand the decisions we must make? Men like us owe it to the world. We are obligated. We can't stop—we can never stop. Without us, none of it means anything. If we were to stop, why, the sacrifices we've made . . . *they wouldn't mean anything.*"

His final words evaporate on the air, but I swear I can still feel the baritone rhythm echoing inside my chest. Men like us.

"Will you come willingly?" I ask again.

A shudder runs through the foliage. Something shifts in the grass behind me. Ten yards away, the earth is vibrating.

A pure-white gap is emerging in the thick folds of grass. As it grows, I see it holds a ramp leading down into the research facility.

He has preserved it.

"Your lab is sterilized. Ready for operation. For a new era. I offer you this invitation. The opportunity to shape a new reality by the power of your mind. Together, we will unleash the future and watch lovingly as it feeds upon the flesh of the old world."

The hazy glow spilling from the ground solidifies into the shine of row upon row of fluorescent lights, test tubes, and cloudy sheets of plastic. I hear the familiar whir of a ventilation hood and I taste my own vomit. I am looking into a cleanroom, its tile floors impossibly white and smooth and unblemished.

The barbed memory is back and this time it is real.

"We can't do this," I say. "I won't do this. It's wrong."

Caldecot leans forward, only an inch, but his eyes are two wells of inescapable gravity. I suddenly feel as if I'm standing on a cliff. As he leans, the world seems to lean with him and a sudden vertigo overwhelms me.

"It wasn't your fault she died," he says.

Her hands were on her stomach when she fell.

My vision quiets and I stumble. My hand lands on his knee and it is cold and hard as stone. I snatch my hand back. The air feels heavy. Like I'm breathing underwater.

"What?" I say, forcing the word out.

"Change is hungry. It *feasts*."

Some part of me is bleeding inside. I'm breathing in gasps. She didn't deserve it, none of them did. *My baby boy . . .*

Could I make it mean something?

"Are you insane?" I whisper.

I do not know who I am asking the question of.

"Your wife's death meant something," says Caldecot. "Fuel for the future. You have only to take the credit, not the blame. You and I—we will make *all of it* mean something."

"The *credit*?" I ask.

My chin dips a few times as confusion coalesces into rage.

"It *was* my fault," I say. "I have no excuse. There is no . . . there can *be* no excuse. I killed her. I killed *him*. The blame is mine. I claim it."

I stop talking, my chest heaving. I can taste my tears.

Caldecot responds, his voice still amused: "Ah, your son. Yes, a shame. But don't you see? You have made another, far more important child. The *creticide*."

My fingers grip the vial.

"Will you come or not?" I shout at this grinning jack-o'-lantern.

Caldecot's languid smile droops to a snarl and back. "You and I will never leave this place. Of that, I guarantee you," he says. "We will stand at ground zero as the world is eaten. While the others die, the light of a new dawn will sear our eyelids away. And you and I will stare into creation and finally and from then on we will know the true face of the world."

His smile returns, blazing and wide.

"The answer is no," he continues. "No. I will not go with you willingly or in any other capacity. Our destiny is here under this diamond sky, and we will face it together."

"No, we won't," I say, pulling my hand from my pocket.

The vial glints. Murder in a bottle.

I pull back to throw it and something nudges my calf. Instinctively, I step over a cord. They are writhing now, all

that blends with my tears to turn the sky into whorls of fading sunlight.

"Please let me out," I croak, and all hope has fled my voice. The gray-green liquid creeps down the vial. Closer to my fingertips.

"You are not locked in here, my friend," says the Caldecot-thing. "The rest of the world is *locked out there*."

Light blooms.

. . . nukes they finally dropped the nukes oh my God . . .

The wires go slack, dropping me onto my knees in a galaxy of silent throbbing brilliance. A new sun is born on the lid of the sphere above. Through the ground, I feel the muted shock waves as a second nuclear warhead detonates against the sphere. And another. The filtered light is paralyzing and beautiful in the way I imagine heaven would be. Wholly beyond the threshold of human experience.

When the flashes fade, we are still living.

Through a rainbow of chaotic dust and debris, the setting sun is collapsing into the horizon now, fat and simmering. A broad tongue of light dances across stippled whorls of ash smeared over the sky. The raging nuclear dust storm outside shimmers and gyrates in the gory colors of the formless void.

Abruptly, I remember a tide of blood. Spreading over impossibly clean white tile. She and I were going to make something from the chaos. Her hands were over her stomach. Our baby boy was growing inside her, strong and slow and waiting to come into this world, but that never happened. He never happened. Never was able to happen.

We make things. We destroy things.

Caldecot's face is turned up toward the detonation. His

teeth flash, brilliant patterns evolving on his face. A single tear etches a radiant path down one gaunt cheek.

The vial is still in my palm.

I throw the flesh-eater crete, and it bounces harmlessly off the back of the stone seat. For a frozen moment, it cartwheels away. Then the vial shatters on the arm of the throne. A starburst of black liquid spatters onto Caldecot's shoulder.

Such a small thing. A vial.

"Oh," says Caldecot, his surprise already fading.

I'm clambering through wire-laced foliage, backpedaling for my life, eyes never leaving the thin man. The crete does nothing for a moment. It's in the long flat part of the exponential curve. Then, like a switch has been flipped, it sinks through his clothes, eating. Metallic flakes, tentative and beautiful, curl up from his skin and launch themselves into the placid air.

In a second, a spreading hole appears in Caldecot's shoulder. Inside, I see flesh and pale bone, but also more wires.

"What a clever crete," he says, and then he wipes the dust onto his fingertips and puts it to his lips. Tastes the crete even as his lips disintegrate into millions of scales that float away like pollen.

"I'm sorry," I say.

"Forgiven," says Caldecot, voice slurring. I can see his molars through a spreading slit in his cheek. His eyes look past my shoulder to the bright laboratory.

"The future is yours," he says.

The flesh-eater is spreading through his body in the helter-skelter fractal exponential manner that is the natural gait of all cretes. Eating Caldecot's neck and jaw. Climbing his face and sending pieces of his chin dropping into his lap. A smoky haze has risen above his throne, the waste heat of the reaction pushing spent particles higher up into the air.

Under the raging light of the nuked dome, I watch the technology consume Caldecot's clothes and flesh from the outside in. Only the wires are unaffected. Left coiled over the throne, they begin to thrum and twitch. The intertwined links of cable rise and slap themselves idiotically against the stone in fading death throes.

The ash plume that used to be a man expands into the still air. Glinting particles form constellations in the flickering shadows. Higher and higher into a divine frenzy of luminescence.

I watch through tear-blurred eyes as the shock waves keep dancing through the dome's surface. The white-hot sheet quivers but remains intact as bubbles of heat claw off it into the atmosphere. The surface glows, absorbing sweeping cataracts of radiation and rendering the nukes harmless. As it heals, the sphere begins to go still and bright and clear. The sun continues its slinking escape over the horizon, taking the light of the world with it.

But a new light has arrived.

It emanates softly from the crevasse in the ground, surging up from under the grass in a pure halo. The room's neatly labeled test tubes each carry a miracle. With the accompanying equipment and notes and data, I see a complete toolkit for the creation of a new world.

On shaky legs, I step down the ramp. Brush my fingers over the layers of hanging plastic. Close my eyes and let the fluorescent glare paint red patterns through my eyelids. The pure white light of the cleanroom envelops me, holding all of the infinite potential of the future.

All of the infinite horror of the past.

Above, a mushroom cloud of atomized jungle is boiling into the atmosphere. Hundreds of miles away, a sonic boom kisses the ocean's surface. A million miles farther on, moving as fast as physics, the blinding light of creation itself races into the vastness.

Mindless, and eternal.

ACKNOWLEDGMENTS

DANIEL H. WILSON

First and foremost, I must thank the wonderful authors who contributed to this collection. It has been an honor to read your work and be allowed to do a bit of futzing. And maximum thanks go also to my coeditor, John Joseph Adams, who made my first foray into anthologies an awesome experience. You're the definition of a pro, JJA. Thanks to my agent, Laurie Fox, for helping to place this book with the great folks at Vintage Books at Random House, and in turn, huge thanks to the robot-loving people there, especially our editor, Jeff Alexander. Always, always my love to Anna and Coraline and Conrad.

JOHN JOSEPH ADAMS

Many thanks to Jeff Alexander, for acquiring and editing this book, and to the rest of the team that worked on it at Vintage Books at Random House; my coeditor, Daniel, for being an enthusiastic and astute editing partner; Joe Monti, for being amazing and supportive, and for finding a home for this project (writers: you'd be lucky to have Joe in your corner); Gordon Van Gelder, for being a mentor and a friend;

Ellen Datlow, for revealing the mysteries of anthologizing; my amazing wife, Christie, my mom, Marianne, and my sister, Becky, for all their love and support; and Carolyn Talcott, Susan McCarthy, A. B. Kovacs, Josette Sanchez-Reynolds, and Vaughne Lee Hansen, for helping wrangle authors and/or contracts. Last but not least, thank you to all the writers who agreed to be part of the anthology, and to all of the readers who make doing books like this possible.

PERMISSIONS ACKNOWLEDGMENTS